CAVE DWELLER

BY WILLIAM NIKKEL

SUSPENSE PUBLISHING

CAVE DWELLER

By
William Nikkel

PAPERBACK EDITION

* * * * *

PUBLISHED BY:
Suspense Publishing

Cover Design: Shannon Raab
Cover Photographer: iStockphoto.com/HARRYKE
Cover Photographer: iStockphoto.com/dndavis

PUBLISHING HISTORY:
JMS Books, LLC., Print and Digital Copy, 2012
Suspense Publishing, Print and Digital Copy, March 2014

ISBN-13: 978-0615988160 (Suspense Publishing)
ISBN-10: 0615988164

For my wife Karen who stood by me every step of the way, my mother for her unconditional love, and the Hawaiian people for their legends and myths.

PRAISE FOR WILLIAM NIKKEL

"William Nikkel's "Cave Dweller" has everything I love: ripping adventure, buried mysteries, and intrigue that spans centuries. Written in a fantastic cinematic style, I read this book in one sitting. Great story, great adventure, great new writer!"

—James Rollins, *New York Times* bestselling author of "Blood Line"

"I must say that William Nikkel knows how to draw you into his story and hold you there.... In many ways Nikkel is like a latter-day Jules Verne, having written a thoroughly enjoyable adventure tale that follows a band of scientists from sunlit coral reefs to the subterranean depths of remote coastal mountains to remarkable discoveries fraught with high danger.... And above all that, this is a thriller with a message—and one as old as the cave-dwellers."

—Gary Braver, bestselling author of "Tunnel Vision"

CAVE DWELLER

BY WILLIAM NIKKEL

PROLOGUE

Sunday, December 7, 1941

Commander Akira stared through the periscope of the eighty-foot long, battery powered mini-sub *I-16*. Saltwater lapped at the scope's lens that probed the surface of the waves twelve feet above his boat.

The order to attack the American fleet had been received: *Climb Mt. Niataka.*

The months of secret planning and the weeks of training... Japan's naval might amassed to deliver a single, decisive blow.

No more waiting.

No more obstacles.

He pulled his eyes from the periscope and focused his gaze on Kiyoshi, who manned the sub's motor controls and flotation valves.

In the dim light he saw the resolve on the young man's oil-smudged face. Like him, Kiyoshi was honored he had been chosen for this mission.

A silent understanding flowed between them.

We will do our duty and, if necessary, die with honor for the emperor.

For a moment, Akira gazed at the photo taped to the periscope just above the eyepiece, remembering his young wife's touch. Yumi's skin as soft and smooth as the silk kimono she wore their last night together.

She spoke proudly of warrior courage and honor, but tears betrayed her pain. She knew they may never be in each other's arms again.

Neither he nor his lone crewman, Kiyoshi, had been specifically designated *kamikaze*. Nor had the eight crewmen of the other four submarines. But he understood how slim his chances were of surviving the attack.

She did, too.

But he could not think about Yumi now.

So far *I-16* had operated undetected from the enemy ships above. But what about the other four mini-subs?

Akira did not know the fate of his eight countrymen. At 0645 hours he'd heard several muffled explosions. Then nothing, only the drone of his sub's electric motor.

Were the explosions depth charges going off?

Had one of the mini-subs been destroyed?

If so, what had happened to the others?

Was his submarine the only one that survived?

Like him, the crews of the other mini-subs accepted the risks. He could not let himself worry about them. His orders were to join the attack and fire his two torpedoes into American warships, once the bombing started.

A single, decisive blow.

Nothing must stop him from carrying out his mission.

He drew strength from that silent understanding.

We will do our duty and, if necessary, die with honor for the emperor.

If he alone survived long enough to successfully complete his objective, the sacrifice would have been worth it.

The enemy fleet will have been destroyed.

Confident of success, Commander Akira returned his eyes to the periscope and peered into the early morning light.

He smiled.

His sub had entered the harbor. He and Kiyoshi would be

honored for their bravery this day.

In the distance, the American battleships were lined up, one beside the other. Cruisers and destroyers held at anchor.

They'd caught the American fleet asleep.

Suddenly—in the sky above—bombers and torpedo planes swooped in low on *Battleship Row*. The first explosions sent dense black smoke billowing high into the air. The attack on the American warships at Pearl Harbor had begun.

Akira aimed his torpedoes and fired.

CHAPTER 1

Present Day

Jack Ferrell straightened in the seat at the helm of his sixty-foot catamaran *Pono* and squinted at the fog that shouldn't have been there.

Amid a seemingly impenetrable mist hugging the water a hundred yards ahead of him, an unearthly glow lit up the darkness.

He rubbed his bloodshot eyes and peered into the night. Normally finely honed, his senses were dulled by lack of sleep and the monotony of sailing miles of flat, open sea.

A frown knitted his thick black eyebrows together, wrinkling his swarthy skin. The phenomenon had to be a figment of his imagination.

No way could this be happening!

His mind searched for answers to the enigma. Red tides, bioluminescent organisms in the ocean. He'd read about milky seas and their incandescence, and the marine bacteria believed to cause them. He'd even seen photographs of them taken from outer space. But he'd never witnessed the phenomena first hand, or anything like them.

They might account for the strange glow, but not the unearthly fog.

Dense fog banks don't form in Hawaii. And they certainly don't glow in the dark.

He checked his GPS and mentally noted the coordinates. No one who hadn't seen the bizarre mist would believe him.

Did he believe it himself?

He could've sworn the fogbank hadn't been there a minute ago. But he had been staring at the heavens, searching the stars in the night sky the way he did whenever he was at sea. Even so, such a glow would surely not have gone unnoticed by his watchful eyes.

Befitting a marine biologist and an adventurer, his curiosity would not let him pass up the unknown. He adjusted his course and headed *Pono* directly for the center of the ghostly apparition.

The dense cloud closed in around *Pono's* twin hulls, leaving the deck slick with moisture, and the rigging dripping wet. At once, the air became quite cool—at least thirty degrees colder than the night air he'd been sailing in only minutes before.

Immediately, goose bumps rose on his bare arms and the breeze that filled *Pono's* sail died.

The boat drifted.

He leaned over the side and peered at the unusually calm water, searching for the source of the light. No squid or any of the other creatures of the sea known to possess bioluminescent qualities.

It seemed the fog itself glowed.

He stood up and stared into the haunting gloom. What he saw defied scientific explanation.

Suddenly, a shrill noise jarred his thoughts.

What…?

Again he narrowed his eyes and stared intensely into the mist, not sure what he heard. It sounded far off, muffled by the heavy dampness blanketing the water.

Then he heard it again.

A woman's scream.

The scream dropped to a whimper. He cocked his ear to get a fix on the woman, but the fog made it impossible.

Suddenly, the mist disappeared, and along with it, the unearthly glow. A warm breeze ruffled and caught *Pono's* sail.

The boat began to move.

Jack grabbed hold of the helm, tightened his big hands on the four-foot chromed steel wheel, and scanned the night. In the dim starlight, he could just make out the white hull and triangular sails of a thirty-foot sloop, fifty yards starboard of him. The boat had keeled over in the breeze billowing its canvas, but it was as if King Trident himself had reached up from the depths and seized the vessel from below. The sobbing came from a woman onboard.

Pushing up with one hand and pulling down with the other, he spun the glistening ship's wheel and pointed *Pono* at the sloop. Then he started the engines and flipped the switch to the electric winch he'd installed to raise and lower the sail. The massive nylon sheet slid down the cable rigging, collapsing on itself in long folds. From inside the cockpit, he held *Pono* on course with his knees pressed tight against the helm, while he tugged and guided the fabric to keep the metal grommets from fouling on the cable.

The woman's whimpers turned to cries for help as *Pono* motored closer to the floundering boat. Jack could read the name, now: *Julie Ann*. And he could see the young woman standing near the stern, frantically waving her right hand. Her left gripped the safety rail.

He worked the throttles to bring *Pono* parallel with *Julie Ann*, careful to keep a twenty-foot gap between them. He didn't want to risk smashing into her hull.

"My brother," she begged, pointing at the water.

Jack dug into the locker under his seat and found the handheld spotlight. He flipped it on and lit up the woman.

His chest tightened. Even if she hadn't pointed, the look on her face told him all he needed to know.

"My brother," she said again in an excited dance at the rail, her index finger pointing wildly.

He directed the beam onto the water and swept the surface with a circle of bright light.

Nothing.

He tried again, and this time he saw a flash of skin. He locked the beam on the head of a man floating face down in the water. His arms were entwined in a section of netting and his body bobbed like a human cork. When it upended a second later, Jack saw the man had been bitten in half below the waist.

He winced, and sucked in a breath between clenched teeth.

His fingers tightened on the spotlight. Immediately he knew what happened. The sailboat's keel had become fouled in a remnant of nylon drift net floating on the waves. When the man had dived overboard to free the boat, the sharks had attacked.

He took the beam off the half-eaten body and redirected it onto the woman gripping the handrail.

"We need to get you aboard my boat," he said. "I'm sorry, there's—" A dog's frantic barking cut him off. The outcry came from the water to the left of the man's body.

He heard the dog bark again and swept the spot in that direction, holding it steady. In the center of the circle of light, a basset hound hung in the water, entangled in the netting. Its front paws were hooked over a half-submerged glass float, and its long ears curled back in the breeze. The struggling hound bayed and howled for help.

Jack threw aside all caution.

Forgetting the sharks that had bitten the man in half, he peeled his sweatshirt off over his head, dropped it and kicked off his deck shoes. He dove into the inky blackness and swam toward the stranded hound.

The heavy net dragged the struggling basset down.

Jack clawed and pulled himself over the nylon web, determined to reach the dog. Three feet away, the doomed canine's nose slipped under the surface of the ocean.

Jack lunged and grabbed a handful of loose skin and fur.

When he pulled the young basset's head out of the water, the dog frantically dug at his arms with its hind claws.

Somehow Jack managed to keep a grip on the nearly drowned pooch. With only starlight to see by, he worked the loops of net free from the pup's short hind legs and wrestled the frightened hound into his arms. He got a lick on the cheek for his effort.

But what had he done?

Suddenly feeling very foolish, he shot a worried glance in the direction of the half-eaten corpse. He and the dog had to get out of the water, fast.

Without wasting a second more, he tucked the squirming dog tight against his body and sidestroked back to *Pono*. Close to the boat, he counted the strokes, concentrating on those last six feet. Only three or four strokes to go.

He'd made it.

Then he heard the woman scream and yell '*Shark*!'

Jack didn't dare slow down or chance a look behind him. He lifted the dog onto the steps in the portside hull and vaulted his one hundred and ninety pound frame aboard. In the next instant he heard a bump against the fiberglass under him and saw a large dorsal fin slice the water, inches from his feet.

He scrambled up the remaining steps and collapsed on the deck. His chest muscles heaved with each lungful of air he sucked in. Again the dog greeted him with licks from a wet tongue. He gave the grateful basset's head a vigorous rub behind its floppy ears.

"You've got to help Brad. Please, help him!" the woman pleaded from her boat.

Her voice got Jack moving. He gave the dog's head one more brisk rub, took a deep breath, and hauled himself to his feet. He hadn't forgotten the guy in the water, and he wasn't insensitive to the woman's loss. But little remained of the man who'd fallen prey to the sharks, and it was far too dangerous to go back in the water.

He found the spotlight and shone it on the woman. "I'm afraid there is nothing I can do for him."

"But…?"

He didn't need to shine the spotlight on the body. Once had been enough to tell him what he needed to know. And even now, he could hear the violent thrashing in the darkness. Nothing remained for him or anyone else to recover.

"I'm sorry, but right now we need to get you on board my boat so I can take you ashore. I'll notify the Coast Guard. They'll do what they can."

"I can't just leave him."

Jack saw her staring at him, eyes begging for the impossible. He feared she might even dive in herself. He had to get her to safety before she did something stupid. "I'm going to move my boat close alongside. You'll have to jump aboard. Can you do that?"

"What?" Her voice shook. "Jump?"

"When I move my boat alongside yours, you'll have to jump aboard," he repeated, more loudly this time. "Can you do that?"

"Yes…yes. I think so."

"Good. I'll tell you when. And don't worry. I'll be there to catch you."

Jack hung a pair of large rubber bumpers over the side, secured them to the railing, and hurried back to the helm.

He eased *Pono's* port side in close.

The bumpers compressed between the hulls and Jack hollered to the woman to jump. He held out his hand and motioned her over.

The woman leaped.

She landed flat-footed on the deck of *Pono*, cartwheeled her arms, and fell back toward the water.

Jack had his hand out, ready. He grabbed her wrist, in a grip hardened by years of labor aboard his father's salmon boat, and heaved her toward him. She collapsed into his arms.

The spotlight slipped from his hand and thumped to the deck. But it stayed on board.

In its glow, he saw her face, young, nice looking.

She clung to him in a bear hug, the way a frightened child would her mother. "I've got you," he said in a soft voice. "You're all right."

She pressed herself against him, and he could feel her heart pounding inside her chest. Terrified. Thankful.

He held her a moment longer. She needed to be hugged. He'd give her that. But he also had to move his boat a safe distance away from the floundering *Julie Ann* while he still could.

"It's all right," he reassured her, easing out of her grasp. He picked up the light and switched it off. His night vision returned, and he led her to the seat in the cockpit where he sat her down. The basset hound jumped into her lap and nuzzled her cheek.

He left the woman and her dog sitting there, and faced the helm. So far luck had been with him. The rubber bumpers had kept the two hulls from crushing against each other. But it was only a matter of time. And there was the netting to worry about.

He reached for the throttle levers, but too late. An unexpected swell rolled underneath *Pono* and slammed her portside hull against the sailboat.

The rubber bumpers flattened.

Fiberglass crunched and grated.

Jack cringed, but stayed focused and eased *Pono* away from *Julie Ann* before another rogue swell rolled under them to finish what the previous wave had started.

A hundred yards out, he throttled back and shut down the engines.

"Let's get you inside the cabin and out of this night air," he said. "Then I'll radio the Coast Guard and fill them in on what's happened."

The woman rose to her feet without comment. He stood there a moment longer, looking at *Julie Ann*. The sailboat listed a few degrees to starboard in the swells, its keel firmly entangled in the nylon netting. The sloop would still be there when the Coast Guard arrived.

His gaze swept the surface of the water, from the boats to the shoreline. A coal black silhouette, Kauai stood out a dimly lit shadow against the dark horizon. No lights shone on the uninhabited cliffs of the Na Pali Coast. Rugged and steep, few people ventured there. And some never returned.

Was there a connection?

He could only wonder. The fog had originated from that very coastline as if by magic, and moved out to sea to engulf *Julie Ann* and her unsuspecting crew.

Perhaps the woman held answers to the mystery.

CHAPTER 2

Jack switched on the overhead cabin light, tossed his sweatshirt onto the table, poured the woman a cup of coffee from the thermos on the counter in the galley, and fortified the strong Kona brew with a shot of brandy. He handed the cup to her and leaned, wet and dripping, against the table with his arms folded across his chest. She had yet to say a word to him since stepping onto his boat. He stood quietly looking at her.

The still unnamed young woman wore cut off jeans and a loose-fitting, white, long-sleeved cotton blouse knotted at the waist. She was prettier than he'd realized topside, when she fell into his arms. Her shirt hid her figure well, but he could tell she had well-rounded breasts to go with the pretty face. Her long brown hair and thick carefully shaped brows matched the biggest chocolate-brown eyes he'd ever seen.

"My name is Jack Ferrell," he said. "Can you tell me yours?"

Tears filled the woman's eyes. She clung to the overgrown puppy who seemed content to be held. She didn't answer.

Jack saw her look right through him. She obviously struggled to accept what happened.

Shock. Disbelief. He could imagine what she felt.

"Take a sip," he said in a reassuring voice. "It'll help."

She raised the cup to her mouth, then set it aside. Still silent, she looked up at his strong tanned face, her eyes pleading.

He hated not knowing what to say. Was there anything he could say to soften the blow of seeing her brother eaten alive?

Doubtful.

Still…

He softened his expression and said, “I’m truly sorry for your loss. I wish I’d arrived sooner.”

The woman let the pup slip from her arms and broke out in great heaving sobs. She buried her face in her hands.

Tears…Jack had to glance away. Not tears.

He resisted the urge to rush over and take her in his arms. A softy when it came to rushing to the rescue of a woman in distress—especially with tears involved—it wasn’t easy. His friend Robert had told him more than once it might get him killed one day.

Maybe.

But she needed him…so did the dog.

He rummaged through a forward storage locker, found his spare blanket, and draped it around her shoulders. It tore at his heart to see her cry. But he knew she needed to shed those tears.

He retrieved his sweatshirt and slipped it on. He poured himself a shot of brandy, slugged it down, and poured himself another which he sipped. He didn’t feel a need to press her for answers.

After a couple of minutes she began to pull herself together. Tears still streaked her cheeks, but the sobs had quieted. He saw her look up at him, her eyes searching his.

“The man in the water was my brother Brad,” she began. “We were sailing the islands in memory of our father. He died a year ago. He named the boat after my mother the year we lost her to cancer.”

Again she broke down, and through tears, gazed pleadingly at Jack. “I told him not to go into the water until we knew it was safe.”

Jack couldn’t understand why anyone would willingly go into the water with a ten-foot man-eating tiger shark cruising about. He tossed back his shot of brandy, remembering he’d just done that very thing…and to save a dog.

Perhaps he should have paused to think before diving in.

Not!

He knew he'd have dove in anyway, and the extra seconds might have been all the shark needed to sink its teeth into him.

He shook off the thought, stepped closer to the young woman, and gently placed a reassuring hand on her arm. She looked like she could use a touch of compassion. She didn't pull away.

"Try a little more of this." He picked up the cup of coffee she'd set aside and worked it into her hand. "I think it'll help."

She took a healthy gulp and handed the cup back to him.

He saw her straighten and brush the tears from her eyes. "Better?" he asked.

She sniffled. "A little."

"Can you tell me your name, now?"

"Lisa. My brother's name is Brad—"

He waited for her to finish. Finally he asked, "Lisa what?"

She swallowed. "Bowman."

"And your brother's?" Even as he asked the question it sounded clumsy and a little ridiculous to him. But the thought she might be married had crossed his mind.

"Bowman," she said, after a second's hesitation. The same as mine." More tears welled in her eyes.

He gave her arm a reassuring squeeze then let his hand slide away. He watched the basset jump back into her lap, worm his way onto her chest, and bury his head and long ears in the crook of her neck. It appeared the hound too wished to help soothe her sense of loss.

Animals…

He smiled at the dog. Amazing.

"If you'll excuse me a moment," he said, looking at Lisa. "I need to radio the Coast Guard and let them know what's happened."

She didn't answer.

When he turned his attention back on the young woman a few minutes later, he noticed she'd finished her coffee. "Care for another cup?"

She shook her head. "No thanks."

"What's his name?" He pointed at the gray and black pile of loose skin and ears in her arms.

She hugged the dog as though the mention of her pet was a reminder he was all she had left. "He's a she, and her name is Rebel."

"Cute," he said. "You mentioned you were sailing the islands."

"We left Maui a week ago. We were heading home."

"So you live on Maui?"

"Brad's been living there, in my parents' house. I moved to California ten years ago to go to college, and stayed on the mainland when I got a position at the museum."

"Museum, huh?" That got him interested.

"The American Museum of Natural History in New York. I have a degree in cultural anthropology."

"I thought anthropologists were grizzled up old men and women with dusty, sweaty clothes, wire-rimmed glasses, and broad-brimmed felt hats to keep the sun off their necks." He knew this was far from the truth, but he was trying to make her laugh.

She managed a weak smile. "I'm a cultural anthropologist, not an archeologist. We're the ones who traipse around the world's jungles in pith hats looking for lost tribes of headhunters. But I don't get out in the field much. My work is mainly analysis and cataloging, which I do at the museum. I leave my fedora and leather jacket hanging on a hook in my apartment."

He chuckled. She had a sense of humor. He liked that. "And I bet they look good on you, too. Me, I'm more of a swimsuit and T-shirt kind of guy."

Her eyes appeared to focus, and he got a feeling she saw *him* for the first time...not just some stranger.

"Suits you," she said with a smile.

The basset stirred on her lap and her gaze dropped to the flop-eared hound. She stroked the fur on the dog's head and got a wet-nosed nuzzle in return.

"That's because I'm on the water more often than not."

She raised her head and looked at him. "I'm sorry, my mind was elsewhere."

"You commented that my outfit suited me," he said. "That's because I'm on or in the water most of the time. I'm a marine biologist. Just spent the last two and a half months doing research in the Northwest Hawaiian Islands. Apex predators. That's my specialty."

Giant jacks, groupers, barracuda, sharks…hunters of the world's reefs. Most people weren't familiar with the term apex predator. He doubted she was. Still, she hadn't asked…yet.

He gave her a moment with her thoughts. And then he had to ask. "If you can, tell me what happened out there."

She pulled the blanket tightly around her, lifted the basset onto her chest, and nuzzled the top of the dog's head. Her eyes filled with tears. "It's all pretty much one big blur. We were on our way back to Maui. Brad thought we could make it as far as Oahu by dark, spend the night there, and sail on to Maui tomorrow. But things started going wrong."

"What kind of things?" His mind began to piece together a possible scenario. Just about anything could happen on the water, and likely as not, would. Surely the dense fog played a big part in the mishap, but what else had gone wrong?

"Everything was fine until this afternoon." She nodded toward shore. "We sailed around the north end of the island then started down the west coast. All of a sudden the wind died. Brad figured we'd motor in so he lowered the sails. We hadn't gone more than a quarter of a mile when the motor quit running. It didn't make any of those weird noises like an engine does when it's going to die, it just stopped dead."

"Your brother checked it out?"

"He spent a couple of hours tinkering with it. The thing just wouldn't run. It wouldn't even crank over."

"Is that when you raised canvas?"

"What?"

"You said you dropped sail. Your jib and mainsail were up when I saw you."

"That's right, just after the motor quit. We hoped to catch

enough of a breeze to keep us on course, which we did. We were moving, but just barely. It was a little after dark when he finally got the engine running. That's when the keel snagged on the netting. I was at the wheel and Brad was below. Had it been daylight I might have seen the floats, but in the dark…"

Jack could sense her frustration. She felt responsible. The truth was, she had nothing to do with it. Drifting sections of nylon netting tear away from the mile-long nets used by many of the world's Pacific fishing fleets and cause huge problems throughout the islands. His feeling on the subject was no secret. He voiced his opinion often and with resolve. Those drifting sections of netting kill indiscriminately, and keep killing as long as they remain in the ocean. In this case, it was not only turtles and fish that died: the netting had claimed the life of her brother.

"Tell me about the fog." The net would be dealt with. He'd see to that. In the meantime he wanted to know about the mysterious, glowing mist that formed where it shouldn't have.

Her eyes narrowed. She hadn't mentioned the fog, and he wondered for a moment if he'd imagined it.

Not likely.

"Brad came up from below deck," she started. "I guess he sensed something was wrong even before I yelled down to him. We could see the floats by then and realized the netting had snagged the keel."

She paused, and he saw her eyes widen. She stared through him, again. Remembering. A mental picture forming.

"The sky was perfectly clear." Her voice sounded hollow, different from before. "Brad saw the fog first and pointed it out to me. The mist seemed to billow up from the base of the cliffs, as though someone had turned on one of those Halloween fog machines. Then it moved out to sea, engulfing us in that eerie light."

Cold, blue luminescence, that's how he remembered it. Unearthly—like a glow stick. "How long did it take for all that to happen?"

"Minutes—five, maybe ten. We just stood and watched. That's when Brad decided to dive in and cut us loose. I tried to convince him not to go in the water, especially after seeing that fog form the way it did. But he wouldn't listen. A minute or two after that he dove in. Then I heard him scream." She gripped Jack's arm, eyes pleading. "He...he...the shark, it pulled him under. And then Rebel jumped in." She buried her face in her hands and sobbed. "I screamed and just froze."

Her tears made it hard for him to just stand there. He wanted to take her in his arms, brush the tears away, and tell her how sorry he was. Instead, he kept his voice firm and even. "That's when I showed up?"

She pulled her hands away and looked at him through her tears. "At least you did something. Even Rebel jumped in to help. I didn't even try."

"You would have died with your brother if you had."

She looked him directly in the eyes. "You didn't."

Jack thought about that. He hadn't died. But he'd come damned close to being killed. "I got lucky." He gave the dog a scratch under the ears. "Rebel was worth it, but I wouldn't want to push that luck."

She smiled at the dog. "Rebel belonged to Brad. He'd only had her a few months. Now I guess she's mine."

"You'll be good for each other."

Jack stepped to the open hatchway and stared into the night. His mind shifted gears, processing what she had told him, what he'd seen. Overhead, stars twinkled in a clear, dark sky with no hint of the mysterious glowing fog that disappeared as quickly as it formed.

He turned and looked at Lisa. "Did the fog have that strange glow to it from the moment it started forming?"

"I've never seen anything like it," she said. "And something else, I thought I heard voices when the mist settled in around us."

Her last comment surprised him. He hadn't heard voices, but had seen the fog. And he knew the unearthly mist had formed suddenly and quite mysteriously.

And that it disappeared just as fast.

What force was at work here?

He'd heard the Hawaiian legends more than once. But he

wouldn't let himself believe local superstition or even that some unearthly magic had anything to do with the strange phenomenon he'd just witnessed. There was a straightforward logical scientific explanation for what occurred. There always was. He just didn't know the answer, but he intended to find out.

CHAPTER 3

Jack tightened his grip on the handrail. A powerful spotlight was sweeping the ocean's surface from a hundred feet up. For the past two minutes he'd watched running lights move through the sky to the south of them. Now he heard the distinctive *wop, wop, wop* of a helicopter's rotors beating the air. They hadn't wasted time getting there.

When the Coast Guard officer told him over the radio they were sending a helicopter, his plan was to take Lisa to port and then return. His plan changed when Lisa insisted on being on site when they arrived. He didn't know if her resolve came from the guts to see a bad situation through to the end, or denial that her brother was dead.

He stepped to the open hatchway leading into the cabin and bumped into Lisa on her way out. She'd obviously heard the arrival of the helicopter.

"Coast Guard's here." He pointed to the light in the sky.

"I know. I heard them." She brushed past Jack and looked up at the helicopter.

They watched the chopper swoop in low and make a slow circle: the downdraft from its rotors beat the ocean's surface flat.

"Mr. Ferrell, this is Lieutenant Rodgers with the United States Coast Guard." The pilot's voice crackled over *Pono's* radio. "Are you in immediate need of assistance?"

Jack could just hear him above the high-pitched whine of the chopper's turbines. He retrieved the microphone from the cabin radio and stood at the hatchway, the cord stretched tight behind him. "This is Jack Ferrell," he said in a calm, even voice. "Owner and captain of the 60-foot catamaran *Pono*. Ms. Lisa Bowman from the sloop *Julie Ann* is safely aboard my boat."

"Roger that," the Lieutenant came back. "A patrol boat is on its way. It should be on scene within the hour. Do you plan to remain here until then?"

"Ms. Bowman would like to take charge of her boat once it has been freed from the netting. She insists she can handle it alone. I'll follow her in. We'll make port in Oahu before she sails on to Maui."

"Roger. We'll keep you posted."

Jack lowered the microphone and watched the helicopter arc away to continue its spiraling search pattern. An exercise in futility. Nothing remained of Brad Bowman's body for the crew of the chopper to find.

* * * *

It was approaching midnight when Jack felt *Pono* slowly swing a hundred and eighty degrees on the anchor line, pointing her twin bows out to sea. He lit up *Julie Ann* with the spotlight and saw the sloop turn and point seawards, as well. In the same circle of light he saw the netting shift directions to follow the incoming tide and noticed the nylon web lose some of its hold on the boat.

He realized the need to take advantage of this opportunity to pull the sloop free.

He scanned the water for the bright shaft of light that would mark the location of the Coast Guard's 25-foot hard-bottomed inflatable, and spotted it three hundred yards away, moving in the opposite direction. He didn't want to wait.

"Time to go to work," he said to Lisa.

"Work?" She rose to her feet where she'd been sitting cross-legged on the deck just forward of the cabin, and frowned back at him. "What do you mean?"

"Your boat. I'm going to try to pull her free of the net."

"Now?"

"Now."

It took a few minutes for Jack to raise anchor, but he finally got it wrestled aboard. He didn't want to think about the damage it caused the coral.

Without stopping to catch his breath, he stepped behind the wheel, started the engines, and eased *Pono* toward *Julie Ann*. He did not want to chance crushing the two hulls together again. What he had planned was chancy enough.

He brought *Pono* around so that her stern faced *Julie Ann's* bow and let the boat idle in gear to maintain position. Then—from twenty feet away—he tossed a grappling hook, tethered to a thick nylon rope, onto *Julie Ann's* deck and hauled the rope in until the hook snagged the railing.

He had her in his grasp. Now he could only hope.

He secured the rope to a stern cleat on *Pono* and inched the throttle levers forward.

Lisa gripped the railing next to him. He saw her lean forward and watch with an intensity strong enough to will the sloop free of the netting. Even Rebel stood howling, with her paws draped over the railing next to her new mistress, doing her part to urge the boat free.

Julie Ann straightened behind *Pono* but the netting refused to release its grip on the keel.

Jack shoved on the throttle levers, coaxing more power out of *Pono's* two engines.

The propellers dug in.

The stern of the catamaran's heavy twin hulls settled a few inches deeper in the water as the line stretched taut.

He saw *Julie Ann's* metal bow rail bend. It was dangerously close to giving way.

"Better duck. The way that rope is stretched, if that railing gives way, that hook will fly back here and take off your head."

Lisa gave him a sideways look and squatted low enough to be protected and still see.

He nodded in the direction of the basset hound. "Rebel, too."

She pulled the dog down from the railing and put her arm around the hound to keep her safe.

He increased power to two-thirds.

The line tightened even more.

He ducked, expecting the hook to fly back at them any second.

But the railing held, and the sloop pulled free.

Jack throttled back to half power and towed *Julie Ann* a safe distance away from the drifting tentacles of netting.

* * * *

The Coast Guard helicopter returned shortly after sunup. An hour later, fuel running low, Lieutenant Rodgers called off their search for Brad Bowman's remains.

"Are you sure you don't want me to call a marine salvage company to remove the netting and tow *Julie Ann* into port?" Lieutenant Rodgers asked over the radio.

"Positive," Jack said. "I radioed the NOAA research vessel *Abraham Lincoln*. She'll be here in two hours to recover the netting."

"Roger and good luck," Lieutenant Rodgers signed off.

Jack watched the orange and white helicopter and inflatable leave the area. It was a stroke of luck that the National Oceanic and Atmospheric Administration's research vessel *Abraham Lincoln* was steaming toward Oahu at this very moment. Like him, it was pulling out of the North West Hawaiian Islands before the Pacific Ocean hurricane season started.

He'd worked alongside the ship's crew for the last couple of months and they were glad to help with the cleanup. Afterwards, he'd dive down and survey the damage done to coral and marine life.

"I guess this is good-bye," Lisa said from the hatchway.

He turned at the sound of her voice. "I can easily tow you in when I'm done here."

"I'll be fine."

"You sure you can manage *Julie Ann* by yourself?" he said, not eager to part ways, but ready to be done with his business there and head in as well.

"I can manage."

"Like I said, I have no problem towing her in for you." He joined her topside, still holding onto the hope she'd change her mind. "And there's plenty of room aboard *Pono* for you and Rebel."

She peered up at him. "I can manage *Julie Ann*. But there is one more thing you can do for me."

"Name it."

"I realize I'm asking a huge favor from you, but could you possibly take care of Rebel for me, maybe find her a good home? I'm always on the go doing one thing or another, and my apartment in New York…well it just won't work out." She held him in her gaze.

Again he felt the seductive power of her eyes. "No problem."

"Thank you, Jack." She drifted her fingers along his angular jaw, leaned up, and pecked his dark, stubbled cheek. "Thank you for everything."

He wanted to say something more, thought he should.

Damn.

Before he could get the words out, Lisa turned and dove overboard without the least bit of concern for hungry sharks.

He touched his check with his fingertips and watched her swim to *Julie Ann* and climb aboard. He'd found her voice pleasant and slightly intoxicating. Her curves inviting. But it was her eyes he remembered most: big and round—the color of chocolate syrup—doe eyes. He wouldn't forget them.

Five minutes later, Lisa emerged topside dressed in a heavy blue pullover and shorts. She leaned on the railing and yelled. "Where'd you say you were sailing to?"

He chuckled and yelled back, "A friend's house on Kaneohe Bay."

She waved, cast off the towline, and motored off in the direction of Oahu.

Jack watched *Julie Ann's* sharp bow slice the swells with no hint of the trouble she had been in just hours before.

He knew people coped with death differently, each in their own way. But he hadn't expected Lisa to dive overboard and sail off like that.

Weird…

Maybe not.

What he didn't understand was her decision to give up that lovable flop-eared hound.

CHAPTER 4

With anticipation and trepidation, Jack watched as the NOAA research vessel pulled the net free of the ocean floor. Next came the arduous task of hoisting the soggy mesh aboard. Jack didn't know how large the piece of netting was, but he did know that there would be tons of it, waterlogged and dripping wet. The job required a sturdy winch and a team of strong men. The NOAA vessel had both.

An hour later the crew winched the last of the netting aboard and piled it on the rear deck. To Jack's disgust—unfortunately as he expected—the net had continued to kill on its voyage across the sea. But a few of the ocean's creatures snagged in the nylon web's deadly grasp had survived. And the crew worked hard to carefully remove each one from the webbing and return it safely to the sea.

No remains of Brad Bowman were found. The sharks had left nothing but a memory for Lisa to mourn.

By five o'clock that afternoon, the crew of the NOAA vessel completed final preparations to return to port.

"We're finished here." Captain Prescott's voice crackled across Jack's marine radio. "You following us in?"

Jack grabbed the microphone and raised it to his mouth. "Just as soon as I check the reef for damage. It could be awhile before I get back this way and you know how I feel about those nets."

"You're not alone. Want us to stick around? Another hour won't make all that much difference."

"Go ahead and start in. I'm just going down for a quick look-see. Then I'll be joining you. I intend to buy you and your crew the beer I promised."

"Sounds good. Just make sure you don't get yourself into trouble down there. I want that beer."

Jack laughed. "And you can buy the second round."

"You're on."

Jack waved farewell. The NOAA crew worked hard. They were men and women—like him—devoted to preserving the oceans and marine life of the world. They'd have to be up early in the morning readying the ship, but tonight they'd toss back a few beers with him—his thanks for a job well done. And he'd deliver, after he checked the condition of the reef.

He slipped his arms into his wetsuit and zipped it up. Even the warm water of the islands would be cool seventy feet down. Next he slipped his arms into the buoyancy compensator strapped to his air tank, hoisted it onto his back, and buckled it tight. Then he stuffed the regulator mouthpiece between his teeth. He bit down on it, took a couple of test breaths, and stepped off the stern of his portside hull.

Thirty feet under, he pulled back and fanned his arms to hold his position. With the sunlight fading topside, he knew his eyes were playing tricks on him. That had to be it. Or carbon dioxide was contaminating the air in his tank.

Not likely.

Forty feet below him—on the edge of his visibility—a rusting hulk, encrusted in barnacles and coral, sat upright on the ocean floor.

The U-boat looked too small to be a full-sized submarine, but he could see the telltale conning tower and periscope. A shred of netting clung to the mast and swayed in the current like a flag in the wind.

A WW II mini sub.

Not a figment of his imagination.

On a visit to the Pearl Harbor exhibit, he'd seen photos of Japanese two-man mini-subs used in the attack: eighty feet long with two bow torpedo tubes, one on top of the other. He knew the role the subs had played, and that all but one of them had been accounted for.

He descended, hardly able to contain his excitement. The ghostly hulk had to be the missing Japanese mini-sub *I-16*. For three-quarters of a century, the sub's fate had remained a mystery—a mystery he now held the answer to.

At seventy feet, he leveled off and removed the last shred of netting from the periscope. The lens remained intact, and he peered into it, not really believing he would be able to see inside the sub. But he couldn't resist the temptation to look. He saw only blackness.

For a moment, he wondered about the remains of its two-man crew. The hatch below him appeared to be closed. If the inner hull remained intact, their skeletons might—at this very moment—be sitting at the controls they'd manned all those years ago.

A ghost ship and a ghost crew.

He stuffed the remnant of net inside his buoyancy vest. It would kill no more.

That done, he spent a few seconds of his precious down time surveying the sub. It had settled onto the sea floor, listing a few degrees to starboard. Corals, barnacles, and a multitude of other marine organisms were working hard to convert the war machine into a life-giving reef—a dichotomy to all the killer boat stood for. Nature's way of making things right.

He continued down and saw several jagged holes in the outer plating. But the years of submersion in saltwater made it impossible to differentiate war damage from corrosion.

On the side of the conning tower—barely visible amid the rust and marine growth—he could just make out the designation painted there by the boat's builders: *I-16*. He traced the numbers with his gloved hand and smiled inwardly.

The missing sub.

He swam toward the bow, recalling that after the attack on Pearl

Harbor, analysts from the United States Naval Institute claimed one of the mini-subs—believed to be *I-16*—successfully fired a torpedo into the *USS West Virginia.*

Were they right?

He wanted a look at the torpedo tubes.

He dropped over the bow, about to peer into the top tube, when he noticed an object round and white, lodged in the coral to his right. Mentally compensating for the magnification caused by the water, he estimated it to be the size of a large grapefruit.

The object looked strangely familiar. Not something that belonged on the reef.

The question of whether or not the sub's torpedoes had been fired would wait. Half-hoping the depth and lighting fooled with his mind, he swam to the enigma.

Carefully, he worked the pale white orb loose from the coral and raised it in front of the faceplate of his mask. In the gloom of the deep, he was staring into a pair of blank, lifeless eye sockets. His suspicions were confirmed.

The skull was the size of a young child's—but fully developed. And the teeth were worn from years of use. Clearly an adults.

Must be the remains of one of the sub's crew, he reasoned. Possibly the tide had washed the skull out of the sub through a split in its hull that he'd missed.

He glanced around. The rest of the bones, what happened to them?

Were they still entombed in the wreck?

He carried the skull with him while he made a quick check of the surrounding reef. It did not surprise him when his search came up empty. He needed help to explore all the nooks and crannies around the boat.

Before heading up, he took a long look at the skull. His first thought was to surface and tell the world about his discovery: the infamous missing Japanese mini-sub from the attack on Pearl Harbor.

But caution made him think better of it.

Despite the distortion of seventy feet of water he could see the uniqueness of the size of the skull—too small even for a chimpanzee.

A cold shiver danced up his spine. He'd share his discovery with the world, but only after he had answers. Now all he had to do was figure out how to get those answers, while at the same time keeping his find a secret.

CHAPTER 5

Jack cut the power to *Pono's* engines and let the catamaran drift the last few feet to the dock at the rear of Robert's house. Before sailing around the island to Kaneohe bay, he'd made port in Waikiki and bought Captain Prescott and his crew the promised beers. He wished he'd cut himself off at two. He was now in serious need of a hearty breakfast and a strong cup of coffee.

His friend Robert stood on the planked pier.

"Toss me the line," Robert called, holding his right hand out in front of him.

Jack waved, hurried forwards, and tossed him the bowline. Then he rushed astern and grabbed the rope coiled there. He hopped onto the pier and tied the aft mooring line to a metal turn-cleat. The bumpers he'd draped over the side of the hull forward and aft gently nudged the edge of the dock.

"You made good time," Robert said, putting a final cinch on the bowline. "It's not even nine yet."

"We got an early start." Jack raked his fingers through the salt-caked strands of his windblown hair, then wiped them on his shirt.

"I did my damnedest to get us here in time to hit you up for a hot shower and a home-cooked breakfast."

"Us?" Robert raised a brow.

"Rebel, remember?" Jack squatted and patted the planks with

the palm of his hand. "Come on, girl."

"Of course, the dog," Robert recalled. "On the radio, you mentioned having her dumped in your lap."

Rebel hesitated at the boat's railing, squatted, and jumped onto the pier.

"Good girl," Jack praised. He rubbed the basset behind the ears then watched her trot off—nose to the wooden deck—in the direction of shore.

"Now, what about breakfast?" Jack asked, facing his friend.

"You're lucky Kazuko likes you. She insisted on cooking enough Spam and scrambled eggs to have leftovers for you and the dog. I've got it warming in the oven."

Jack slapped Robert on the back. "Kazuko does like her Spam?"

Robert grinned. "And Rebel? You know your dog deserves the best."

"My dog?" Jack looked at the basset squatting on the grass at the head of the pier. He'd grown fond of the hound, but hadn't really thought of her as his. She didn't fit his idea of a water dog. Her short legs were more suited for digging. But she was awfully cute and well behaved.

"Yeah…your dog," Robert reaffirmed. "You said the girl you rescued—what was her name, Lisa?—gave her to you."

"I believe Lisa's words were to find Rebel a good home. So in a way, yeah, you're right. The dog belongs to me."

Rebel was nosing the planks in their direction. "See." Robert pointed at her. "The hound is attached to you already. She can't be away from you longer than it takes her to pee."

"Looks that way, doesn't it?" Jack's stomach growled loudly enough to draw a look from Robert.

"Damn," Robert said. "We'd better get some food in you."

Jack craned his neck, peering in the direction of the house. "And speaking of that lovely woman of yours, where's Kazuko? She's home, I hope?"

"Inside in her office working, the last time I checked."

"Good. I have something I want to show you both." Jack jumped aboard his boat, ducked into the cabin, and retrieved the skull, which he had wrapped in a beach towel to protect it. He cradled the bundle, the way a running back does a football, and rejoined Robert on the pier.

Robert nodded at the towel. "What have you got there?"

"I'm not sure." Jack kept the skull wrapped tight. "But I know I have a story to tell you that you won't believe."

"Not another one?"

Jack couldn't resist a broad grin. "This one you'll really like. And it doesn't involve someone wanting to kill you."

"Yeah…right. Well let's roust Kazuko from her computer and have a look at whatever it is you've got. Christ, you're holding onto that thing as though you're afraid it'll jump out of your arms."

"You'll know why, once you've had a look at it."

"By all means let's hurry, then. I'm not sure I can stand the suspense."

"Smartass."

Robert shrugged. "You're the one who came here with all the cloak and dagger stuff."

They caught up with Rebel, and the three of them walked toward Robert's house. When they reached the boathouse sheltering Robert's yellow and white de Havilland Beaver, Jack nodded at the vintage floatplane bobbing on its pontoons. "How's the plane running?"

"Like a top," Robert said. "You entertaining thoughts of going up in her?"

Jack shrugged. "Who knows?"

Inside the house, Jack placed the bundle on the koa-wood dining table and helped himself to the food warming in the oven, while Robert went in search of Kazuko. He piled Rebel's share on a plate and set it on the floor. She dug into hers and he carried his to the table.

"She'll be out in a minute," Robert said as he joined Jack at the table. "While we're waiting, you can tell me about this girl you saved."

"According to her, she's a cultural anthropologist, with a position at the American Museum of Natural History in New York."

"I suppose she's pretty?"

Jack grinned. "Not in a *Vogue Magazine* way, but she is pretty. She's in her late twenties, five foot four or five, with brown hair that hangs a few inches below her shoulders. And the woman has the biggest chocolate-brown eyes I've ever seen."

"I swear," Robert shook his head, "you and your women!"

"Good, you helped yourself." Kazuko called out from the hallway.

Jack got up and walked over to her with his arms open. "As always, the hostess with the mostest. And I have to say, you look magnificent." He hugged her. "Rebel and I thank you."

The dog appeared at their feet, and they looked down at her. She barked once, rose onto her short hind legs, and planted her oversized front paws on Kazuko's bare thighs.

Kazuko reached down with both hands and rubbed Rebel behind the ears. "You're quite welcome."

"I hate to intrude." Robert swept a hand in the direction of the table. "But I believe you have something you want to show us?"

Jack laughed. "Sure do."

They took seats at the table, and Rebel curled up at Jack's feet. Jack pushed his plate to the side and slid the bundle in front of him. "First let me tell you how I came to find what I'm about to show you."

"Not again." Robert shook his head slowly from side to side in obvious frustration. "Show us already."

"Relax, buddy. When I spoke to you on the CB I only gave you the abridged version of what happened. It'll save a lot of questions later if I start from the beginning."

"Ignore Robert," Kazuko said. "I'd love to hear what went on out there on the water. Robert only told me you rescued some girl and her dog."

"That's close to what I told him, but there's more...a lot more."

He started by describing the unearthly fog that should not

have been there. Then, without omitting even the smallest detail, he described the events leading to the discovery of the skull. When he was done, he carefully unwrapped his find and cradled it in the palms of his hands with the hollow eye sockets staring at Robert and Kazuko. For a long moment neither of them said a word, their gazes locked on the tiny skull.

"What gives?" Robert's expression turned to oak. "Someone killing children?"

Kazuko also looked confused.

"That's what I thought at first," Jack said. He extended his arms across the tabletop and offered the remains to Kazuko. "Take a closer look and tell me what you think."

"Scientifically?"

"Scientifically."

"You know this isn't my field of expertise."

"You've had the same classes I have. Give it a shot."

Kazuko concentrated. "Modern humanoid. Quite small. Childlike." She took the skull from Jack's hand and rotated it in her fingers, carefully examining every feature. "But the teeth are different from those of a young child. They appear worn. An adult."

"What are we talking about, here?" Robert shot a questioning look at Kazuko, then Jack. "A midget? A dwarf?"

"I'm not sure," Kazuko answered.

"But it could be?"

"Perhaps."

Kazuko handed the skull back to Jack. "You think this could be remains from one of the sub's crew?"

"The thought crossed my mind." Jack studied the skull for the hundredth time since finding it. "But I don't think so."

"It has to be," she said.

"Does it?"

"What other explanation is there?" Robert asked.

"That I don't know," Jack said.

"Well I know one thing for sure." Kazuko nodded at the skull. "We're only guessing. You need to show this to an expert in the field."

"Or turn it over to the police," Robert urged.

"No police," Jack said right back. He didn't even have to think about his answer. "Not yet, anyway."

"And let me guess" Robert probed. "For the time being you're not going to share your discovery of the mini-sub?"

"No."

Kazuko settled back in her chair. "You have that look, Jack."

"He's already made up his mind," Robert quickly added. "I can tell. And that look you see in his eyes is the look he gets when he's about to involve me in one of his harebrained schemes."

"We need to find out what I have here, first." Jack returned the skull to the towel. "Then we can talk about harebrained schemes."

"I agree we need to know more," Kazuko said. "Do you have a person in mind to contact?"

Jack stroked his chin. "I know just the person, if I can reach her."

CHAPTER 6

A week later, Jack watched woman in a red, low-cut evening gown walk through the doorway of Millstones on Robson Street in downtown Vancouver. He'd dined with the same woman two years ago. Several male patrons stopped in mid-bite to stare at the contours of her voluptuous figure, emphasized by the close fit of her dress.

In her stiletto heels, Dr. Sienna Conti stood a full five inches taller than the average male, and an inch above Jack's six-foot frame. She was perfectly proportioned, and her silky, shoulder length, dark brown hair could have put her in shampoo commercials. Her full, soft lips made a man want to kiss them.

No one in the restaurant would have guessed she was a renowned and highly respected paleoanthropologist and evolutionary biologist from the University of New England in Australia.

He recalled how he had loved looking at her standing on the stage, lecturing on the evolution of man. And how much he truly enjoyed the conversation they shared during dinner later that night. The woman's scientific achievements were legendary.

Now that he thought back on that night, Jack was sure he would have made a play for her—or at least done more than just flirt—had it not been for the half-dozen colleagues seated at the table with them. They'd all competed for her attention. But then he must have made more of an impression on her than he believed at the time. When he spoke to her on the phone a week ago to explain what he needed, she had a vivid recollection of him and that night.

Jack rose from his seat trying not to stare and glanced around the restaurant. "A bit fancy for my taste."

"Who said you have taste, Jack?"

He looked at her and felt a shiver of uneasiness, dressed as he was in his khaki Dockers and loaner restaurant tie and sport coat.

She smiled. "Jack, I do believe your hands are shaking."

They weren't. She obviously had a playful side to her. Confidence, beauty, class. And the ability to joke when appropriate. He liked that.

"I'm sure it's that dress" he said. "You look positively stunning." He slid the chair out for her. "Have a seat and I'll order us drinks."

Sienna eyed Jack up and down. "You look good, too. All that time you spend at sea obviously agrees with you."

Jack scoffed. Did she know what she was doing to him? "If that's the case, how come I'm the only one who's nervous?"

She batted her eyes. "What makes you say I'm not?"

The woman knows.

He chuckled. "Because your hands aren't shaking."

She gracefully took her seat and watched him fumble with the chair across the table from her and sit down. "I do believe you're more nervous than I am."

"I'll get over it." He took a sip of ice water to cool his hormones.

"Jack, I have to say, I'm flattered. The moment I'm in the market for a man, I'm looking you up."

They both laughed.

"Let's order before we get ourselves into trouble," he said. "Then you can tell me all about that skull I sent you. If I remember right, on the phone the other day you used the word unbelievable."

She nodded. "First of all, the skull's not from a child, as size would appear to indicate. It's from an adult female, thirty to forty years old. Close examination revealed unique cut marks on the left occipital condyle. The occipital condyles articulate with the first cervical vertebrae"

"You're saying the head was cut off?"

"Not cut off, bitten off. The cut marks were consistent with shark bite."

"So the head was bitten off by a shark?"

"More precisely, the body was bitten off from the head."

"I can see that. The shark—probably a full-grown tiger—takes the woman's body into its mouth and bites down, severing the head. Death by shark attack; makes sense. But you could have told me that over the phone."

"I could have, but there's more. And this is where it gets intriguing." She glanced around, then leaned close to Jack and said in a hushed voice, "Are you familiar with the island of Flores between mainland Asia and Australia and the discovery of an 18,000 year-old skeleton nicknamed Hobbit?"

He wondered why she was lowering her voice. The discovery she spoke of was not a secret. "I read a short article on the discovery in 2003 when it first happened." He kept his voice low to match hers. "*Homo floresiensis* is the name discoverers gave a new species of human. She was what, three feet tall with a brain smaller than a chimpanzee's?"

"That's the one."

His forehead knotted. "You're not implying—"

"Let me explain," she said, before he could question further. "Hobbit lived during a time when modern humans—people like you and me—were on the march around the globe. That makes her unique. At first the scientists thought they had discovered the bones of a child, perhaps three years old. Then they realized it belonged to a full-sized adult. The pelvic structure told them Hobbit was female, and tooth wear confirmed she was adult. They estimated her weight at just fifty-five pounds. And you're right about the brain. They calculated it to be less than a third the size of a modern human's."

"Doctor Conti, I know where you're going with this, but it can't be."

"Humor me. And call me Sienna."

Jack liked the direction this relationship was heading. "I'd love to, Sienna."

"Careful. Those big hands of yours will start shaking again."

He glanced at his hands. They were fine. She'd done it to him again. "Okay, I'm humoring you."

Her lips curled into a hint of a smile. "As I was saying, the island of Flores was never connected by land bridges to either Asia or Australia. Even during periods of low sea level, Flores was separated from other landmasses by at least fifteen miles. Until the 1990's, when researchers used modern techniques to date tools first discovered by Theodor Verhoeven in the Soa Basin on Flores, most scientists believed no people could have reached Flores. Until some 4,000 years ago, when modern humans came along with the brainpower to build boats. Those test results dated the tools to about 840,000 years ago. They prove Verhoven's claims that human ancestors reached Flores long before modern humans landed there. *Homo floresiensis* was one of those early human ancestors."

"Which leads to the question of how did they get there ahead of modern man if their brain was roughly the size of a grapefruit?"

"Precisely. What's even more interesting is that well-flaked spearheads were also found. That suggests Homo floresiensis—though his brain was much smaller than his Homo erectus ancestors—was much smarter. In January 2007, a computer model of Hobbit's brain showed frontal lobes with big convolutions—a trait linked to higher thought. And unusually large temporal lobes, which handle hearing, memory, and emotion."

"So am I to understand they were as smart as you and I?"

"Maybe even smarter about some things. Their brains were highly developed and advanced in ways different from the human brain of today."

"And *Homo floresiensis* existed side by side with modern man," he thought aloud. "Maybe that's what drove them to Flores. They were trying to stay one step ahead of their larger, stronger cousins." He took a breath, mulling over what he said. "I'll buy that. But Flores is over three thousand miles away from Hawaii. There's got to be some other explanation."

She shook her head. "Your skull is *Homo floresiensis*, Jack."

"You're sure?"

She leaned closer. "That's not all. It's primitive—like Hobbit—but modern. The skull you found didn't come from someone who's been dead thousands of years…or even a hundred years."

He waved her words away. "Impossible."

"But a fact just the same."

"That would mean some of Hobbit's relatives survived long after they were thought to be extinct."

"Maybe there is something to the legends."

"Legends?"

"According to geologist working on Flores, a volcanic eruption some 12,000 years ago could very well have been responsible for the demise of *Homo floresiensis* in the part of the island where Hobbit's bones were found, along with other local fauna, including the dwarf elephant called Stegodon. The archeologists who discovered her, however, suspect that *Homo floresiensis* may have survived longer in other parts of Flores to become the source of the *Ebu Gog* legend told by the local people."

"*Ebu Gog*?" Jack scrunched up his face. "Never heard of it."

She rolled her eyes. "Not it, Jack. According to legend, the *Ebu Gog* are small, hairy, cave dwellers matching what we know about *Homo floresiensis*. They were even believed to be present when the first Portuguese ships arrived there during the 16th century. Furthermore, these strange little creatures were reportedly last spotted as recently as the late 19th century."

"I can see where you're going with this," Jack interrupted. "Who—"

"I'm only telling you what I know," she said before he could finish. "There are other reports, too. For instance, on the island of Sumatra, people have reported sighting a one to one-and-one-half-meter tall humanoid they call the *Orang Pendek*, which a few professional scholars take seriously. Two amateur explorers even claim to have recovered footprints and hairs believed to be from the *Orang Pendek*."

Another Big Foot sighting, only *Little Foot* in this case. He didn't know what to think, but she had him intrigued. "I'm sure they did DNA testing?"

"Analysis yielded mixed results. Experts who believe in the find feel both the footprints and the hairs are from a previously undocumented species of primate, but DNA analysis of the hairs found only human DNA."

"Contamination by the people who handled the hairs?"

"That's one possible explanation. Another is that the scholars supporting these sightings are merely seeing what they want to see."

He grinned. "And you?"

Sienna smiled back. "If the stories are correct, the *Orang Pendek* may also be modern Flores men still living on Sumatra. What I can't explain, is how this skull ended up in the water off Kauai."

Their dinners arrived and conversation between them stopped as they concentrated on eating.

Halfway through his steak, Jack pointed his fork at her. "You know this means someone got to Hawaii ahead of the first Marquesan and Tahitian settlers."

"You're not thinking *Homo floresiensis*?"

"That's exactly what I'm thinking."

"Interesting but unlikely."

"Now who's the skeptic? You ever hear of the *Menehune*?"

"Of course I have. But you said it yourself, we're talking thousands of miles of ocean."

"Why not? If their survival was threatened on Flores and—if you believe the reports—other islands as well, what's to keep a few of them from sailing away to find a new land? Columbus did it. The Marquesan and Tahitian settlers did it. Why not *Homo floresiensis*?"

"The Polynesians were experienced seamen in ocean-worthy boats. *Homo floresiensis* didn't have the knowledge."

"Columbus got lucky. So did the Polynesians. Who says *Homo floresiensis* didn't have the knowledge and skill to do the same thing?"

"The skull does suggest it. But...?"

"But nothing."

She did not answer right away. Finally she said, "You have a flight back tomorrow?"

"First thing in the morning. Why?"

"You stumbled onto a find that defies explanation. One that needs to be presented to the scientific community."

"It will be. I'm just not ready to do that yet. And I'm asking you to keep it secret a little longer. Are you willing to do that?"

"You can trust me. I might have been the one to tell you what you found, but the right to tell the world about it is all yours."

"Will you hold onto the skull for me? I don't want anything to happen to it."

"Sure. I'll keep it locked up until you instruct me otherwise." She dug out a gold pen and a personal business card from her clutch-purse and scribbled a number on the back. "This is my private number. Call me."

"I can't thank you enough." He took her card and tapped it against his hand. "The skull might be the only bones down there. And it might or might not be connected to what happened on the water that night. But one thing's for sure, something not entirely of this world went on out there and I'm going to get to the bottom of it."

CHAPTER 7

Jack stood on the sidewalk outside the Honolulu International Airport baggage-claim area. He switched on his cell phone to call Robert who was waiting in the short-term lot. He and Kazuko were anxious to hear about the skull.

Robert pulled to the curb five minutes later, and Jack was glad to see Kazuko with him.

He tossed his bag in the back and climbed in. Robert studied him in the rearview mirror. Kazuko sat sideways in her seat, looking at him.

"Aren't you going to ask how my flight was?"

Kazuko inched around a little more. "We want to hear about the skull."

"So you don't want to hear about the hijacking and how I was forced to have sex with three voluptuous flight attendants?"

"Nice try," Robert said. "Tell us about the skull."

"Have it your way." Jack settled back in his seat. "You drive and I'll talk."

Once they were settled into the flow of traffic out of the terminal, Jack told them the story.

Robert looked at him in the mirror. "Surely you're not saying Sienna believes that skull you found belongs to *Homo floresiensis*?"

"That's exactly what I'm saying."

Kazuko settled back in her seat. "Ireland has its leprechauns, Scandinavia has its trolls, we have the *Menehune*...every culture has its enigmas. Stories, Jack. That's all they are."

"Stories, maybe." Jack shifted his attention to Kazuko. "But some of them have at least some probability of being true. The existence of *Homo floresiensis* supports it."

"I know how your mind works," Robert said. "You believe those stories. And you're thinking this *Homo floresiensis* creature migrated to the Hawaiian Islands from Flores and that skull you found is the proof."

Jack glanced back and forth at Robert and Kazuko. "I don't know how that skull ended up in the ocean off the coast of Kauai. But I do know the skull came from a three-foot humanoid believed to have survived well into the 19th century. Now there might be some answers down there and there might not. I won't know that until I check. And that's exactly what I'm going to do...first thing in the morning. The question is, are you going with me?"

* * * *

The next morning Jack, Robert, and Kazuko stood in the cockpit of Jack's sixty-foot catamaran. With Jack at the helm they watched the eastern sky turn from blush to coral to bright crimson. Tentacles of orange and red wrapped themselves around a mantle of clouds, sending a spray of color into the morning sky. Seventeen miles to the west, Niihau—*The Forbidden Isle*—remained a dark shadow.

"Red sky in the morning," Robert said. "Sailor take warning."

"That's what they say." Jack looked up at the rigging, then glanced down at the compass and checked their heading. "But I don't think we're in for stormy weather any time soon. Nothing but smooth sailing, bright skies, and clear water for us...according to the Channel Nine weather man, anyway."

"You honestly think there's more down there—besides that Japanese mini-sub, I mean?"

"We'll know in a couple of hours. And to answer your question, yes I do. That skull didn't just drop from the sky."

"I wish we'd brought someone else along with us to remain topside and man the boat," Kazuko interjected, her lips downcast in disappointment. "That way I could have dived with you."

Jack sympathized with Kazuko. With luck, he and Robert would solve the enigma of Hawaii's *Menehune* legend. To not be down there with them when they did made her feel left out of the action, and for good reason. Staring into the depths from the deck of a boat, not knowing what's going on seventy feet down, is both nerve wracking and anticlimactic.

But then again, the dive might not turn up anything new—other than giving Robert an opportunity to look over the mini-sub, which Kazuko wanted to do as well. But the wreck of *I-16* wasn't going anywhere for some time. Before the sunken WWII derelict was raised from her watery grave, Kazuko would have plenty of opportunities to look it over. He'd make sure of that.

"You're a capable diver," Jack told her. He didn't want to sound chauvinistic and he hoped what he was about to say didn't come out that way. "But…I don't know, I'd just feel better if Robert made the first dive with me. Not knowing what we are going to run into, I'd be too worried about you."

"And you're not worried about me?" Robert gasped, doing his best to feign hurt.

"No offense, buddy. She's way prettier than you. And you know how I feel about the ladies."

"Sure, always riding to their defense. And I'm left watching your back."

Jack patted Robert on the shoulder. "That's why I want you with me down there. Someone has to make sure I don't go sticking my hand into the wrong hole."

"Right. And you get the girl in the end," Robert said, still playing along.

"Wrong, you've got the girl." Jack pointed at Kazuko.

Kazuko's long, dark hair glistened in the breeze like waving threads of black silk. Her dark almond-shaped eyes were sparkling pools of oil. And her flawless brown skin, bronzed by the rising sun—a tribute to her island heritage—stood out in contrast to her father's fair-skinned Japanese ancestry. Her lips curled into a smile when she returned their gazes.

"What are you two gawking at? And you Rebel?" She brushed wild strands of hair from her face.

"A goddess," Robert said. "And none of us is going to let anything happen to you."

Kazuko leaned down and petted the top of Rebel's head. "Rebel is absolutely precious, but you two are completely nuts. Nothing bad is going to happen out here on a fine day like this!"

* * * *

Jack idled *Pono* along and watched the longitude and latitude change on the screen of his GPS. When the coordinates appeared, that would put him directly over the sunken sub, he shut down the engines and dropped anchor.

The catamaran swung around on the anchor line, putting her bow into the incoming current. Jack calculated the sub lay about fifty feet to port of their position. Four hundred yards astern of them, the rugged mountains of the Na Pali Coast stood out like a scene from *Jurassic Park*.

"Beautiful, isn't it?" Jack said.

Robert took in the sight. "Just where I'd expect to find a twelve thousand year-old skull."

"According to Doctor Conti, this one's a mite more recent than that."

"I feel like Faye Wray in King Kong," Kazuko added.

Robert wrapped his arm around her waist. "Relax. That overgrown chimp's not getting his hands on you unless he can swim."

"Speaking of swimming," Jack said. "Tide's on its way in. Mind you don't get swept ashore by the current."

"I'm not the one to worry about," Robert scoffed. "You're the one who takes chances he shouldn't."

Jack grinned. "And I'm the one who gets the girl, remember?"

"I heard that." Kazuko stepped over to where they were huddled round the dive equipment. "Is that all you two talk about, girls?"

Jack squatted and began checking the dive equipment Robert had assembled for him. "Not me. Robert brought it up."

"Like she's going to believe that," Robert said. "Now, if you don't mind, I'd like to get wet."

Jack ran his hands over his Sea Quest buoyancy compensator, making sure the tank was strapped tightly to its mount, and that the inflation valve and buckles worked properly. Once he'd done that, he checked his backup regulator to see that it was in place. Having an octopus setup, providing a secondary regulator to breathe through in an emergency, was easier and safer than buddy breathing. And it was indispensable if your primary regulator failed.

Next, he lifted his new Scuba Pro Mark 12 regulator and purged a burst of air through it…and one more for good measure. Then he inserted the rubber mouthpiece into his mouth and tried a couple of breaths.

He trusted Robert's compressor. But he didn't want to chance getting a dose of bad air. He'd been down that route once before and it had almost killed him. Fresh air from the tank flowed freely into his lungs.

Satisfied the equipment was functioning properly, he pulled the regulator from his mouth and let it hang by the air hose connected to the tank. "The depth here is around seventy feet. That'll give us about forty-five minutes of downtime before we need to worry about decompression."

"Even if it comes to that there shouldn't be a problem." Robert peered at the numbers on his pressure gage. "My tank reads right at three thousand PSI. Yours should read the same. That'll give us close to an hour and a half's worth of air if you don't suck yours dry chasing after a beautiful raven-haired mermaid flashing her bushy eyebrows at you."

Jack frowned at Robert. "Are you feeling particularly testy this morning or what? We let that subject drop, remember? Besides, you and I both know you're the one who's always sucking your tank dry."

"Is that right? A bottle of Don Julio says I'll be calling you Hoover when we compare pressure gages at the end of the dive."

"You're on."

"It's a bet then."

Jack pinched the fabric of Robert's wetsuit. "Nice."

"My birthday present from Kazuko. Titanium lined three millimeter with a matching three millimeter hooded vest."

"Figures you'd have the best. I'm still using the five millimeter I bought a couple of years ago."

"Works doesn't it?" Robert smiled and clapped Jack on the back. "Let's get wet."

The two friends sobered up the moment they strapped on their dive gear. They'd made countless dives together during their six-year friendship, and both of them respected the ocean for its wondrous beauty…and its power to kill.

"We'll take a quick look at the sub, then I'll show you where I found the skull," Jack said. "We'll fan out from there and see what we find. And keep a check on our downtime. I'll do the same."

"See you down there." Robert adjusted his mask, bit down on his regulator mouthpiece, gripped the railing, and stepped off the stern of *Pono's* portside hull.

"Don't take any chances," Kazuko said from behind Jack. "I want both of you back aboard safe and sound."

"No worries." Jack waved his hand at the sky. "You said it yourself. Nothing can go wrong on a beautiful day like this."

He inserted his mouthpiece, repositioned his mask, and stepped into the water.

CHAPTER 8

From just a few feet down, Jack could see the mini-sub sitting on the ocean floor. Robert hung in the water ten feet below him staring at it, clearly mesmerized by the sight. Jack caught up with his friend and they proceeded down together.

They circled the periscope the same way Jack had the day he discovered the sub. His fascination remained.

They released another burst of air from their buoyancy compensators and lowered themselves onto the hatch cover. Robert tugged on the locking wheel. It didn't budge.

Jack pointed out the *I-16* painted on the tower. Robert flashed him the okay sign with his thumb and middle finger.

Robert took the lead and swam the length of the two-man sub. Along the way, he rubbed flakes of rust from the hull with his gloved hand and pounded on the metal skin with his knuckles. Each rap sent a thud of solid metal to their ears.

Jack knew the thought going through Robert's mind. He'd come to the same conclusion. The skull did not come from inside the sub. The only breach in the hull was where it had rusted through from the outside. The inner hull remained intact.

Leaving the WWII derelict behind, Jack led Robert to the recess in the reef where he'd discovered the remains. They knew from his initial search, there were no other bones in the immediate vicinity, but he and Robert planned to begin a broader search from there.

Jack removed his mouthpiece and purged air into the small inflatable buoy he retrieved from the pocket on his buoyancy compensator. He let the float's lead anchor sink to the bottom and watched the connecting line play out. The buoy hovered three feet above the coral, giving them a spot to guide off of. He flashed Robert a thumbs up.

With an arm's length separating them, they swam a circular search pattern that spiraled out ten yards with each pass around the buoy. Their depth fluctuated between seventy and eighty feet. Forty minutes later, their grid—like an expanding wheel—widened a hundred yards, revealing nothing of significance.

Jack signaled a halt and surveyed the reef. The undersea landscape stood out a drab greenish brown, giving the impression the reef was dying.

He knew it to be far from the truth. Water absorbs light. Red was the first to go, then orange, yellow, green, blue, indigo, and finally violet. The corals here looked remarkably healthy.

The rogue section of drift net had done its killing above, not down here.

He noticed Robert peering into shadows in the coral twenty feet away. He checked his watch. They had time.

Leaving his friend to search the area he'd focused in on, Jack checked the compass strapped to his wrist and swam into a break in the reef in front of him. It was like following a riverbed on a direct line to the coast.

After a couple of minutes of looking and finding nothing, he began an arch that would take him back to Robert's location. A sudden surge in the current swept him sideways. Had he not been on the bottom of the ocean off the uninhabited Napali Coast, he'd have thought a huge gush of water had been expelled from a giant pipe.

The unexpected current surprised him. He swam into it, kicking hard to hold his position against the rush of the tide, and scanned the reef, not sure what he was searching for.

Then he spied the source of the surge: a hole, six or seven feet across, that looked like a dark shadow in the cleft of a wall of coral to his right.

An overwhelming desire to probe the cause of the freakish phenomenon kept him from swimming free of the current. The muscles in his legs began to cramp. Finally, the surge trickled off to nothing. He floated a few seconds, peering into the opening.

Suddenly, he felt himself sucked toward the hole.

He tried to swim away, but couldn't.

The powerful vacuum dragged his feet inside.

He kicked with every ounce of strength he had and dug at the water with the palms of his hands, trying to claw his way out.

No use. The reef swallowed him.

He reached out desperately and grabbed a rock outcropping at the mouth of the cave and held on.

* * * *

Fifty feet away, Robert glanced at the orange dial of his DOXA dive watch. They had been down forty-five minutes. Time for them to head up. He looked over at Jack just in time to watch him disappear feet first into a dark cleft at the base of the reef.

What the hell?

It took a moment for him to realize what happened. Then it hit him. A cave…Jack had been sucked into a cave.

He felt a shift in the surge, but nothing strong enough to cause him to drift more than a few feet back and forth. The current had to be significantly stronger where Jack was, for the hole to swallow him like that. He couldn't imagine what was causing the anomaly.

Without a second's more hesitation, he swam as fast as he could toward Jack. When he neared the hole, he felt the surge pull him in that direction. Twenty feet ahead, the opening loomed black and foreboding.

It'd be tricky avoiding the suction. Then he saw Jack's body disappear into darkness.

His friend was gone.

He quickly brought his flippered feet around to position them between him and the mouth of the cave. Then he kicked hard with his long powerful legs and backstroked to keep from being sucked inside. And from fifteen feet away he was just able to hold his own against the current.

For what seemed like an eternity, he stared at the black hole. It'd only been seconds—he knew—but plenty long enough for the full impact of what had happened to tear at his guts.

Then he saw his friend's gloved hand gripping a rock at the entrance.

His chance.

Robert approached the opening from the side. With the current tugging at his body, he reached around and grabbed Jack's hand; then he leaned in and peered at his friend. In the gloom of the cave, he could just see Jack's eyes on the other side of his faceplate: wide open and expectant.

Jack winked as if to say, *What kept you?* Then his hand slipped from Robert's grasp and his eyes opened wide in horror.

As did Robert's.

In the next instant, Jack disappeared into blackness.

"No!" Robert's scream sent a stream of bubbles to the surface.

He pressed closer to the opening.

Gone.

He had two choices: Surface and hope Jack made it out okay on his own or stay and help his friend. Only one choice was acceptable in his eyes. Help his friend. But he couldn't risk becoming trapped himself.

Precious seconds ticked by.

He pondered his options. Surface for fresh tanks and return with a safety line or let himself be sucked into the cave with Jack and hope that together they could make it out alive.

The problem was, they were already at the point of having to decompress or surface. If he went up now and brought down fresh tanks they had a chance. They would still have to decompress, but they would have extra tanks to ensure they had the air to do it with. If he entered the tunnel without the extra tanks and they used up the air supply they had left just getting out, they might both drown, or at best have to surface and suffer the excruciating pain of the bends.

He checked his decompression gauge. The needle touched red.

Time's up. He had to make a decision or waste another fourteen minutes decompressing at fifteen feet.

He needed the extra tanks. Now!

He took one last look into the black void of the tunnel and kicked hard for the surface.

CHAPTER 9

Jack felt as if he were being sucked into the nozzle of a fire hose. At first he tried to fight the current, but he quickly discovered that was an exercise in futility. All he did was exhaust his air supply. The only choice he had was let the flow take him and hope for the best.

He pointed his flippers in the direction of the current, flattened himself, and tucked his arms to his sides like fins on a torpedo. Within seconds, absolute darkness engulfed him.

Jack never suffered from claustrophobia, and early on in life had learned to master his fear and rely on it to heighten his senses. But here, in this black tunnel, the walls he couldn't see closed in on him. Never before had he felt so helpless, frightened, and alone.

And even though he breathed in—heard the hiss of air pass through the regulator in his mouth, tasted its cool freshness—his system starved for oxygen.

Or was it in his mind?

His chest tightened.

He thumbed the switch on the end of the mini dive-light tethered to his wrist.

Silt swirled in the narrow beam. But the small electric torch did little to light the way.

In the gloom of this watery hell, he concentrated on breathing: slow rhythmic breaths that flowed naturally in and out of his lungs.

All the while, he was reassuring himself that his deadly predicament would turn out all right.

Rocketing through the underwater tunnel, he understood the phenomenon. Five million years ago, a tube formed when red-hot lava flowed into the sea and crusted over. The sea now surged back and forth through that tube with the rise and fall of the tide.

This was not the first time he'd been sucked into a lava tube, and he relaxed somewhat, knowing he would be able to ride the current out the way he'd ridden it in.

Not unlike a wild ride at a California water park.

The passage snaked inland, and several times his flippers careened off the wall. At first, he'd been worried about slamming into jagged rock outcroppings, but dismissed his concern when he realized the lava had been worn smooth by eons of sand and silt washing back and forth in the tube.

But what if the tunnel suddenly narrowed to the size of a basketball? He'd be jammed into the opening by the current.

A cork in a bottle.

His heart raced with the thought of what it would be like to suffer a slow agonizing death, hopelessly stuck there.

In several places the tunnel did narrow—giving him the impression he was passing through the center of an hour glass—but each time he made it through with room to spare.

It felt like the ride would go on forever. But he knew that would not be the case.

A moment later the current slacked off. He mentally prepared himself for the inevitable change in direction of the surge. He'd simply turn with the tide and ride the current out feet first.

His nerves tensed.

That's when the tunnel opened up on him.

At once he realized he'd been spat out into a large cavern.

But how large?

And where on earth was he…?

He flashed his dive light around. The narrow beam would not touch the surrounding walls.

All at once it dawned on him that, suspended in absolute darkness with only a stab of light illuminating the silt swirling in the water four feet in front of him, he should not have had a sense of direction. But oddly enough, he did.

It wasn't absolute darkness. A dim glow filtered down to him, and when he looked up, he saw the reflection of surface water.

An air pocket.

New questions flooded his brain.

Jack tried to not let his overactive mind run amuck and imagine all sorts of screwy possibilities. At best they would only be guesses.

He needed concrete answers.

He thumbed a valve on his vest and shot a burst of air into his buoyancy compensator. It was easy for him to accept the presence of a grotto deep within the lava tube.

But not light.

Slowly, he ascended above the current that would have carried him back the way he'd come. He had no idea how large an air pocket had formed or even if the air was breathable. It didn't matter. His curiosity wouldn't let him pass up the opportunity to check it out.

And there was still the riddle behind that mysterious luminescence, above.

With his hand raised to shield his skull from cracking on a low ceiling of rock, Jack eased his head out of the water.

* * * *

Robert surfaced astern of the catamaran. His decompression gauge showed red, and he knew he should have swum straight to the surface from the mouth of the cave. But he also knew that a hundred yard surface swim, while bogged down in scuba gear, would have sapped his strength and wasted minutes he didn't have. He'd chosen to push the limit of his downtime and angle his assent to come up at the boat.

He peeled back his mask and saw Kazuko staring down at him from the stern railing. Her brow furrowed. At once he realized she'd been watching his bubbles rise to the surface...*one set of bubbles.* Rebel had her over-sized front paws hooked over the railing next to Kazuko.

The basset hound howled at his appearance as though she, too, knew something bad had happened to Jack.

He spit out his regulator and yelled, "Jack's been sucked into a cave. My tank's low on air. Hand me down a fresh one and the nylon rope inside the locker under the seat there."

"I knew something was wrong! I've rigged a tank with Jack's old regulator and it's ready to go. But it doesn't have an octopus set up."

"Give it to me. I've got to get back down there. And toss me a real dive light. The little piece of shit I have with me isn't cutting it."

"Can you see him?" she said, rummaging in the storage locker beside her. "Is he all right?"

"He's too far inside to tell."

She tossed him the rope. "For God's sake, how'd it happen?"

He had no intention of wasting precious minutes discussing what happened. There would be time for that when Jack was safe aboard the boat.

"Later," he hollered and unbuckled his buoyancy compensator and tank. He handed it up to Kazuko. "Now hurry and get that tank."

"Okay! Okay!" she yelled back at him. She turned and disappeared from sight.

A few seconds later she reappeared and lowered the tank to him. "Do I need to radio for help?"

"Not yet." He turned in the water and scanned the surface behind him. "Jack might have already made it out of there on his own."

She looked. "I don't see any bubbles."

Robert hadn't truly believed she would. "I'm going down. I'll swim into that cave and pull him out if I have to. When we come up we'll need to decompress. With this full tank we should have plenty of air. But just in case, tie a line to that last tank. Lower it to fifteen feet and keep it there."

Kazuko dropped the light to him. "Whatever you do, be careful."

He buckled on the fresh tank, repositioned his mask over his eyes, tucked the rope under his arm, and used his free hand to fish the regulator from the water.

Dammit, Jack!

He purged a shot of air through his regulator and looked up at Kazuko through his goggles.

He saw her brush a tear from her cheek.

"I'll tug two times on the rope when we get to the tank," he said. "You should be able to see us at that depth and know he's with me. If I tug three times, call the Coast Guard and tell them we have a diver emergency. Better yet, call them anyway and give them a heads up. Every second will count."

Without another word, Robert bit down the mouthpiece, ducked his head under the water, and kicked for the bottom.

CHAPTER 10

Stunned, Jack slid his mask onto his forehead and looked around. The odor of salt, rotting seaweed, and fish guts hung heavy in the air. He didn't bother using his tiny dive light. The narrow beam would have been welcome in darkness, but it wasn't needed. An unearthly glow, like the one he'd seen the night he pulled Lisa from the floundering *Julie Ann*, lit up a large open gallery in a kind of twilight—as if the sun were about to rise on some distant subterranean horizon.

The sight was almost more than his mind could comprehend. He stared at it, unblinking.

Overhead, a domed ceiling arched fifty feet or more above the surface, of what he could only describe as a mini sea. Sheer walls of dull grey rock rose out of the water a couple of hundred feet to each side of him. He'd surfaced inside a flattened Neolithic superdome.

Thirty yards in, a wall-to-wall stretch of white sand sloped out of this mini sea, six or eight feet above the tide line. With the rise and fall of the surge, small waves curled and broke along the pristine beach. And just beyond the slope of sand stood a cluster of what looked like fat mushroom caps.

Jack dropped his gaze from the grandeur of the cavern for a moment and scanned the blue-white sheen on the surface of the water.

A miniature milky sea.

No other explanation fit.

Or did it?

He cupped a double handful of seawater and peered into it. Countless fine threads of light—some an inch long—swirled like an alien soup.

He smiled, opened his fingers, and let the water splash back into the sea. To be certain, he used the flat of his hands to cut semicircular swaths along the surface of the water. The wakes behind his palms showed black.

Now he knew for sure. This was not an algal bloom of a red tide, distributed vertically through the water column that lit up when agitated. The blue-white luminescence existed only at the surface and glowed undisturbed.

How had such a concentration of bacteria formed here?

For now, he was satisfied just to know the source of the light. Other answers would come in time.

He swam toward the beach. When his feet touched bottom, he slipped off his flippers and waded ashore. A few feet above the waterline, he dropped his fins and mask, unbuckled and shrugged off his buoyancy compensator and air tank and stood them up in the loose sand.

Feeling as if he'd just landed on a foreign country, he turned in a complete circle, taking in the vastness of the cavern. Then he remembered he'd brought his digital waterproof camera.

He dug the compact Canon out of a storage pocket and flashed a few pictures. Then he climbed the sandy incline.

From the top of the slope, he gazed inland with a renewed realization of something mysterious and exciting. He hadn't spied a field of giant mushrooms or anything close to being a mushroom. In front of him, a half dozen huts, little more than four feet high, littered the area—grass roofs looking like golden domed caps sitting atop fat stalks.

But why build huts? It didn't make sense for someone to put up walls and a roof with no foul weather to keep out or a need for shade.

He scanned the sand and saw hundreds of tiny depressions.

Footprints.

He didn't know how long the tracks had been there. In a place without rain or wind, it could have been thousands of years.

And what about the huts? The people who inhabited these squat little homes could not have been more than three feet tall.

Homo floresiensis.

More questions without answers.

He faced the water. From that vantage point he could see two ponds—one on each side of the flooded grotto—separated from the main body of water by low rock walls. Each pond measured approximately seventy-five by a hundred and fifty feet. Obviously, the inhabitants of the subterranean village had practiced aquaculture...*or still did.*

Could it be possible?

It was easy for his mind to run wild, imagining a long lost race of little people occupying the village while they harvested fish, lobster, octopus, and other seafood from the ponds.

Caught up in the magnificence of it all, he turned toward the cluster of huts and hollered, "Hello."

His voice echoed in the cavern, then fell silent.

All he could hear was the gentle lapping of the waves on the beach behind him.

He walked to the closest hut and knelt down. Then he pulled back the multicolored cloth flap covering the doorway, and peeked inside, using his mini dive light to illuminate the interior.

He saw a raised sleeping area, folded netting, wood bowls, and painted gourd pitchers for carrying water. Everything appeared neat, clean and orderly, as if the inhabitants had just stepped out.

A chill crept up his back. He rose to his feet and looked around.

It felt as though he was being watched.

His mind again.

Then he heard the murmur of voices.

He hurried to another hut, threw back the flap, and flashed his light around the interior. He was sure he'd catch someone hiding inside, or prove his imagination was running wild.

Nothing...

No real surprise there.

He stood, looked toward the other huts, then glanced at his watch. At best estimate, he had been inside the grotto ten or fifteen minutes. There was so much to explore here, he regretted having to go. He feared that once he left this subterranean Brigadoon, it would vanish.

But he had to believe that wouldn't happen, and promised himself he would come back. And when he did, he'd come prepared.

Jack snapped pictures of the hut's interior, the doorway, the surrounding village, and the fish ponds. No one would be able to say this place was a figment of his imagination.

When he had the documentation he needed, he walked back down the slope of beach to his dive equipment. There, he turned and peered at the roofs of the village one last time, reflecting on what he'd seen.

He grinned.

Robert and Kazuko would scoff at the story he was going to tell them. That would change when he showed them the photos. He'd enjoy seeing their jaws drop.

For the next half minute, he stood next to his tank and eyeballed the water, trying to imagine the ride out. He had surfaced at sea level, but he hadn't been there long enough to bleed off the nitrogen that had accumulated in his body. He would have to decompress once he was clear of the tunnel.

Do I have enough air?

He suddenly became very concerned about the pressure remaining in his tank. The gauge read five hundred pounds. If the current going out of the tube was as strong as the one coming in, he'd have enough air to make it out, but not enough to decompress.

That meant enduring the bends.

Not a welcome thought. He couldn't even imagine what it would be like to be crippled for life. Perhaps it would be better to drown.

Jack buckled on his buoyancy compensator and tank, positioned his mask on his forehead, and carried his fins into the water. Ten feet in, he pulled them on and put the mask over his face. He bit down on his regulator's mouthpiece, and ducked below the surface.

His only thought now was making it out alive.

What he feared most had happened. The tide was beginning to wane, and he knew at once the ride out was going to be slower than the ride in.

It took a moment for the surge to build for its trip out. He didn't wait.

He kicked into the tunnel and the moment the current changed direction, he let it sweep him seaward.

The ride lasted only a few seconds.

Again, the current changed directions, and he kicked and stroked hard to keep from being sucked back into the grotto. With the aid of the illumination from his mini dive light, he could see he held his position.

Barely.

A few seconds later, the surge flowed out and thrust him forward on its bid for the sea. He relaxed and let it take him.

Full in its grip, he could feel the current had lost some of its intensity.

Again the surge flowed in from the sea. He felt like a load of laundry in a washing machine.

He swam against it. And like before, he kept himself from moving backward. But fighting the current caused him to suck up what little air he had.

The tide continued to surge back and forth with increased regularity until it dissipated to almost nothing.

Slack tide.

In those minutes between the changing of the tides, he'd have to swim. That meant using more air.

Air he couldn't spare.

With no light at the end of the tunnel to point the way out, he had no choice but to rely on his instincts and track the gentle ebb and flow of the almost nonexistent current to maintain his course. Hoping he did not come to a fork in the tunnel. And praying his air supply held.

Seconds passed, or was it hours? And still no end in sight.

He knew each breath he breathed could be the last. The air in his tank had to be dangerously low. But he couldn't allow himself to worry about that. He needed to swim.

All at once, he felt a drop in his airflow.

The unexpected sensation caused him to stop swimming.

Was it getting hard to breathe, or was it his imagination?

An overreaction brought on by a heightened sense of need, he hoped.

He took a shallow breath, straining to see the end of the cave, and continued to kick and claw his way out.

Only more blackness.

Then, past another bend in the tunnel, he saw it. The faint blue circle of open ocean.

A sense of relief flooded over him with the realization he'd make it. Now all he needed was enough air to hover at fifteen feet for fourteen minutes: the time it would take him to decompress.

With renewed vigor, he swam hard. It would be a close thing.

Then his air cut off completely.

Helplessness gripped him like an iron claw tearing at his gut, but he was not about to give up. The bends were inevitable, but he still might live.

Holding his breath he swam on. He'd have to remember to exhale once he left the cave and started his ascent.

He dry swallowed, fighting for the extra seconds it would give him.

His lungs screamed at him to breathe.

Another second passed. If only he could take a breath!

His mind worked as if mired in molasses—his thoughts dreamy, detached. He knew that any second his body would demand he take a breath, even though there was no air to breathe.

Then he would involuntarily suck in a lungful of water.

In a flash of understanding, he knew what it felt like to be powerless to prevent the inevitable.

He was going to drown.

CHAPTER 11

Jack's lungs burned and still he swam hard, trying to make it to the light. The beat of his heart was a loud thump…thump…in his ears.

Just a little farther.

His head hummed. The humming grew louder.

Thump, thump, thump!

The pain in his chest became unbearable.

He bit down on the mouthpiece of his regulator and frantically sucked in as he swam.

No air.

He dry swallowed.

It did no good. Nothing he tried worked now. His brain demanded he breathe.

He jerked the regulator from his mouth and clamped his hand over his lips.

The tunnel opening tilted and spun as though some giant hand twisted the earth's crust to keep him from making it out.

Oh God…

* * * *

Jack expected agonizing coughing, chest wracking, and hacking with no relief. Only more saltwater that would bring more coughing and hacking...and finally death.

Instead, he breathed with the fish. He was one of them now.

Impossible.

But he was breathing just the same.

Was this heaven? Had it been ordained that he should forever inhabit the ocean he loved?

Or was this purgatory for him...a halfway point to an even more heavenly place?

There was the bright light he'd heard about...a dazzling white light that blinded him.

And he clutched an arm thick with muscle.

The Savior's arm?

The fog inside his head began to clear. The light moved away and he could see darkness.

He could still breathe, but something didn't fit. This wasn't heaven or even purgatory.

He was...

Robert's masked face and sandy blonde hair came into focus.

Jack clutched the regulator in his mouth and took a couple more breaths. His friend had found him.

His mind clearer now, he noticed Robert didn't have a reg in his mouth; that he wasn't breathing off Robert's octopus set up. He passed the regulator back to his friend.

Jack clamped his lips together and waited while Robert took two deep breaths.

The final effects of cerebral hypoxia cleared when more O2 in the air from the tank found its way to his brain.

He felt the regulator being thrust back into his mouth.

Exhaling in a burst of bubbles, he took two deep breaths and handed it back. They were buddy breathing.

Alive, thanks to Robert.

Now that his mind was working again, Jack analyzed the situation. They were taking turns breathing through his old Mark V. Robert must have switched out tanks. But that didn't explain why he used the old regulator setup that didn't have a backup reg.

It didn't matter. He was alive, thanks to his friend's quick thinking.

But they still had to decompress. He hoped that with both of them breathing from the same tank, there'd be enough air.

Again, Robert offered the regulator.

Jack took his two breaths, passed it back, and looked around. In the glow of the dive light dangling from Robert's wrist, he searched for the extra tank he hoped to find lying on the floor of the tunnel. It would be an easy matter to attach the regulator on his empty tank to a full one and swim out with the new tank tucked under his arm like a football.

There wasn't one.

His next thought was to attach his octopus setup to Robert's tank.

A piece of cake.

He found his regulator and raised it for Robert to see so that he would know the plan.

That's when Jack noticed he'd bitten clear though the rubber mouthpiece.

Robert took the damaged reg into his hand, rotated it in front of his faceplate, dropped it, and pulled his own regulator from his mouth.

Jack took his turn. They'd have to buddy breathe all the way to the surface.

But they'd make it.

Providing they had enough air.

Fifteen feet below the stern of the catamaran, they found the tank Kazuko had lowered for them. Jack exhaled a sigh of relief in a flurry of bubbles. He seized the regulator attached to it and gently bit down on the mouthpiece.

He looked up through the clear blue water at the bottom of *Pono's* twin hulls bobbing in the gentle swell…so close he felt like he could reach up and touch them.

They beckoned to him, and he wanted to race to the surface and breathe in great heaving lungfuls of the fresh air above. But he would have to wait another fourteen minutes.

It seemed to Jack like a lifetime, but fifteen minutes later he and Robert were back aboard, feeling more like his old self. Rebel nuzzled his hand for a pet of reassurance. He was only too happy to give her a scratch behind the ears.

"You frightened me and Rebel half to death," Kazuko said, her hands planted on her hips.

Jack chuckled, partly because Kazuko included Rebel as if the dog actually knew something was wrong, but mostly because he was positively elated just to be alive.

"Scared shit out of myself when I ran out of air," he offered. "In fact I'm still finding it hard to believe I made it out of that cave alive."

Robert handed him a bottle of water. "You were knocking on heaven's gates when I found you, that's for sure." He motioned for Jack to drink. "Another second and I would have been too late."

"Okay, you're safe." Kazuko still had her hands on her hips, but now her eyes had narrowed. "I still don't know what happened down there. So tell me."

Jack recognized her matter-of-fact voice and stern look. Her need to know details replaced the concern she showed a moment ago. That's how she wanted it to look, anyway. He knew her far too well. She trembled inside, like him.

"I love you too, Kazuko." He stood and hugged her. "Sit down and relax. You're both going to find what I have to tell you hard to believe."

Kazuko took a seat next to Robert and quickly wiped away a tear.

Jack smiled and said, "Disney could make an absolute fortune off of the ride I just took…at least the ride in. I wouldn't recommend the ride out to my worst enemy."

He explained how the unexpected surge had sucked him into the cave. He described rocketing through the lava tube in darkness but didn't feel a need to tell them how terrifying an experience that had been for him. They knew.

"And if you think that's something, take a look at what I found at the other end." He switched on his digital camera and showed them the photos of the grotto and the village of tiny huts. "What do you make of these?"

Kazuko glanced from Jack to Robert. "From the looks of it, that hut can't be more than four feet tall."

Robert turned the camera screen toward him and pulled it close. "Shit, you're right."

"Close," Jack said. "I figured it to be about four and a half feet."

Robert turned and looked toward shore. Kazuko joined him.

Jack followed their gazes to the rugged coastal mountains. He knew they were trying to visualize the grotto. The lava tube had to lead into one of those mountains. There was no other explanation. Otherwise the cavern would have been flooded.

"There has to be another way in," Robert said. "I sincerely doubt whoever built those huts entered the way you did."

Kazuko laid her hand on Robert's arm. "Those huts are so small. Do you think a bunch of kids found a way in and built that village, playing native?"

"Kids didn't build those fish ponds," Jack scoffed before Robert could answer her. "Hell, from the size of some of those stones, *I'd* have trouble picking them up."

"Jack, you have that look." Kazuko peered into his sea-blue eyes. "You think that village was built by *Homo floresiensis*, don't you?"

Jack shrugged. "No wind, no rain…those huts could have been there a long time."

"The footprints, maybe," Robert said. "But I doubt the huts would last. Humidity, rot…I think they'd collapse after a few years."

Jack looked Robert square in the eyes. "Not if they were maintained."

Robert laughed openly. "You nutcase. Do you really believe there is a lost tribe of little people living down there?"

"Not there. I'd have seen them.

Robert shook his head in obvious disbelief. "God, you're serious."

"It's not out of the question." Jack gripped the railing and stared inland. A mental picture formed. "The Waimea Canyon and the Na Pali Coast are rugged and rarely traveled. Hell, there are caves all over the place. And you said it yourself. There must be another way in. Maybe the grotto is a transient village they occupy when they go there to harvest food."

"I'm not saying I buy into such a wild notion," Kazuko said. "But I do agree it's not totally out of the question."

Robert glanced from Kazuko to Jack. "You're both nuts."

Jack grinned. "We'll find out when we go back in."

CHAPTER 12

Jack stood at the helm, tossing his plan around in his mind for the millionth time. The three of them had agreed to explore the grotto and the mystery surrounding the tiny village. The question was how best to carry out the expedition.

The long boat ride back to Robert and Kazuko's house gave the three of them plenty of time to discuss the matter and hammer out a plan.

With *Pono* safely tied to the dock, they took their conversation inside the house. They hadn't yet come to a full agreement.

"I still believe it would be best to proceed in secret," Jack said. "Think about what'll happen the moment we go public with the discovery of the mini-sub and that subterranean village."

"Television crews, news people, and every rubbernecker imaginable will be flocking to the site, hoping to capitalize on the find," Robert conceded. "But I think exposure can be minimized if we go in low-keyed. And that way we won't have to sneak around."

"We're not going to be sneaking around. We're just going to be conducting scientific research without telling anyone."

"And if something goes terribly wrong down there," Robert's eyes reflected his concern, "who's going to know or even think to come looking for us?"

"Nothing's going to go wrong."

"That's what you said about the dive."

"We'll be prepared this time and we'll go in at slack tide."

"I'd rather find another way in that doesn't require swimming a trunk full of equipment in through a submerged lava tube."

"I agree. You fly us over the area and we'll take a look. If we see a possible way in, great. We'll hike in and check it out. If not, that lava tube has been there thousands of years. It'll still be there."

"We'll need to put a team together," Kazuko added, raising her index finger to her lip in thought. "Scientists who know what they're looking at. Experts, all of them. And they'll have to agree to keep quiet about it until it's time to fill the world in on what we've found. That'll be the tricky part. If even one person leaks the fact that we are proceeding in secret, we're sunk. At that point, we'll have been better off going public."

Jack realized Kazuko had been giving his plan careful consideration. Unlike Robert, she wasn't completely against it. "I think Sienna will be willing," he said. "And she might suggest others who'd want to join us."

"Sienna?" Robert arched an eyebrow at Jack. "You're on a first name basis, are you?"

Jack pictured himself sitting across the table from her at dinner. "The last time we talked, I was."

"Why does that not surprise me?" Robert studied Jack, letting the comment hang while he twisted the cap off a bottle of Foster's beer. "You actually believe a group of top-notch scientists will drop what they're doing and fly here, at their own expense, to take part in a secret expedition to find a lost tribe of little people their peers believe extinct? Based on your word that they exist. It's not going to happen…even if I pick up the tab."

Jack snagged a bottle of beer from the refrigerator and pointed the neck at Robert. "Not entirely on my word. Sienna examined the skull and drew her own conclusions. And I have the pictures to support my theory."

Robert scoffed. "Still…"

"I believe we can pull it off." Kazuko's voice reflected certainty that hadn't been there a moment ago. "And you—my dear, sweet lover—are going to finance the expedition."

"Me!" Robert nearly choked on a sip of beer. "I was only speaking hypothetically."

She smiled. "That's what you thought."

Robert ran the back of his hand across his chin and wiped away a dribble of brew. "You know I'm up for a good adventure, but do we really need a bunch of high-priced scientific experts along? Sienna, sure, if she'll even agree to join us. But wouldn't it be better to draw a line there?"

Jack laughed. "So we agree to keep the venture a secret." He raised his bottle the way a man would offer to shake hands.

Robert shrugged and clinked the neck of his bottle against Jack's. "We keep it a secret. But only if Sienna goes along with the idea."

Jack looked at Kazuko. "You okay with this?"

"You get Sienna," she said, "and you'll hear no complaints from me."

"Deal." Jack chuckled. "And no worries. You know how it is with me and the ladies."

* * * *

Jack hated having to wait to call Sienna. But by the time he, Robert, and Kazuko agreed on a plan the night before, it was too late...or too early. He doubted she wanted to get a call from him or anyone else at 3 A.M. her time.

He took a sip of coffee, set his cup down on the deck next to him, dug her card from his wallet, and tapped it against the fingers of his left hand. The sky over Kaneohe Bay showed the first colors of the day: roses and pinks, with a blaze of orange peaking above the eastern horizon. Early morning in Hawaii, but not in Vancouver.

He flipped the card over and silently read the number she'd written on the back. The fate of their expedition hinged on her curiosity.

Sienna's phone rang a half dozen times. "Hello," she said, before the call went to voice mail.

"Sienna…Doctor Conti, this is Jack." He breathed in to calm himself, partly out of apprehension about her response to what he was about to ask her, and partly because her voice was as provocative as the rest of her. "Did I catch you at a bad time?"

"Not at all. And you can call me Sienna, remember?"

"How's your schedule over the next week or so?'

"I was just packing to fly home. I leave Vancouver tomorrow."

"Australia?"

"Sorrento, Italy—my parents' villa. That's where I fell in love with archeology. As a family, we used to spend our summers diving ruins in the Mediterranean. But Pompeii got me hooked."

"You're a diver, too. That's good."

"It's been a while. Anyway, that's not why I'm going. I took three weeks off to spend the summer with them."

"What would you say if I asked you to lay over in Oahu for a few days on the way?"

"Hawaii's not exactly on the way, Jack. Does this have anything to do with that skull you found?"

"You haven't told anyone about it, have you?"

"I gave you my word, remember?"

"Sorry. I shouldn't have asked…"

"Stop worrying," she said. "Now, I'm sure that's not why you called. What's on your mind?"

"I found more."

"More? What do you mean more?"

"I found a subterranean village. Sienna," he swallowed. "The huts couldn't have been more than four-and-a-half feet tall."

"What? Where?"

"A village with huts no taller than my chest. Sienna…a village built for little people." He tried to calm his excitement. "In a grotto inside a mountain on the Na Pali Coast of Kauai. Directly inland from where I found that skull."

"That's not possible."

Jack could almost see the incredulous look on her face. "I have pictures."

The phone went silent. A moment later Sienna said, "Please tell me you can e-mail them to me?"

"They're downloaded on my laptop. I'll do it right now...while we're on the phone."

She gave him her e-mail address and he typed in the commands. "You should have 'em."

"I'm opening them, now."

"Take your time." He wished he were there to see the wide-eyed look on her face when she got her first glimpse of the pictures. By now he was sure her lovely brown eyes were narrowed in intense scrutiny.

"This is amazing, Jack. Talk to me."

He told her about the lava tube, being sucked through it, and the discovery of the grotto and village, but not that he had almost drowned in the process. When he'd finished relating his story, he said, "We plan on going back in, Sienna. And we want you along with us."

"When?"

"As soon as I can put together a team of experts."

"Who's the *we* you referred to?"

"Two friends of mine, Robert and Kazuko. Kazuko's a marine biologist with the University of Hawaii. Robert's her...well he might as well be her husband. Plus he's my best friend."

"And you say you're trying to assemble a team of experts to go along."

"You're the first...if you agree, that is."

"I don't know. The skull...tiny huts on a beach inside a grotto on Kauai. You realize the scientific community is going to have a field day with this?"

"Only if we tell them. I'm not planning on sharing the discovery until I know more about it."

"You're doing this in secret? Why?"

Jack feared this is where he might lose her. "All I can say is it's a feeling I have. And I'm counting on you to help me pull it off."

"This is new territory for me. I'm not accustomed to sneaking around."

"But you have…"

She did not answer right away, and Jack knew he'd pegged her correctly.

A few seconds later she said, "Let me get back to you."

CHAPTER 13

The ring tone from Jack's phone jarred him from his thoughts. He glanced at the incoming number on the display screen and recognized Sienna's private line. It had been two and a half hours since they talked.

He flipped open his cellular and said, "Please tell me this is good news."

"I'm in."

Jack breathed a sigh of relief and settled back in the padded deck chair, on the lanai facing the ocean at the rear of Robert's house. "You've made my day. How soon can you be here?"

"There are conditions, Jack."

"Name them."

"You're in charge of logistics, and I'm in charge of the dig."

"I kind of figured it that way."

"And I can bring along a couple of colleagues to assist me: Regan White, a forensic pathologist and close friend I've worked with on numerous occasions, and Tumra Baruti, a geologist."

"Not a problem, providing they agree to keep quiet about what we're doing."

"If I tell them to, they will."

"Okay. But before I forget, do they scuba dive or at least swim? There's a strong likelihood we're going to have to enter by way of the ocean…through that submerged lava tube I told you about."

"I got that impression by the way you talked. Regan dives…and Tumra says he swims like a fish."

"Not certified?"

"No. But he's not worried providing someone experienced shows him how."

"I can do that. So we're good to go, then?"

"Not yet. Finances…I assume you have a backer. You'll need equipment and you'll have to compensate my colleagues for their airfare and time. And they'll need a place to stay when they get there."

"You sound skeptical."

"Not skeptical. I just want to be up front about this."

"I wouldn't expect less."

"Good. If I thought it was going to be any other way, I wouldn't be joining your expedition."

"Is there anything special you need?"

"You can buy me dinner when I arrive."

"Champagne, oysters on the half shell…"

"Jack, it's only dinner. We have a lot to talk about."

"What gave you the idea I thought it would lead to more?"

"And what made you think I was implying sex?"

His grip on the phone, tightened. He took a breath and relaxed. "How's McDonalds sound?"

Sienna laughed into his ear. "Make it Burger King and you're on."

"You do like messing with me, don't you?"

"Why Jack, whatever gave you that idea?"

"This is going to be fun. When are you going to arrive?'

"Tomorrow morning."

"And your colleagues? Or do I need to arrange flights for them?"

"I took the liberty. They arrive the day after."

"Good. We'll have time for that dinner."

"I'm trusting you on this. So are my friends," she said, the tone of her voice serious. "I hope you're not taking us on a wild goose chase."

"No geese down there," he said matter-of-factly. "Just a beach littered with tiny huts and a lot of questions that need answers."

"I take it you'll be picking me up at the airport?"

"E-mail me your flight itinerary and I'll be there."

"Just be on time. I don't like spending more time in airports than necessary."

He closed the cover on his cell, sighed, and slumped into the cushion of his chair. Responsibility for the expedition's success weighed more heavily on him than he had imagined. But he remained buoyed by confidence in his assessment of the find. This was not a hoax, and for sure no troop of Boy Scouts had built that village as a weekend hideout.

The sound of the door sliding open made Jack turn and look. "About time you got up," he said to Robert who stepped onto the lanai, carrying a cup of coffee. "I've been sitting here two hours waiting for you to join me."

"I was on the internet half the night." Robert stifled a yawn. "So who were you talking to?"

"Sienna." He couldn't resist a smile. "She's agreed to join us. And she recruited two colleagues to come along."

"Good. I think we're going to need them." Robert settled into a chair. "Last night Kazuko and I got to talking about those tiny huts, and Kauai and its legends, and well…I went online to see what I could find. You know that little valley we saw off to the left of the cliffs where the grotto's located? That's the Honopu Valley. Guess what else it's called?"

Jack saw the sparkle in Robert's emerald green eyes. He'd found something good. "Just tell me already."

"*Valley of the Lost Tribe.*" Robert leaned back, his lips spreading into a grin. "It's believed to be the last ancestral home of the *Menehune*."

The tiny huts, the grotto, the rugged cliffs, the valley…images flashed through Jack's mind like a slide show. "Damn."

Robert pursed his lips and made a sucking sound with his cheek.

"Guess it's time for me to get out my check book."

Jack raised his hands in a gesture of helplessness. "Sorry about that. I never intended for you..."

"Relax buddy," Robert said, cutting him off. "Kazuko came up with the idea we need some high-priced talent along; and she's also the one who decided I'd pay."

Jack shrugged. "You know the irony of it is, that if we hadn't been friends before you inherited your money, I just might have resented the fact you were rich and would never have gotten to know you."

"We should both thank my grandparents, then." A faraway tone in Robert's voice hinted at a fond memory of the couple. "They left me the money."

"God love 'em." Jack rocked forward and planted his elbows on his knees. "And since we're on the topic of money, do you feel like going for a ride in that vintage floatplane of yours this morning? There has to be another way into that grotto. I'm thinking we can fly over the area and try to spot a cave that looks promising."

"Let's stop and think about what we're doing." Robert raised a halting hand in front of him. "Don't get me wrong. I have no problem fronting the money for this expedition. Lord knows I'd do most anything for Kazuko. But I keep getting the feeling we should just leave things the way they are. The lost tribe part of it, anyway. The sub can be salvaged and put on display, and the crews' remains returned to Japan. But the skull should be locked away where no one will find it...or better yet, buried and forgotten."

"That's why I want to go forward in secret. I have the same reservations as you. But I do think we need to proceed with the project. Questions need to be answered. And the possible existence of a race of little people, living unnoticed among us, is only one of them."

Robert shrugged. "Just a thought."

Jack stood and clapped him on the back. "Relax buddy. This is going to be fun."

"I've heard that before."

Jack flashed a toothy grin. "Let's fly."

CHAPTER 14

Robert's vintage de Havilland Beaver skipped and bounced across the light chop in Kaneohe Bay. In spite of being strapped in tight, Jack felt compelled to hold on as if his life depended on it.

Robert laughed. "Relax. This is nothing. You oughta be with me when the water's rough."

Jack shot him a sideways look. "No thanks."

Within seconds the sturdy plane rose above the waves. Seawater dripped from the twin pontoons as Robert steered the yellow and white floatplane into a wide sloping curve that would put them on a direct course to Kauai.

Below, dark-skinned canoeists stopped paddling to gaze up at the plane. Jack peered down at them through the Plexiglas window in his door. He waved. "I don't think they like sharing the bay with you."

"They've seen the plane before. But I guess it still makes them nervous to see it skip across the water in front of them."

The sky was a deep azure with only a spattering of puffy gray clouds along the Ko Olau Range. Thirty minutes later, the long white lines of breaking surf and the turquoise of shallow water over the reefs disappeared from sight behind them. Below there was only the dark blue of deep water.

Jack loosened his seatbelt a couple of inches and relaxed to the drone of the reliable 450 hp Pratt & Whitney radial engine. "Even if this flight turns out to be an exercise in futility, the ride alone is worth the effort."

"It *is* beautiful up here." In the distance Kauai stood out like a slate-gray shadow on the horizon. Robert nodded toward the windshield. "And it looks like clear skies all the way."

An hour later, Robert dipped the nose of the de Havilland Beaver and swooped in low over Waimea Canyon—the Grand Canyon of the Pacific—a Shangri-la of jungle-like glens, tucked amid deep sculptured valleys. Several miles ahead loomed the rugged mountains of the Na Pali Coastline. Fluted walls of basalt, with razor-sharp ridges rising thousands of feet above sea level—battlements against the Pacific beyond. Undeniably spectacular. But they were focused on a small area around one jagged mountain on the coast.

"That's all state park property down there," Robert said with a nod of his head. "Even if we do find another way into that grotto, it'll be hell getting an archeological permit."

"All the more reason for secrecy."

"I knew you were going to say that."

Robert honed in on the coordinates as the sun reached its zenith. Noon by their reckoning was the best time of the day to be in the sky and looking at the ground. There would be no shadows cast by a slanting sun.

They flew in a low arc over the section of mountains they believed held the grotto. Jack gazed down at the sharply sculpted landscape through a pair of ten-power field glasses. One gorge looked the same as the next: no cave entrance, only steep palisades no one in their right mind would dare climb.

Robert steered his floatplane out over the water and swung it back inland on a course in line with the submerged lava tube. Below them, under seventy feet of water, rested the mini-sub where it had lain undiscovered for nearly three quarters of a century.

Jack peered out the side window, trying to catch a glimpse of the sunken hulk. All he saw was the sea.

"Don't worry," Robert said. "The sub's right where we left it."

Jack's friend had read his mind. "For a while longer, anyway."

Robert nodded ahead. "Might want to pay attention. Here we go."

He approached the beach twenty feet above the water and rode the wind current in a steep climb over the towering cliffs.

Jack scanned the ground with his binoculars but saw nothing. Just more dense foliage and impossibly steep palisades.

Beautiful and lush to the eye, but deadly to anyone who falls trying to explore them.

He lowered the field glasses to his lap and rubbed his eyes. "Where in hell is that damned cave?"

"It's down there," Robert said, looking out his own side window. "We're just not seeing it."

Jack settled back in his seat and let out an exasperated breath. "I have to admit, this isn't quite what I imagined."

"The mountain peaks of Kauai are one of the wettest spots on earth—over four hundred inches of rain a year. Multiply that by about five million years and it makes for one hell-of-a-lot of erosion."

"And a damned good hiding place."

"That, too."

Robert banked the plane in a tight circle over the area and flew back out to sea to make a second pass. He made his turn and followed the same course inland. And again they crested the cliff.

From out of nowhere, a pair of black tour helicopters—giant gnats against a blue sky—appeared in front of them.

Robert pulled back on the yoke.

The propeller clawed the air.

The vintage craft climbed another two hundred feet just in time to avoid a midair collision.

"Jesus." Jack jerked his head to the side and eyeballed the closest helicopter as it veered away from them. He couldn't see the passengers' faces, but knew they had to have been scared witless. Like him.

Robert leveled out. "What do you think?"

Jack glanced over at his friend sitting calm behind his dark glasses. "I think they ought to outlaw those things when we're flying around up here."

"That's not what I meant."

Jack scanned the foliage-choked landscape. "I think we need one of those helicopters so we can get down nice and low."

"You do, huh? Check this out, dickhead."

Jack shot Robert a look. "Who—?"

Robert nodded at his side window. "Look."

Jack craned his neck against the restraint of his seatbelt and saw one of the helicopters rise up next to them. "Is that guy buzzing us?"

Robert turned the wheel and put another fifty feet between his wingtip and the chopper's rotors. "I'd say so," again he nodded at the window, "if that's any indication."

Jack saw the pilot and a young male passenger extend their middle finger. "Yup, buzzing us. Want to report him?"

"Let the wiseass show off for his passengers…*this time*. If he does it again, I'll call it in."

"Maybe we should head back…give him his air space. I have a feeling we could fly around up here all day and it wouldn't do us any good."

"I'm inclined to agree." Robert banked the de Havilland Beaver in a sweeping turn that put them on course home. "We'll just have to settle for a nice plane ride."

"You call this nice?"

"Okay, exciting. And, you got to satisfy your curiosity."

"It was a long shot, but we had to look."

"And now we know."

"You knew we weren't going to find anything when you flew us here, didn't you?"

"There was always a chance I was wrong."

"You wrong?" Jack huffed. "Well, it figures the cave would be hard to spot. Otherwise some curious hiker would have stumbled onto it by now."

"My thought is it's been hidden by design."

"You just might have hit the nail on the head." Jack raised the binoculars to his eyes, leaned to the window in his door, and scanned the hillsides as they slid past. "Especially if someone wanted to stay lost."

"Like a tribe of little people?"

CHAPTER 15

Robert swooped in low over his house before circling out over the water of Kaneohe Bay to set down with fuel to spare. Jack noticed a familiar looking sloop tied up at the end of the dock in front of his catamaran, and he had his eye on the thirty-foot sailboat as they motored to the dock. He could read the name clearly, now: *Julie Ann.*

"Looks like you have company, Jack." Robert said.

"This should be interesting." Jack faced him and grinned. "I had no idea she would show up here."

"Then I don't feel bad that no one was home to greet her."

Jack checked his watch: three fifteen. "Kazuko's not back yet?"

Robert cut the engine and let the starboard float drift the final few feet to the dock. "I don't expect her home till after seven." He unbuckled his harness and slapped Jack on the shoulder. "Look at the bright side. At least your lady friend waited for you."

Jack shrugged off his harness, opened the door and stepped onto the float. He leaned down to grab the rope to secure the plane.

Lisa chose that moment to hop from her boat to the planked walkway. "Hi, Jack. Surprised to see me?"

Jack almost fell into the water when he lost his balance while giving her a double take. He caught himself, straightened, and turned to enjoy the sight.

Lisa stood ten feet away, clad only in an orange thong bikini bottom, designer sunglasses, and a large-brimmed straw hat. A towel draped around her neck and down the front of her, covered her nipples. Her exposed mounds of flesh, tanned golden brown, glistened with sweat.

Robert climbed from the plane and stood next to Jack, looking. He rested an arm on Jack's shoulder and leaned close. "Jack old buddy, you're the only guy I know who can spend three months at sea doing research, sail home in the middle of the night, and on the way, save a damsel in distress, solve a seventy year-old World War II mystery, shock the scientific community with the archeological discovery of the millennia, and end up with the girl and her dog."

"Sounds plum amazing when you put it like that." Jack handed Robert the mooring line, took a half step in Lisa's direction, paused, looked back at Robert, and winked. "But that does seem to be the case."

She met Jack half way and slipped her arms around his neck. "I hope you don't mind me showing up here like this."

He leaned into her and kissed her cheek. Then he pulled back and eyed her body up and down. You can show up like this anytime."

She gave him a playful shove. "I was sunbathing, silly. What I was talking about was showing up here, at your friend's place."

"But of course. And speaking of showing up here, how'd you find it?"

"Simple. I remembered you told me he had a house on Kaneohe Bay. I just sailed in and looked for your boat. You can't exactly hide a sixty foot catamaran like yours...especially when it has the name *Pono* scrawled in two-foot-tall green and gold letters on the side of her hulls."

"I'm glad you're here." Jack moved to the side and with a sweep of his hand, gestured toward Robert. "Lisa, this is my close friend Robert Foster."

Robert looped the mooring line around a cleat on the pontoon and stepped forward, smiling. "Glad to meet you, Lisa."

Lisa pulled the towel tight over her breasts and offered her hand, which he shook. "Nice to meet you, Robert. I apologize for the way I'm dressed…or not dressed in this case. But I wasn't exactly expecting someone to drop in from out of the sky."

"Don't give it another thought."

"Thank you, but I should have been more considerate." She peered down at herself then refocused on Robert. "It's just that I like to take advantage of the sun every opportunity I get. And I must say, you have a lovely home."

Robert glanced from Lisa to the house and back. "Thank you. The house is old but comfortable. The best part is, it's next to the water and we have our own private pier. Which as you can see is indispensable."

"And practically non-existent in Hawaii." Jack put his arm around Lisa's shoulders. "Let's head up to the house and get something cold to drink."

She ducked under his arm and stepped back. "Excuse me a moment while I slip on a T-shirt and shorts. It'll only take a second."

They watched her leap aboard her boat and duck into the cabin. "You sure can pick 'em," Robert said.

"More like she picked me."

"Well, she's pretty. I'll say that much. But I don't know. Seems kinda odd, her latching onto you like this."

"Not so odd when you think about it."

"Right. You are her white knight."

Jack crossed his arms in front of him and nodded in the affirmative. "And I didn't even have to slay a dragon."

Robert chuckled. "Yet."

* * * *

The sky over the water turned a light shade of rose when the sun set on the other side of the island. Mai Tais were the order of the evening, and Jack set fresh ones in front of Lisa and Robert. He fixed one for himself and retook his seat next to Lisa. Rebel lay at his feet.

"I think she's taken a liking to you," Lisa said, with a hint of envy.

"Seems so." Jack locked eyes with the basset peering up at him with her head flattened on the deck, ears spread wide like wings. He'd grown attached to her, too. He hoped Lisa wasn't going to ask for Rebel back.

Robert's cellular chimed, drawing Jack's attention away from the dog.

"That's Kazuko," Robert said when he glanced at the display.

He stepped to the barbeque and chatted while he turned the two dozen monstrous shrimp sizzling on the hot grill. When he was done flipping, he said, "Dinner's ready. And we have company."

He listened a moment longer, smiled, and closed his phone. "She'll be here in a few minutes."

"Perfect timing." Jack shot Lisa a quick grin. "Now you get to meet the brains of the family."

"Don't let Kazuko hear you say that," Robert said. "I've got her fooled."

"You only think you have her fooled."

Robert chuckled. "Right again. I'm going to take the shrimp inside and toss the salad."

From the table on the lanai, Jack and Lisa could hear dishes clanking in the kitchen. Lisa slid her chair back and stood up. "Shouldn't we help?"

Jack had been staring at her lips for two hours wanting to kiss them. With Robert in the kitchen it seemed like an opportune moment to take advantage of the privacy.

"In a minute." He stood in front of her, took her in his arms without saying more, and pressed his lips to hers. Her lips met his with the same burning desire and parted. Their tongues touched. The kiss built in intensity, and Jack pulled her tight against him.

"Ahem." Kazuko coughed in the doorway of the glass slider before stepping onto the lanai. "Have I just ruined a moment?"

Jack released Lisa to arms' length and glanced over his shoulder at Kazuko. "Yes. But that's okay." He turned and faced her. "Kazuko, meet Lisa. The woman I told you about."

Lisa adjusted her T-shirt and offered her hand. "My pleasure.

And I must say, you have a wonderful place here."

Kazuko shook Lisa's hand and gave her a long look. "Thank you. It's nice to meet you. You're everything Jack said you were."

Jack sucked in a breath. He knew the sting of Kazuko's tongue when she didn't like someone or something. The jury was still out on Lisa. The next few seconds would determine how the evening would go.

"I'll take that as a compliment," Lisa said.

Kazuko's expression softened a little. "I understand you're an anthropologist."

"I hold a degree in cultural anthropology, but I'm afraid I don't get into the field much."

"Jack told us you work at the American Museum of Natural History in New York."

"Cataloging. Not exactly the career I planned on."

"Food's ready," Robert said from the doorway. "If someone would take these plates and silverware, I'll bring it out."

Lisa stepped past Kazuko and took the dishes and silverware from Robert's outstretched hands. She then carried them to the table and began arranging the place settings. "I understand you're a marine biologist." She set the last plate in front of Jack and winked at him. "And that you work for the university."

Jack caught the look from Lisa. She knew she was being sized up. Knowing she was okay with Kazuko's probing and that she was playing along, took the pressure off him. He could breathe now.

"Don't let this skirt and jacket fool you." Kazuko smiled. "I spend a lot of my time in the field. My specialty is invertebrates. Currently, my research involves reversing the depletion of Hawaii's reefs."

"Sounds challenging."

"Very," Kazuko said with resolve. "Now, if everyone will excuse me a minute, I'm going to slip into something more comfortable."

When Kazuko was out of earshot, Lisa chuckled at Jack and said, "She's protective of you, isn't she?"

"You noticed." He gave her a peck on the cheek. "Thanks for

understanding. Now excuse me while I give Robert a hand."

Over plates heaped with barbequed shrimp, rice, and salad, they talked about their jobs. Even Robert, whose more-than-substantial means allowed him to avoid the eight to five grind, added to the conversation with stories about his volunteer work with the Pacific Whale Foundation. There was no mention of the planned expedition into the grotto. And when they were done eating, Lisa helped Kazuko clear the table.

"Mind your manners while we're gone," Kazuko said. "We'll stick these in the dishwasher and be right back."

* * * *

Lisa followed Kazuko into the kitchen. The two of them were alone together for the first time and she knew there would be questions.

"You're probably wondering why I came here looking for Jack?" she said before Kazuko could ask.

Kazuko took the dishes out of Lisa's hands, set them in the sink, and began rinsing them. "The thought had crossed my mind. You're a pretty woman. I'm sure you have your choice of men."

The corners of Lisa's mouth curled into the hint of a smile. "Jack rescued me and well, I kind of just bailed on him out there. I felt I owed him more…something."

"Owed him?" Kazuko turned and leaned against the counter, facing Lisa. "Jack did what Jack does. Somehow he always manages to be in the wrong place at the right time. I doubt he feels you owe him."

Lisa averted her face and opened the dishwasher. "I got the impression he was attracted to me."

"Attracted." Kazuko chuckled. "Don't take this wrong. Jack likes women. Women like Jack—for obvious reasons. When it comes to that he's an open book."

"And that concerns you."

"Let's just say Robert and I kind of watch over him."

Kazuko handed Lisa the rinsed dishes one by one and watched

her arrange them in the dishwasher. "I'm sure you miss your brother?"

Lisa swallowed a lump that rose and lodged in her throat. "Brad and I were inseparable. I miss him dearly."

Kazuko placed a reassuring hand on Lisa's shoulder. "I can only imagine. Perhaps I shouldn't have asked."

Neither of them spoke while Lisa loaded the last of the dishes in the washer.

When the machine was on and washing, Lisa turned to Kazuko and said, "Tell me about this other side of Jack. The side that's not an open book."

Kazuko gave her a long appraising look. "You've seen the congenial, unpretentious Jack—humorous, impulsive, easygoing, always quick to help." Her eyes narrowed as though she looked into the past. "But there's a cold, efficient Jack, as well."

* * * *

The sound of clanking dishes was a signal to Robert and Jack that the women were out of earshot.

"She seems nice," Robert said. "Maybe I judged her too quickly."

"She *is* nice." Jack glanced in the direction of the kitchen.

"Still—"

"Look," Jack said, cutting Robert off. "I'd appreciate it if you gave Lisa a chance."

"I think we're doing that, Jack."

Jack considered Robert's comment. "Yeah, I guess you are."

Robert settled back in his chair. "So tell me, how are you going to handle Lisa? She's obviously staying the night."

"I'll just ask her what her plans are and go from there."

"Don't forget, you're meeting Sienna at the airport tomorrow afternoon. And if I remember correctly, you two have a dinner date."

"I haven't forgotten." Jack peered through the glass slider at the two shapes in the living room. He faced Robert. "Honestly, I'm not sure what to do about Lisa."

CHAPTER 16

Jack lay wide awake on his bunk aboard *Pono*. He and Lisa had kissed long and passionately at the edge of the dock where her boat was tied and then she had bid him good night. He could still taste her on his lips.

Damn.

Why'd she have to be young and pretty?

And why did she have to stir his blood the way she did, now, with the expedition ahead of him?

He first became aware that someone had stepped aboard *Pono* when he felt an almost imperceptible shift in the pitch of the boat. He sat up on his bunk, gripped the handle of the short-barreled .357 under his mattress, and waited.

A couple of seconds later he heard her whisper, "Jack, are you awake?"

Damn right I'm awake!

He released his hold on the gun, smoothed back wild strands of his hair with his fingers, and smiled. He'd considered going to her boat and asking her the same thing. Obviously they both had the same idea. But she'd beaten him to it.

Jack slid on his faded swimsuit and stepped topside. Lisa stood at the open door to the salon, staring in. The three quarter moon shone bright behind her, sending a slab of cool white light into the cabin. "I was just thinking about sneaking over to see you. You must have read my mind."

She stepped inside. "You think I could let the evening end with that kiss? My God, I've been an absolute mess inside myself this past hour."

His gaze focused on her short lightweight cover-up and the "V" of exposed flesh from neck to bellybutton where the robe overlapped. The moonlight gilded her brown hair, her bronzed skin.

He sucked in a breath.

"Three quarters of an hour, to be exact." He grinned, letting himself breathe. "Not that I was counting the minutes."

"You, too?"

"That was no goodnight kiss."

She stepped close and put her arms around his neck. "No it wasn't."

* * * *

Jack hopped onto the dock in the glare of the rising sun. He arched his back and rolled his shoulders to stretch his sore muscles. With the nail marks covered by his shirt, no one would know he had just gone three rounds with a crazed sex machine.

He glanced at *Julie Ann*. Lisa had slipped from his bunk while he slept. He assumed she had left under the cover of darkness and that she was back aboard her boat.

It was nice of her to make it easy for him to not have to make any awkward explanations to his friends.

He turned and waved to Robert who watched him from a chair on the lanai. He'd have bet a hundred dollars Robert waited to see which cabin Lisa emerged from.

She'd stolen his thunder. Still, there'd be questions and a comment or two.

Coffee first.

Rebel bounded up to Jack halfway along his trek to the house. He paused, and bent down to let her plant her front paws on his thighs. She licked his arm, and he scratched her head and stroked her neck.

"Good girl." He helped her down and continued walking. The basset trotted beside him with her ears flapping.

"I see she's still here," Robert said to Jack when he walked up to the table. "She sleeping in or did you leave her handcuffed to your bunk?"

"Can I at least get a cup of coffee before you start in on me?"

"Help yourself. I'll wait."

Jack poured himself a cup of coffee from the carafe sitting on the table, slid back a chair, and took a seat. "What makes you think she's on my boat?"

"I know you. A pretty girl, less than a hundred feet away." Robert shook his head. "You wouldn't pass up an opportunity like that. And the two of you do have a history."

"You talk like we're old lovers."

"Old or new, if the shoe fits…"

"Well," Jack scoffed. "It so happens I don't know where she is. I assume she's on her boat."

"Boat's here, she's here. Kazuko and I were kinda hoping she had someplace she needed to be."

"Did you expect her to leave in the middle of the night? Geez, you talk like you don't like her."

"Jury's still out on that one. She seemed decent enough at dinner last night, but I'll have to reserve judgment until I know more about her. From the way Kazuko talked, she's not at all sure what to think."

Jack stared into the dark Kona brew in his cup. Robert and Kazuko made a habit of looking out for him. Robert deserved the truth. "You were right, you know?"

"Right?" Robert scrunched his face. "Right about what?"

"She slinked aboard my boat last night and there's no way in hell I can begin to describe what happened after that."

"I knew it," he said, unable to contain a broad grin. "You had sex written all over your face when you walked up."

Jack chuckled. "That's putting it mildly."

"Is that right?" Robert's expression sobered. "Well, don't get too used to it. The woman lives in New York, remember? She has a job there."

"I haven't forgotten."

"All right then, any idea what you're going to do?"

"Do?"

"About Lisa. Is she going to just hang around here working on her tan while you cavort about with Doctor Conti on the other side of the island?"

Jack wondered if he'd made a mistake inviting Lisa along on the expedition. He'd purposely held off telling Robert, hoping to avoid a sordid rebuke from him by waiting for the best possible moment to break the news. Now he found himself in a corner. If Robert pressed him any harder, he'd have to tell him.

"I'm not sure there's a problem," Jack said, stalling. Lisa still had not made an appearance. Maybe she would back out of going along. If only he could talk to her and find out how serious she was about joining them.

"No?" Robert arched a brow, clearly surprised. "Last night she neglected to say when she's leaving. Did she mention to you when that would be?"

"Not exactly." Jack steeled himself for the inevitable. "You see, I kind of invited her along."

Robert rocked forward almost knocking over his coffee cup. "Kinda invited! What the hell does that mean? Either you did, or you didn't."

"She's a cultural anthropologist. This is right up her alley. And it would do her good to get some field experience."

Robert made a face, and Jack could tell by the look he got, his friend didn't like what he heard. No surprise.

"Just how much did you tell her?" Robert narrowed his eyes in the direction of Lisa's boat.

Jack glanced over his shoulder at the sloop and saw Lisa hop from her boat to the dock and stride their direction with the lithe and grace of a jungle cat. Thank God she had on yellow shorts and a white sleeveless top and not the thong.

"Not much," he said. "In fact I was quite vague."

"Well, she's your problem. We can only hope it works out all right."

"I'm sure it will. She seems to have her shit together."

"She can sail. And by the way you're moving this morning, she's good in bed. Beyond that, the woman's a bunch of talk."

Jack was glad Robert couldn't see the scratch marks. He held his gaze on Lisa. "You're right. Talk's cheap. But we need to give her a chance. She's had it tough. Both of her parents are dead and her brother was ripped to pieces right in front of her. It's a wonder she's able to hold it together at all."

"It'd be easier for me to accept her if she was an emotional mess. And I'm sure Kazuko agrees."

Jack shot a hard look at Robert. "Is that right? Just because she's not sitting in a corner somewhere, blubbering, it doesn't mean she's not hurting inside. You know how it is after a funeral. Everyone who can, screws their brains out. Maybe she's using this sex-thing with me as a coping mechanism."

"If that's the case, more power to her. I just hope she doesn't turn out to be dead wood in search of someone to show her a good time. Everyone on this mission is going to have to carry their weight."

"And I don't want to get sucked into second-guessing her intentions every step of the way. Now let's drop the subject and move forward with our plans. Like you said, she's my problem."

"Your problem." Robert chuckled. "This is going to be fun to watch."

"Is that so?"

"You bet."

"Guy talk?" Lisa asked from ten feet away.

Robert slid his chair back and stood up. "Good morning. Join us for coffee."

Lisa winked at Jack. "I'd love to."

Jack felt a shiver creep up his spine. A simple wink from her and he was on his feet to slide the chair next to him away from the table and hold it for her. He couldn't believe it.

"Thank you." She drifted her finger nails across the back of Jack's hand and settled into the chair.

Jack wanted to pull away, but couldn't. It was as if her touch had welded his hand to the back of the chair. All he could do was think about those nails digging into his back.

He noticed Robert's lips curl into a hint of a smile.

Dammit!

"What's so funny?" he asked even though he knew what Robert was thinking. Everyone would be expected to hold his or her own and already he was pulling chairs out for her. He quickly retook his seat.

"Am I missing something?" Lisa glanced back and forth at the two men.

"Nah," Robert said. "It's just nonsense between Jack and me."

She fixed her eyes on Jack. "Let me guess, a little harmless fun at my expense?"

"Robert knows you slipped aboard my boat last night."

She raised a brow. "Oh? What else did you tell him?"

"I didn't tell him anything. The wiseass guessed it."

She smiled at Robert and winked. "Then he doesn't know about the whips and chains."

Robert shifted in his seat. "Jack tells me you're joining us on our little excursion into the unknown."

"He invited me along, yes. And I accepted. But he never did tell me where we're going or why. He—"

"Good morning, Lisa." Kazuko stepped onto the lanai and set a platter of freshly sliced fruit and a stack of salad plates on the table. "Did I hear you say you were going somewhere?"

Robert shot her a look out of the corner of his eyes. And before Lisa could answer, said, "Jack invited her along on the expedition."

Kazuko arched a brow at Jack and said, "Naturally you accepted."

"Jack insisted it falls in my area of expertise," Lisa said in a professional tone of voice that hadn't been there a moment ago. "And last night you all but told me I need field experience."

Jack watched Kazuko spear a couple of slices of papaya for herself and take a seat in the chair next to Robert. From the way she stabbed the fruit, he could tell she was not happy with him. But she spared him a snide remark. Apparently she wasn't all that mad. It was time to get down to business. And what he had to say might save them all some discomfort.

"We need to finalize some details," he said. "Lisa, I might've invited you along a little prematurely. You're welcome to join us, but first you need to agree to some things."

Lisa held Jack in her gaze an extra heartbeat, then focused on Robert and Kazuko. "I said 'yes' to coming along, because I thought all of you wanted me to be part of the team, and because I was sure I could contribute."

An uncomfortable silence fell on the table. A few seconds later Kazuko said, "I'm sure you understand why we're cautious about taking you along. There is a lot that can go wrong. This is not just a simple trip into the woods to look for lost trinkets."

"When you said *we*, I assume you're speaking for Robert as well."

"She is." Robert rested his forearms on the tabletop. "We like you, Lisa. But we don't know anything more about you than what you told us last night. And Jack...well...what you two have cooking might only complicate things where we are going."

Lisa crossed her arms against her chest. "I know you're protective of Jack. He's your friend; I understand. But I assure you our relationship is not going to interfere in any way. You tell me what it is I need to agree to and if I have a problem with any of it or if you absolutely don't want me along, I'll bow out. No hard feelings."

Jack watched Robert and Kazuko exchanged glances. They both nodded.

"All right," Jack said. "I'll explain everything. But first my friends and I need to know if you can keep a secret?"

CHAPTER 17

Jack used the long drive across the island to convince himself everything would work out fine. He eagerly anticipated Sienna's arrival on Oahu and now regretted not having had time to prepare her for the recent addition to the group. With a little more talking, Lisa had managed to ingratiate herself with Robert and Kazuko. But Sienna had handpicked the colleagues she wanted along. She might not be receptive to Lisa joining them.

And I promised to buy her dinner.

Dinner would be cocktails and Chinese takeout at Robert's house with the five of them sitting around the table on the lanai. Right now lunch and a cold beer were more in order. Especially since he'd shelved his romantic thoughts about Sienna.

It turned out he'd timed his arrival perfectly. He stopped outside the baggage claim area twenty minutes after Sienna's plane landed and dialed her cell phone number. She answered on the second ring.

"You made it?" he said, pleased she was not standing at the curb waiting for him.

"I've collected my bag, and I'm on my way out. Please tell me you're not calling to let me know you're going to be late?"

"I'm right outside."

"Prompt. I like that."

"That's me." He grinned into the phone. "When you walk

outside, look to the left. I'm the tall, good-looking guy in the tan shorts and the lime-green aloha shirt, standing by the yellow 4-door Wrangler Unlimited."

Less than a minute later Sienna stepped out of the baggage claim area, her roller bag in tow. He spotted her immediately. A vision of class and comfort, she wore an off-white, short sleeve cotton blouse, light brown corduroy jeans and dark brown boots. A matching corduroy jacket was slung over the handle of a leather briefcase she carried with her left hand.

Very nice, but a little warm for Hawaii. Then he remembered she'd flown in from Vancouver.

He waved and hurried to help with her bag. Back at the Jeep, he opened the passenger door for her.

"Nice to see there's a gentleman left in the world," she said, flashing a flirty smile.

Perfect. More points.

He tried to resist a grin, but the corners of his lips curved upward just enough to betray his delight. "I slay dragons, too."

"Let's hope we don't run into any." She slid onto the seat and folded her long legs in. "I'd hate for that Tommy Bahama shirt to get scorched."

Jack laughed. "Me too. It's the only one I own."

He climbed in on the driver's side and drove away. "You do realize you look more like a model on vacation than a scientist here to work. Everybody was staring at you back there."

She looked at him and laughed. "They wouldn't if they saw me in my work clothes. I'm quite a different person in the field."

"Is that right?" He turned his head to the side and looked at her. "Maybe not as much as you think."

"What I think is you've been at sea too long, sailor." She focused her gaze on the windshield. "So, where are you taking me?"

"A place downtown for lunch, if you're hungry. It'll give us some time alone to talk. After that, Robert and Kazuko's house on Kaneohe Bay. You'll be staying in their guest bedroom."

"You're staying there too, I suppose?"

"On my boat. It's tied up to their dock."

* * * *

Looking at Sienna sitting across the table from him, Jack realized his personal life had recently become very confusing. He was glad he hadn't discarded his romantic thoughts about her, and that they were where he could get to them if the opportunity presented itself. For now, though, they'd stay on a shelf in the back of his mind, where he'd tucked them.

Why do women have to be such a distraction?

There was no way he could undo his affair with Lisa—not that he regretted it—but he needed to keep their relationship from escalating to the point where romantic entanglements interfered with the success of the expedition. Too much was at stake for him to allow that to happen.

He ordered himself a beer and Sienna a glass of iced tea. When their waitress walked away, he settled into his chair and put his mind on business. "I told you I thought we'd have to swim in through the lava tube. That's the case, I'm afraid. Robert and I did a flyover of the area. I'm sure there's another way in, but we couldn't see it."

"This whole secrecy thing, I don't get it. I told you I'd go along with your scheme, and I will. But what's it all about?"

He glanced around at the other patrons in the room. No one appeared to be paying even the slightest bit of attention to them. He looked at her. "There's a valley there. You know what they call it?"

"Jack—"

The smile slipped from his face. She obviously did not want to play guessing games.

"*The Valley of the Lost Tribe*," he said. "It's believed to be the last ancestral home of the *Menehune*."

He saw hers eyes focus on his. He'd piqued her interest. "If a tribe of little people built the huts I saw, and the fish ponds," he continued, "and if they're still around, and if we find them, I don't want the world to know about their existence until we're ready to tell them."

"That's a lot of ifs."

"You of all people should understand my concern. From day one mankind has exploited his fellow man. History proves it. What one man has, another man wants. Look what happened to the Native Americans, the Hawaiians. Progress is going to happen and there's no way to stop it, but we at least need to know what we're dealing with here, before we turn the world loose on it."

"Certainly a noble thought, Jack. And one I believe in, or I wouldn't have agreed to come. I just wanted to hear you say it to be sure we're on the same wavelength."

"I assure you we are. And Robert and Kazuko feel the same way. I assume your two colleagues are onboard with this as well?"

"They are. That's why I picked them. And speaking of colleagues, there'll be one other person joining us. Michael Tomkin, a veteran caver. I thought he'd be an asset to the team, since he's led several expeditions into the Ora Cave on New Britain, an island off the coast of Papua, New Guinea."

"I've read articles about that cave. Good call. Since we're on the subject of team members, I invited Lisa Bowman, a cultural anthropologist, to join us."

"Ah, the woman you rescued."

"You remember."

She smiled and said, "Let me guess, she's pretty?"

Her eyes did not waiver from his. Was he being judged, or tested? She had him pegged, but he couldn't be obvious about it. "She works at the American Museum of Natural History in New York. And if it weren't for her and her poor dead brother becoming stranded out there, I wouldn't have found that skull. And we wouldn't be sitting here."

She stared at him long enough to make him feel uncomfortable. He'd love to know what she was thinking.

"All right," she finally said. "By my count that makes eight of us."

Jack quietly breathed a sigh of relief. He wouldn't let her down. "A world renowned and beautiful paleoanthropologist, a forensic pathologist, a geologist, a veteran caver, a cultural anthropologist, two marine biologists, and an adventurer…four women and four men, a well-rounded team of professionals, if you ask me."

Sienna gave him a knowing nod. "Let's make sure we keep it at that." Not waiting for an answer, she dug into her briefcase and pulled out two manila envelopes. She opened one and removed several 8 x 10 enlargements of the huts in the photographs Jack had e-mailed to her.

He'd been wondering why she had carried her case into the restaurant with her, and now he knew. The blowups made the huts look even more impressive.

"You see these carvings," she said, pointing to the poles framing the doorway to a hut in one of the photographs. "And these, and these." She pointed out similar carvings on the doorways of huts in two other photos.

He leaned close. "Yeah, now that you point them out, I do. Okay, educate me."

"Not so fast." She lifted the flap on the other envelope and removed another stack of photos. "Take a look at these."

He studied the second set of prints and slowly thumbed through the first group of pictures. He took a photo from each stack and held them up side by side, glancing back and forth at them, then looked up. "The carvings look identical. Where did these photos come from? And what are the carvings on?"

"A ten thousand year-old wooly mammoth tusk," she smiled, "from a dig in Finland."

CHAPTER 18

Jack stood next to Sienna at the front door of Robert's house and knocked. When there was no answer, he used his key to unlock the deadbolt, then stood to the side to let Sienna walk in ahead of him. He followed right behind her, toting her suitcase. His friends were expecting them.

Rebel's nails clicked on the tile floor as she raced toward them. He glanced in the direction of the hound, and through the back slider noticed Robert wave them outside. Rebel nuzzled his ankles, and he squatted to give her the customary scratch behind the ears.

"Looks like everyone's on the lanai," he said to Sienna.

Sienna stooped and added her fingers to the scratching. Rebel licked her hand, happy to have the extra attention. "Adorable dog." Rebel was giving her arm a bath, now. "Is she yours?"

Jack realized he must have failed to mention the dog when he told her about his discovery of the skull. "Mine and Robert's and Kazuko's," he said. "It's more like she belongs to the house."

"She's certainly lovable."

"She likes you." He nodded toward the lanai. "Let's step outside and I'll make the introductions."

Robert stood at the back slider, waiting for them. He stepped aside, and Jack and Sienna walked onto the lanai. On his way through the doorway, Jack caught an approving nod from Robert.

They wouldn't be disappointed.

"Everyone," Jack announced with a motion of his hand. "This is Sienna. Sienna, this is Kazuko…your hostess." Again he used his hand for a pointer. "This is Lisa. And the ugly guy standing next to you is Robert. I've warned you about him."

"Warned?" Robert scoffed. With a backhanded wave at the empty chair closest to him, he offered Sienna a seat. "You need to know something about Jack. He lies."

Kazuko stood up and reached out her hand. "Doctor Conti, it's an honor to meet you. My suggestion is that you pay no attention to either one of these two guys. They're incorrigible when they're together."

"I'll keep that in mind. And please, call me Sienna." She smiled at Kazuko and shook her hand. At almost the same time her gaze settled on Lisa.

Lisa slowly rose from her seat, eyeballing Sienna from head to toe.

Jack recognized what was going on: one lioness sizing up another. Sienna had to have picked up on it, too.

Damn.

"An honor, to say the least," Lisa said and slowly offered her hand.

Sienna gave Jack a sideways glance before stepping forward and shaking the young lady's hand. "The honor, I'm sure, is mine."

Kazuko gave Jack a hard look and maneuvered between the two women. "I'm sure you'd like to freshen up after your flight. I'll show you to your room."

Sienna turned without another word to Lisa. "That would be nice. Thank you."

* * * *

Jack felt uneasy. He stared with unseeing eyes at the bottle of chardonnay in his hand.

Was Sienna the cause? Lisa?

For the past half hour, he'd paid close attention to Sienna's interaction with Lisa, while the group exchanged small talk. It seemed Lisa tried hard to appear relaxed. But more than once he noticed an appraising look in her eyes that made him believe she was uncomfortable with Sienna being there.

Was she really that jealous, or was it something else?

He remembered the scratches on his back. Had she intended them to be a type of brand to show her claim on him as a lover?

He hoped not.

"Jack, the wine."

Robert's voice jarred him from his thoughts. He saw his friend looking at him. So were the others.

"Oh yeah," Jack said and filled their glasses. Then he set the bottle down on the table, stood up straight, and raised his glass. "Here's to a successful expedition."

Sienna, Robert, Kazuko, and Lisa met his toast with equal enthusiasm.

"You already know I've put a lot of trust in you, Jack," Sienna said when she lowered her glass. "You've filled me in on bits and pieces of your plan, but that's it. This would be a good time to lay it all out on the table."

"You're right about that," Jack said, back on track now. "It's a shame the other team members won't arrive until tomorrow, but we shouldn't let that hold us up. We'll fill them in on everything when they get here."

Seated back in his chair, he glanced around the table and saw everyone looking at him. This was his show. "We're going to be entering the grotto by way of the lava tube I was sucked into. Robert and I flew over the area yesterday, hoping to find another way in; we didn't. That leaves us with no other choice."

"I'm as adventurous as the next person," Lisa groaned, "but I can't see us letting ourselves be sucked into the grotto the way you were."

"We won't. We'll be going in at slack tide. And we'll be using underwater scooters with lights. There should be plenty of time for us to make it through the tunnel before the surge becomes a problem."

"And if we don't?" Lisa asked nervously. "What if there isn't enough time?"

"You'll make it through just fine." He held her firmly in his gaze a moment. She needed to trust him.

When the corners of her mouth curled into a smile, he faced the group. "Now I know everyone is not an experienced diver," he continued, speaking primarily for the benefit of Lisa and Sienna. "That shouldn't be a problem—diving together and keeping an eye on each other. And you won't be hauling any supplies. Robert and I will take care of that before any of you go in. All you'll need to concentrate on is the dive."

"I'm sure I don't need to ask this," Sienna said, "but you do realize there is no way we can do a full workup of the site in one or two days? If we find what we hope to find, it'll take months, maybe even years."

"I think we all know that," Jack sighed inwardly. "You're in charge of the dig so I'll let you make the final decision on how long we stay down there. Robert, Kazuko, and I were figuring three days to a week. It's our feeling we should have a good idea of what we're looking at by then."

Sienna fiddled with the stem of her glass. "Let's plan on five days," she said a few seconds later. "Since you'll be hauling the equipment and supplies underwater, we'll take in the minimum amount and hope for the best. With eight of us working, that should give us plenty of time to do the initial workup."

"I assume we're using your boat," Lisa said. "Surely you're not going to leave it anchored off the coast unattended for a week?"

"A friend of ours named Kimo will sail *Pono* to Lihue. He'll return in time to be there waiting for us when we come out, which now will be five days. He's a damned good captain and we can trust him to keep his mouth shut."

"And if we need him sooner?" Lisa asked.

"Outside communication is a problem. We can't talk through

dirt and rock. The best we could do at that point is have one of us swim out and make a call on Robert's satellite phone."

"And what if one of us gets hurt?"

Lisa was obviously on a roll. It seemed to Jack that she'd saved all her questions for this exact moment. He couldn't help wondering why she hadn't shared her concerns with him before now.

He scanned the people seated at the table. His gaze settled on Sienna, who was focusing on Lisa. When Lisa posed her questions to him, he noticed her glance in Sienna's direction.

Is that it?

He glanced back and forth at the two of them. They were looking at each other, now.

Is Lisa putting on a show for Sienna's benefit?

"My colleague Regan White will serve as team doctor," Sienna offered quite matter-of-factly. She arched a brow at Jack. "Let's just hope you don't have to make one of those emergency calls you were just talking about."

"And who is Regan White?" Lisa asked.

Jack noticed Sienna's eyes narrow at Lisa.

Damn.

"That's my mistake," he said, to ease the tension brewing between the two women. "I should have explained who the other members of the team are. Regan White is a forensic pathologist."

"So she is a medical doctor," Lisa probed.

"That's right," Jack said. "Tumra Baruti, a geologist, will also be joining us tomorrow. So will veteran cave explorer Michael Tomkin."

"Think of this as a camping trip," Robert quickly added. "We can *what-if* ourselves to death on this thing. Underground or five miles into the woods, it's not that different."

Jack slid his chair back and stood up. "We have all evening to think about the expedition and hash out any issues that come up. What I'd like to do right now is have Sienna share an interesting bit of information she's uncovered. I tell you, this adventure of ours just keeps getting better."

He excused himself from the table and retrieved Sienna's briefcase for her. She opened it on her lap, removed the two envelopes of photos she'd shown Jack earlier in the day, and set the case on the tiled deck.

With everyone looking on, she spread the first set of photos out on the table where they could be seen. "These are blowups I made of the huts Jack found. I want you to look closely at the carvings on the poles framing the doorways."

The photos were shuffled from one person to the next until everyone—even Jack who'd already seen them—had viewed the enlargements. When their eyes rose to meet hers, Sienna removed the second set of photos and laid them out. "Now take a look at these."

Lisa was the first to comment on them. "I've seen these. Not the photos, the actual tusks. My—they were on loan to the museum. The carvings are on wooly mammoth tusks found in Finland."

Jack picked up on Lisa's slip of the tongue. Curious. "Was there something you wanted to add?"

Lisa scanned the group. Her gaze settled on Sienna. "I'm not quite as naive about what's going on here as I led you to believe. I'm sure Sienna is familiar with the name Dr. Bradford Whittingham the Third."

Sienna nodded. "The famed Archeologist and Paleontologist who discovered the tusks in the pictures, there."

"He's my father. Bowman is my married name. I'm divorced."

"Brad, your brother," Jack added, "was Bradford the Second? And his last name wasn't Bowman."

She cast a sheepish glance at her hands. "My father wanted him to follow in his footsteps."

"And you?" Jack asked.

"He was more interested in my brother. My goal was to prove him wrong."

"My God," Kazuko said, "why the secrecy?"

Lisa managed a smile. "I wanted you to accept me for me, not because of my father's achievements."

"I suppose we owe you that," Sienna said. "So tell us, what's your opinion about what we're looking at here?"

Lisa brightened. "The carvings on the tusks look identical to the carvings on the huts in the grotto."

"Precisely. And?"

"And you're saying that since these carvings match, it implies that while modern man as we know him migrated across Asia to North America, *Homo floresiensis*—a species of little people hardly more than three feet tall—were doing the same thing. And that these little people somehow migrated to Kauai."

"I'm saying the carvings suggest it, nothing more."

The group exchanged looks.

"Legends are born from real life experiences," Kazuko said matter-of-factly. "Either as stories conjured up by someone seeking to explain the unexplainable, or from unusual sightings that occur unexpectedly. For years people in Hawaii have reported seeing child-sized humans dressed in red loincloths, cloaks, and helmets like those worn by the ancient chiefs. Most of the stories that circulate concerning *Menehune* are based on the ancient legends or tales of the small people on Kauai. The island is famous for its *Menehune* Ditch. Maybe there *is* something to those legends after all."

Hearing Kazuko come around to his way of thinking made Jack smile. "So the *Menehune* legend isn't just a bunch of stories now, huh?"

"It makes you wonder."

"Well," he said, "the *Menehune* sightings here in Hawaii may or may not be factual. But if there is a tribe of little people inhabiting that cave, we're going to find them."

CHAPTER 19

Jack felt his heartbeat quicken. They were rapidly approaching their destination off the rugged Na Pali Coastline.

"There it is," he said to Kimo, who stood next to him in *Pono's* cockpit. "The Na Pali Coast."

Kimo stood with his face to the wind and scanned the shoreline, with the breeze curling back wisps of his long, gray hair. "I've lived on Maui all my life. I've heard stories about Kauai passed down by my grandfather's grandfather. But this is the first time I've seen this part of the coast."

Jack pointed. "That little valley over there, according to Robert, it's called *The Valley of the Lost Tribe*. Farther in, there are rock platforms, taro fields, sacred altars—a regular metropolis. It's believed to be the last ancestral home of the *Menehune*, the ancient ones. It's primal." He raised his hand in front of him, thumb and forefinger extended with a half-inch gap between them. "And we're this close to proving their existence."

"Are you sure this is something you should be doing?"

"I have concerns. But there's too much knowledge to be gained here to walk away from it."

Kimo focused pensively on the coastline. And after a long moment he said, "There is an ancient native legend that speaks of the giant tiger shark Apukohai that guards the waters of Na Pali.

It is said that enemies who ventured here were thrown from those cliffs to pay for their transgressions." He turned and looked Jack in the eye. "Be careful what you search for."

Jack felt the power of Kimo's words. Lisa's brother, the tooth marks on the tiny skull; maybe there was something to that legend. But he hadn't considered himself or his team to be transgressors. Not until now.

He let Kimo's comment hang in the air without reply. The only sound was the creak of rigging and the splash of water against the twin hulls. Powerful. Serene.

From somewhere inside the cabin, a verbal outburst from Michael Tomkin interrupted the serenity in the cockpit. "For a short fella," Kimo said, "the man has spunk."

Tomkin could not have been more than five foot one, and Jack doubted the man weighed more than a hundred and thirty pounds with his shoes on. He definitely did not fit the image of the famous caver Jack had expected to see waiting for him at the airport. And even though Sienna held the hard-bodied explorer in high regard, it did not change Jack's opinion that the man needed to cut his caffeine consumption in half.

"I agree with you," Jack said. "The guy's been giving Robert a bad time for the past half hour."

"I think he just likes to hear himself talk."

"He's opinionated, that's for sure."

"He's going to be hard for you to get along with."

Jack thought about that. The same concern had crossed his mind a number of times in the twenty-four hours he'd known Tomkin. Especially since the brash thirty-year-old caver put the make on Lisa every chance he got.

Damned Aussie.

He could hardly blame the man for dogging Lisa, though. She was definitely a head-turner. Then again, so were Sienna, Regan, and Kazuko. And only Kazuko was spoken for. Still, Tomkin concentrated on Lisa. But did that mean he'd be all that difficult to get along with?

Jack decided to reserve judgment.

"Not necessarily," he said. "Tomkin just has a problem with how Robert's been instructing Tumra on how to dive. He thinks Robert's going about it the wrong way."

"Maybe he should try listening for a change. I'm going forward to check on the equipment."

Jack patted Kimo on the back. "You do that. We'll be anchoring in about fifteen or twenty minutes."

Tomkin picked that moment to exit the cabin and join them in the cockpit. Jack and Kimo heard him grumbling under his breath. Kimo shot a knowing glance at Jack, climbed onto the starboard hull, and stepped toward the equipment piled on the deck forward of the cabin.

"The man's going to die," Tomkin spat.

Jack wondered if he should reconsider his opinion of the red-haired caver. The man displayed an arrogance that was hard for him to warm to. "You're talking about Tumra?"

"Who else? Your friend Robert in there"—he nodded toward the cabin—"is teaching Tumra how to dive all right, but nothing about cave diving. I've dived in dozens and I tell you, it's not some pleasure dive in thirty feet of water inside a clear-blue lagoon, with lots of pretty fish swimming around. Those walls can close in on you like a vise—squeeze the breath right out of you. And then there are all the big and little nasties you can run into inside a cave. If the man gets into trouble, he won't be able to just swim to the surface and poke his head out and take a breath."

"Tomkin, relax. There's no need to scare the poor guy."

Tomkin locked eyes with Jack. "The man deserves to know what he's in for."

"Tumra only needs to know the fundamentals of diving for what we have planned." Jack did not look away. "Robert will take him down and make sure he's comfortable with the dive equipment before he ever enters the cave. Keep in mind I've made one trip through that lava tube already. As long as we have plenty of air, there's nothing to worry about. Besides, you, Robert and I will ferry in the equipment before anyone else goes in. That'll give us a chance to check the cave for those *nasties* you mentioned."

"You said the walls of the cave are smooth? I've dived some lava tubes and those walls were anything but smooth—like bloody sharks' teeth sticking out everywhere. Cut you to pieces if you aren't careful."

"Not this one. A few bumps and ridges here and there, but yeah, there's none of the jagged outcroppings you'd expect to find."

"But you haven't been back for a closer look. The way you talked you didn't have a lot of light with you when you were sucked in."

Tomkin's pessimism made Jack glad he hadn't mentioned running out of air and almost drowning. The Aussie would've had a field day with that information. "I assure you, we'll have plenty of light this time around."

"Can I offer a suggestion?"

"Of course. I want everyone on the team to be comfortable with giving input whenever they feel it's necessary."

Tomkin smiled. "Okay, mate. When we get inside and start exploring the cave, let me call the shots. I'll feel better."

Jack didn't have to think it over for long. Tomkin was conceited and arrogant, but he was an expert in the business of cave exploration. "I can live with that."

* * * *

Jack stood with his back to the five-foot tall crane assembly he and Robert had mounted on the leading edge of the fiberglass deck joining *Pono's* twin hulls. The other team members were gathered around the four equipment canisters, stacked just forward of the main cabin. Like him, they were in their mid thirties—except Lisa—and in good physical health. Seeing them standing there, willing and eager to go, did a lot to relieve his concerns about the coming dive and whatever they might encounter inside.

The group eyed him expectantly, even the dog.

"We've been over everything already, but let's do it again," he said. "I—"

"We're all professionals in our jobs," Tomkin interrupted. "Let's get inside that hole and go to work."

"We'll be doing that soon enough. I just don't want there to be any confusion when we do."

"Sure, whatever." Tomkin glanced at the sky. "But I gotta warn you. This sun, if I stay above ground much longer I'm liable to get a tan."

Tomkin's comment brought a chuckle to the lips of everyone on deck except Jack.

"Tomkin, redheads don't tan." Jack smirked. "They burn. Try sunblock 45. There's a big bottle of it inside."

"You're wrong about redheads not tanning," Tomkin corrected. "A few do. But I'll give you that one, providing you do something for me."

"What's that?"

"Call me Michael. If we're going to spend a week underground with each other, we should at least call each other by our first names."

Jack realized he'd been calling everyone by their first names except Michael Tomkin. He'd been content to simply call him by his last name. It must have been his pride getting in the way, or petty jealousy. Whichever it was, he'd have to work on putting the issue behind him. If he didn't, it would be a long five days. Besides the man deserved his respect, even if he was cocky and rubbed him the wrong way.

"You're absolutely right. From now on, it's nothing but first names."

"Does that mean I can't call you shithead?" Robert spoke up. "Even if you're not acting like one."

This time Jack laughed. So did everyone else. "Shithead is definitely out," he said. "Butthead is all right, though."

"Well then, I suggest you and Michael quit acting like a couple of buttheads and let's get on with the expedition. Time's a wasting."

"Right." Jack scanned the group. "As you know, we'll be

underground five days. The four waterproof cases you're sitting on contain the equipment and supplies we'll need. They're color coded for convenience: yellow for the scientific equipment, green for the food, blue for the water, and red for camp supplies and batteries."

"Keep in mind," Michael warned, "without batteries we're finished before we get started. So protect them. Unless you want to work by torchlight, providing we have torches."

"Unless I misunderstood, the grotto was lit up by bioluminescent bacteria," Regan said, glancing from Michael to Jack. "Is that not the case?"

"Four days ago it was. But I have no idea what caused the massive collection of bioluminescent bacteria inside the cavern, or how long such a concentration will last. Milky seas have been known to last days at a time. It's been four. Your guess is as good as mine."

Jack saw Regan exchange looks with Tumra and Lisa. He understood their concern. Spending almost a week, or even a day, inside a dark cave didn't appeal to him, either. He'd done that. Once was enough. Michael, on the other hand, seemed to be at home in a hole underground. Sienna *had* made a good choice in inviting him along.

It didn't change the fact the guy irritated the hell out of him.

"Relax." He raised his hands in front of him and pressed down in a gesture to calm their concerns. "We have more than enough battery operated lanterns and replacement batteries. No one is going to be left in the dark."

"When do we dive?" Tumra asked with equal concern. "Robert told me he was going to take me down ahead of time so that I could get comfortable with the scuba equipment."

"The tide is on its way in now." Jack checked his watch: a few minutes before one. He looked directly at Tumra. "It'll be that way for another couple of hours. That's when you and the others will make your descent, the lull between tides. In the meantime, Robert will take you down for your checkout dive." He glanced at Lisa, then Regan. "I'd encourage any of you who'd like a refresher course to join them. And while you're doing that, Michael and I will be getting the equipment ready to go over the side."

"And if we get caught in that surge you talked about?" Regan asked.

"You won't," he reassured her. Refocusing his attention on the entire group, he added. "And before I forget, when you begin your descent you'll see the mini-sub. Look at it all you want on the way down, but don't stray. The sub is not the focus of this mission. We're heading straight to the lava tube."

"I've made a lot of dives," Regan said. "It's damned tiring. I'll be doing good just to make that long of a swim in the few minutes we have. Not to mention the difficulty we're going to have just getting this equipment inside."

"That's why we have those." He pointed his finger at four powerful battery-powered, underwater scooters lined up along the bow rail. "Robert, Michael, and I will use the scooters to ferry the equipment in. Then we'll return with them and take you inside with plenty of time to spare. Once we've made our final descent, Kimo will wait two hours to make sure we're safely in and then leave. He'll return five days from now and be waiting topside to pick us up."

"So once we're inside the grotto," it was Regan talking again. "That's it? No radio communication, no contact with the outside world?"

Jack held her gaze. He liked the fact that she asked questions. But they'd been asked and answered when the group sat together at the dinner table the night before. He wanted to believe her apprehension would subside, once everyone was safely inside the grotto and sifting through clues to the existence of the *Menehune*.

"That's right," he said. "We'll be on our own."

CHAPTER 20

Jack stood with his bare back to the sun and cranked the handle on the manually operated winch, mounted to the small crane. Even Rebel watched with interest when the last canister, packed with supplies, splashed into the water at the bow of the boat.

Robert had chosen well. Each canister was the size of a large steamer trunk and constructed of high-impact plastic, with a durable rubber seal which was watertight down to a hundred and fifty meters. They'd tied lead weights to the outside of the cases to give them neutral buoyancy in the water. A battery-powered, underwater scooter was strapped to the lid of each one.

He peered down at the canister and watched the cable slacken. The three other canisters bobbed at the end of the ropes tethering them to the bow safety rail. Treading water in swimsuit, mask, and fins, Michael unhooked the canister and let it float with the others. The canisters had been heavy and cumbersome on the boat, but in the water they moved easily.

Jack retrieved his T-shirt from where he'd draped it over the railing, and used it to mop his broad chest. The scuff of footsteps on the deck behind him made him turn and look. He sucked in a breath when he saw Lisa standing there. She'd shed her tight-fitting shirt and shorts and stood dressed in a yellow bikini which flaunted enough exposed skin to leave little to the imagination and a lot to be desired. Way too much for his liking, with Michael sniffing around.

He glanced toward the cabin. Kazuko, Sienna, and Kimo were standing at the stern railing staring down at the water—no doubt watching the divers' air bubbles rise to the surface.

He looked back at Lisa. "I thought you might want to take advantage of the checkout dive."

"Robert has his hands full with Tumra and Regan. Besides I made several dives with my brother the week before he..." She blinked several times and looked away.

Jack took her in his arms and pulled her against him. Her skin burned hot against his. He felt himself become aroused at her touch. He closed his eyes tight and held her.

Damn!

"Are you going to be okay with this?" he asked in a soft voice.

She nestled the side of her head in the mat of dark hair on his chest and gripped his muscled biceps. "Just hold me a minute. I'll be fine."

He brushed strands of her hair from his lips and held her. "No one will think badly of you if you go to Lihue with Kimo. There will be other expeditions into the cave."

She dug her nails into the flesh on his arms and pushed him away. "I want to be here with you on this one, Jack. It's important to me. I finally have a chance to actually do something besides cataloging someone else's find."

"How nice," Michael interrupted from the boarding ladder. He sloshed onto the deck, dropped his wet fins and mask next to Jack's feet, and brushed back his dripping hair with his fingers. "If you like, I can strike up the barbie and open a bottle of wine. Maybe even find some music on the radio for you and the Sheila to dance to."

Jack let go of Lisa and faced Michael. "How about I just throw you back in the ocean and hold your head under water for a few minutes?"

"No fun in that, mate." Michael clapped a wet hand against Jack's shoulder and stepped past him. "What do you say we get you suited up so we'll be ready to haul that equipment in when Robert finishes his checkout dive?"

"I was just waiting on you," he said to the back of Michael's head.

Michael stopped, turned, and arched a brow at Jack. "Is that what you were doing?"

Jack met Michael's arched brow with a narrow-eyed look of disdain.

Damned Aussie.

Jack didn't want to play. "Do yourself a favor and give it a rest." He draped his T-shirt over his shoulder, brushed past Michael, and headed for the cabin.

"Testy bloke," Michael muttered to Lisa.

When Robert, Regan, and Tumra broke surface a few minutes later, Jack had his full-body wetsuit pulled on up to the waist, and his mask and fins piled next to his scuba tank. The hair on his chest glistened with sweat. "Let's do it," he said to Michael.

"About bloody time," Michael groused.

Working together, they helped each diver out of the water, lifting their tank and regulator setup from their back and shoulders after they'd unbuckled their buoyancy compensator. Robert climbed aboard last.

"They're good to go," he said, shrugging off his own dive equipment.

"Did they like the mini-sub?" Jack asked, taking Robert's apparatus from him.

"Hard to keep their attention on me, but I managed. How'd you and Michael make out?"

"We're good to go when you are."

"Give me a few minutes to breathe some of this nice warm air and gulp down a bottle of water, and we'll get this show on the road."

Jack gave Robert a friendly slap on the shoulder and faced Kimo. "Let's swap out these tanks."

"I'm way ahead of you."

Jack noticed Kimo had already brought three replacement tanks topside. He smiled. "Damn good day for a dive."

Fifteen minutes later, he stood at the bow, suited up and ready to go. Rebel sat looking at him, and Robert and Michael were already in the water. He gave the dog a pet and shook hands with Kimo. "So you and Kazuko will have the others ready when we get back?"

"Don't worry. You just take care of yourself."

"I will, old friend. Ask the gods to watch over me."

"I'm not sure they'll listen." Kimo's normally stoic expression cracked into a smile. "But I will, anyway."

"I'll take all the help I can get." He gave Kimo's hand another shake then pulled on his mask. He strapped on a caver's helmet with a powerful headlamp, bit down on his regulator, and dropped into the water.

Proceeding according to plan, Jack took charge of the blue canister. Since it contained their water supply, it was the heaviest, and probably the hardest to handle. Robert—being his equal in size—held onto the red case with the camping gear and batteries. Michael—the smallest of the three—was ready to go with the food. Given each case's neutral buoyancy, Jack didn't expect weight to be a factor. But he wanted to be prepared.

The three of them started down slowly, each riding his cargo like a kid on a bobsled. Jack was glad to finally be in the water, but couldn't deny his apprehension about going back into the lava tube. His first trip had almost cost him his life.

Their angled descent took them over the mini-sub, and Jack once again found himself staring at the periscope.

A sudden prickly sensation chilled the water inside his wetsuit.

In his mind, a vision of the Japanese captain, staring back at him from inside the boat, came to life. A ghost ship with a ghost crew, condemned to sailing the ocean depths forever.

He shook off the chill and glanced at Michael, ten feet to his right. The man was facing the sub, and he kept staring at it as they cruised past. It had to be killing him not to be able to investigate the sunken hulk.

Ten feet above the seafloor, Jack leveled off and increased his speed to max. He glanced from left to right and saw Robert and Michael match his speed. He felt relieved to have the sub behind them.

Fifty feet away, the entrance to the lava tube loomed like a giant mouth. He slowed at the opening and entered cautiously, waiting for the dread of once again being inside the lava tube to settle on him. But that didn't happen.

The powerful beams from the head lamps on their scooters probed deep into the darkness, casting bright light where none had existed. The sides of the shaft were the way he remembered them: for the most part smooth, scoured that way by eons of silt flowing in and out with the tide. Brightly colored fish, startled by the light, darted about looking for cover where little existed. A lobster studied them from a crevice under a rock on the floor.

This was nothing like his first trip into the tunnel. Before, he'd been sucked into the lava tube totally unprepared. This time he wasn't alone, and they were going in with bright lights, powerful scooters to pull them along, and plenty of air. The only thought on his mind now was the thrill of what awaited them at the other end.

He increased speed.

The tunnel—ranging from three to four meters in diameter—snaked its way to shore over three and a half football fields away. Even at slack tide, enough silt remained suspended in the cave water to cut their vision to ten meters, but not enough to cause concern that they might have trouble navigating the passageway.

A piece of cake.

With the three of them proceeding one behind the other, he led them deeper into the lava tube., He felt the walls close in on him when the shaft narrowed in a few places to within a couple of meters. There was just enough room for them to navigate the passage on their makeshift sleds.

His first time through—in the dark with silt swirling around him—he'd been oblivious to the tightness of the space. In the light, he felt his chest tighten from the sensation of tons of rock pressing down on him.

He thought about the inexperience of the divers waiting for him on the boat. If one of them were going to have a problem, this is where it would happen. And even the slightest mishap in here could quickly turn the expedition into a deadly disaster.

Trying not to think about that, he pressed on. And in the distance he saw a faint light.

The grotto.

The mystery behind the high concentration of bioluminescent bacteria might never be explained. But that was of no concern at the moment. What mattered was it continued to light up the cavern for them.

Jack ran his canister aground on the soft white sand thirty yards in, and stood up in knee-deep water. They had no time to spare, but he wasn't about to cheat himself out of a quick look around. He removed his helmet, peeled back his mask, and scanned the grotto. Robert and Michael did the same.

The cavern's grandness awed Jack the way it had his first time in. He flashed Michael a big glad-we-made-it smile and said, "Is this how you pictured it?"

"Not even close. I've seen some really awesome caves, but this place is bloody amazing." He glanced at the domed ceiling, fifty feet overhead and the walls, two hundred feet away on either side of him. Then he turned in a circle, his eyes wide open and alert. "You could fit two rugby fields in here easy. And those huts," he raised a gloved finger and pointed, "they're half the size of what you'd expect to see."

"How about you, Robert. Glad you came along?"

"Damn right I am." He took a few steps up the slope in the direction of the closest hut and stopped. "And you're right. A troop of boy scouts didn't build those huts."

"You can have crow for dinner." Jack nodded at his canister. "Right now, let's get this gear ashore and head back for the others. We don't have a lot of time to spare."

Michael turned and peered at the water, appearing to stare into the lava tube they had just passed through. "Let's just hope nobody suffers from claustrophobia."

CHAPTER 21

Fifteen minutes later they were motoring back toward the lava tube on their scooters, with the other members of the team in tow. Jack lay atop the fourth canister, with Lisa firmly grasping the waist strap of his buoyancy compensator. He watched the others strung out ahead of him, like a school of seals diving for the reef. Thirty feet below, Michael held the lead position, with Tumra holding onto him. Kazuko and Sienna were a few feet behind and to their right. Robert and Regan were farther back on the left.

Jack felt the discomfort of pressure building on his eardrums and slowed his descent to give Lisa and himself time to equalize the pressure. He noticed Robert had slowed, no doubt for the same reason, and so had Kazuko. Not the case with Michael. He continued on down, seemingly oblivious to the pressure change. That might work for him. But what about his passenger?

Tumra held on a few seconds longer. Then, all at once, he let go of Michael and kicked frantically toward the surface.

"*No…*" Jack's warning dissipated in a stream of bubbles.

Without waiting to see Michael's reaction, Jack steered toward Tumra and saw Robert and Kazuko do the same.

But no one was close enough to stop Tumra from bolting for the surface.

Suddenly, Tumra stopped kicking. It looked as if the Egyptian had suddenly remembered something he'd been taught. Then Jack saw him reach up, pinch his nose, and shake his head to clear his ears.

Good man.

Jack wanted to strangle Michael. If Tumra had panicked to the surface, the Aussie's cockiness could have hurt the man or even killed him. An air embolism, caused by too fast an assent, was a serious matter.

Kazuko and Sienna reached Tumra first. Robert and Regan arrived a second later. Slowed by the resistance of the canister, Jack was still a couple of seconds away from them when he saw Tumra—his olive skin paled by the ordeal—flash the women the okay sign and motion them back toward their scooters.

Relieved, Jack sighed into his regulator with a burst of bubbles. He bit down on the mouthpiece when he saw Michael roar up to the group and stop. Robert grabbed Michael's arm and shook his head, obviously upset.

Jack's first thought was to let Robert give Michael hell. He had it coming. But twenty-five feet under water was no place for a fist fight. He sped over to them, motioned for Lisa to stay with the canister, and stopped next to Robert. He took hold of his friend's arm and wouldn't release it until Robert let go of Michael. Both Robert and Michael seemed to calm down.

Jack looked at Tumra. The gutsy Egyptian swam over, flashed him the okay sign, and jabbed his index finger toward the bottom.

This was no way to start an expedition, and for a moment Jack considered surfacing. But he knew they needed to keep going. He glanced at each member of the team.

They all flashed the universal thumb and index finger signal for okay.

Michael gripped the handles of his scooter and pointed it toward the seafloor. He waved Tumra over.

Jack grabbed Michael's hand. When Michael looked at him, he let go and pressed down with both palms in a gesture to take it slow.

Michael nodded.

Jack moved aside to let Tumra swim in behind Michael and take hold of the waist strap of his buoyancy compensator.

Jack swam back to the canister and assumed his position atop it. Lisa took her place. The others paired up with their assigned partners and followed Michael down in the same order as before.

Everyone took it slowly.

Less than a minute later they entered the lava tube. The powerful lights on their scooters lit up the rock walls. And when the team drove deeper inside, total darkness closed in behind them.

Jack kept a watchful eye on the string of divers. He had no idea whether Lisa or any of the other passengers had their eyes open or not. A part of him hoped they had them squeezed shut. They had already suffered one mishap. Now he feared one of them would panic in the tight confines of the shaft.

So far so good.

Then the walls began to close in on them.

He realized they were approaching the first location where the passageway tapered to a couple of meters.

His breathing quickened.

The group ahead of him entered the narrow shaft with plenty of room to spare. Regan's head came up, but everyone held on.

Now it was his turn. Riding the canister made the going tight for them. He'd been through the passage with a canister once, and knew they would make it. He hoped Lisa trusted in that.

The shaft closed in on him.

Just a few feet more.

Seconds seemed like hours.

He felt the weight of the rock crush the breath out of him. Still, he navigated the bulky canister through the passage with precision. All at once the tunnel opened up. Lisa had not moved.

Two more to go.

Another few feet and the shaft pressed in on them, but not as much as before. They scooted through.

That left just one narrow passageway for them to negotiate: a hundred and fifty feet of tunnel that made you feel as if you'd been flushed through a sewer drain.

This was the section Jack dreaded most. After it, the grotto was an easy ride away.

They entered the rock pipeline, and it appeared they were going to make it through without any problem.

Suddenly—directly in front of him—Regan let go of Robert.

Jack eased off on the throttle and drifted to within a couple of feet of her. He sensed her panic, and needed to get to her, but couldn't squeeze past the canister attached to his scooter.

The walls closed in on him.

His heart raced.

Dammit!

He pinched his eyes shut.

Breathe. Slow even breaths.

Struggling to keep his own claustrophobia at bay, he helplessly watched Regan frantically pound on the lava walls with her fists.

Through the corner of his mask, he saw Lisa swim up next to him.

He looked more closely. She, too, watched in wide-eyed horror.

It took a moment for Robert to react, but he was at Regan's side in seconds. She continued to flail at the rock, though not as frantically as before. He grabbed hold of her head and made her look at him. She calmed down. He pointed first to her eyes, then his.

From only a few feet away, Jack could clearly see Robert close his eyes, indicating for her to do the same.

Robert's ploy seemed to work: he was able to take Regan's hands and moved them to the waistband of his buoyancy compensator. The moment she had a firm grip on the strap, he took hold of his scooter and sped them both forward.

Jack glanced at Lisa's eyes through the faceplate of her mask. To his relief they were brown, focused, and unbelievably calm. Regan's bout with panic hadn't affected her.

A minute later he and Lisa surfaced inside the dimly lit grotto. He was glad to be out from under the weight of all that rock. In here he could breathe.

Ahead of him, Robert and Regan climbed out of the water. The others stood on shore, oblivious to what had occurred with Regan.

It was no doubt for the best.

He held onto that thought and motored ashore.

They'd all made it safely inside, but not without mishap. And they had five days to go.

Anything could happen.

CHAPTER 22

Sienna scrambled to the top of the beach and stood with her back to the group. In front of her, the tiny huts she'd seen in the photos dotted the floor of the cavern. The sight numbed her mind. Activity continued behind her, but she only had a vague awareness of the other members of the team sloshing ashore. She wasn't even aware Regan had panicked.

She turned and saw Robert pointing a finger at Michael. The others in the group were gathered close around him.

"That was a stupid stunt," Robert said, loud enough for everyone to hear. "What were you trying to prove taking Tumra down that fast?"

"We were doing fine, mate." Michael straightened in front of Robert. "And get your finger out of my face. Tumra agreed to tap me on my back if he had a problem. He never did."

Kazuko stepped next to Robert and placed a calming hand on his shoulder. Robert glanced at her and after a long moment, smiled. He looked at Michael again and said in a calm tone of voice, "This was only his second dive, if you count his checkout dive. You should have known better."

"That was my fault," Tumra said. Deep-set and intense, his almost black eyes accentuated the beak-like appearance of his nose. "I should have signaled to him that I was having a problem."

"I don't need you to defend me," Michael groused.

"And we've had enough mishaps for one day," Jack said. He turned to Regan. "Are you okay?"

"Now that we're out of there, yes." Regan wiped the salt water from her face with her hands and combed her fingers through her wet hair. She inhaled a deep breath and let it out again. "Never thought that would happen. That narrow tunnel caught me off guard, is all."

Sienna heard Regan's comment and only then realized something bad had happened to her in the tunnel. She raced down the slope and stopped in front of her colleague. She brushed stray strands of damp strawberry blonde hair from Regan's face and peered into her turquoise eyes. "Are you sure you're all right? What happened?"

"My claustrophobia kicked in." Regan's tone was apologetic.

Jack, Robert, and Michael exchanged looks.

"But you're okay?" Sienna probed.

Regan smiled at her. "I'm fine now, thanks to Robert."

Sienna exhaled a sigh of relief, marched up the slope and faced the research team. From up there, she stood a full head taller than everyone else. They needed to stay focused. "Listen up, people. We've had a full day, but I want to set up camp and complete an initial assessment of this site before we sleep."

Jack walked up the slope and stood next to her. A man of his word, he said, "She's in charge now, folks. I suggest we get to work."

Kazuko, Regan, and Lisa turned their heads, taking that moment to scan the grotto. Tumra slipped on his black-rimmed glasses and joined them. Obviously, with all that had been happening on the beach, they had yet to fully appreciate the magnificence of the sight.

"I never imagined it looking like this," Regan said.

"Or smelling." Tumra fanned his hand in front of his nose.

"That's the smell of the sea." Kazuko chuckled. "Nice, huh?"

"I'm with Tumra," Lisa did some nose-fanning of her own. "That smell will definitely take some getting used to. But this place *is* amazing."

"That's for sure," Regan agreed. "There is something here for everyone."

Kazuko edged past Michael and began to unbuckle the scooter strapped atop the green canister which Jack and Lisa had been riding on. "I suggest we start with the tents and cooking supplies. If those fish ponds are even half as productive as they look, we're having seafood for dinner."

"I'll go for that," Tumra said. "Sure beats MRE's."

"What, you don't like Meals Ready to Eat?" A hint of sarcasm showed in Michael's voice.

"Do you?" Tumra stepped to the other side of the canister and went to work dropping the lead weights.

Michael laughed. "Lobster for dinner and nobody thought to pack wine."

* * * *

Sienna chose an open, flat area to the right of the village to set up camp. A half-hour later the area was dotted with the blue nylon domes of their seven two-man tents. Every member would have his or her own tent, except Robert and Kazuko—each one providing a bit of privacy in a commune of eight.

Aluminum camp stools had been unfolded in front of the tents, as well as the cooking gear and the scientific equipment that had been arranged on top of the empty canisters that now served as work tables.

Jack walked toward Sienna, who stood facing her new workbench, and watched her power up a digital camera.

"Home away from home?" he asked.

She turned at the sound of his voice. "I've been aching to start to work on these huts. Want to join me?"

No way would he pass up the opportunity for a few minutes alone with her. "Your lead, Doctor."

She started walking toward the nearest hut, and Jack fell into stride next to her. The incident with Regan in the lava tube concerned him. He had his own problem with claustrophobia, but had remained in control. Regan had lost it.

"Regan commented on her claustrophobia kicking in," he said. "What was that all about?"

"Why not ask her?"

"I wanted to hear what you had to say."

"And what makes you think I know?"

"I have a feeling you know more about Regan than you let on."

"She has a tendency to be claustrophobic at times."

"No shit. Why on earth didn't she say something—or you, since you knew she suffers from the condition?"

"We talked about it. She honestly didn't think it would be a problem."

"We're likely to encounter other narrow spaces before we finish our work here. What then?"

Sienna stopped and looked him in the eyes. "She assured me that won't happen."

"And if it does?"

"It won't. She has medication. I'll make sure she takes it."

Jack saw the resolve in Sienna's eyes and decided not to press the issue further. Instead, he grinned. "Let's take a look at those carvings."

She continued walking toward the nearest hut. "You won't say anything to her, then?"

"I won't," he assured her. "But I can't speak for Robert or Michael."

"Can you talk to them about it?"

"The first chance I get."

"I think that's best." She dropped to her knees at the entrance flap of the hut. "She's upset enough about her behavior as it is."

The Regan issue was closed, for now. He'd leave it that way, but he couldn't help feeling it would come up again. Then what?

He put the thought out of his mind and watched Sienna run her fingers over the carvings on the poles framing the doorway. It dawned on him that the carvings were not present anywhere else on the hut. He asked, "Is there some significance in the fact that these carvings were only done on the doorways?"

"It could possibly be a prayer to their god or gods—early civilizations usually had several to watch over their home. Or it could be some kind of record of their lineage."

He chuckled. "Like one of those needlework signs you see in people's houses: 'Bless Our Happy Home.'"

"I'm certain these carvings have deeper meaning than a simple needlepoint phrase hung in someone's living room."

"This is what brought you here, isn't it?"

"All I'm going to say is, you and your beginner's luck! These carvings could turn out to be the single most important part of the discovery. Your name will be in all the science journals."

"I'd be happy just knowing what the carvings mean."

"You might have to settle for having your name in *National Geographic*. Epigraphers—people who specialize in interpreting ancient engravings—are still working on the carved mammoth tusks found in Finland. So far no one has been able to decipher them."

"Maybe the key to that enigma lies somewhere in these huts."

"We'll never know until we look." She took several pictures of the carvings before turning her attention to the sheet of multi-colored kappa cloth covering the opening. She gently fingered the coarse material and snapped two more pictures. Then she pushed the flap aside, snapped several pictures of the interior at different angles from the doorway, and crawled inside.

Jack held the flap back and looked in at Sienna. Even with her sitting down, there was no more than a two or three inch gap between the top of her head and the ceiling. "What's it like in there?"

"Like I'm sitting inside a doll's house."

Jack furrowed his brow.

"I meant, do you see anything?"

"None of the tools I'd expect to see." She snapped another couple of pictures. "Only a painted gourd bowl or scoop hanging from the wall."

"I saw one of those gourd scoops in the hut I peeked into when

I discovered this place. There were also wooden bowls, netting, and a raised sleeping area."

"Not in this one."

"Whoever built this hut must have taken their stuff with them when they moved on." He turned and nodded in the direction of the hut sitting on the edge of the village, near the center and closest to the beach. "That's the hut I saw the artifacts in. Let's take a look in there."

Jack straightened and waited for Sienna to crawl out of the hut. He looked to see what the other team members were doing. Kazuko and Lisa stood on the rock levee, eyeballing the fish pond closest to their camp. Tumra sat on a stool in front of his tent, with his laptop open on his knees. Robert and Michael were organizing the dive gear. Regan sat, Indian style, on the sand by her tent, the first-aid kit laid out in front of her.

He was glad for the minutes alone with Sienna. He might not get another opportunity.

"Ready," he asked, when Sienna stood up next to him.

She took a photo of the ground between them and the next hut and pointed at the small depressions while she walked. "Too bad the village was built on soft sand. Otherwise we might have gotten some photographs of foot impressions—even made some plaster casts to show off to the public."

"You can tell they were made by feet the size of a child's, but I know that's not good enough," he said and looked to the rear of the cavern. "Perhaps we will have some luck when we explore the rest of the grotto."

"You're still stuck on the *Menehune* idea, aren't you?"

"You have to admit, the findings point in that direction." He shrugged. "But being a scientist, I know we need conclusive evidence to convince the world of their existence."

Sienna dropped to her knees in front of the doorway to the second hut. "Confidence, Jack. We've only just started."

"Patience was never one of my virtues. But I'm learning."

"You'll need to if you're going to play this game."

He watched her begin the examination process, and then go through each step with the same meticulous precision she'd used on the first hut. He'd have just flipped up the flap and taken a look inside.

And now he thought about it. That's why he missed the carvings in the first place. He doubted he'd ever have the patience to sit for days, or even hours, brushing away soil to expose a single artifact.

Finally she moved the flap aside and poked her head in. "This is where you saw the artifacts you mentioned?"

"He squatted next to her. "Positive. Why?"

She turned her head and looked squarely at him. "Everything's gone, even the bed."

CHAPTER 23

Sienna backed out of the doorway of the last hut, and Jack let go of the cloth flap. From the way she moved, he already knew the answer to the question forming on the tip of his tongue.

Nothing.

"You don't have to tell me," he said. "Bare as Old Mother Hubbard's cupboard."

She shook her head at the hut. "Doesn't make sense."

"Unless…"

His comment brought a sideways glance from Sienna. He knew what was coming.

"Not *Menehune*?" she said with a tone of skepticism.

He shrugged. "Got a better answer?"

"Legends and fairytales, Jack. Someone came in here ahead of us and took the artifacts, that's all."

"Then explain the footprints." He pointed at theirs amid all the others in the area. "Ours are the only full-sized prints here."

"I don't know. Maybe it's kids playing a joke."

"Kids didn't build these huts. And they certainly didn't make those carvings."

Sienna scanned the miniature village. "No, they didn't."

Jack saw lanterns flicker on at their camp. He glanced up at the ceiling as though he were looking at the sky. "We're losing our light."

"I noticed it's been getting steadily darker," Sienna agreed. "What do you make of it?"

"The bioluminescent bacteria must be dispersing. It's a miracle of nature the stuff lasted this long. What do you say we join the rest of the group?"

They hurried back to the others, as the cavern beyond the reach of the lanterns fell into darkness. Michael met them at the edge of camp and handed them their hard hats and headlamps.

"From now on, no one goes anywhere without their helmet and light," he said. "Especially the helmet. Don't want people cracking their skulls open."

Jack took his, slipped it on his head, and said, "Thanks."

Michael's gaze shifted from Jack to Sienna, and back to Jack. "I apologized to Robert for what happened with Tumra, and now I want to apologize to you."

"You and Robert worked things out, then?"

"We did. There was no excuse for what happened. And he was right. I should have known better."

"I'm glad to hear you say that."

"We're all novices in one way or another down here, I can't forget that. It's important we work together."

"How's Regan?" Sienna nodded toward her colleague, who stood in front of the camp stove adjusting the flame under a pot.

Michael turned and looked. "She seemed a bit down earlier. I think she was embarrassed about what happened to her."

Sienna laid her hand on Michael's arm. "You didn't pressure her about it, did you?"

Michael smiled. "She assigned herself camp cook. Promised to whip us up an epicurean's delight. Not sure what that is, but I'm guessing it'll be good."

"She didn't tell you she's a gourmet cook?"

"Seems she left that part out."

"You ordered lobster, right?" Jack pointed. "I'd say Kazuko delivered in spades."

Michael turned and chuckled. "Bloody hell, mate."

They could just make out Kazuko and Lisa walking toward them from the fish pond. Kazuko carried a lobster in front of her, with both hands gripping its back. Even in the gloom and from a hundred feet away, Jack could tell the lobster had to weigh every bit of twenty-five pounds.

Regan trotted down to the two women. She laughed and faced the camp. She waved. "We eat good tonight, folks," she joked.

Sienna waved back and hurried over to them.

"Regan appears to be her old self," Jack said. He clapped Michael on the back and said, "Come on, let's take a look at that bug."

"You're not worried?"

Jack frowned at Michael. "About what?'

"Regan's claustrophobia." Michael exhaled an exasperated breath. "You saw what it can do."

Jack scanned the enormous chamber. "Not in here."

Jack walked away, and Michael followed. They joined the others, who stood in a half-circle in front of Kazuko and Lisa.

"...and there are plenty more like it," Kazuko finished. She held the lobster up for Jack and Michael to see. "I was just telling them about the fish pond. It's teeming with life. I've never seen anything like it. Believe it or not, there are at least a hundred more like this one in there...some even bigger. And huge schools of mullet the size of your forearm."

"She's not exaggerating, Jack." Lisa was all smiles. "I saw 'em. It took both of us to pull this monster from the rocks—had to use a couple of hooked sticks we found down there to pry him loose. That fish pond is an engineering marvel and I bet the one over there is no different."

Everyone peered into the darkness, looking in the direction of the far pond.

"Regan," Sienna spoke up, refocusing their attention. "I've tasted your lobster. It's excellent. You did yourself proud."

Robert took the lobster from Kazuko who struggled to hold it up. "If you're ready to work your magic, I'm starved."

Regan blushed. "You'll relish every bite."

Jack stood back and watched everyone march up the slope to camp. All in all, it had been a good first day.

Standing there a moment longer, he starred into the darkness at the rear of the cavern. Glowing water. A village full of empty, child-sized huts. Missing artifacts. Hundreds of tiny impressions in the sand. Fish ponds teeming with life. What next?

* * * *

Jack poked his head out of his tent and glanced around. He'd thought he heard sand crunching, like someone walking in front of his tent. The cavern was dark except for a single beam of light coming from a headlamp, thirty feet away. A bright circle lit up the side of the hut nearest camp—the one he and Sienna had found the gourd bowl in.

He crawled out to see who it was.

Lisa had blown him a kiss when they retired to their respective tents. A part of him hoped it was her, luring him out into the dark. He glanced toward her tent and heard her gentle snoring.

Just as well.

He switched on his headlamp and aimed the beam at the ground in front of him while he walked. The last thing he wanted to do was crash into the camp stove or work table.

"Couldn't sleep," Sienna said, with her back to him.

He stopped next to her. "You knew it was me?"

"Your cologne?"

"I'm not wearing cologne." Jack was confused.

"Precisely."

"That was a delicious dinner. Regan's a great gal."

She turned to look at him. "I heard you guys talking. You're going to scout the back of the cavern, tomorrow."

"There has to be at least one other tunnel leading in here."

"It's hard to believe nobody knew this place existed."

"Other than the little people who built it, you mean?"

He could have kissed her. "So you do believe in the existence of *Menehune*?"

"Let's just say I'm glad you insisted on keeping the find a secret."

"Speaking of secrets. That incident with Regan's claustrophobia—that tender little moment between the two of you, when you found out what happened—I'm guessing you're more than mere colleagues."

"Haven't you wondered why you and I were never more than just friends?"

"Yeah. But I chalked it up to you wanting to keep our relationship on a professional level."

Sienna turned and placed a hand on Jack's cheek. "You're hard to resist, Jack."

He took her hand in his and kissed it. Now that the woman's love life was out in the open—at least as far as he was concerned—he couldn't begrudge Sienna her lifestyle. He loved women, too.

"No one needs to know," he said. "Unless you choose to tell them."

Sienna touched her hand where he'd kissed it. "You're a dear for saying that. We'll see."

Behind them, Lisa sat on her heels, watching from the darkness of their camp.

She slipped back into her tent, unnoticed.

CHAPTER 24

Jack crawled from his tent and stood up in the light from lanterns. The activity in camp awakened him from a bad dream. At least, he hoped it was a dream and not a vision of events to come.

Out of habit, he glanced up expecting to see a morning sky. He saw only rock and shadows.

Not a good way to start the morning.

He yawned and focused on the camp stove, looking for the coffee pot. Robert had it in his hand, filling a cup.

"I'll take one," Jack said, his voice thick with sleep.

Robert poured a second cup and met Jack halfway with it. "You look tired. Too much fun yesterday?"

"It was at that, wasn't it?" He took a couple of sips and nodded at his cup. "Four or five more of these and I ought to be good to go."

"You didn't sleep?"

"I dozed a little and finally drifted off around four or five. And speaking of not sleeping, what were you guys jabbering about out here last night? If I hadn't been trying to sleep, I'd have joined you."

"When?"

"Must have been about three."

"I don't know about Michael and Tumra, but I was sound asleep at three."

Michael walked up holding a day pack in his hand. "Don't know about Michael, what?"

"Jack asked what we were talking about last night," Robert explained. "I told him I was asleep."

"And what time was that?"

"About three," Jack turned his attention to Michael. "I thought I heard you guys out here, whispering."

"Not me, mate. I was dreaming about a blonde with tits the size of melons."

Jack looked back and forth at the two men. "Forget it. Must have been dreaming."

"I prefer mine." Michael smiled. "Drink up. I want to get started."

Jack glanced at his watch. It felt early.

Michael slapped him on the back. "Trust your watch, mate. It's after seven. That's the problem with caves. No bloody sun to wake up by. Let's move." He turned and walked away.

Jack glanced at Robert.

"Don't look at me." Robert gave a sideways shake of his head. "I have a feeling he's like this all the time."

* * * *

Jack slung the strap of his day pack over his broad shoulder and scanned the grotto, looking for Lisa. He didn't want to leave camp without at least telling her good morning, but every time he looked for her she was somewhere else.

He hated to think she was avoiding him.

The sound of her voice made him turn. He saw her on the other side of camp, talking to Kazuko. They appeared to have struck up a friendship.

That's a step in the right direction.

Finally he could relax. Robert and Kazuko were family to him. And of the two, Kazuko was the most opinionated. Get on the good side of her, and you were in.

"She likes her," Robert said, hefting his own pack.

"Who?"

"Kazuko. She thinks Lisa is all right."

"You?"

"I'll let you know."

"You going with me and Tumra?" Michael asked. "Or do you two plan on hanging around here and playing with the women?"

Screw you, asshole! Jack was sure Robert had thought the same thing.

"Lead on," he said, and slid on his helmet.

Michael took off toward the rear of the cavern.

"Don't mind him," Tumra said on his way past Jack. "He's short."

Jack chuckled and fell in stride behind Tumra. Robert followed behind them.

Once they left the light of camp, Jack noticed the ominous feeling the cavern took on in the dark. The beams from their handheld flashlights and headlamps cut bright swaths through the inky blackness, but beyond loomed a foreboding world of shadows and darkness.

A few minutes into their trek, Jack heard the generator sputter to life behind them. He turned and saw the village light up. The women weren't wasting any time getting to work.

His spirit warmed. So far the grotto had been one mystery on top of another. With luck, the day would reveal answers to some of those mysteries.

"Let's go, Jack." Robert slapped him on the back.

"It's all quite amazing, isn't it?"

"And hard to fathom."

"You got that right." Jack fell back in line and hurried to catch up with the men in front of him.

Farther in, the sand floor stretching across the cavern turned into rock. Michael called a halt and scanned the area.

"We're there," he announced.

"Where is 'there'?" Robert asked, coming to a stop next to Jack.

"The cavern is shaped like the horn of a goat," Tumra said. "Look up and you'll see the ceiling is now no more than ten or fifteen feet above our heads. The walls are maybe a hundred feet away from us on either side."

Jack aimed both of his lights at the slate-gray basalt ceiling and saw it pressing down on them. How would Regan react to that? He glanced around. Wherever he looked his headlamp lit up rock.

"So," he said, "the lava tube should be someplace close."

"Unless it sealed itself off."

"It's here," Jack reassured him. "The people who built that village and those fish ponds had to get in some way. And I don't think they came in the way we did."

"No shit," Michael chimed in. He jabbed a thumb at the darkness to his right. "You and Robert look over there. Tumra and I will check around here. And stay together. I don't want to have to come looking for you because you wandered off alone and got hurt."

"You don't let up, do you?" Jack said.

"When I'm exploring a cave, I take it personally if someone on my team gets hurt."

"Come on, Jack." Robert tugged on his arm.

Jack bit back his frustration and pointed his light at the stone wall. "Let's find that cave. Maybe there'll be a hole I can push him into."

"That's the spirit."

After a couple of minutes Jack's light fell on an opening to a cave. "Damn, this has to be it."

Robert added his light to the passageway. "Unless there's more than one."

Jack looked at Michael and Tumra. He saw the beams from their flashlights and headlamps dance like light sabers in a Star Wars movie fight scene. "They're still looking, so I'm guessing this is the only one."

"I'll call them over." Robert raised a cupped hand to his mouth.

Jack reached up and gently grasped Robert's wrist. "Let's have a peek inside, first."

"You sure that's wise?"

"Can't hurt."

Jack stepped into the pitch-black passageway and Robert

followed him. Their lights lit up the tunnel. Jack pointed his flashlight at the floor.

"What are you looking for?" Robert asked.

"Foot prints. I promised Sienna I'd try to find some."

"You won't find any here. Floor's solid rock."

"I can see that. Let's go in a little farther."

They cautiously crept another twenty meters, their light beams crossing and crisscrossing the darkness.

Jack visualized the lava tube Robert and he had ventured into on Kahoolawe the year before. A glazed oval tunnel, that looked as if a giant had pressed down on it with the palm of his hand.

There was some evidence of glazing here, but very little compared to the lava tube on Kahoolawe. The walls and ceiling were craggy, dark gray rock—typical of what most people would expect the inside of a volcanic cave to look like. But the floor was worn smooth in a path that wound its way around boulders and jagged outcroppings.

The question that nagged him was, who walked here? Was it some fanged, red-eyed creature of the underworld, or a lost tribe of little people?

A warm breath of air moved through the tunnel.

The cave was alive.

Robert gripped Jack's arm. "Time to get Michael and Tumra."

CHAPTER 25

Jack stopped. His long-time friend was right. They had gone far enough without the others.

He turned and angled the beam of his headlamp up so that he wouldn't blind Robert. "You got that feeling too, huh?"

"All I know is, my gut tells me this is far enough for now."

"I have to admit, it's not quite what I imagined."

"It's everything I imagined. Let's go."

A pair of headlamps and flashlights met them at the entrance to the cave. Jack knew he'd get shit from Michael.

"Do you enjoy pissing me off?" Michael groused.

"What? Did you think we got lost?" Jack felt his face heat up.

"Just don't take off like that, again. Okay, mate?"

"And *you* stay away from Lisa." As soon as he said it, Jack felt foolish. But what the hell, it irked him that the man dogged her every chance he got.

Michael laughed. "So that's what this is all about!"

"Right, *mate!*" Jack directed his headlamp in the man's face. "Are you okay with that?"

"Touchy bloke," Michael muttered to Robert and Tumra, and pushed past Jack. Several feet into the cave, he stopped and turned to the three men who had yet to move. "You just going to stand there?"

Jack caught a hard look from Robert that told him he'd made an ass out of himself.

Damn.

He regretted his anger had surfaced here, now. *But dammit…*

Exhaling a calming breath he said, "I guess it's my turn to apologize."

"No worries. Now—if you're done—I suggest we get a move on. We have a cave to explore."

The path they walked was worn smooth, and easy to travel. Even so, Michael took it slowly, pausing frequently to shine his light into the shadows.

Jack judged the tunnel to be five or six meters across, and almost as many tall at the center. He was anxious to discover if this was indeed a passageway out. But like Michael, he didn't want to overlook anything that might be of importance to the mission.

His focus was centered on the pathway ahead of him when something plopped on his helmet. Worried, he stopped walking and pointed his light at the ceiling of the tunnel.

Another drop splashed on his forehead.

"Shit, it's raining," he said, swiping away the water with the back of his hand.

Robert laughed. "That water is probably older than you are."

Jack scanned the area with his lights. Water dripped from fractures in the basalt. Rain leaching into the lava tube from the strata above was continuing its journey underground through cracks in the floor.

"What do you think?" he asked Robert over his shoulder. "How long does it take for water to percolate through a couple of thousand feet of rock?"

"More time than we have, I'm sure."

"Well put." Jack fished a bottle of water from his backpack. He unscrewed the cap, took a long drink, and held it out to Robert. "At least we don't have to worry about dying of thirst."

Robert waved off the offering and dug out a bottle of his own. "That's one thing off the list, anyway."

"Come on, gentlemen," Tumra said, walking past them. "Michael's on the move again."

Jack watched him for a few steps then turned to Robert. "Think I should lighten up on the Aussie?"

"Let me put it to you this way. A group of us went fishing with a guy once who couldn't keep his line in the water. Every time someone would catch a fish, he'd run over to where they were and cast his line in. By the end of the day we all caught fish except him. Turned out he never had his line in the water more than five minutes at a time."

"So you're saying I need to keep my line in the water and not worry about him?"

"You've already hooked the fish, Jack. You just haven't realized it, yet. Now let's get going."

Michael and Tumra had already disappeared from view around a bend where the cave made a left turn. They could see the glow of the two men's lights, but not the men. Robert set a fast pace to catch up, with Jack following closely.

Robert and Jack rounded the corner expecting to see more black rock. They gasped at the sight that greeted them.

"What the—" Jack managed.

"Don't ask me," Robert offered. "I've seen pictures of them in books, but that's it."

Michael and Tumra stood fifty meters ahead with their lights trained on a formation that looked as if a million gallons of tapioca pudding had oozed from the wall and hardened into overlapping mushroom caps. Water dripped into a pool at the base.

No one talked. For a long moment Jack and Robert stood transfixed. A constant *drip, drip, drip* echoed in the cavern.

Finally, Jack began walking forward. He still hadn't said anything. His eyes were focused on the formation. The entire expedition was worth a single look at this marvel of nature.

The grotto had been spectacular enough, now this. He could only imagine what they would find next.

The toe of his shoe hooked a crack, and he stumbled forward.

Robert kept him from falling by grabbing hold of his pack from behind.

"Careful, Jack."

Jack glanced over his shoulder at his friend. "Magnificent, isn't it?"

"Sure is. But you don't want to break a leg getting there."

"What?"

"Watch where you're stepping."

"Oh, yeah." Jack pointed his light at the path and kept it there the rest of the way.

He stopped next to Tumra. "What do they call it?"

"Flowstone." Tumra used his light beam like a pointer. "It's the most common cave deposit, and is almost always composed of calcite or some other carbonate mineral."

"But what causes it to be shaped like that?"

"Flowstone forms from flowing water." Tumra explained. "Thin layers of calcium carbonate and other cave minerals form when the water loses its dissolved carbon dioxide. Those thin layers initially take on the shape of the underlying rock. But the formation tends to become rounded as the layers thicken."

"Is it always the color of bleached coral?"

"Not necessarily. I've been in caves where it formed in thin brown and beige sheets called cave bacon. It can be red if there's a lot of iron in the water."

Robert stepped to the edge of the pool to get a closer look. "I didn't even know formations like this existed inside lava tubes."

"They usually don't. And when they do form, they aren't nearly this big. This is by far the largest one I've seen."

"And that's the problem," Michael added. He pointed his flashlight at a slit less than a meter wide. "It's practically sealed off the cave."

"Oh, I don't know." Jack eyed the slot. "Looks like we can squeeze through. Besides, the path leads right to it."

Michael stepped to the narrow slit and lit it up with his light. "Me, maybe." He faced Jack and smiled. "You'd better suck it in. It's going to be tight."

Michael shrugged off his pack, held it in his hand, and slipped into the slot with no trouble at all.

Jack did the same with his pack and edged in right after him.

Almost immediately, his chest tightened under the sensation of all that rock bearing down on him. He breathed in and out, forcing from his mind the feeling of being crushed to death. It had turned into a battle of wills between him and the Aussie. He was not about to let the narrowness of the gap keep him from making it through to the other side.

He saw Michael slide into the chamber beyond.

Only a few more feet to go.

His shirt snagged, and he sucked in a breath.

"Problem, Jack?"

"A minor inconvenience is all." He forced past the restriction, tearing his shirt on the sharp-edged rock.

He popped out of the grove and glanced around. The cavern opened up on this side of the flowstone. A dozen columns of calcite, forty feet tall, stood like pillars holding up the mountain. A pool of water, the size of a large irrigation pond, stretched the length of the left side of the cavern. There seemed no end to nature's natural wonders.

He heard Robert scrape free of the rock. It was hard to take his eyes off the sight of the cavern. When he finally turned to look, Robert was completely through and Tumra was sliding out. The three of them stood together.

"Let's hope we don't run into any more crevices like this," Robert said, fingering a hole in his shirtsleeve.

Jack peered down at his own shirt, looking for the tear he knew was there. The beam of his headlamp lit up an object on the pathway at their feet.

What…?

He bent and picked it up.

Michael's bone-handled pocket knife.

He'd seen the Aussie cleaning his fingernails with the jackknife the evening before. He figured it'd slipped out of the man's pack. He held it out for him to see. "You dropped your knife."

Michael narrowed his eyes at Jack. "So you took it."

Jack furrowed his brow. "What are you talking about?" He pointed his light at the path. "I tell you, I just now found it, right there on the ground."

"You're not fucking with me?"

"Honest, I found it right there. What's the problem?"

"I looked for my knife this morning and couldn't find it."

"I figured it had dropped from your pack."

"That's the second place I checked."

Robert moved nearer to get a look at the knife. "Where'd you see it last?"

"On the work table with the rest of the equipment. I laid it there last night after dinner."

They all exchanged glances.

Jack took one more look at the knife and handed it back. "If you didn't drop your knife here, who did?"

CHAPTER 26

Jack scanned the cavern of pillars. He could have sworn he heard something other than the incessant drip, drip, drip of water. Deeper in the cave, where his light wouldn't reach, the scuff of a footstep on rock? Someone whispering?

He cocked an ear toward the sound.

Nothing.

He exhaled the breath he'd been holding and sidestepped into the narrow slot they had come through only minutes before. The others were ahead of him, already on their way back to camp. This time everyone moved with purpose and no one gave anyone a hard time. They'd been in full agreement on the decision to join up with the women before proceeding farther into the cave.

If his team were on the verge of a discovery of great significance beyond what had already been found, the women should all be there to share in it.

With his thoughts on who dropped the knife, his chest didn't tighten on him the way it had the first time he squeezed through the narrow slot. And when his shirt snagged, he sucked in and slid past the protrusion without a second thought.

Five feet of crevice remained when he saw the three men waiting for him in the open tunnel beyond. His mind should have been on sidestepping those last few feet as quickly as possible, but surprisingly it wasn't.

He wondered if he would have had the same difficulty negotiating the narrow passageway if he were half as tall and a hundred and fifty pounds lighter. He pictured a species of human being three feet tall and weighing fifty-five pounds.

No doubt someone the size of a small child could scamper through the crevice with no problem at all.

"Hurry up and slide your ass out of there," Robert said. "I want to get the women and be back here before old age sets in."

Jack realized he'd stopped moving when his thoughts wandered to the little people. He quickly edged his way out of the crevice. "I was just thinking—"

"You're thinking what we're thinking," Michael cut Jack off. "Let's go."

Jack stood his ground. "Don't ever cut me off like that again."

Michael stopped. "What's your problem? You think someone or something walked through here ahead of us. I do, too. So do Tumra and Robert. We need to get the women and hurry back here if that's what we're going to do. Or we just proceed without them."

Jack knew at once he'd let Michael get to him, again. And worse yet, the man was right. They did need to get a move on.

Damned Aussie.

"You two done?" Robert sounded irritated.

"They are," Tumra answered. "Or they can stay here."

"Michael's right." Jack swept a hand in the direction of the pathway. "After you."

He glanced over his shoulder at the narrow opening, unable to resist one more look.

* * * *

Sienna stood up in front of the hut where she was performing the workup, and wiped beads of sweat from her brow with her forearm. When she lowered her arm, she saw the men's light beams, bouncing along in the darkness at the rear of the cavern.

To her, they looked like miners parading home after a day's work. But they hadn't been gone a day or even half a day. What was up with that?

She feared that wasn't a good sign. "Ladies," she announced to the women squatted a few feet away, "the men are back."

Lisa tapped Regan on the shoulder and they rose from their knees to look.

Regan walked a few steps and stood next to Sienna. "So soon?"

"Something must have happened."

Kazuko wandered up from the fish pond and joined the three other women. "Did I hear you say the men are back?"

Sienna pointed. She could just make out their silhouettes now. "Let's wait for them at camp."

Regan passed out bottles of water to the men as they trudged into their encampment. "Drink up guys. You know how important it is to stay hydrated."

The men shrugged off their packs and plopped down on stools. The humidity of the cavern had sapped their strength. They needed to catch their breaths.

"Well?" Sienna prodded. All four women stared at them, waiting for an answer.

"There's a tunnel just like we figured," Jack said. "We followed it in about a quarter of a mile, maybe a little more."

"Did you run into a problem?"

"Not what I'd call a problem. There's a path worn into the rock." Jack looked at Sienna and nodded. "A well worn path."

Sienna's eyes sparkled in the lantern light. She could see the tribe of little people who built the village walking that path, in their travels to and from the grotto.

She stroked her chin with her fingers. "Do you know how many pairs of little feet it would take to wear a path in rock?"

"I'm guessing." Jack grinned. "Say ten or twelve thousand years' worth?"

"We're still confused about why you're back so soon," Regan said. "If there's a path, I think you'd have followed it to see where it led."

"We would have if it wasn't for what we found." Jack motioned a hand at Michael. "Show them."

Michael dug into his pocket for his knife, and held it out in front of him where they could see it. "This."

Regan knitted her brow. "I'm not following. You found your knife?"

"On the trail." He looked at the three other men, they all grinned.

Sienna could tell Jack and Michael were toying with her. Robert and Tumra were smiling broadly and, she could see they enjoyed the game as well. It was time to put an end to their nonsense.

"Out with it," she said. "Or Regan will see to it you're eating power bars for lunch."

"I left it on the table last night." Michael slid the knife back into his pocket. "This morning I couldn't find it."

She narrowed her eyes at the men. "One of you is playing a trick?"

Jack stood up. "I thought I heard the guys talking out here this morning around three. They assured me they were asleep."

The gravity of what he said sank in. She scanned the face of each member of the group. "Someone was in our camp?"

"And they dropped the knife on the path," Tumra said.

Sienna, Regan, Kazuko, and Lisa all looked at each other.

"This could very well be the discovery of the millennium," Jack continued. "We wanted you women in on it."

"Or a great big hoax," Lisa spoke up.

"You're forgetting the carvings," Sienna reminded her. "They're real. And so are these huts."

"And so was the skull," Jack added.

"None of us can deny the authenticity of the find," Robert said. "The belief that a lost tribe of little people might exist in here is what brought us together on the expedition in the first place. But Lisa could be right. Some kids or even a couple of homeless people could have slipped into the grotto last night and taken the knife. The only—"

Sienna raised a hand to stop him. "Before you say more, I know where you're headed." She scanned the group and saw them all staring at her. They had to be thinking the same thing.

"Yeah," Jack said as if confirming her thoughts. "We won't know the truth until we see what's at the end of that path."

Sienna glanced at each of the women. "What do you think, girls? Ready for a little hike?"

"We can always come back here," Regan said. "The answer to this riddle—it seems—lies at the end of that path."

Kazuko stepped over to Robert and hooked her arm around his. "We're getting nowhere standing here."

Sienna smiled at Kazuko. The four women had been standing in a tight group facing the men. And that's how it had always been for her: women against men—in the scientific community, in life. But here—in just a few quick steps across the soft sand—Kazuko had dissolved that line. Here, the men and women were one team working together, not two.

"Let's do it," she said.

CHAPTER 27

Jack stood at the entrance to the cave with his compass open in his hand. He turned and squinted in the direction of their camp and the village of tiny huts. A black void swallowed the beam of his headlamp, as though nothing existed beyond its reach. The instant they shut down the generator and switched off the lanterns, darkness enveloped the cavern like a moonless night.

How eerie it must have been for those who first ventured here with only a flaming torch to light the way!

Is this how the grotto looked to the little people when they first walked here?

It was difficult to imagine himself in their place. If he were half his size would he venture this far into the mountain, with only a burning stick to light the way? Man feared the dark. Was it that way for the little people? Or had they relied on darkness to survive?

"I suggest we pair up before we go any farther," Michael announced.

Michael's voice pulled Jack from his thoughts. He quickly stepped over to Lisa. "I'm all yours, partner."

"Forget it." She swept her light over the other team members. "You've got some nerve. That's for sure."

"What are you talking about?"

"I saw you and Sienna together last night."

The beam of her flashlight settled on each pair as they formed up. Kazuko stood next to Robert, Regan and Tumra had their heads together, whispering while Michael and Sienna moved a few steps into the cave, their lights probing its dark interior.

Lisa crossed her arms tight against her breasts. "Shit!"

"So that's why you've been avoiding me. You're jealous." Jack chuckled. "Sienna's the last person you should be worried about."

"Go to hell. Her hand was on your cheek. You kissed it."

Jack grinned and adjusted his pack. "Trust me. We're just friends, that's all."

"But—"

He moved her day pack farther up on her back—more bottles of water, more power bars, more batteries, kneepads, and a roll of toilet paper—a heavy load like the others. But they wanted to be prepared.

"Now the straps won't cut into your shoulders as much," he said. "Let's get going."

A gentle rush of warm air, like a breath from a sleeping giant, curled back a strand of Jack's hair when he and Lisa walked up to Michael and Sienna. "That breeze," he said to Michael, "I felt one like it when Robert and I entered the cave earlier."

"Caves breathe," Michael explained. "It's a change in barometric pressure. In this case, every time the ocean surge rises and falls back there in the grotto, the pressure inside the cavern changes, sucking air in and out through the other end of this tunnel."

"That means the tunnel definitely leads outside," Jack said, matter-of-factly.

"I'd call that a reasonable assumption."

Michael turned and faced the rest of the group. Obviously speaking for the benefit of the women, he said, "Sienna and I talked it over. We'll take it slow, but there's no reason to spend a lot of time exploring ground the guys and I covered earlier."

"You're that sure of yourselves?" Regan asked.

"I'm quite sure of myself," Michael said. "But that doesn't mean we didn't miss something in the shadows along the way. So keep your eyes peeled. And watch your footing. The path we'll be following is well worn, but the floor of the cave is littered with loose rocks, pot holes, and crevices."

Lisa giggled. "Pretty much like crossing the street in New York."

Jack laughed with her. "Only without the traffic."

"I'm serious when I say be careful," Michael continued. "A broken leg would really ruin your day."

"I think we get the idea," Kazuko said. "We're all professionals. Now I suggest we get going. Robert and I have a dinner date."

"And I'm cooking," Regan added. "So I agree."

"Lisa?" Michael looked at her now.

"We're not doing any good standing here."

"In that case, keep together." Michael turned and set a fast pace, with Sienna following close behind him.

Few words passed between the members of the group on their trek along the path. Everyone seemed intent on getting through this first leg of the journey and on to the cavern of pillars Jack had described to the women over lunch back at their camp.

When they arrived at the giant flowstone, the women grouped at the edge of the crystal pool, awed by the calcite formation as the men had been the first time they saw it.

"You were right," Sienna said to no one in particular. "This is amazing."

"Quite," Tumra said loud enough for all the women to hear. "A flowstone formation this size is rare in lava tubes. This is the largest one I've seen."

Regan snapped a couple of digital photos, then ran the beam of her flashlight down the length of the flowstone to the narrow opening between it and the far wall. The smile slipped from her face.

She snapped another photograph. "I suppose you expect me to go through there?"

Michael stepped sideways in and out of the narrow opening. "Piece of cake, really. As slim and trim as you are, there's plenty of room to slide through."

Sienna must've noticed the stricken look on Regan's face,

because she stepped to her colleague's side and laid a reassuring hand on her shoulder. "You can do this. I'll go first and you follow right after me. We'll never be more than a couple of feet apart."

"Let's go now," Regan pleaded in a whisper. "I don't want to be the last person through with everyone waiting for me on the other side."

Sienna peered into Regan's eyes. "You're sure about this?"

Regan smiled

Sienna and Regan rushed past Jack and Michael and slid into the aperture without saying a word to them.

"Wait!" Michael called out to them. "Take off your packs!"

Too late.

The two men looked at each other.

Michael sidestepped into the slot after the women. Jack hurried behind him.

At the opening, he turned to the other members of the team and announced, "We're on the move."

He waited for Lisa to join him before following Michael into the fissure. He could hear Sienna and Regan joking and giggling.

So that's what that stunt was all about.

He'd been curious how Regan would handle the narrow slot. The two women had apparently figured out a way. Laugh their way through.

Clever girls.

Suddenly the giggling stopped.

* * * *

Sienna heard Regan gasp.

She turned her head and looked. They'd been giggling like schoolgirls and edging their way through the crevice without a hint of trouble. Now Regan stood paralyzed.

"Just keep moving," Sienna urged. "You're all right."

"It's my pack. I'm stuck."

"Relax. Breathe in and out."

"I can't. My chest…it feels like a ton of rock is sitting on it."

"Yes, you can." Sienna reached back and took Regan's right hand in hers. "Try to pull your arms out of the straps."

"Is she all right?" Michael called out from the other side of Regan.

"Leave her alone," Sienna said. "She's fine, just working through a little problem, is all."

"I thought we were going to make it," Regan gasped.

"And we are," Sienna reassured her. "Just shrug your arms out of the straps and let the pack fall to the floor."

Regan worked her right arm free.

"Good girl," Sienna praised in a calm voice. "Now the other one. Just let the pack fall."

"I'm trying."

"Relax and work the strap off your shoulder."

"I can't breathe."

"Yes you can."

"Sienna!"

"Don't worry, sweetie." Sienna wrapped her hand around Regan's. "Just slide this way and the pack will slip right off."

"It won't." Regan took a half step toward Sienna. The strap slid from her left shoulder, but the pack remained stuck. "I think—"

"Keep coming."

She took another step and Sienna moved with her. "That's it."

The pack slid down Regan's left arm to her hand. She held it next to her. "We did it!"

"You did it." Sienna kept hold of Regan's hand and slid out of the crevice, dragging Regan with her.

Sienna turned and wiped a tear from Regan's eye.

Regan's lips curled into a shaky smile.

"I'm proud—" Sienna abruptly stopped talking and peered deep into the cavern of pillars.

Regan leaned close. "I heard something, too."

Beyond the reach of their light beams, blackness hid the answer.

CHAPTER 28

Jack moved shoulder to shoulder with Michael and Lisa followed closely. The moment they emerged from the slot, he left Lisa's side and brushed past the Aussie, in a hurry to get to Sienna and Regan.

Ten feet in front of him, the two women stood as still as the rock pillars, their light beams fixed on the darkness at the other end of the cavern.

He stopped in his tracks and whispered, "What's wrong?"

Sienna held a hand up in a signal to be quiet.

He crept to a stop beside her and added the beams from his headlamp and flashlight to the two women's. The darkness swallowed the light.

Nothing...

He held his breath and listened.

Drip, drip, drip.

Another couple of seconds passed, and he let himself breathe.

He leaned toward Sienna's ear. "Talk to me."

"Something's out there," she said.

Jack studied the shadows within the reach of his light.

"We thought we heard talking," Sienna added.

"Regan, too?"

Clearly annoyed, she shone her headlamp in his face. "We both did."

The harsh light made Jack squint. “Relax. I heard it, too. Right before we returned to camp to get you.”

Sienna shot him a look.

He realized he should have told her. “You’re right,” he said. “I should have mentioned it. But I couldn’t—”

Out of the corner of his eye, he saw Michael step toward them, with Lisa a stride behind him. He let the subject drop and stepped back to let the Aussie through.

Michael eyed him as he went by.

Jack didn’t look away, even in the glare of Michael’s headlamp. He wasn’t going to let the man get to him

Michael turned and faced the group. He raised a hand. “This is as far as the guys and I went. From here on we take it slow and careful.”

“Where’d you find the pocket knife?” Lisa had stopped a few feet from Jack, Sienna, and Regan. She already had her headlamp and flashlight trained on the cave floor at her feet.

Michael pointed with the beam from his flashlight. “About where you’re standing.”

She kept her lights on the pathway, walked several feet past Michael, then stopped and scanned everyone’s faces. “No tracks. Nothing.”

“Everybody,” Michael said, “take a break and drink some water. And don’t let your imagination get the better of you.”

Sienna leaned into Jack and whispered, “I swear we’re being watched.”

Regan moved in close. “I feel it, too.”

Jack glanced back and forth at the two women. A chill raised the hairs on his arms. He tried to dismiss it, but couldn’t. “Earlier, I thought the same thing. But like Michael said, maybe it’s our imaginations.”

Sienna exchanged glances with Regan, then looked at Jack. “All three of us?”

Robert stepped up and clapped Jack on the shoulder. “It’s probably the cave wind playing games with your ears.”

Jack eyed his friend. "You heard us talking?"

"So did Kazuko."

Kazuko edged in closer. "No reason to scare the others."

Jack looked at Sienna and Regan. "We keep this to ourselves—at least for now."

"Agreed." The response was unanimous.

Jack took a couple of steps away from the group and peered into the coal black depths of the cave. Whoever—whatever—they were watching from the darkness, even now.

* * * *

The team moved cautiously around the calcite pillars. Michael took the lead, with Jack and Lisa walking right behind him. Sienna and Regan followed a few feet back. Robert, Kazuko, and Tumra brought up the rear.

The cavern was—at Jack's estimate—about the size of a big-city train station. And searching its vastness made the going slow.

With each step, he kept a wary eye on the shadows, as he scanned the dark cavern with his lights.

There was still the question of the voices.

Even if not everyone had heard them.

For the tenth time, he looked over his shoulder to check on the group members walking behind him. Robert, Kazuko, and Tumra picked their way through the columns to the left, a dozen feet away. Their light beams danced in the darkness like a laser show.

A rustling sound brought Jack to an abrupt halt. His heart lurched. He pointed his flashlight. Darkness swallowed the beam.

Everyone stopped.

"You heard something?" Robert asked.

"I did." He pointed his light. "Out there."

"I tell you, it's nothing," Michael insisted.

Jack wasn't convinced.

Another rock broke loose and clattered to the floor farther in the cavern, beyond the reach of their lights.

Lisa stomped past Jack and hurriedly scanned the shadows to the right and left of Michael.

From the way she rushed past him, Jack got the distinct feeling she wanted to be the first person to discover whatever lay ahead.

"Slow down, partner." He stepped round one of the pillars and hurried to catch up with her.

She stopped with a huff and looked at him. "Do you know what we're on the verge of here?"

"Yeah. A broken leg or worse, if you don't slow down."

"The Nobel Prize, Jack." Her brown eyes sparkled with tiny flecks of gold in the light from his headlamp. "It's so close I can taste it."

He hadn't seen that gleam in her eyes before. From the moment she agreed to join the expedition he'd been wondering how she would react. It felt good to see her excited. But it also concerned him.

"Maybe, maybe not" he said. "Nobody is to know about any of this until I say so, remember?"

"How can you be so obtuse?" She reached for his hand, took it in hers, leaned close, and whispered. "It's right in front of you. Grab it—for us."

He hadn't stopped watching her eyes. A kid's at Christmas, that's what they reminded him of. This was the first real quest of its kind she had been on. It was natural for her to be keyed up by the prospect of making such an important discovery. Still…

"We'll grab it." He weighed his words, not wanting to douse the fire raging inside her, just to tone it down to a controlled burn. "All of us, and one step at a time."

She let his hand slip from hers. "If you say so."

Michael had forged ahead. Without saying more, Lisa hurried to catch up with him.

Jack shook his head. She'd break something yet.

When they approached the end of the cavern, Jack felt the walls and ceiling close in on him even before his lights lit up the rock. Not the first time his sixth sense had warned him something was wrong.

He glanced around nervously, half expecting to see a dozen pairs of glowing eyes peering at them from the darkness.

Nothing...

Just more rock and more shadows.

"Slow up, folks." There was no mistaking the caution in Michael's voice. "I don't like the looks of this."

Jack would never question his intuition again. He edged past Lisa and stopped next to the Aussie. "What's the problem?"

"That." Michael aimed the beam of his flashlight at the ceiling.

The cavern had narrowed to a tunnel, large enough to drive a Volkswagen bug through with an inch to spare on the sides and a foot above. Plenty of room for them, providing they were careful not to hit their heads.

He eyed the circle of light. It was obvious what concerned Michael. A jumble of cracked rock formed an arch above the entrance.

A sprinkling of gravel sifted from a crack and fell to the floor in front of them. Small rocks littered the pathway.

Shit!

"What do you think?" Jack asked over his shoulder. He averted his gaze from the jumble of stones at the top of the archway, turned, and looked at Tumra. "Do we chance it?"

"It's not stable, that's for sure. But no telling how long the rock has been like this." Tumra stepped forward, adjusted his glasses, and looked more closely. "What I don't understand, is why it fractured. The surrounding stratum appears solid."

"Have a look at this," Sienna called out from off to the left, as she snapped a photo.

Everyone looked. The beam from her flashlight lit up a circular disk, recessed a couple of inches into the wall of stone next to the archway. The disk was four or five inches in diameter, with chiseled symbols similar to the carvings they'd seen on the doorways of the huts.

"Breadcrumbs," Robert said. "At least we know we're on the right track."

Kazuko shot him a sideways glance. "Not exactly a scientific explanation."

"But true, just the same," Jack said. "The question is, can we make it through without the ceiling caving in on us?"

"If we hurry and watch our heads," Tumra answered. "It's the return trip that concerns me. The tunnel could collapse behind us."

"And if it doesn't?" Lisa questioned.

Jack gave her a long look, remembering her comment about the Nobel Prize. He shot a glance at Michael, hoping to hear his thoughts on what they should do, and saw Lisa dash past him and into the tunnel ahead.

"What are you waiting for?" She turned and motioned for them to follow. "I say, go for it."

"That was a fool thing to do," Jack said. He glanced at the other members of the team. "What's the verdict?"

Michael spoke up. "We've come this far. We keep going."

"Tumra?" Jack wanted confirmation from the geologist.

"We go in single file, and we tread lightly," he cautioned

"All right." Jack locked eyes with the Aussie. "Michael, you and the women go first. If these rocks give way before we're all inside, I want someone with the women who knows what he's doing. Robert, you and Tumra go next. I'll bring up the rear."

One by one, the members of the team cautiously ducked through the archway. Finally, it was Jack's turn.

More gravel fell to the floor in front of him.

Shit!

He stooped through the archway and joined his companions. They stared at him in a way that made him think they half expected him not to make it through alive.

He stood, formulating a witty remark, and swallowed it when the floor under his feet began to shake.

The mountain around them rumbled.

"Go!" Jack shouted. But he didn't need to. Everyone stumbled deeper into the tunnel ahead of him.

The rock ceiling gave way and crashed to the floor. Dirt billowed up, sending the team into a coughing spasm.

Jack stopped and peered into the gloom behind him, straining to see through the thick cloud of dust.

Particles swirled in his light beam. Beyond that, nothing.

He hacked up another lungful of dust, rubbed the grit from his eyes, and waved his hand in an effort to fan the sifting dirt away.

Finally the dust settled enough for him to make out the passageway.

Tons of rock blocked the tunnel.

There was no returning to camp.

CHAPTER 29

Jack watched another half-dozen rocks clatter to the cave floor a couple of meters in front of him. He glanced up at a jumble of stones that somehow remained in place. Dust and gravel filtered down from cracks.

He raised his hand to his mouth and stifled a cough. Thank God the entire mountain hadn't come down on them.

Another rock fell…more dust and gravel.

The mountain might collapse yet. He needed to move his ass.

He turned to join his teammates. But before he could take a step, a rock the size of a golf ball clipped him on the bridge of his nose. The cave exploded into a burst of tiny lights. His ears rang.

He staggered backward like a punch-drunk prizefighter, and shook his head, trying to get his mind to focus.

His vision cleared—at least he wasn't seeing stars.

It took another second or two for him to be able to stand without feeling as if his legs were going to give out under him.

He staggered forward and felt gloved hands gripping his arm and shoulder.

"You okay?" Robert asked.

He nodded, still dazed. "Now I know how Goliath felt when David nailed him with a rock from that sling."

"Goliath died, remember? And so will we, if we don't move

our asses."

Jack raised a leaden arm, pointed the way, and took a shaky step. "I'm with you."

"Sure you are."

In one quick motion, Robert ducked under Jack's arm. He tucked it around his neck, held onto his hand, and walked him into the cave. Fifty meters in, they caught up with the other members of the team, where they'd stopped to regroup inside a small cavern.

With one look at Jack and his bloody nose, Regan took several quick steps toward him. Kazuko rushed ahead of her and took hold of Jack's free arm.

"Have him lie down," Regan ordered. She glanced over her shoulder. "And grab the first aid kit from my pack over there."

Lisa already had the kit in her hand. "It's here." She handed it to Regan and kneeled next to Jack. She switched off his headlamp, peeled off his helmet, lifted his head onto her lap, and cradled it.

The other members of the team gathered close around them.

"Do something!" Lisa snapped. She stripped off her gloves, dropped them in Jack's helmet, and set it aside.

Regan furrowed her brow at Lisa in a what-do-you-think-I'm-doing look, but said nothing.

Jack brushed the side of his hand across his upper lip, smearing the twin trickles of blood flowing from his nostrils, and eyeballed the red stain on his glove.

"Stop messing with it." Regan peeled off her gloves and shined her light into his eyes—first one then the other.

With a nod of satisfaction, she focused the beam on his nose. After a couple of seconds, she dug into the first aid kit.

Jack peered through the glare of lights at the expectant faces looking down at him. The attention took him aback. But the best part was having his head in Lisa's lap.

He smiled up at her and said, "This almost makes it worth being smacked on the nose."

The grin slipped from his face when Regan pressed a folded gauze pad to his bloody nostrils.

"Is it broken?" Lisa sounded concerned.

Regan placed Jack's hand on the gauze pad to hold it in place. "I don't know. Possibly. But I will say his nose probably won't be as straight as it was."

Michael stood up with a huff. "Everyone take a break. Drink some water and eat a couple of power bars. You'll need the energy." He slid his pack from his shoulders, fished out a bottle of water and leaned the pack against the far wall. Then he walked deeper into the cave.

Jack rose to a sitting position with help from Lisa, accepted a clean gauze pad from Regan, and gingerly dabbed at his nostrils. When he checked the pad, there was only a trace of red.

Robert pulled a water bottle from his backpack and handed it to him.

Jack twisted off the cap and eyed the bottle. "My throat's so caked with dust I don't know if I can even swallow." He took a gulp, and another. Several drops trickled from the corners of his mouth. Water never tasted so good.

He carefully swiped the back of his hand across his mouth and nodded at Michael. "Sensitive fella, isn't he?"

"He has a point," Robert said. "And it looks like you have more than enough nurses to take care of you."

Jack peered up at him. "Not you, too?"

Robert chuckled. "I'd hate to see you get too spoiled." He turned and faced Kazuko. "Let's find us a comfortable spot to sit down."

"It's for sure he doesn't need us," Sienna said. She and Tumra walked away.

Regan snapped the first aid kit closed and joined them.

"I hate to say this," Michael called out, walking back to the group. "But it looks like we're going to have to find some other passageway out of here. That way's a dead end."

Tumra stood up. "What do you mean a dead end?"

"Just that. A rock the size of a car is blocking the tunnel."

"Another cave-in?"

"Can't tell. But no way are we able to move it."

"There has to be another passage," Sienna demanded.

Regan stood next to her, supporting what she'd said.

"There is." Jack reassured them from where he lay with his head resting in Lisa's lap. He wondered if Sienna and Regan were thinking about the voices they'd heard. He was.

He propped himself up with his arm. "I say we don't waste any more time talking, and start looking. Perhaps back there." He pointed the water bottle in the direction of the cave-in. "Maybe, with all that dust, we missed the passage."

"Take care of your nose," Robert said. "I'll check it out."

Jack's nose hurt like hell, but he wasn't going to just lie there while everyone else searched the cavern for a way out. He put down his water bottle, forced his legs under him, and slowly worked his way onto his feet in spite of Lisa's repeated objections.

She stood up beside him and held onto his arm.

He didn't really need her to steady him, but he didn't pull away. *Damn, she felt good!*

He forced himself to ease his arm from her grasp, and gently brushed his palm along the back of her hand when her fingers slid across his skin. "I'm good," he told her. "Thanks."

She locked eyes with him. "Any time."

The way she looked at him didn't help. He shifted his gaze to the stone floor at his feet. "Would you mind helping me find my helmet and flashlight?"

Lisa squatted and picked up his hard hat. She retrieved her gloves from inside and handed it to him. "Here you go."

"How about my flashlight? I dropped it here someplace."

She swept the floor with a circle of light from her headlamp. "I don't see it."

Jack slid on his hardhat and switched on his headlamp, adding his light to the search. The rock wall behind Lisa lit up. He turned, and when he brought his head around, a shadow swallowed the circle of light.

What...?

He squinted and stepped closer.

A hole.

He knelt down and pointed his headlamp inside. It wasn't just a hole, it was a tunnel.

"Everyone!"—he looked over his shoulder at his teammates—"I found our way out of here."

The other members of the expedition crowded around Jack, staring at the tunnel opening, no more than two feet wide and four feet tall.

Regan's hands began to shake. She looked at Sienna. "I can't go in there. Not yet. Not after…"

Sienna took Regan's hands in hers and squeezed them. "Perhaps one of us should check it out first." She shone her light on Michael. "You know, to make sure it's safe before we all crawl in there."

"I'll go." Jack scanned the floor with his headlamp. "Did someone pick up my flashlight? It seems to have disappeared."

"Use mine." Sienna handed hers to Jack.

"You can't go alone," Michael said. "That's the rule. We don't explore anywhere by ourselves."

Michael's headlamp moved, causing Jack to look in his direction.

Dropping onto his kneepads, Michael edged in front of Jack, tugging his pack along with him.

"Okay." Jack grabbed Michael by the arm, making him pause. "We both go."

"You're hurt. Let me." Robert snatched up his pack and took a step toward the opening.

Tumra had his pack in hand as well. "I think I should go, too."

"Enough already," Jack said. "Everybody pay attention—" He caught a concerned look from Kazuko. Clearly she did not want Robert to go into the tunnel.

"Robert," Jack continued, "I'd feel better if you remained here with the women. Tumra—you, Michael and I will check out the tunnel."

"Novices." Michael shook his head and crawled inside on his hands and knees.

Jack mentally shrugged off the Aussie's comment and followed his lead.

"I'm coming, too," Lisa announced, and ducked in right behind Jack.

Jack stopped crawling and glared over his shoulder at her. "The point of our checking out the tunnel is to make sure it's safe for the rest of you."

"I'm not staying behind, Jack. Now get going."

There was no mistaking the resolve in her voice.

Damn her hard headedness!

Not happy with her decision to join them, Jack continued on.

The four of them crawled on their hands and knees for a couple of minutes, taking their time following the tunnel. Jack was sure Michael slow-played it for their benefit. He was glad of that—and of the Aussie's foresight to add leather gloves and kneepads to the list of supplies.

"You notice anything different about this tunnel?" Tumra called out from the rear.

Jack had kept an eye on the rock around him. The last thing he wanted was to end up in another cave-in. But rock was rock. The only difference he'd noted was the size of the cave. It had remained constant.

"It took you this long to see it?" Michael questioned Tumra from in front.

"Not hardly. I was just waiting to see if anyone else noticed the marks before I pointed them out."

"What are they talking about?" Lisa asked Jack.

"I don't know," he muttered over his shoulder.

He scanned the rock trying to figure it out, but couldn't.

In a voice loud enough for Tumra and Michael to hear, he said, "Why don't you two enlighten the rest of us?"

"Take a good close look at the rock," Tumra answered. "Tell me what you see."

Jack looked more closely and this time noticed the symmetrical striations.

Tool marks.

"My God!" he called out. "The tunnel's manmade."

"Precisely."

CHAPTER 30

Jack rose to his feet next to Michael and arched his back, thankful to be out of the tunnel. They had crawled on their hands and knees perhaps two hundred feet. A little more than the distance from the goal post on a football field to the fifty-yard line. Physically, it felt like a mile.

Playing mole—it turned out—was not his game. He'd let Michael be the one to go back for the others. The Aussie actually enjoyed this shit.

He glanced around. They stood in the shadows of a cavern, dimly lit by the beams of their headlamps. He judged the chamber to be about the size of a large living room. The walls and ceiling were toothed with jagged basalt. The floor was smooth by comparison, a natural geologic formation, unlike the rock drainpipe they had just crawled through.

When Lisa's headlamp emerged from the tunnel, he stepped back and watched both her and Tumra crawl out and go through the same back stretching exercise he had.

"Man was definitely not meant to walk on all fours," Jack announced, to no one in particular.

"Or woman," Lisa quickly added. She stepped past him and flashed her light around the cavern.

He watched her body move inside her shorts and shirt when

she walked. Her vitality was intoxicating.

God, he was falling for her!

"This is amazing," Tumra said, from behind Jack.

Tumra's voice made Jack turn and look at the Egyptian. He was almost glad for the interruption. "What's that?"

"This tunnel. It's been chiseled through solid rock." Tumra ran his fingers over the edge of the opening. "Amazing. And how'd they know which direction to dig, to link this cavern to the lava tube at the other end?"

For a moment, Jack considered the difficulty of the task. He and the others had been walking inland—he knew that from checking his compass. And it had been a gentle ascent. But he had absolutely no idea where they were inside the mountain.

He shrugged. "Maybe it was blind luck."

Tumra stripped off his helmet and combed his fingers through his curly black hair. "Even with modern tools and a lot of manpower, that's a hell of a lot of work to go to on the remote chance of running into another cavern. And if this tunnel is as old as I believe it is, the people who dug it didn't have jackhammers or dynamite."

"An industrious bunch, that's for sure," Michael commented.

"To say the least. And look at this." Tumra pointed at a saucer-sized stone disk, like the one they'd seen in the cavern of pillars, imbedded in the rock wall a foot above the opening. Mysterious symbols, similar to the others they'd seen, were chiseled into its surface.

"Interesting…" Jack swept the cavern with his light. "What do you think, Michael? Do we go back for the others?"

The beam of Michael's headlamp moved back and forth, as he checked both ends of the chamber.

"This room is like the hub of a spoked wheel," he said. "We have tunnels branching off in three different directions. Four, if you count the one we just came through. I say we check 'em out first."

Jack looked. The openings were uniform in shape and about four feet high. Each of them manmade, like the one they had crawled through. Industrious, indeed. "So, do we flip a coin or what?"

Michael glanced at him and stepped to the tunnel directly across from them. "To do that, it'd have to be a three sided coin."

"You know what I mean." Jack frowned.

Damned Aussie.

Jack couldn't believe how easily Michael irritated him. He walked over to join him at the tunnel.

"I'll check this one," Tumra said.

"And I'll have a look in the one over here," Lisa added.

"Remember," Michael cautioned, "no one searches alone."

Jack saw Tumra head toward the opening on the right and Lisa walk in the direction of the one on their left. He watched a moment longer and saw her squat and peer into the roughly hewn aperture.

He was about to turn away, when she screeched and stood bolt upright.

Her outcry shattered the silence.

"What's wrong?" Jack called out as he hurried to her side.

Michael and Tumra followed after him.

"I saw something—a shape." She pointed a shaky finger at the tunnel. "In there."

Jack squatted and probed the darkness inside the shaft, with light from his headlamp and hand held flashlight.

Nothing.

Michael and Tumra leaned close, adding the beams of their lights to Jack's. The walls, ceiling, and floor of the tunnel came into view, but a hundred feet in there was total darkness.

With Michael and Tumra looking over his shoulders, Jack searched the shadows.

Still nothing.

"What did you see?" Jack stood up and faced Lisa. "There's nothing in there but rock and more rock."

"Something alive," she looked down at the tunnel opening, illuminating it with her headlamp, "I don't know."

"Could have been a shadow moving with your light," Michael added. "If you haven't noticed, they do that. Of course, a good imagination helps."

"It wasn't my imagination." Lisa pointed. "Something in there shied from my light. I'm just not sure what."

"What or who?" Jack mumbled. Someone had taken that knife. He'd heard voices in the cavern of pillars—so had Sienna and Regan. Now Lisa had seen something shy from her light inside that tunnel.

Menehune?

He wanted to rush in after them.

"So you believe me?" she asked, looking at Jack.

"I don't doubt you a bit." He fought back his enthusiasm. "We're not alone. And haven't been, from the moment we entered the grotto."

"Your little people?" Michael questioned.

"We've all felt that way," Tumra spoke up. "That's the only explanation that fits with the stuff that's happened. It's just that none of us has been ready to admit it."

"Until now," Jack said.

Lisa started toward the opening in the rock wall. "I say we go after the little critters and catch one. Can you imagine what it would mean for us, if we actually took one back for everyone to see?"

Jack caught that same glint of excitement he'd seen in her eyes earlier. But the way she talked worried him.

Dammit!

"The Nobel Prize, again?" He huffed. "Get off it, already. If we're right and the *Menehune* do exist, they aren't animals to be put on display. They're humans, like you and me."

"Not exactly like us," Michael said. "But you're right, they're not animals to be caged."

"No one deserves that." Tumra took a step back, looking at Lisa as though she had suddenly grown horns. "Not even an animal."

She stared at them incredulously. "What's wrong with you men? Don't you know how much money can be made off a discovery of this magnitude? The Nobel prize is only the beginning."

Jack clenched his jaw

Dammit!

"I can't believe what I'm hearing," his tone reflected disappointment. "What we're doing here, it's not about money."

"No?" She glared at him from behind her headlamp as though daring him to answer. "If not money, what?"

Jack thought the motive for the expedition was understood by everyone. He glanced at Michael and Tumra, then back at Lisa.

They all looked at him.

"Searching for the truth is what scientists do," he explained. He struggled for clarification. "Curiosity, understanding—to learn something about the world that we might otherwise not know. That's what this expedition is about."

"Right," she scoffed. "That crap sounded good in school, but I've learned it doesn't buy you a thing. Money is what's important, Jack."

This was not the woman he had wanted to get to know. He shifted his gaze back and forth at the two men standing in front of him. "Tell me you don't agree with her."

"We agreed to keep what we found here a secret, until we knew what we were dealing with," Michael answered for both of them. "Now we have an idea what that is. But we're not sure."

"And when the time comes to decide what we do with that information," Tumra added, "it won't be just us making the decision." He started toward the opening they'd crawled through minutes before. "I'm going back for the others before we go any farther."

Lisa rushed to catch up with him and planted a hand firmly on his shoulder. "Let's see what's in that tunnel first. We can always go back for the others."

He stopped and faced her. "We're a team, Lisa. Everyone should be here."

"He's right," Jack said.

Before Lisa could comment further, Tumra dropped to his knees and crawled into the tunnel.

Lisa obviously didn't want him to go. She took a step toward him as he disappeared from view. "Wait."

When Tumra didn't answer, she squatted with her hand against the wall for support and peered into the tunnel. Her palm rested squarely on the stone disk. And when she leaned forward, the disk slid inward inside a circular slot.

A deep rumble reverberated through the cavern.

The ground under their feet shook.

Small pebbles rained down on them.

Jack jerked Lisa away from the opening and dropped onto all fours. He opened his mouth to yell a warning and heard the Egyptian scream.

Jack's eyes widened. "Tumra!" His cry was lost in a crash of falling rock and dust.

Michael appeared on his knees next to him.

Their lights lit up the jumble of stones filling the cave ten feet in. The dust-choked light from Jack's headlamp settled on the waffle sole of a hiking boot, protruding from the pile.

"No!" Jack started into the tunnel on his hands and knees.

Michael lunged forward and tackled him. "Don't."

Jack peered back at him. "What are you doing?"

"I've experienced cave-ins before. I'll go."

Michael quickly crawled inside.

From the entrance, Jack watched him probe Tumra's ankle with his fingers. "Is he alive?"

"I'm not getting a pulse." Michael backed out just in time to avoid being crushed when more rocks crashed down in front of him.

Jack made a move toward the tunnel. "We—"

"He's dead, Jack." Michael grabbed Jack's shoulder and held him there. "There's nothing we can do for him."

For a second or two, Jack stared in disbelief at the opening to the tunnel.

Then—as if a switch had been flipped on inside the recesses of his brain—he snapped his head around and looked Michael square in the eyes. "Robert and the others, they're trapped!"

CHAPTER 31

Jack stood, clenching and unclenching his fists, his forehead pinched. Tumra dead—this *couldn't* be happening. And his friends were trapped in a cavern on the other side of a wall of rock that it would take a crew of men days to move.

Michael huffed out a breath. "Bloody hell."

Jack shot a scathing glance at Lisa.

She raised her hands in front of her clearly expecting him to hit her. "I had no idea. I swear—how could I?"

Jack fought to control his anger. She couldn't have known. But that was of little consolation.

Tumra was dead.

Because of her.

He turned his attention to the stone disk, pressed into the rock wall. "What the hell's with that?"

Michael sniffled and straightened. His brow furrowed. "A trigger." He fingered the polished sides of the cylindrical depression. "Some sort of booby-trap, I imagine."

"Why would they do that?"

"Bloody hell, mate," he shook his head and shrugged, "take a guess. You keep asking me questions like I'm supposed to have the answers."

Lisa stared at the disk. "You believe me, don't you? I didn't know."

Jack ignored her comment and paced the stone floor. "We've got to get moving. Get some equipment in here—something!"

"They have enough water and power bars to last them several days, if they play it right." Michael picked up his pack and slung it over his shoulder by one strap. "Grab your pack and let's go. Jack, you choose the tunnel."

Lisa found her pack and lifted it by the straps. "What about the expedition, the little people? We're not going to let the chance of a lifetime slip through our fingers, are we?"

Jack narrowed his eyes at her. "We get Robert and the others out alive. That's all that matters now." He stepped toward the tunnel where Lisa saw movement.

Lisa rushed over and grabbed his arm, stopping him. "Think about it. All those workers down here, the news—we'll end up with nothing."

"Nothing?" Jack couldn't believe what he was hearing.

"That's right. Nothing! This is my chance to prove myself to my father. He has to know."

"Your father's dead. So is your brother. You have to prove yourself to no one."

Her expression hardened. "There's me."

Jack wrenched his arm free of her grasp. "Stay here and search all you like." He shot a glance over his shoulder at the Aussie. "Come on, we'll take this one."

"You can't mean that," she pleaded.

"Listen to me." Jack drew a breath. "The expedition's over."

"But—" Again she reached for his arm.

Jack jerked away and ducked into the tunnel.

Michael raised a brow at her. "Coming?" He dropped to his knees and crawled in behind Jack.

Jack heard the shuffle of kneepads on the rock behind him, saw lights reflect off the rock. He didn't care who followed him—Michael, Lisa, or both of them. They could come or stay. He was going to get help for his friends.

Some fucking white knight I turned out to be. I led my friends into a rock tomb.

Several hundred feet in, the tunnel he was crawling through opened into a natural cave, twenty feet in diameter. He stood and took a quick look around. A scuff of rock let him know Michael and Lisa had crawled out behind him. He didn't feel a need to check.

Directly ahead, glazing—similar to what he'd seen in the lava tube they started out in—appeared like a silver and green blister on the walls and ceiling. He could hear water dripping, and he could feel a warm cave wind. This tunnel was definitely not manmade. And somewhere up ahead it opened to the outside world. The breeze was evidence of that.

But how far ahead?

And how big was the opening?

He took off at a fast walk. His headlamp and flashlight pointed at the trail worn into the stone floor. Every few seconds he glanced up to see where he was going, but there was no probing the shadows for clues into the past. His thoughts focused on finding a way out and getting help for his friends.

A hundred feet in, he caught the sole of his boot on a crack and tripped. He stumbled forward and righted himself just before he landed face-first on the stone floor.

"You might want to slow down just a bit," Michael said from a few feet behind Jack.

Jack kept his headlamp trained on the path in front of him and said, "We have to get out of here and fast."

"Right," Michael said, speaking to the back of Jack's head. "But break a leg and you'll do no one any good. Least of all our friends trapped back there in that cave."

Jack knew Michael was right, but he plunged on amid the black depths of the mountain.

Still, the going was slow. All too often, the narrow path meandered around a boulder or rock outcropping, causing him to waste precious time going around the obstruction. To speed up the pace, he resorted to hopping atop the obstacle and bounding off the other side.

Anything to keep them marching forward at the fastest pace possible.

Michael continued to follow Jack's lead. Lisa followed him. She had fallen quiet after the scene back in the cavern.

Finally, after another ten grueling minutes, she asked Jack, "How much longer are you going to stumble around in this darkness? You don't even know where you're going. We need to take a break and talk about it."

"No we don't," Jack said over his shoulder. "We keep walking until we find daylight. Then we walk some more."

"I'm guessing Robert has the satellite phone?" Michael questioned.

"In his pack." Jack did not break stride. Nor did he look back. "We'll have to hike out of the valley to get help."

Jack no sooner got the words out of his mouth when the pathway curved to the right at the base of a sofa-sized rock, not unlike several he had crossed along the way.

He hopped onto the rock the way he had before. It wasn't until he was about to step off the other side that he saw the danger.

He cartwheeled his arms backward to keep from tumbling over the edge headfirst.

Michael, having seen Jack fighting to keep his balance, reached up and grabbed Jack's belt at the back of his pants.

"Easy, mate." Michael held on until Jack stepped back down off the rock.

"Thanks," Jack gasped, planting his hands on his knees to stop his legs from shaking. His whole body shook. "That was close."

Michael stepped around the stone protrusion and looked. "Bloody hell…"

Jack joined him. "You can say that again."

Lisa huffed to a halt behind the two men. "It's about time we stopped."

Neither Jack nor Michael answered. Their eyes remained firmly locked on what lay ahead of them.

She frowned, edging between Jack and Michael, and peered over their shoulders. "What are you looking at, anyway?"

The two men pointed their flashlights. "That!"

Everyone's light beams crossed and crisscrossed inside a fissure that split the cavern three feet in front of them—a gigantic crack in the earth that must have opened up sometime after the lava tube had formed.

Jack swallowed hard as he eyed their only way across the forty-foot chasm: a bridge that looked more suited for someone the size of a child.

He reached in front of Lisa, tapped Michael on the arm with the end of his flashlight, and pointed. "Seems we don't have a choice."

"Bridge looks a mite shaky to me." Michael shot a nervous look at Jack. "We'd better take it slow and easy. And we go one at a time."

Jack didn't argue with Michael's assessment. He motioned the Aussie forward with a wave of the beam from his flashlight. "You're the expert."

Michael looked at Jack in the face. "That's a ripper."

"You're kidding, right?" Lisa looked back and forth at the two men and took a step backward.

"Me first," Michael smiled, "then you. If it holds us, it'll probably hold Jack. And if it doesn't—" He shrugged.

She stood her ground. "I'm telling you, I'm staying here until the two of you are across and I know that thing's not going to fall apart under me."

Jack was past arguing. They needed to get a move on.

"Let's just get across the damned bridge." He waved his flashlight, motioning for Michael to go ahead.

Michael glanced at both of them, turned, and stepped onto the bridge—first one foot, then the other.

The bridge held. He glanced over his shoulder at Jack and Lisa. "Piece of cake."

Jack admired the Aussie's guts. "Tell me that when you make it across."

"Pushy bloke, aren't you?" Michael took another step, and

another.

The bridge creaked under his weight.

When Michael stepped onto solid ground at the other end, he looked across the chasm at Jack. "Your turn."

Jack wasn't sure, but swore to himself he saw Michael grinning at him.

Aussie smartass.

Jack realized he was starting to like the guy. He breathed in deeply, blew the breath out in a gust, and stepped onto the bridge.

The wooden structure creaked underfoot. This was nothing like he'd imagined. It was far worse.

He was halfway across when he felt the bridge shake.

"What the—!" he muttered and held on.

"No!" Michael called out from the other side.

The bridge continued to shake. Confused, Jack focused his headlamp on the Aussie. What'd he mean, *no*?

Michael's face lit up in the light and it seemed to Jack the man was looking past him.

Jack chanced a glance over his shoulder.

Lisa had stepped onto the bridge.

She took another step.

He whipped his head around and scanned the bridge in front of him.

Twenty feet.

He took a cautious step forward, then another, and another. He had to get off the bridge.

A beam cracked below him.

"Wait!" he hollered to warn her off.

"I'm not staying over there by myself." Lisa brushed past him, practically putting him over the railing.

Jack heard another crack and saw a rough-hewn support beam fall into the crevasse. The bridge was coming apart under the extra weight.

Another beam broke and fell.

There was no time to waste. He got his feet moving and noticed

Lisa approaching the other side. Michael stood there with his hand out, waiting.

Only a few more feet.

Jack felt the bridge giving way under him. Lisa would just make it, but there was no way he would unless he jumped.

To avoid colliding with Lisa, he leaped off the bridge at an angle to the solid ground ahead. The remaining wooden supports splintered and collapsed under him.

The shattered bridge tumbled into darkness below.

Jack landed flat-footed on the edge of the precipice.

With a sigh of relief, he twisted his body around and peered into the black depths of the bottomless pit behind him. There was no going back, at least not that way.

When he turned to join Michael and Lisa, the edge of the chasm broke under his weight.

He jumped.

Too late. The ground beneath him collapsed.

His right side and forearms slammed against the floor of the tunnel as his legs slid into the fissure. The flashlight flew from his hand, bounced, and clattered out of sight.

He began to slide.

Frantically, he groped for a handhold—anything!

His fingers dug in, but the cave floor crumbled in his grasp. He was slipping over the edge and couldn't stop himself.

CHAPTER 32

Helplessness gripped Jack like an iron claw. In that instant, he knew he was going to die.

Not like this, I'm not!

He dug his fingers into the floor of the cave, clawing.

There was nothing for him to hold onto.

His body dropped into the chasm.

Then his fingers hooked on a solid outcropping of basalt.

With nothing below him but certain death, he hung by his left arm from the edge of the precipice. He could feel the burn in his muscles from the strain.

Dirt and gravel trickled down on him from the ledge above. Rocks bounced off his helmet and shoulders.

He ducked his face to keep the grit from getting in his eyes, and coughed out the dust that found its way into his throat.

With his right hand, he groped the ledge for a handhold and clawed with the toes of his boots.

The cliff face crumbled under his efforts. He was alive, but he would never make it out of the crevasse without help.

He looked to his left, and in the light from his headlamp, saw Michael on the edge of the fissure helping Lisa to her feet. She hadn't gone over the edge when the bridge fell.

He opened his mouth to yell for help. Before he got a word

out, he saw Lisa shove Michael over the edge. His shriek fading into the depths.

Unable to believe what he was seeing, he watched the Aussie's body tumble and disappear into the abyss.

Nooo—!

His mind screamed, but no words came out.

Stunned by what he saw, he hung there in disbelief. Lisa had murdered Michael in cold blood, and for what? The Aussie had saved her life!

He felt his chest hollow as if his heart had been ripped from it. And for a moment, he stared in shock at Lisa.

Then the burn in his muscles cleared his mind.

She was the only one who could save him, and he'd just watched her shove Michael to his death.

Drenched in sweat, his fingers began to slip.

He wouldn't be able to hold on much longer.

"Lisa!" he called out, straining to maintain his grasp.

She stood motionless and stoic—like the calcite pillars they'd seen—not even a glance his direction.

"Lisa!" he called out, again. She was his only hope—even if she had just killed the Aussie.

"Please." His voice reflected his desperation.

It was then he saw Lisa straighten up and slowly turn to look in his direction. And in that moment when their eyes focused on each others', he knew.

She would let him die.

His jaw muscles clenched. Not if he could help it.

Again he groped the ledge with his right hand, and again the rock crumbled in his fingertips. He dug rock and gravel from the wall of the precipice with the toes of his boots. There was nothing solid for them to hook on.

Finally, the strain on his fingertips was more than his ardent will to survive could overcome.

His fingers slipped from the handhold. She was killing him, too. He closed his eyes as he felt himself fall.

In that instant, a pair of strong, calloused hands grabbed his wrist, stopping his plunge to certain death.

Jack's eyes popped open.

He didn't hesitate a second to dig the toes of his boots into the wall of the precipice. And this time he found a protruding rock stable enough to support his weight.

When he looked up, his headlamp lit up the face of a bearded man with a head the size of a child's and soft blue eyes that betrayed his dark skin.

It took a second for Jack's mind to grasp what happened.

Menehune!

He saw the cave dweller turn his head and in a language not exactly Hawaiian, speak to someone behind him.

Another dark-skinned bearded man appeared at the edge of the chasm. He stood maybe four feet tall, was barrel-chested, heavily muscled, and matted with course black hair on his chest, arms, and legs.

Jack still struggled to grasp the situation. This was happening! The little people were real. Not the overactive imagination of a man falling to his death.

Together the two cave dwellers pulled him out of the crevasse and onto solid ground. He could not believe their strength. They had lifted him effortlessly from the cliff face.

The two men took a couple of steps back and cocked their heads at him.

Jack couldn't speak. He just stood there, filling his lungs with the dank air of the tunnel and letting it out, too stunned by what had just happened, too mesmerized by the sight of the little people, to do anything but breathe.

A few long seconds later, he wiped the dirt from his eyes with the back of his hand and looked at them with curiosity. These were not the fairytale creatures depicted on billboards throughout Hawaii.

He saw them as being little, but they were not exactly that. They were short compared to him—the tallest standing about forty inches from head to foot—but their bodies were heavily muscled—not unlike a chimpanzee's. But that was their only similarity to the knuckle-dragging primate.

These men were unmistakably human. They each wore a loincloth to cover their genitals, and sandals to protect their feet. And each of them had a large knife stuffed into their waistband.

More *Menehune*—men and women—crowded close to stare at him through intense brown eyes. They seemed to appear from the shadows, from the very rocks themselves. Several of the little people held fiery wooden-handled torches above their heads.

He noticed that the women were unmistakably smaller than the men—most of them no more than three feet tall and not nearly as hairy. They were bare breasted and wore short, simple kappa-cloth skirts tied at the waist on one side. They wore the same fibrous sandals as the two *Menehune* who'd pulled him to safety.

Lisa stood tall among the band, and he noticed her hands were behind her back as if they were tied. A leather gag quieted her. Two bearded men pointed spears to keep her captive.

He didn't need to hear her muffled pleas to know she was terrified. He could see the fear in her wide-eyed expression.

In any other situation he would have been concerned for her safety. But not this time. She'd been content to let him die—she'd have killed him just as surely as she had the Aussie.

Only he hadn't died.

He scanned the band of little people, his eyes coming to rest on the barrel-chested, blue-eyed cave dweller.

He was alive, thanks to the *Menehune*.

Again, he turned to Lisa and saw the fear in her eyes. He couldn't deny that a small part of him didn't like seeing the young woman suffer. Even if she were a killer. But that was as far as his compassion took him. There'd be no heroics from him.

No white knight was coming to the rescue.

Lisa's fate lay in the hands of her captors. And seeing her two male guards jab their spears at her, it was obvious they were not moved by her beauty or the fear in her eyes.

The men stood as tall as children, but their five-foot-long spears were not toys. They held them on Lisa with purpose.

But why only her?

He thought it odd no spears were pointed at him.

Studying the faces looking his direction, he thought about what that might mean. They trusted him—or appeared to—but their stern expressions told him there was much for him to be concerned about.

Several images of what that might be popped into his mind, and were dismissed just as quickly. He'd deal with circumstances when they arose. Right now he was glad to be alive.

And he couldn't wait to thank the burly blue-eyed *Menehune* who had saved him.

But with all those little faces looking at him and the blurred memory of what had just happened whirling in his head, it was impossible for him to concentrate or even know what to do next.

Did he even have a choice?

The blue-eyed cave dweller stepped forward. It appeared he wanted to say something.

Jack noticed that Blue Eyes was the tallest and most muscular male in the group, and the only one who didn't have dark eyes.

Was he their leader?

He struggled to stay focused. "*Aloha*," he said with a smile and reached out in a gesture to shake hands.

The blue-eyed cave dweller and his band took a step back.

Jack withdrew his hand. He should have known they'd be leery of him. He let his arms hang at his sides. "I mean you no harm."

Nostrils flared.

Jack held his tongue. The *Menehune* obviously did not share his enthusiasm to communicate.

Steady eyes bore into him with loathing. This was their world. And now he knew what it felt like, being the unwanted minority.

But they had saved his life. He couldn't believe the *Menehune* would have come to his aid if they intended him to die.

"*Aloha*," he said again, and pointed his headlamp on the different faces. He got glares and suspicious looks from most of those he saw.

But not all of their faces were filled with hatred.

The barrel-chested cave dweller standing in front of him did not shy away this time. And although he was a full head taller than most of his clan and powerfully built, his eyes softened with understanding, like those of a caring father.

"*Hiti mai*," he said in a low guttural voice, then turned and waved a muscled arm at the group in a clear sign for them to go.

Jack stood for a moment and watched Lisa and the band of little people trail off ahead of him with one of the torch bearers in the lead.

"*Hiti mai*," the cave dweller said, with more urgency in his voice this time and waved him forward.

Jack understood: the *Menehune* was telling him to go with them.

Hiti mai. He silently repeated the words to himself. He had an idea what they meant. But where were the little people taking him?

CHAPTER 33

Jack stepped past the barrel-chested cave dweller with the blue eyes and followed the departing group. The little guy stood his ground waiting for Jack to fall in line.

The two of them exchanged glances. The *Menehune* had not drawn his knife or threatened Jack in any way. But it was obvious he didn't have a choice in the matter.

With Jack's stride being twice that of the *Menehune*, it was hard for him to keep from stepping on their bare heels. He slowed to keep pace and eyed the string of little people walking in front of him. Nothing about them was comical, but he couldn't help smiling.

With an image of Disney's seven dwarfs marching off to work locked in his mind, he considered whistling their tune in Snow White. It fit in a twisted sort of way.

But the smiled slipped from his face when his thoughts returned to Robert and the others.

He was their only chance.

And time was running out for them.

He swiveled around and faced the cave dweller who was urging him forward. "Hold on a minute. My friends," he jabbed his index finger in the direction they'd just come from, "they're trapped back there."

The cave dweller listened, furrowed his brow, and pointed

toward the group walking ahead of them. "*Tata'i*."

"You don't understand. They're trapped. They need help."

Again, the cave dweller pointed. "*Tata'i*."

"But—"

The burly *Menehune* gripped the handle of the dagger in his waistband and slid it out an inch. "*Tata'i!*"

Jack raised his hands. He didn't doubt the little guy's ability to use the knife. "All right, all right," he said over his shoulder and started walking. "Just keep that pig-sticker where it is."

The *Menehune* kept his hand on his knife and fell in stride behind him.

Minutes stretched into more minutes, and deeper into the bowels of the mountain they walked. With each step, the rock overhead pressed down on Jack with increasing intensity until he could feel the weight of the entire mountain on his shoulders.

Would he ever be able to find his way back to his friends?

Another hundred yards in, the floor of the lava tube steepened, far steeper than any of the paths he had walked getting there. It wasn't long before he became winded. And in spite of his desire to rush ahead for help, he longed to take a break.

This was no climb for the weak hearted.

But the pace of the *Menehune* did not falter.

He pushed through his pain and fatigue and thought about the race between the hare and the tortoise with the tortoise plodding forever forward.

And that's what his captors did. They meandered around basalt outcroppings the size of cars and over slabs of rock that appeared to have fallen from the ceiling of the cave. And always in silence. There was no conversation among the clan when they walked.

He couldn't help wondering how many trips a day the little people made up and down the trail.

Did they always walk it in silence, a solemn trek to the grotto to harvest the bounty of the sea?

Was the reticence of the group brought on by the presence of intruders into their world?

He could only wonder.

A drop of sweat from his forehead stung his eye. Even though it was cool inside the mountain, he was sweating like a pig. Humidity and exertion taking its toll, he was sure.

He paused to wipe the back of his hand across his brow.

"*Tata'i.*"

Jack glanced at the burly little fellow behind him. His stop had caused the hairy cave dweller to grip the handle of his knife, again. Apparently they didn't get tired.

He continued up the trail and at last, he could see Lisa and the *Menehune* ahead of him disappear from sight over the top of the rise. The lava tube had leveled out. He hoped that meant they were nearing the end of the trail.

To Jack's disappointment, the trek did not end there. Instead, the tunnel branched off to the left. The *Menehune* leading the procession had already made the turn.

At least they were headed downhill.

This branch of the lava tube was smaller than the other one—maybe ten feet in diameter. But the slope down was every bit as steep, and he had to watch where he put his feet. A task complicated by the loss of his flashlight and the dimming of his headlamp.

He grew frustrated with the tiny steps he had to take. The footholds were more suitably spaced for the stride of the *Menehune.* For him, it was like walking on stairs in an elementary school, with the steps too far apart to take two at a time and too close together to be able to walk at a normal pace.

Taking the chance that he wouldn't stumble and fall, he took his eyes off the trail and peered into the torchlight ahead. The lava tube meandered downward like a string of spaghetti. Without knowing his destination or exactly where he was inside the mountain, it was impossible for him to determine in which direction they were heading. For all he knew they were walking toward the coast.

But that wouldn't make sense. They'd climbed high inside the center of the mountain and were now headed downhill. He felt certain the lava tube led inland.

Finally the tunnel leveled out. And what he saw a hundred meters ahead made him gasp.

Daylight!

With freedom that close, it took every ounce of willpower he could muster to keep from sprinting toward the opening. He was confident he could outdistance the short-legged cave dwellers before they could stop him, but caution told him to wait until he was outside and in the clear.

They continued along the path another thirty or forty meters, then—to Jack's surprise—the lead *Menehune* entered a tunnel on the right.

He had only one choice. He'd have to make a run for it.

His body tensed.

Damn!

Before he could take even one step toward the opening, half a dozen spear-toting guards positioned themselves between him and the exit.

For a fraction of a second, Jack considered making a break for it anyway. The sharp-pointed spears made him change his mind.

Swallowing his disappointment, he stepped into the side tunnel, hoping to see another way out of the mountain.

That wasn't the sight that greeted him.

The short passageway led into a chamber the size of a small-town movie theater. Fiery torches stuck into holes chipped at an angle into the walls, bathed the cavern in warm flickering light. Shadows wavered, as if in a mystical dance lost to the world.

He paused to take in the magnificence of it all.

The floor that spread out before him was paved in smooth rectangular stones fitted tightly against each other. Forty feet away in the middle of the room, a round pit six or eight feet across and lined with stones blackened by smoke, sat in the center of a circular depression twenty feet in diameter and a foot deep. The ceiling over the fire pit domed into a chimney that had been dug through the side of the mountain. Everywhere, the dirt and rock bore tool marks like those he'd seen in the two tunnels he had crawled through earlier. The chamber had been chiseled out by hand.

This was a gathering place for the clan.

A rush of activity drew his attention to a handful of frail, gray-haired men and women, about three feet tall, who stepped forward and greeted the *Menehune* band with smiles and claps on the shoulder.

In the center of it all, a hunched man, wearing a red and yellow feathered cloak and supporting himself with a carved staff a foot taller than he was, stood at the front of a group of elder men gathered close behind.

"*Tapata'i*." The command came from the silver-haired man in the feathered cloak.

The *Menehune* guarding Lisa and him stopped and formed a circle around them. The elder had apparently ordered them to wait.

Jack listened to a spattering of hastily spoken words he didn't understand. He saw fingers pointing—at him, and at Lisa. Heard more talk, and saw more finger pointing. The crack of the old man's staff against the floor ended the discussion.

Without another word, Lisa and he were ushered toward a five-and-a-half-foot-tall opening in the far wall. The other *Menehune* in the room stepped back as Lisa and he walked past.

At the entrance to the cave, he stopped and looked back at the room. All eyes were focused on Lisa and him. His barrel-chested escort—joined by the half-dozen spearmen who had blocked the exit to the outside—stood ready, with his hand gripping the knife wedged in his waistband.

"*Tata'i*!"

Jack hesitated, scanned the crowd of *Menehune*, and locked eyes with the silver-haired man in the feathered cloak. This might be his only chance to plea with his captors to let him go.

No good. The resolve on the faces of the six *Menehune* spearmen—especially the mean-faced guard on the right, with the grotesque white scar angled across his lifeless left eye—said it all. He had no choice other than to obey.

He turned and ducked inside the cave.

A few feet in he glanced over his shoulder to see if Lisa had followed. She had. And since she was a good six inches shorter than he was, she could almost stand straight. He wasn't so fortunate.

Before he could turn his head back around, he and Lisa were prodded forward by the guards. They were clearly prisoners. The question now was where they were being taken.

Following the passageway deeper into the mountain, he was surprised to see a dozen similar sized tunnels branching off to his right and left. Three-foot-tall holes—like doorways in a hotel—lined both sides of the tunnels.

The passageways—he imagined—provided access to the clan's living quarters. When he ducked his head to peek inside one of the openings, his suspicions were confirmed. They were entrances into bedroom-sized dwellings.

Clearly, he was in the heart of their underground village. What he still didn't know was what they had planned for Lisa and him.

He cautiously eyed the deadly spears.

The *Menehune* had saved him. Now they stood between him and getting help for Robert and the others.

Once again, he felt like turning and making a run for it.

But he knew what that would get him.

He stopped and faced the cave dweller who'd saved him. Maybe he could make the man understand. "You don't know what you're doing. I need—"

The quickness of the spearman to Jack's right took him by surprise. The guard thrust his five-foot lance.

Jack jerked away in time to keep from being stabbed in the chest, but the sharp metal point sliced his right bicep.

Shocked by the sudden, unprovoked violence of the attack, he clutched the bloody wound, stumbled backward, and fell to the floor.

Lisa screamed.

He rolled onto his back and stared up at his attacker.

The grim-faced sentry stood over him and raised his spear.

CHAPTER 34

Jack threw his blood-soaked hand up in front of him in a feeble attempt to ward off the deadly plunge of the spear. Pain had yet to register: survival was his only thought.

"*Tapata'i*." The blue-eyed, barrel-chested cave dweller reached out and seized the shaft of the spear.

Jack watched his attacker step back. The burly cave dweller had saved his life, a second time.

Perhaps...?

He sat up, cradled his bleeding arm in his lap, and pointed his bloody index finger at his rescuer, then at himself. "Friends," he gasped.

The cave dweller looked at him, but did not respond.

Jack cringed as a surge of pain settled in.

He fought through it, and again pointed. This time he rapidly moved his finger back and forth between them, eager to make the cave dweller understand. "Friends," he repeated, his voice clearer this time. "You and I—friends."

"*Tata'i*." Blue Eyes took his turn to point.

That was not the response Jack was hoping for. The burly cave dweller pointed into the depths of the tunnel.

He stood up. Lisa was led into the gloom and he followed.

The passageway ended in a cross tunnel with two small

openings like those in the tunnel behind him. Only these had doors constructed of woven limbs resembling bars on a cage or jail cell.

The two *Menehune* guarding Lisa stripped her of her pack and hardhat and ushered her at spear point through the small doorway to his left. Another guard opened the door on the right for him and leveled his spear.

Jack did not mind being ushered along by the cave dweller who'd saved his life, but he wasn't about to let himself be manhandled by the six spear toters bullying them.

"Just back the fuck off!" he hissed and looked around.

Scarface moved in closely, spear lowered and ready.

Jack had a feeling the mean-faced guard had been waiting for an excuse to put his spear to use again.

He braced himself.

Scarface locked gazes with him.

Jack almost wanted the ugly fucker to try and stick him again. But he wasn't going to give Scarface the chance.

With his eyes focused on the tip of the spear, Jack stripped off his pack and hardhat and handed them to the blue-eyed cave dweller. When he chanced a quick sideways glance at him, he thought he saw him smile.

"*Taa atu!*" The mean-faced spearman pointed at Jack's dive watch.

Jack narrowed his eyes, unbuckled his Seiko, and handed it over. Three feet tall or ten feet tall, the guy had no right to stab him with that spear.

He took one more look around, dropped to his knees, and crawled inside.

The dwelling was shaped like an earth and stone igloo. Circular and domed, it was ten feet wide across the floor, with a three-foot-tall entrance. A raised bench or sleeping area had been carved into the far wall to the left of the door. It was barely large enough for him to curl up on. An oil lamp, on a small ledge directly in front of him, flickered just brightly enough to cast the recesses of the room into shadows. The place reeked of damp earth.

Definitely not the Ritz.

He discovered he could almost stand straight if he stood in the middle of the floor. A foot to either side of that, and forget it. The room was more suited for the hunchback of Notre Dame. The men who'd chiseled out this dwelling hadn't anticipated housing six-foot tall prisoners.

He squatted by the door and peered between the wooden bars like a caged animal.

There was no chance of escape, not under the intense, watchful eyes of the six guards positioned along the wall opposite the cells. They wouldn't hesitate even a second to stick him with their spears, especially the scar-faced cave dweller. He'd bloodied his. And there was no mistaking the loathing in his one good eye.

He scanned the passageway, looking for his barrel-chested champion. If he could get through to anyone, he'd be the one. The little guy had saved his life twice. There had to be a reason.

All he could see were the resolute spearmen.

He settled wearily onto his butt and sighed. The adrenalin rush that had got him this far was rapidly being replaced by fatigue. His ribs and arm ached, his nose hurt, he was hungry, thirsty, and he desperately needed sleep.

But he feared that if he closed his eyes, he might not open them.

Kimo's words echoed inside his head: *Be careful what you search for.*

Never had words been more true.

The responsibility for Tumra and Michael's deaths—everything that had gone wrong from the moment they swam into that lava tube—clearly rested on his shoulders, and rightfully so. Exasperated, he rested his forehead on his arms draped across his knees.

"Jack."

Lisa's soft voice brought his head upright. This was the first time she'd spoken to him since pushing Michael into the crevasse.

Shit!

The woman was a murderer, but hearing her call his name was comforting just the same. He wasn't there alone.

"What?" He asked.

"I'm scared."

"You should be."

"Aren't you?"

"Why'd you kill him?"

"I don't know," she answered after a brief silence.

"You can do better than that."

"Honestly, I don't know what I was thinking." Her voice was a whisper, apologetic. "It was like—like I wasn't myself."

"Not yourself." He scoffed. "What a crock of shit."

"Easy for you to say." Her voice raised a notch. "You need to know my father was a bastard. He always put my brother first. Not me, him—even when I showed I was better than he was."

Normally he'd have been compassionate. But not this time.

Damn her!

Lisa's ability to manipulate men matched her sexual talents. Savage. Primal. He was sure now that's all it'd been between them: raw animal lust.

"You let me fall." He couldn't forget she had stood there and watched his hands slip from the ledge. It was the same as killing him.

She didn't answer.

"You let me fall, Lisa. Why?" he demanded.

"You saw me kill Michael," She finally admitted.

Jack thought her voice sounded almost childlike and pictured the doe-eyed little girl caught with her hands in the cookie jar.

Fuck!

"I was frightened, Jack. I'm sure you understand," Lisa continued in her little-girl voice.

She might have been frightened by having been caught committing murder. But that isn't what made her kill Michael. He was sure she knew exactly what she was doing when she pushed the Aussie into that crevasse.

He scoffed. "Lisa, you gave up your right to understanding when you killed Michael."

"Please, Jack. Can you forgive me?"

It was that little-girl voice of hers again. He wanted to feel sorry for her, but couldn't. "No. Not ever."

The passageway fell quiet.

He closed his eyes and swallowed hard to dislodge the lump that rose in his throat. What next?

* * * *

Jack hadn't moved from where he sat at the doorway to his cell. Tumra dead. Michael murdered. His friends trapped. And him a prisoner. He'd set out on this expedition fascinated by the prospect of discovering a lost tribe of three-foot-tall cave dwellers. How could everything have gone so horribly wrong?

He buried his face in his hands and listened to the quiet, half expecting to hear the pounding of drums. The natives were definitely restless.

So was he.

Lisa had not said a thing to him since he told her he'd never forgive her. It was still hard for him to accept the fact that such a beautiful, vibrant and sexual creature had turned into a cold blooded killer.

But she had. And she'd answer for what she'd done.

Right!

Till now, he hadn't really thought about what he would tell the authorities if he ever got out of his cage. He had no proof of Michael's murder, the cave-in, or the existence of the *Menehune*. Only his word.

The *Menehune*. He chuckled to himself. Would anyone believe him?

With that thought, a shiver turned his skin to goose flesh.

And if something happens to me…?

He gingerly probed the gouge in his bicep, recalling how close he'd come to being killed.

Too close.

He was relieved to discover the bleeding had stopped, but his arm and shirtsleeve were soaked with blood.

His blood.

He narrowed his eyes at his guard.

The scarred, dark-skinned face stared at him.

Jack knew he couldn't afford to dwell on the possibility he might not make it out of the *Menehune* village. But he couldn't pretend his life wasn't threatened. If he wasn't alive to go for help, Robert, Kazuko, Sienna, and Regan would die a slow, agonizing death.

And lovely doe-eyed Lisa—if she managed to survive—would be free to tell whatever story she thought fitting.

Not if I can help it!

His mind dredged up every ugly scenario his imagination could foster, but he wasn't going to concede his fate. He was sure the gnarl-eyed spearman across from his cell door wanted to stick him in the guts with that spear. But someone else was clearly in charge here.

Jack had seen him.

He would be taken before the clan's high chief. That's how it always turned out in movies. That's when he would make them understand. He'd just have to pray that the silver-haired *Menehune*, with the cloak and staff, was infinitely more sympathetic than the mean-spirited guard staring at him.

A shuffling noise moving through the tunnel pulled Jack from his thoughts. Firelight flickered on the walls. Someone was coming.

Suddenly hopeful, he pressed his face to the bars. The burly, blue-eyed cave dweller's face stood out in the torchlight.

He was glad to see him.

What he didn't like was the smirk on old Scarface. Perhaps this wasn't the meeting he'd anticipated.

CHAPTER 35

Jack stood and arched his back, careful not to crack his head on the low ceiling. Even though he was a head too tall for the passageway, he was out of the close confines of his cell.

Thanks to the blue-eyed cave dweller.

Now they needed to take him where he could stand without having to stoop over. He'd already had his nose broken, his ribs cracked, and his arm sliced. He didn't need to add a broken back to the list of damage done to his body. He hurt too much as it was.

He caught an anxious look from Scarface. There was no doubt in his mind the thug was aching to use his spear. He might get his chance, but not yet. Blue-Eyes was clearly running the show.

"*Hiti mai.*" Blue-Eyes turned and began walking back the way he'd come.

Jack saw the six guards move toward him, spears at the ready. It was obvious he was supposed to follow along.

He took a step and stopped. There had to be something he could do to ease the tension. Trust, and that started by addressing each other by name.

"Wait," He called out to Blue-Eyes. "What is your name?"

The cave dweller turned and looked at him.

Jack took the man's silence to mean he did not understand. He didn't want to call him Old Blue Eyes. That name was taken.

He pointed at himself and said, "Jack." Then he pointed at Blue-Eyes and waited for him to fill in the blank.

Only a stare.

Jack repeated the process and waited.

"Matapolu." The man pointed at himself. He smiled and aimed a calloused finger in Jack's direction. "Jack."

Matapolu. Jack silently repeated the name. He already looked to the short man as a sort of friend. Now he could at least call him by name, even if the man didn't understand English.

"*Tata'i.*" Jack said, remembering the word Matapolu used.

Matapolu's blue eyes opened wide then returned to normal.

Jack took the response as a good sign.

"*Tata'i,*" he repeated in a soft tone of voice.

Matapolu smiled, turned, and continued walking.

Jack couldn't resist smiling himself. His use of that one word considerably narrowed the gap between him and Matapolu.

His mood brightened as he followed Matapolu through the tunnel. He was sure he was being taken to the large communal chamber he had walked through on his way to his cell. Around the corner lay the way out.

When Matapolu led him into a side tunnel he hadn't been in, his empty stomach twisted into a knot.

Where was Matapolu taking him?

He glanced around as if the answer was scribed in the walls. To his surprise, he saw symbols chiseled there. In the torchlight he couldn't tell for sure, but he'd have sworn they matched the carvings he'd seen on the doorways of the huts in the grotto, as well as the Mammoth tusks in the photos.

The interpretation of the carvings remained a mystery, but he was certain of one thing, he was being taken somewhere special.

Buoyed by optimism, he followed Matapolu with renewed curiosity.

Like the communal chamber, the floor here was paved. The armed warriors led him about fifty feet along the cobblestone path, before stopping at an arched entrance leading into a larger room beyond. The stone blocks forming the arch bore the same chiseled symbols plus some he didn't recall seeing.

At the head of the procession, two guards carrying long spears stepped forward. Matapolu stood quietly while they assumed their posts next to the arch: one on each side, their backs to the wall.

With a nod of satisfaction, Matapolu faced Jack and said, "*Hiti mai.*"

It seemed nothing more needed to be said. Matapolu waved Jack in and stepped through the archway ahead of him.

At once Jack recognized the chamber for what it was. It did little to help him maintain his optimism.

The room was about two-thirds the size of the clan's communal chamber. And, instead of having a single large fire pit in the center, a smaller pit sat on either side and slightly to the front of two tiers of six-foot long stone benches along the right wall.

A twenty-foot long stone bench formed a half circle against the wall to the left. A single stone bench, about four feet long, sat in the middle of the room. An arched doorway, showing a dim flicker of light, loomed against the far wall.

A dozen flaming torches protruded at an angle from sockets spread around the wall. Fire crackled in both pits.

The *Menehune* held court here. He was being put on trial.

Matapolu stood a few feet to the right of the archway and pointed at the bench in the center of the room. "*Taiamu*," he said, looking at Jack.

Jack narrowed his eyes at Matapolu, and at the same time noticed a familiar engraved saucer-sized disk in the wall behind the cave dweller.

He remembered the disk Sienna had pointed out at the sight of the first cave-in, and the one Lisa had pushed, causing the rockslide which killed Tumra.

Another booby-trap?

Of course. He tried to recall if he had seen others like it on his way here. He couldn't be sure.

He stepped to the bench and stood quietly while he watched

twin threads of smoke rise and disappear into a hole in the ceiling.

"*Taiamu!*" Matapolu pointed more anxiously.

Jack had no problem understanding he was being told to sit. He took a seat on the end of the low stone bench and crossed his legs in front of him, Indian style, to keep his knees from hitting him in the chest. He watched the gnarl-eyed spearman walk over and stand behind him.

Still waiting for an opportunity to poke me with that spear, huh?

He smiled and extended his middle finger. Some languages are universal. He was sure his guard got the message.

The *thwack* of a spear shaft against rock drew Jack's attention to two warriors standing next to the opening in the far wall. A moment later, he saw the silver-haired *Menehune* in the feathered cloak step into the room, his carved staff clacking on the cobblestones in front of him. In addition to the cloak, he wore a red-feathered helmet, reminiscent of ancient Hawaiian royalty.

But where were the drums? There were always drums.

Jack knew he'd been right in his assumption. Here was more than a *kahuna* or a chief. He was quite possibly the last surviving *Menehune* king.

Chief or king, one thing was for certain. In this subterranean world, old Silver Hair was in charge.

Jack fidgeted on his stone seat. He didn't know if he should stand or sit in the presence of the *Menehune alii*. His impulse was to stand. But Matapolu had motioned for him to sit.

He kept his butt firmly planted on the bench, hoping he wasn't making a mistake, and watched the high chief lead five elders across the room to the two benches. They were followed by the two warriors with spears.

The high chief sat down on the top step, flaring his cloak around him, and tapped his staff against the stone step at his feet. The five elders stepped forward, one at a time, and took seats on the bottom step. When they were seated, two warriors armed with spears positioned themselves one on each side of the *alii*.

Jack did not need a translator to know he was about to stand in judgment before the *Menehune* court.

He wouldn't let them see him sweat.

A full minute went by and still no one spoke. The only sound was the crackle of the flames.

The suspense broke when Lisa stepped into the chamber a couple of feet ahead of the men guarding her. A dozen *Menehune* spectators filed in seconds later and took seats on the half-moon bench behind him.

It made sense for Lisa to be there, but he was surprised she'd been brought to the room after he was already seated. Surely, in the eyes of the *Menehune*, Lisa and he were the same: both tall outsiders and a threat to the clan's existence.

So why were we brought in separately?

He pondered the question while he watched Lisa sit down on the other end of his bench. There was no way the *Menehune* could know he was not like Lisa.

Or did they?

A crack of the high-chief's staff on stone hushed the crowd. His expression hardened. "*Malu mate tanata loa*."

Matapolu stepped to the bench in the center of the room. Jack noticed he had on a brown and tan, *kapa* cloth, shawl-like garment draped over one shoulder and knotted at the waist on the opposite side. A golf-ball-sized green crystal pendant hung from a heavy gold chain around his neck.

He'd lost sight of Matapolu for a minute and realized that during that time he'd slipped into his ceremonial *kihei*.

They meant business.

Matapolu faced the high chief and five elder advisors. With a casual sweep of his hand, he motioned at Jack and announced, "*Aoe*."

Jack had no idea what had been said. But he needed to believe in Matapolu and hoped the man was speaking on his behalf.

Matapolu aimed a calloused index finger at Lisa. "*Lima Toto*."

The sting of those two words made Jack cringe. He could only guess what they meant. But from the way Matapolu spoke them, they weren't good.

He almost felt sorry for Lisa.

For the next minute, Jack listened to a flurry of conversation among the five *Menehune* elders. The high chief listened, intently.

The words were spoken softly, making it difficult for Jack to make them out. What he did hear he didn't understand.

Without a word the high chief stamped his staff on the stone step, ending the conversation.

Jack held his breath.

The high chief stood up, pointed his staff at Lisa, and said, "*Mate*."

Mate. Jack repeated the word to himself, searching his limited knowledge of the Hawaiian language.

Nothing.

Then it hit him.

Make.

He knew that word. Death!

Like hell!

He exchanged glances with Lisa.

Had he and Lisa both been sentenced to die, or just her? He wasn't sure. It didn't matter. The *Menehune* weren't going to execute anybody if he could help it. Not even Lisa. She'd stand trial in a real court of law.

Seeing the high chief sweep the end of his staff in the direction of the doorway, Jack knew they had been dismissed.

He wasn't ready to leave the chamber. He'd face whatever fate awaited him, but only after he'd had his say. His friends were still trapped in that tunnel. They needed his help or they'd die.

"I know you don't understand me," he began from where he sat on the bench. "But I have to try. And I hope you can tell by the tone of my voice, I'm desperate. My friends are trapped in a cave. They will die if you don't release me so I can get help. Do you understand? You have to let me go."

The crack of the high chief's staff on rock was the answer Jack got.

Jack bolted to his feet. "But they'll die if you don't—"

The gnarl-eyed guard leveled his spear at Jack, stopping him mid-sentence.

Jack balled his fists and angled his body to his attacker.

The guard jabbed his spear at him several times.

Jack stood his ground, but didn't force the confrontation. The guard would obviously take immense pleasure in skewering him with that spear. That wasn't going to happen. Not without a fight.

He glanced around. All eyes were on him.

Matapolu took a step toward him and raised a hand at the guard.

Jack let himself breathe when Scarface backed away. But he didn't drop his guard, not yet.

He saw the angry guard huff and wave his spear at Lisa. That was all it took to get her moving. Wide eyed and staring, she headed for the doorway.

Matapolu fell into step behind her, and Jack knew enough to follow him out.

In the tunnel a few feet beyond the entrance to the council chamber, Matapolu raised a hand and said, "Hoopau."

The guards, who'd fallen in line at the archway, halted the procession.

Matapolu turned and peered up at Jack. They locked eyes. He pointed into the tunnel and said, "*Tata'i*."

Jack stood there and watched Matapolu walk back into the council chamber. He'd seen hope in the man's eyes.

The guards continued on, and Jack followed behind Lisa. After a few steps, he glanced back at the archway and saw Matapolu standing in the center of the room addressing the high chief.

* * * *

Jack crawled back into his cage. He couldn't believe how weary he was. Even his hair hurt. He'd pay twenty dollars for a bottle of water and one of the power bars in his pack.

If I had twenty dollars.

His wallet was tucked in his bedroll in his tent inside the grotto. Needing money was not something he'd considered when they set out to explore the lava tube.

Looking out at his guards, he doubted cash meant much to them, anyway.

He curled up on his tiny sleeping platform, with his head resting on his arm and facing the door. At least his oil lamp sill burned. He hadn't been confined to the uncertainty of total darkness.

He closed his eyes and listened to the unearthly quiet of the tunnel.

A minute later he thought he heard sobbing. He cocked an ear and listened more intently, eyes wide open.

It was Lisa, she was crying in her cell.

And for good reason. The high chief had just sentenced her to death. And now that he thought about it, maybe that death sentence included him. The council's final decision remained a mystery.

Locked there in his hole all he could do was wait and prepare himself for the worst.

And pray he was right about Matapolu.

The barrel-chested cave dweller had stood beside him in the council chamber, not his accuser, but his defender. Or so it had seemed.

Was he there now, arguing for leniency?

Did his words mean anything to the high chief?

He had to believe they did. Matapolu clearly held a position of importance within the *Menehune* clan. He was the one who stood before the high chief and pleaded his case. His spoken word had kept Scarface from using his spear.

Or had he misjudged the man completely?

He'd find out soon enough.

CHAPTER 36

Jack slid his legs over the edge of the tiny sleeping platform and sat with his forearms resting on his knees.

He inhaled a deep breath and exhaled it in a loud rush of air.

The cold of the stone pallet had seeped into every joint in his body, making him wish he'd been sitting. But he had found some comfort in curling up with his knees to his chest, like a baby inside his mother's womb.

His mother.... It seemed like forever since he had seen her.

He buried his face in his hands, scrubbed the grittiness from his eyes, then stroked back his hair. He peered at the doorway and saw guards posted in the passageway.

The flame on his lamp flickered. It had dimmed.

He checked the oil in the lamp and found it almost gone. He saw several *kukui* nuts sitting on the shelf and eased one into the fragile flame. The nut caught fire and the flame rose, bathing the room in a warm light.

It made sense to him the *Menehune* would burn the nut from the candlenut tree. Hawaiians had depended on the oily nut as a source of light long before the advent of electricity.

Stifling a yawn, he glanced at his left wrist to check the time and saw a line of pale skin.

Annoyed his watch had been taken from him, he squatted in

front of the door and leaned close for a better look. A different guard stood across from his cell. They'd changed shifts.

At least the spear-toter with the grudge had been replaced.

He rested his elbows on his knees and massaged his temples. He'd dozed off. But how long had he slept? And was it day or night? Time was running out for Robert and the others and it might already be too late.

But he refused to believe that.

A shuffle in the passageway outside his cell drew his attention back to his door.

The scrape of feet on rock grew louder.

He heard talking and frowned.

No way.

He cocked an ear.

"Do you think Jack and the others are back here?"

"I'd say so, unless they found a way past these guards."

The voices brought him to his feet, and his skull cracked on the ceiling. He massaged his scalp.

It can't be!

He promptly forgot about the bump on the head, dropped to his knees, and peered through the gaps between the wooden bars. The portion of tunnel he could see beyond the guards was empty. The guards stood steadfast at their posts.

No matter how hard it was to believe, he knew he wasn't hearing things. "Robert! Sienna!" he called out. "Is that you?"

"Jack!" Robert hollered back from around the corner. "My God, I can't believe it! You all right?"

Sienna, Kazuko, and Regan chimed in with Robert, expressing their own concerns and joy.

Jack pressed his face to the bars, straining for a better look. He still couldn't see his friends but firelight, growing brighter by the second, danced on the wall of the tunnel. They were definitely walking toward him.

"Yes! Yes!" he yelled. Unable to contain his excitement, he shook the wooden bars, rattling his door. "What about you guys?"

"Nothing wrong with us that won't wash off," Kazuko answered cheerfully.

He relaxed onto his heels and exhaled the breath he'd been holding.

Thank God!

Finally, two armed guards—followed by a smug-faced Matapolu—led the procession around the corner. Robert, Kazuko, Sienna, and Regan walked in a tight group behind them. Two more guards brought up the rear.

A tear welled in Jack's eye, and he wiped it away with the tips of his fingers. Never had a sight looked so good.

"Lisa!" Sienna called out.

Jack saw Sienna's look of confusion when there was no answer.

Matapolu stopped and raised a hand, silencing Sienna and the others. The guards held them back, and Matapolu stepped to the door. He still wore his smile. "Friends," he said.

Jack was taken aback by Matapolu's use of the word. He reached through the bars and eagerly offered to shake hands. "Yes! Friends."

Matapolu eyed Jack's hand, reached, and shook it. "Friends," he repeated and stepped back.

Jack was surprised by the power in such a small hand. He remembered how those same small hands had saved him from falling into the crevasse.

A guard stepped forward, untied the rope securing the door to Jack's cell, and held the door open. Jack backed away and squatted, facing Robert and the others as they were ushered inside. At once the cell became incredibly small.

"I see they took your gear, too," he said, noticing that their packs, hardhats, and headlamps were gone.

Robert glanced at the low ceiling. "Back there in the cave. It's too bad. Looks like I could use my hardhat."

"No shit." Jack fingered the tender lump on his head. "I've already cracked my skull."

Careful to keep his head low, Robert edged in next to Jack, took a seat on the rough-hewn rock floor, and folded his long legs in front of him, Indian style. Sienna and Regan—both tall for women—had a similar problem standing. Kazuko being five inches shorter made out a little better. But she still had to watch her head. The three women sat down in a semicircle on the floor, facing the men. Kazuko sat on the end closest to Robert.

Everyone talked at once. The chatter and a million questions were directed mostly at Jack.

Before he could make sense of it, a flurry of activity on the other side of the cell door drew their attention to the passageway. They fell silent at the sight of the commotion.

Four *Menehune* approached, with a tightly wrapped and tied woven palm-mat bundle suspended between them on two long poles supported on their shoulders. They carefully laid the bundle on the cobblestone floor. Dirt-caked black hair protruded from one end, waffle-soled boots stuck out of the other. There was no blood, but the person wrapped in the palm mat was obviously dead.

The *Menehune* walked away without uttering a word.

"Tumra," Jack said, more as a comment than a question.

"We watched our hairy little friends out there pull his body from the rubble," Robert answered. "We had no idea who'd been buried in the cave-in. We were worried you all might be dead."

Robert's expression suggested that he was only just now realizing that a member of the team was unaccounted for. His expression tightened. "We saw Lisa in the cell next door. Where's Michael?"

"Michael's dead." Jack looked at his hands. He couldn't quite bring himself to tell Robert that Lisa had murdered the Aussie.

"So Lisa's okay?"

Jack glanced at the expectant faces looking at him.

"I called out to her," Sienna added, her expression one of confusion. "But she didn't say a word. She actually scooted away from the door as though she wasn't at all happy to see us."

"She probably isn't." Jack stared at his friends for a few more seconds, wanting to put off the inevitable. "Lisa killed Michael. She murdered him."

Robert huffed out a breath. "What do you mean, murdered?"

Jack locked eyes with Robert. "She pushed him into a crevasse, plain and simple. I watched her do it."

The women gasped.

He looked at them, feeling the need to say more. "I know what I saw. She killed him."

Robert shook his head from side to side. "But that doesn't make sense!"

"That's she's a murderer?" Jack didn't like having to talk about Lisa. And he was even sorrier that he'd invited her along.

"Anyone is capable of killing, Jack. You of all people know that. What I meant was, it didn't make sense for her to kill him."

Jack stared at his hands. "She would've let me die, too. Matapolu, the *Menehune* who brought you here, saved me."

"She wanted you both dead?"

Jack looked at Robert. The anger building inside him made it easier to talk. "Tumra was dead. You guys were sealed in that cave. Michael and I were the only ones who stood between her and whatever money and fame were to be gained from the discovery. That's what she was after."

"I don't care what the relationship was between Lisa and her father," Sienna said. "Fame—wealth—they're no excuse for murder."

"What caused that cave-in, anyway?" Robert asked suspiciously.

Jack knew his friend and knew where the question was leading. "That was an accident. My guess is, the *Menehune* have rigged booby traps all through these tunnels. Lisa triggered it, but only when she unknowingly pressed on a stone disk that released the rocks." Jack scanned the group. "And speaking of booby traps, how'd you guys get out of that cave?"

"The *Menehune*—if that's who they are—dug us out," Sienna offered. "What we couldn't figure out, is how they knew we were trapped there."

Jack thought about how he'd pleaded with Matapolu and the high chief and his council of elders to let him go so that he could get help for his friends who were trapped. Had they understood him, or was there some other power at work here?

"I told them," he said.

"But they don't speak English." Sienna glanced at Regan and Kazuko. "We tried talking to them and they just looked at us."

Jack studied the guards in the passageway outside the cell. "That's what I thought, too."

Robert followed Jack's gaze to the guards. "Interesting, to say the least. First they set booby traps to keep out pesky neighbors. Then they save you and dig us out. Our hairy friends seem to be full of surprises."

"What's important," Jack said, "is that you're here, safe and sound."

"You're right—" Regan cut herself off in mid-sentence. "Your arm—you've been hurt!"

Jack looked at his bloody sleeve. "The mean-looking guard with the scarred eye took a dislike to me."

Regan probed the tear in Jack's shirt. "You've got a nasty slice in your bicep, but it's stopped bleeding. Still, I'll need to bandage it."

"Go ahead and tear off—"

Regan ripped off the ruined sleeve before Jack could finish his sentence.

He watched her deftly fashion a bandage over the wound.

"Looks like you'll live," Robert said, when Regan tied off the makeshift dressing. "So what else did we miss?"

Jack's stomach growled loudly enough for the other team members to hear. "Dinner, for starters.

Robert sighed. "You mean breakfast."

"What in hell is the time, anyway?" Jack asked, glancing at his friend's bare wrist.

"It was a quarter till five when they took our watches," Kazuko said. "I know, I checked before I handed mine over."

"They didn't feed you?" Regan asked.

"Not even one of my own power bars."

"That reminds me." Robert pulled a mashed power bar from his pocket. "Back there in the cave, before they dug us out, I had my fill of these things. I shoved this one in my pocket when I was too lazy to stick it back in my pack. Have at it."

Jack tore open the wrapper and scooped the gooey power bar into his mouth with his tongue. "I'd have given you a hundred dollars for this, you know," he said between bites.

"You can owe me," Robert told him. "So what else has happened?"

Jack told them about Lisa's and his meeting with the high chief, and how Matapolu had spoken on his behalf. "At least that was the feeling I got," he said.

"And what did the high chief have to say?"

"He pointed his staff at Lisa and said one word: *Mate*."

Robert furrowed his brow.

"You sure that's what he said?" Kazuko asked.

"I'm sure."

"*Mate*." She repeated the word as if thinking. In the next breath, her eyes widened. "*Make*."

"That's right," Jack said. "Death!"

"The chief sentenced her to death?" Sienna questioned, alarmed.

Jack nodded. "I think Matapolu told him she murdered Michael."

"And you?" she asked.

"I'm not sure."

"Nobody is executing anyone!" Robert snapped.

"My sentiments exactly," Jack agreed.

"Good." Robert lowered his voice. "Now tell me, what's your plan for getting us the hell out of here?"

CHAPTER 37

Jack didn't have a plan.

Yet.

He sat staring at the palm mat bundle lying in the passageway across from the cell. It was hard not to. The *Menehune* had left Tumra's body there for a reason.

What reason?

He wished he could talk to Matapolu.

"I've been going over some of the words I've heard the *Menehune* say," Kazuko announced. "I think I'm making some sense of them."

Kazuko's voice drew Jack's gaze away from Tumra's body. He saw that she'd scooted next to Robert, who had his arm around her shoulders, his attention focused on her.

The sight of their tenderness toward each other made him smile.

His eyes wandered back to the body. "How's that?"

She leaned forward, out of Robert's outstretched arm. "You remember the *Menehune* word *mate*? As you know, I speak fluent Hawaiian, but it's modern Hawaiian. That's what confused me. There's no *K* in the ancient Hawaiian language. They used a *T* instead, which is consistent with Polynesian societies. You also know the Hawaiians didn't have a written language prior to the arrival of the missionaries."

Jack was intrigued by what she was saying. "Yeah, keep going."

"The missionaries," she continued, "changed the *T* to a *K* when they put the Hawaiian language into its written form."

"So if you change the *T's* to *K's* you can talk to them?" Sienna asked.

She nodded. "Enough to get a point across, anyway."

"Then I say we try it on the guards," Jack said. "Tell them we want to talk to Matapolu."

"And find out if they plan on leaving Tumra's body there," Regan suggested. "It'd be best to not have him decomposing five feet away from us."

"I second that," Robert added.

Jack saw them staring at the body. "I can't believe they just left him here. Poor guy."

"His death hurts," Sienna spoke up. "He was my friend. So was Michael. I invited them along. If you don't mind, I propose a moment of silence in their honor."

They all bowed their heads.

"A terrible way to die," Sienna said a few long seconds later as she raised her head. "And now, folks, I suggest we try communicating with the people we came here to find."

"Let me see what I can do." Kazuko squatted at the doorway and put her face to the wooden bars.

Jack, Robert, Sienna, and Regan huddled close behind her and watched.

Kazuko glanced over her shoulder and caught a go-ahead nod from Jack. She faced the guard standing across from the cell and, speaking in Hawaiian, asked to speak to Matapolu.

The guard cocked his head, but didn't answer.

Kazuko repeated the phrase again, only more slowly this time as she concentrated on replacing K's with T's.

Jack heard her stumble on the pronunciation of a couple of words, but figured the guard understood because he spoke back to her.

"What'd he say?" Jack whispered into her ear the instant the guard finished talking.

"He says Matapolu is sleeping. He'll return when he wakes up." She looked over her shoulder at Jack. "I think."

"What do you mean 'you think'?"

"They don't exactly speak Hawaiian. And it's not just a matter of inserting T's for K's. It's a mixture of Polynesian languages."

"But you communicated?"

"I got the impression from the guard that he didn't really want to talk to me."

"Or maybe he wasn't supposed to," Robert added.

"Matapolu is the only *Menehune* who's spoken directly to me," Jack said. "Not even the high chief."

Kazuko turned and joined the huddle. "It was the same with us."

"In some primitive cultures, only special or high-ranking members of the tribe are permitted to speak to outsiders," Sienna said.

Regan flashed a shaky smile. "Yeah, the witch doctor. And it's usually when they light the fire under the giant pot of water."

Jack pictured the Tarzan movies he'd liked when he was a kid. "Sounds like you've watched one too many late-night jungle movies to me."

Sienna narrowed her eyes at Jack and laid a comforting hand on Regan's arm. "We're all a little nervous. But to my knowledge, the Hawaiians didn't practice cannibalism."

"I won't deny I'm concerned for all of us," Regan said. "But I was only kidding when I made that witch doctor comment."

"Maybe not as much as you think," Jack told her with total seriousness. He regretted the frivolous comment that'd brought him the hard look from Sienna. "Matapolu just might be some kind of shaman or *kahuna*. From what I've seen, he clearly holds a position of importance within the *Menehune* clan."

"I hope that's the case," Kazuko said. "He's definitely the one to give us the answers we need."

"Then we'll have to wait," Robert said.

"Yeah," Jack agreed. "But for how long?"

* * * *

Jack sat slumped against the wall, facing the barred doorway. The nap he'd had before Robert and the others showed up had taken the edge off of his need for sleep. Kazuko lay curled up with her head on Robert's lap. Sienna and Regan sat close together with their legs pulled tightly against their chests and their heads resting on their knees.

Two strong couples. Each person with someone they could lean on. He hoped that someday he'd be blessed with that kind of relationship.

He'd spent enough long hours on the water by himself to become intimate with loneliness. At times he had been almost comfortable with it. Other times, it had ripped at his guts like an iron claw.

"I can't help feeling sorry for her," Sienna said, raising her head from her knees.

"You mean Lisa?" Jack questioned. Sienna must have known he was awake.

"She looked so lost when I saw her watch us walk in."

"Personally, I'd prefer to not think about the woman."

"You know we'll have to take her with us."

"Straight to the nearest jail. When we get out of here. Who knows when that'll be?"

"We'll get out of here," Robert said.

Jack looked at his friend. "I didn't know you were listening."

"Been thinking."

"About getting out of here?"

"No. About your *Menehune* friends."

"Who says they're my friends?"

"Matapolu saved your ass, didn't he? And didn't you two shake hands and call each other 'friend'?"

"All right. But I know at least one *Menehune* who doesn't like me. The fucker speared me in the arm. He'd have stuck me in the guts if I hadn't moved."

"Be angry at him then. But don't judge the others by his actions."

"Point made. So what was it you were thinking about?"

"Even if they don't call themselves *Menehune*, I think it's safe to say they are the source of the legend. And I'd say they've lived up to their reputation of being diligent and efficient workers. These caves weren't dug overnight. I also think there is more to them than we're seeing."

"I've been thinking the same thing."

"As I have," Sienna spoke up. "I've been giving considerable thought to those carvings on the huts in the grotto. We know who carved them, but not what they mean. I do know they're not just decorative carvings put there by a primitive cave dweller trying to fancy up his place."

"Speaking of those carvings," Jack said. "On my way to meet with the high chief in the council chamber, I saw symbols that matched them perfectly, chiseled in the rock walls."

"And don't forget they matched the carvings on those mammoth tusks," said Regan.

"If I remember correctly," Jack added. "That's what brought you here?"

"And for good reason," Sienna shot back. "If we decipher those carvings we can set the anthropological community on its ear. We know now, the discovery on Flores was only one small piece to a much larger puzzle. I'm certain the information contained in those carvings traces the migration of a species of little people who became the source of myths and legends in cultures throughout the world."

"I recall you being skeptical about the existence of *Menehune* when I suggested it in the grotto. Fairytales, legends—I believe that's what you called them."

"It's hard to deny their existence when they save your life."

Jack smiled. "I just had to rub it in."

"So I understand where you're going with this," Robert said. "You're ready to believe cousins of these little people migrated across the globe. And in doing so, they became the source of all the little people legends."

"That's what I'm saying," Sienna confirmed.

"And you need to solve the riddle behind the carvings to prove it?"

"I'm certain they hold the key to it all."

"Like Jack said, we came here because of the highly probable connection to the carvings on the mammoth tusks," Regan offered. "None of us can deny that connection, or that a species of little people, related to the ones here, most likely carved them. I, too, would like to substantiate that theory."

"When you think about it," Jack looked at Regan then Sienna, "didn't matching the carvings on those mammoth tusks to those on the huts in the grotto do that?"

"To a degree," Sienna answered. "But how? When? Where? Why? The answers to those questions lie within those carvings. You might not like hearing this, but I for one would be content to stay here awhile."

"Did I hear right?" Kazuko lifted her head from Robert's lap. "You want to *stay* here?"

Robert helped her sit up. "You were listening?"

"How could I not?" She rubbed her eyes, and then smoothed back her long silky black hair, hooking the wild strands in place behind her ears. "You guys weren't exactly whispering."

"What are your feelings?" Sienna asked, looking at Kazuko.

"I'm not excited about staying here longer than I have to, that's for sure. But I would like to learn all I can about the little people responsible for so much Hawaiian folklore."

Sienna nodded. "Face it, there's much to be learned here. And I've been on enough digs to know the secret to the *Menehune* and much, much more lies within those carvings."

CHAPTER 38

Jack smelled the food before he saw Matapolu and two female *Menehune* step to the door of the cell.

A troop of guards paraded into the passageway directly behind them and relieved the sentries posted there. Jack was happy to see the ill-tempered guard with the scarred face was not among them.

"Friend," Matapolu greeted them through the openings between the bars, and stepped back when a burly guard approached and opened the door.

"Friend," Jack eagerly replied. He was surprised when Matapolu stepped into the crowded cell.

Kazuko rose onto her knees and in her modified Hawaiian said, "We want to talk to you about this place, we want to learn from you."

There was a long moment of silence. Jack exchanged looks with the rest of his group. Everything—even their lives—hinged on their ability to communicate with the *Menehune*.

Matapolu turned his head, giving each of them a good, long look.

To Jack, it seemed as if the short man were peering into the very heart of their souls, to judge their worthiness. He felt a shiver of uneasiness when Matapolu's gaze settled on him.

Was it an insult in their society to have a woman speak so freely to him?

Did he even understand what Kazuko had said?

He held his breath.

Without a word, Matapolu stepped from the cell and waved in the two *Menehune* women carrying the trays of food.

Jack let himself breathe out. The food smelled wonderful, but he couldn't deny his disappointment. Their effort to engage his hairy friend in conversation had failed.

He watched the two women set the heaped platters on the floor, in the center of the cell. This was his first close look at the *Menehune* women. The one nearest to him flashed a sideways glance his direction and smiled. She had eyes the color of coffee and firm softball-sized breasts. Both women appeared comfortable with their partial nudity.

Again, he was taken aback by the hairiness of the women in the clan. Like the others he'd seen, the hair on their heads was black, thick, coarse, straight, and cropped just above the shoulder. Short black hair covered their arms from elbow to wrist. Tufts of that same black hair protruded from their armpits, giving way to a strip of fine black fuzz extending a third of the way to their waist. More black fuzz spread across their abdomens just below their bellybuttons and thickened where it disappeared from sight beneath the modest swath of kappa cloth. Hair, like the hair on their arms, covered their legs.

His first impression of the women he'd seen in the tunnels was that the added body hair made them appear primal and unkempt, in a Neolithic sort of way. Now he felt ashamed for having thought that. With their smooth, chocolate brown skin, high cheekbones, full lips, and even white teeth, they were actually quite striking.

He caught the woman with the softball-sized breasts eyeing him, and held her in his gaze as she backed out of the chamber.

Matapolu spoke from the other side of the bars and Kazuko interpreted. "He says we eat first, talk later. He'll return when it's time."

Jack frowned at her. "What does he mean by that?"

"When it's time." She shrugged. "That's all I can tell you."

Jack looked at her with a blank expression that turned into concern. He didn't understand the delay. And worse yet, he feared they had just been given their last meal.

He duck-walked to the doorway, pressed his face against the wooden bars, and peered into the passageway at Matapolu's retreating body.

What were the Menehune up to now?

Robert said, "Something's bugging you."

Jack pushed off from the door, giving Matapolu one last look, and faced his friend. "Nothing, really. It's just that I don't trust them."

"You need to eat," Regan suggested. "You might feel differently with a full stomach." She glanced around nervously. 'And it'll take your mind off this tiny room."

Jack picked up the uneasiness in her voice. He'd also felt the room close in on him with the five of them crowded inside. She was doing well to keep her composure.

He scooted over to the platter and breathed in through his nose. "It certainly smells good."

"It *is* good," Sienna said. She looked past Jack at Regan. "Shredded deep-pit pork, if I'm not mistaken."

"As good as any I've eaten," Regan acknowledged.

Jack saw Sienna look anxiously at Regan. She was obviously concerned about her partner's claustrophobia inside the tight confines of the cell.

That makes two of us.

He fingered up a steaming wad of meat and dropped it into his mouth, while his stomach growled in anticipation of the food. Sienna was right. The meat tasted delicious. He chewed, pausing periodically to savor its flavor. Then he washed it down with a cup of water poured from a metal pitcher the *Menehune* women had brought.

He licked his lips and reached for another mouthful. "It's called *Kalua* pig here in the islands."

"Make sure you have some of this fruit." Kazuko was already on her second slice of papaya.

Jack chuckled at her attempt to mother him and stuffed the wad of meat into his mouth. When he had finished chewing, he swallowed and reached for a banana. Peeling it, he noticed Kazuko staring at the food.

He knew her well enough to know something was preying on her mind. "The fruit not agree with you?"

Kazuko gave a slight shake of the head. "Looking at all this food, I couldn't help wondering whether Lisa was given something to eat. Guilty or not, she deserves to be fed."

Robert, Sienna, and Regan glanced at Kazuko, but continued to chew their food with no response. Jack caught a wink from Robert that said 'you're on your own, buddy.' Knowing that Lisa had murdered Michael, they didn't share Kazuko's concern.

He shrugged. "And worrying about her solves nothing."

"Hey," Sienna interrupted. "Did anyone take notice of these platters?" She pointed at a bare spot on the plate where the meat had been eaten.

Everyone leaned close.

"Symbols like those in the carvings we've examined." Regan shot a knowing look at Sienna. "The platters are engraved with them."

"That's not all," Jack said.

They all exchanged glances.

He answered the question reflected in their eyes. "They're made of gold."

Robert turned to Jack. "I know what you're thinking. You do realize there are no natural gold deposits in Hawaii?"

Jack was confused. Robert was right. But the gold had come from somewhere. Where?

"You're assuming that the *Menehune* made these platters," Kazuko pointed out. "Perhaps they only engraved them."

Robert scoffed. "You don't just find gold platters lying around."

Glad that Kazuko had forgotten about Lisa—at least for the moment—Jack gripped the edge of the meat platter with his thumb and forefinger and pressed down. The rim bent easily. "*Solid* gold platters," he corrected.

Sienna gazed at the platter on the floor in front of her and rubbed the yellow metal with her finger. "If the *Menehune* somehow managed to get their hands on enough gold to make these platters, and smelted them on their own, we're looking at a culture capable of almost anything."

Jack gingerly rubbed his injured bicep. "That would explain the metal spear points."

"I didn't recognize them as being made of gold," Robert said. "At least not the ones I saw."

"And not the one that cut me," Jack added. "But it was definitely metal, and it was razor sharp."

Kazuko made eye contact with Sienna and asked, "Wouldn't the *Menehune* be exposed to the same technology the rest of us are?"

Sienna nodded. "It'd be a logical assumption to say they have knowledge of modern technology, yes. And they might even possess the intellect to duplicate it or come up with something on their own, but where would they get the materials to make—" She put her index finger to her lips in thought and added, "Let's say, electricity?"

"They wouldn't," Jack assured them. "Not living a secret existence inside these caves."

"I say we eat now and worry about that, later," Robert suggested. "Who knows when we'll eat again?"

Sienna fingered a morsel of meat, and again examined the mysterious symbols engraved on the gold platter. "Jack, a while ago you mentioned you thought that there was more to these people than we were seeing. I think you've got your answer."

The room fell quiet while they ate. The platters were nearly empty when Sienna said, "We have to figure out a way to convince Matapolu they can trust us."

Her comment was the exact thought going through Jack's mind. He wanted to believe he was wrong not to trust the *Menehune*, but it was logical for them to want to protect their way of life. "I doubt anyone over three feet tall has ever given them reason to trust anyone but their own kind."

"We can hope all we want that they'll open their arms to us,"

Robert said. "But time is limited. We need a backup plan."

Jack looked at him. "Like jumping the guards?"

"Exactly. It should be relatively easy for the two of us to overpower them and take their spears."

Robert's confidence made Jack raise a brow. "Keep in mind, they pulled me out of that crevasse. They're not weak, by any stretch of the imagination."

"Surprise will be on our side."

"And what if we have to hurt them to do it?"

"If it comes to that, it'll mean they've given us no choice."

Jack mentally prepared himself for the worst. And should it come to that, he'd make sure the gnarl-eyed *Menehune*, who'd been quick to cut him for no good reason, was the first to go down.

"So we do what we have to," he said with resolve.

Robert locked eyes with him. "You bet."

CHAPTER 39

Jack sat cross-legged at the doorway, waiting for Matapolu to return. The food had quieted his stomach, but not his mind. Robert, Kazuko, and Sienna appeared to be coping with their captivity, but Regan exhibited increased discomfort at being confined in the tiny cell.

When he saw Matapolu coming, he was glad the wait was over. He held onto the hope Matapolu was his friend, and that their predicament would be resolved without bloodshed.

His or theirs.

"Here comes our friend," he said to Kazuko when Matapolu stepped into the passageway outside the cell.

Again, a guard stepped forward and opened the door. Matapolu quietly stood back while the same two *Menehune* women entered their cell and removed the empty trays.

Jack caught another coy look from the large breasted woman and smiled at her.

When the women had left the passageway, Matapolu stepped to the doorway. Jack sat back and listened to Kazuko greet their friend. And heard Matapolu rattle back in *Menehune*.

Jack took the quickness of Matapolu's response as a sign he and Kazuko were communicating at last. He had no idea what they were saying to each other, but did recognize the words "*hiti mai*" when Matapolu spoke them. He was sure they were going to be taken somewhere.

Where?

"He says we're to go with him," Kazuko announced to the group. "That we have much to talk about."

Matapolu stood back and waved them out. Being the one closest to the door, Jack crawled out first and squatted next to Matapolu to wait for the others to follow.

The first thing he noticed was the attitude of the guards. Even though they stood ready with their spears, they did not close in around him the way they had before. It appeared to him that he and his friends were no longer being viewed as a threat to the clan.

He welcomed the opportunity to show the cave dweller that they could be trusted.

Regan crawled out next, followed by Sienna, Kazuko, and Robert. Matapolu had to move sideways in the passageway to give them room. When they were all out, Matapolu looked up at them and said, "*Tanata Loa.*"

Kazuko chuckled. "They call us *The Tall Ones.*"

Robert glanced at the ceiling pressing down on them. "I'd say that fits."

"Ask him if we can get moving," Regan said, her voice strained.

It was as though Matapolu had read the urgency in Regan's voice. He turned and led them along the passageway. At the intersection with the main passage, Jack peered over at Lisa's cell and saw her sitting on the other side of the door with one hand gripping the wooden bars.

Hatred and disgust were there for what she'd done, but he couldn't help feeling a tinge of sadness for the young woman whose wiring had got crossed somewhere along the line. He stopped walking, bringing the procession behind him to an abrupt halt.

"Matapolu." Jack pointed. "What about Lisa?"

Matapolu stopped and cocked his head at him, then looked at Lisa.

Jack waited, sure Matapolu knew what he was going to be asked.

"*Pepehi tanata*," Matapolu said in a hushed, firm voice. "*Pio*."

"He said she's a murderer," Kazuko translated, flatly. "And that she is their prisoner."

When Kazuko had finished translating, Matapolu turned and continued through the tunnel, as though nothing more needed to be said. Robert and the women followed.

Jack took one more look at Lisa and fell into line. Behind him Lisa shouted, "Kazuko, Sienna, Regan, the man's a liar! I didn't kill anyone! Don't leave me here!"

Jack did not turn and look. He noticed that no one in front of him did either. Her pleas trailed off with their footsteps.

His concern for Lisa gave way to curiosity. They were entering the area of the tunnel where the *Menehune* had chiseled out their living quarters.

He noticed oil lamps burning in some of the dwellings and heard idle chatter, much like a person would expect to hear in any household where family gathered. Here the doorways were covered with cloth flaps, not bars. Some of the flaps were folded back, and he could see shadows of *Menehune* moving around inside. Snoring resonated from a few of the darkened dwellings.

This was not the type of activity Jack had expected to see. He was sure it was daytime outside this subterranean world, yet here in the *Menehune* village its occupants behaved as though it were time for bed.

All very Rockwell like, but why hadn't he seen this type of activity within the dwellings the evening before, when he was being led to the council chamber?

The answer occurred to him as quickly as the question: it had been late evening.

They're creatures of the night!

The *Menehune* roamed the outside world under the cover of darkness to conceal their existence.

But then stories of *Menehune* encounters were commonplace in Hawaii.

Now that he thought about it, how many of those stories were real? And how many were imagined?

The passageway fell quiet as they left the underground village behind. The only sound was the scuff of shoes shuffling along the corridor and the crackle of the torch in the hand of the guard in front of him.

Jack watched with concern as Matapolu walked past the tunnel leading to the council chamber and into a tunnel on his right. A hundred feet in, a half-dozen entrances—three on each side—loomed dark and empty. Unlike the dwellings they'd passed, there was no life here.

Only the stench of death.

Had Tumra's body been brought here?

Jack huffed out a breath through his nose, trying to rid himself of the smell while he eyeballed the familiar looking symbols chiseled into the stone above each opening.

Were the symbols a prayer for the dead—a warning from the gods watching over the bones of the *Menehune's* ancestors?

He could only wonder.

Perhaps he would know in time, but right now he wanted to get to where they were going. He was beginning to feel like a hunchbacked priest weaving his way through the catacombs of Italy. Only without the rats.

He wondered if the rest of the group felt the same way.

Surely they did.

Jack could not imagine where they were being led, but he was glad to be leaving the rooms of the dead behind.

Seeing the tunnel make a turn to the right, Jack got the impression that they had circled around the dwellings where the other *Menehune* were preparing for sleep. He began to wonder if these were Matapolu's private quarters. He clearly held a position of respect within the clan and if he were equal to a shaman, it made sense for him to live separately from the main village: The underground equivalent of living at the top of a mountain.

Twenty feet farther in, a stone arch framed the entrance to a larger, dimly lit room. Symbols like the others they'd seen adorned the stone blocks framing the doorway. There was no doubt in Jack's mind, this was a special place.

Matapolu led them inside. And when he reached the center of the room, he stopped, turned, and faced Jack and his four friends. He raised his arms in a gesture that brought the troop to a halt a few feet inside the archway.

Jack glanced around the chamber, but his thoughts were on what lurked in the shadows. He still didn't trust Matapolu. They'd walked to this place in total silence. He'd thought Matapolu would be eager to talk to them, knowing Kazuko could translate his words. But there had been no chatter along the way, nor even now.

Strange.

But then, maybe not.

They'd learn the motive behind Matapolu's actions when he was ready to talk. They'd been brought to this chamber for a reason other than standing in judgment before the high chief. That in itself was promising. He'd be content to stand without having to stoop over to keep from hitting his head.

The group fanned out on either side of Jack. Robert stood next to him, leaned close to his ear, and whispered, "I take it this isn't the council chamber you talked about."

Jack took a closer look at the dimly lit room. It was round and domed like the council chamber but smaller, perhaps twenty feet in diameter. A doorway to their left opened into what he figured were Matapolu's private sleeping quarters. But he was looking at something else.

"My guess is that this is a religious sanctuary," he said, without turning to Robert. "Check that out."

"I am." Sienna spoke up before Robert could answer. She stood staring, with her mouth agape.

Ten feet away to the group's right, a green crystal, roughly the size and shape of a football standing on end, sat on top of a two-foot tall stone pillar. A narrow beam of sunlight from above encircled the crystal with light, causing it to glow as though an ethereal flame were burning at its core.

Visually tracing the beam of sunlight to the ceiling, Jack noticed a round shaft about, two feet in diameter, had been dug out at an angle so that light from the outside could enter.

Amazing.

But what he saw next left him awestruck. Hundreds of the mysterious symbols had been chiseled into the ceiling.

This truly is a magical place.

Perhaps at last they would learn the truth behind the *Menehune* legend.

CHAPTER 40

Jack's final shreds of doubt that Matapolu was a holy figure—a *kahuna*—within the *Menehune* clan, disappeared. It was time for the short, blue-eyed cave dweller to provide them with answers.

His look at Kazuko asked her to translate for him, but Matapolu's hushed voice cut him off before he could open his mouth.

He listened to the *kahuna* talk.

"Roughly translated," Kazuko offered without being asked, "Matapolu is the keeper of the sacred stone. He says he brought us here to discuss the future of his people."

Sienna glanced from Kazuko to Matapolu. "What does he mean 'the future of his people'?"

"I'll ask," Kazuko said.

Again she translated and Matapolu answered. "He says they are all that is left of the *Menehune*. When they are gone, there are no children to take their places in this world."

Until now, Jack had not thought about the absence of children within the clan. It dawned on him he'd only seen adults.

"Why aren't there any children?" he asked.

It was as though Matapolu had anticipated Jack's question. "We are the last," he continued, with Kazuko translating. "It is forbidden for us to make children. The numbers of our people are too few. Without other *Menehune* tribes to marry into, the babies are born deformed or dead."

"You realize he's talking about inbreeding?" Sienna whispered.

"Sure I do," Jack said. "And since all the adults I've seen look healthy, my guess is, the deformed children didn't live long."

Kazuko's right hand shot up, gesturing them to stop talking. She continued to translate. "Before *The Tall Ones* came to our lands in their giant double-hulled boats, our numbers were many times what they are now. Our people flourished. For generations we lived alongside *The Tall Ones*, and shared with them the knowledge given to us by *God's Stone*. Some learned, but many were hesitant to give up their old ways. Over time, *The Tall Ones'* numbers grew, and we were driven from one island to another, until all that remained of us were those who sought refuge inside caves deep within these mountains."

"What do you mean?" Kazuko asked in her modified Hawaiian. "*The Tall Ones* drove you from your lands?"

Her voice choked with emotion while she translated. "There were warriors among *The Tall Ones* who craved power. They took the best lands for their own and enslaved the *Menehune* who remained. The men forced themselves on our women. Some of the *Menehune* women became wives, and bore children. But those children lacked the knowledge of *God's Stone* and took on the ways of *The Tall Ones*."

Matapolu stopped talking and walked toward the green crystal. Sienna seized the moment of quiet. "Tell him we want to know about the carvings. And when he mentioned *God's Stone*, was he referring to that green crystal? Gosh, I don't know where to begin."

Kazuko translated Sienna's questions to Matapolu. He faced the group, and with a sweep of his hand, indicated the carvings on the ceiling. "This is the story of my people. We have been called many names by many cultures. Here, we are the *Menehune*."

He pointed to a section of carved symbols directly above their heads, and they all looked up. "In the time before our awakening," he went on, "the first of my kind moved toward the great sheet of ice and it was there they encountered the tall yellow-haired ones, with horns on their heads and long flowing mustaches. The fair-haired ones were much larger and stronger than my people, and even then we were cautious of them. But like them, my ancestors were nomads in search of food. Their tools were crude and made of stone, and being smaller with only simple weapons, they could not kill the large animals that roamed the land in vast herds. They learned to benefit from *The Tall Ones'* superior strength, and at night they would sneak into their camps and steal meat. You must know, this was before there was a written language. What I am telling you was passed down in the memories of my ancestors. It was later put into writing. The carvings you see here."

"What about *God's Stone*?" Kazuko asked in English, eyeing the glowing crystal. She immediately repeated the question to Matapolu in her modified Hawaiian.

"I will get to that," he said. "The little people who became *The Chosen Ones*—my direct ancestors—settled in a great valley on the edge of the ice fields. It was in that valley they discovered the glowing stone." He pointed at the green crystal. "*God's Stone*."

"Moldavite," Regan spoke up for the first time. "Grail stone. Legend has it, moldavite was the green stone in the Holy Grail. Matapolu's ancient ancestors must have settled in the Moldau Valley of what was at one time Czechoslovakia. That's the only place it's found."

"Moldavite. Grail stone," Jack said. "I've never heard of it."

"That's because you're not into crystals," Regan said. "There are people who believe Moldavite is the only gem to be sent to earth from the heavens. And that there are people here on earth who were not originally from here."

"You're talking aliens," Robert cut in.

She nodded and continued, "The belief is that they're from the Pleiades, Sirius, Orion, and other galactic systems. The thought being that in order for the earth to heal itself, new races of beings are needed. These souls—incarnating on earth for the first time in a physical body—need a way to be grounded in the unique energies of this planet. Moldavite supposedly helps them do that."

Jack scoffed. “Alien souls on earth. Some sort of cosmic ten commandments sent here from heaven. I find it all a bit hard to believe.”

Matapolu stood quietly listening to the verbal exchange between Regan and Jack. And in a display of exasperation, he exhaled a long, drawn-out sigh.

“Yet you must believe,” he said, in almost perfect English.

Jack forgot what he was about to say and looked the *kahuna* squarely in the eyes. Robert, Kazuko, Sienna, and Regan stared.

“You speak English?” Jack said, breaking the silence that had descended on the room.

“Yes. At night when we go to where *The Tall Ones* live, I listen to them talk. The stone helps me understand.”

“The grail stone?” Jack confirmed.

“*God's Stone.*” Matapolu pointed at the football-sized crystal sitting on the stone pillar. “See how it glows. Within its heart burns the power of God. But you have to believe to feel its potential.”

“Let's say I believe,” Jack said. “Why the *Me Tarzan you Jane* act? You could have told me you spoke English and spared me and my friends here one hell-of-a-lot of grief!”

“It is forbidden for us to speak your language. We have watched *The Tall Ones* desecrate this world. It is believed you are the evil ones sent here to destroy all that is good.”

“Surely you don't believe that?” Sienna said.

“I believe there is evil among all the tribes of the world, just as there is good. And I believe there are deeds done every day that are truly evil, even when they were intended to be good.”

There are a lot of evil, nasty people in this world. Jack couldn't have agreed more. And he refused to believe the *Menehune* were beyond reproach, no matter how much he respected Matapolu's words.

He narrowed his eyes. “But that's not the case when it comes to the *Menehune*?”

Matapolu shook his head, bowed it sadly, and fingered the Moldavite crystal hanging from the chain around his neck. “I fear evil exists, even here among *The Chosen Ones*."

No shit. Jack had been on the receiving end of the evil asshole's spear.

Scarface!

"If that's the case," Jack said, "why aren't they punished or run off?"

"Only among the last generation has this evil surfaced. And then it is focused against *The Tall Ones*. High Chief Hootano and his council of elders do not see this as a bad thing the way I do."

"Evil deeds done in the name of good," Robert reaffirmed. "As you've pointed out, your people and ours are not all that different."

"The same." He nodded. "But also different. The *Menehune* do not destroy the earth by taking all that it can give, leaving nothing for future generations. You have already seen a small sample of our accomplishments."

"The fish ponds in the grotto," Kazuko offered.

"Yes." A smile creased Matapolu's face. "There, and many places around the islands."

Jack hadn't forgotten about the engineering accomplishments the *Menehune* were credited with, but he couldn't accept Matapolu's claim that they'd built all of the ancient fish ponds found in the Hawaiian Islands. "You're saying the *Menehune* built *all* the fish ponds?"

"Built, no. Responsible, yes. As I said, there were those among *The Tall Ones* who learned from us."

Jack felt as if he'd been taken full circle. "And yet they drove you here."

"Sadly, yes. For six hundred years we've lived in these caves."

"And everything you're telling us is written here on the ceiling?" Sienna asked.

"That and more. See those three circles linked together? They represent the three layered nature of the human soul: the earth, sea, and sky."

"Carvings like these have been found in northern Europe," Sienna said. "But no one—not even our top scholars—has figured out how to interpret them. Can you explain why?"

"Only through the power of *God's Stone* can they be read."

"Then what you're saying is there are other people who possess or possessed this," Jack pointed at the green crystal, "*God's Stone?*"

"In the beginning when my ancestors became *The Chosen Ones*, there were three stones like the one you see here. Only the purest, most believing man in the tribe could touch them without burning his hands. And it was through him that *The Chosen Ones* learned the power of *God's Stone*. Eventually the tribe split in a quest to spread the word. Three holy men—said to have been chosen by *God's Stone*—carried forth the stone for each tribe. This one was carried here."

"But the Moldau Valley is full of moldavite crystals," Regan pointed out. "Just like the one you wear around your neck. People claim they have certain calming qualities, but nothing like what you're talking about. And nowhere have I read about one that glows."

"That is true." Matapolu lifted the green crystal suspended from the heavy gold chain around his neck. "We have wooden chests full of crystals that have been passed down through countless generations. But only three contain the word of God. The one you see here," he pointed to the glowing crystal atop the pillar, "the one that remained with the people in the valley of *The Chosen Ones*, and the one carried north. The others are mere conduits of the power contained within the heart of *God's Stone*."

"You talk of taboos," Jack said. "And how the *Menehune* believe we are the evil ones sent to earth to destroy all that's good. Yet you brought us to this room for a reason. Why, Matapolu, why did you bring us here, if we're so bad?"

Matapolu's barrel chest heaved another sigh. "Because my people are dying, and I believe you can help us."

CHAPTER 41

Lisa let her hand slip from the wooden bars. Jack had been her last hope for freedom, but he had walked away, leaving her there to rot. She *had* wanted him to die at the crevasse; and she most certainly would have left him to the mercy of the *Menehune*. Even so, she couldn't believe he'd abandoned her, knowing they had sentenced her to death.

Who do these hairy little moles think they are?

She looked around her cell, thinking they should be sitting in cages, not her. After all, the *Menehune* were freaks of nature—throwbacks to an inferior species of man that should have died out long ago. They should be put on display alongside the wooly mammoth exhibit at the Museum.

The thought made her smile. She could see the smug look on the curator's face knowing he had the only living *Menehune* exhibit in the world.

The bastard.

Maybe he'd smile for once. Not that it would matter. She'd be famous, and rich. She could look down at him and the other academics who snubbed her, and have the last laugh.

Her thoughts were interrupted by a quiet, almost indistinct shuffling in the passageway outside her cell. The sound had evidently alerted her two guards as well because she saw them look to their right, in the direction Jack and the others had taken.

She pressed her face to the door and peered through an opening between the wooden bars, hoping it was Jack sneaking back for her. Then frowned when she saw the *Menehune* with the scarred face walk towards her. He carried a small oil lamp with a single flame.

What is that repulsive animal doing here?

A surge of nausea made her close her eyes. She *would* fight before she would let them lead her to her death. A tear welled under her eyelids. This couldn't be happening!

She scooted to the far wall of her cell and kept her eyes fixed on the doorway. Her hands began to shake. She would fight them. But how much fight did she have in her?

She'd spent hours cramped in her cell, with hunger and thirst eroding her strength. She'd seen the platters of food and smelled the meat the two *Menehune* women had carried to Jack and the others. But no food had been brought to her. That she needed nourishment meant nothing to the creatures holding her captive.

Again her thoughts turned to Jack. All he had to do was rush to her rescue the way he did that night on the ocean when she'd pushed her brother to the sharks.

She felt a tinge of loss picturing the scene. It wasn't that she had wanted her brother dead. At times she actually enjoyed his company. But he'd left her with no choice. So it was his fault. He never would have given her the money their father willed to him.

Maybe if she had one more chance to explain—offer to give Jack a cut of the money—he would be there for her.

She frowned at the thought. Not a likely prospect.

He left me here to die.

Or so it seemed. She wondered if he would have left her for the sharks that night if he'd known she had just killed her brother for money.

Probably.

But ten percent—a hundred thousand dollars—was a lot of incentive.

Not that he'd have lived to spend it.

Outside her cell, the stocky *Menehune* with the scarred face stood next to the two spear-toters who had been guarding her. She heard them whisper back and forth. It struck her as odd that they talked so quietly, when she couldn't understand what was being said.

The conversation ended when the disfigured *Menehune* faced her cell. She saw him narrow his eyes at her.

What the—?

She held her breath—afraid to even breathe—and worked her legs under her, ready to spring. They were not going to get their hands on her.

Her cell door rattled open, pulled aside by one of the guards. The two guards stepped in, their sharp, pointed spears leveled at her. Scarface entered behind them. She could see the resolve in their eyes.

She let herself breathe.

"Get away from me!" She raised her chin at Scarface who now stood to the side of the two guards.

He waved her forward.

"Buzz off asshole! I'm not going anywhere with you!" She kept her chin up, not expecting him to understand what she had said. But he *would* understand her look of defiance and the tone of her words.

"You will come with me, now."

His use of English—though heavily accented—stunned her.

"Come," he said and took a step closer.

Her stomach tightened into a queasy knot. She did not even want to think about him touching her.

She raised her chin at him and shook her head from side to side.

"We talk." Again, he waved her forward.

"We can talk here," she said, collecting herself.

"Not here." The tone of his voice sharpened. "You will follow me."

She wasn't going with him anywhere. She nodded at the two guards holding the spears. "They speak English too?"

"Yes."

"And the others?"

"We all know how to speak English."

"Then why wait until now?" It infuriated her to learn she'd been forced to sit dumbly through that spectacle in the council chamber.

"It is taboo for *Menehune* to speak the language of *The Tall Ones*."

She smirked. "So you're breaking one of your laws by talking to me like this?"

His answer was a cold hard look.

The warmth of satisfaction coursed through her. This scar-faced mole is no better than I am. "Tell me your name."

He puffed out his chest. "Topena."

"Well, Topena." Crouched on the earthen floor, she was face to face with him. They locked eyes. "You can go fuck yourself. That's what you can do—you—you revolting creature!" She worked up a wad of saliva with her tongue and spit it in his face.

Spittle trickled down the side of his nose and across his lips. He wiped it away with the back of his hand and waved the two spearmen forward.

Lisa recoiled when the tips of their sharp spears thrust to within inches of her face. Sheer terror widened her eyes and she flattened her back against the unyielding stone wall. She did not regret spitting on Topena, and only wished she could get her hands around the ugly little fucker's neck.

She closed her eyes.

Topena gripped her jaw. "I would be careful if I were you. If it had been up to me I would have killed you and the others while you slept in your tents."

The touch of Topena's calloused fingers made her open her eyes. The tips of the spears remained poised inches from her face. She reached up and slapped his hand away. "If that's the case, why didn't you?"

"That fool Matapolu. But he is not here." He bared his teeth in a sadistic grin. "Only me."

"If you're going to kill me, then do it."

"What you tell me will decide whether you live or die." He backed up a step. "But we cannot talk here. Others might hear."

She didn't believe him for even a second. She had already been sentenced to death by the high chief. Nothing could change that. But going with them might provide her with an opportunity to escape.

Her stomach growled, reminding her it had been many long hours since she'd eaten. "You starve me, then you come here expecting me to cooperate?"

"You will eat, I promise."

Topena stepped out of the cell, carrying the oil lamp with him. The two guards backed out behind him and waited for her.

Lisa stayed put for a couple of seconds to let her courage build. When she'd steeled herself enough to follow, she dropped to her hands and knees and crawled out, emboldened by her hope for escape. Now that Jack and the other members of the expedition had abandoned her, the only choice she had left was to play along with Topena.

With the single flame from Topena's oil lamp for light, they proceeded into the main passageway. Lisa followed Topena, who silently crept along, trying not to be heard. Both guards followed closely behind, spears leveled and ready.

A chorus of snoring greeted them, yet her body clock told her it was daylight outside this subterranean hell.

So they *were* creatures of the night.

They quietly slipped past the darkened dwellings. Lisa thought about calling out to the sleeping *Menehune*, but decided against it. Nothing good would come from it.

A minute later they approached the side tunnel that she remembered led to the council chamber. Straight ahead of her lay the darkened passageway which opened onto the communal chamber and her doorway to freedom.

She mustered her strength to make a run for it. But a burly *Menehune* with a spear stepped out of the shadows to block the way and a second one moved into view next to him.

The fucker! Her one chance to escape and Topena had anticipated it.

The two guards fell into line with them when they turned into the side tunnel. Topena's plan was falling into place. What other surprises did he have in store for her?

In the dim light of the oil lamp, the passageway seemed cold and foreboding: some evil lay ahead. The flame danced on the images scribed on the walls, taunting her to look at them. But she couldn't bring herself to face the carvings that had once fascinated her.

They, too, mocked her.

Now all she could think about was getting away. She would do whatever she had to.

Anything!

At the far end of the tunnel—on the other side of the archway—the glow of a fiery torch, held by a lone *Menehune* standing in the council chamber, lit the room in a pale golden light. Anger replaced fear. And she cursed herself for leaving the safety of her cell.

If this was an elaborate trick to lure her to her death, she would take that vile creature Topena with her.

When she stepped into the council chamber, the *Menehune* with spears fanned out in a half-circle between her and the archway. She turned to face them and noticed that the six conspirators—including Topena, who stood at the center—were the six spearman who had escorted Jack and her to their cells the afternoon before.

Her legs threatened to give out, but she somehow found the strength to stand her ground. For the moment, anyway.

"What now?" she managed to ask.

Topena pointed at the stone bench in the middle of the room. "We talk, then you eat."

She had no desire to sit on the same bench she was sitting on when the high chief sentenced her to death. "How about I eat first?"

"Sit!" He took a step toward her, his insistence pressing her onto the bench. "Tell me what the others have planned."

"I've noticed the way you glare at Jack. You don't like him, do you?"

"I think you all should be killed."

"I know. You told me." She stood up, hoping it gave her an advantage to look down on him. "Just what is it you think I can do for you?"

"Matapolu's mind is poisoned."

"Poisoned?" She had an idea what he meant, but wanted to keep him talking. "What do you mean, poisoned?"

"For as long as I can remember, he has been our *kahuna*—the keeper of *God's Stone*. His words at the council yesterday convinced high chief Hootano to let Jack live a little longer even though it is *Menehune* law he must die."

"Yet your high chief was content to let me die?"

"He could see no good in you."

"But you do. And you want something from me that you can take to your King to convince him Jack must die."

"And *The Tall Ones* with him."

"I'm listening."

"As I said, Matapolu's mind is poisoned. Even now he plots with them against the good of the *Menehune*."

"Why not just go to the high chief and tell him what's going on?"

"Because of this." He pointed to his scarred lifeless eye. "When I was young, I went against his wishes and ventured far from here to the village of *The Tall Ones*. I killed one of them to keep from being captured. But I was cut in the fight and the King feels my blood runs too hot to be trusted."

"I see." She had to smile. "So without a statement from me, your word is shit to the King?"

"If by that you mean he will listen to you, yes."

"Why would my word be any better than yours if he and Matapolu could see no good in me?"

"You can convince him you will stay here and be his wife. He needs a son and our women are forbidden to have babies."

She stumbled backward. "You sick, ugly sonofabitch! Why would I want to do something as revolting as that?"

Without turning to look, Topena waved the five guards closer. And smiled as they leveled their spears at her. "Because you want to live."

CHAPTER 42

Everyone except Matapolu stood in stunned silence.

Jack struggled to understand how he thought they could help. What could he and the others possibly do to help the *Menehune* avoid the inevitable? No one cheats death in the end. That's a fact of life.

"People die," he told Matapolu. "There's nothing I or any of us can do to stop that from happening."

"We will all leave this world one day, that is true. But we would like to live out our last days free of worry that *The Tall Ones* will find us—as you did. I fear your coming here will bring others of your kind, those who will seek to take what is not theirs—to destroy what they do not understand, to change those things that do not need to be changed, and make us live the way they do."

Matapolu stopped talking and his pleading eyes sought their understanding. He continued, "You cannot be blamed for those things we fear. Your intention—I believe—was to learn, not to destroy, or change. But sadly, there are many *Tall Ones* who do not believe the way you do."

"We did come here to learn," Jack said and took a step forward. "We found a skull from one of your people—a woman—in the reef outside the lava tube that led us into the grotto."

"Mele." Matapolu bowed his head, clearly saddened. "She was

taken by the great shark Apukohai."

"The shark god of Kauai?"

"You are familiar with the story?"

"I was told the giant tiger shark Apukohai guards the waters of Na Pali."

"That is the legend. We of course do not believe Apukohai is a god. There is only one god, and his essence lives in the green stone. But the great shark exists. We've seen him."

Jack pictured the shark that almost got Rebel and him. "So have I. But how did Mele fall prey to Apukohai?"

"There are women among my people who want to bear children. Maternal instincts die hard. My sister's daughter Mele was one of them. A year ago she allowed herself to become pregnant. Enraged by her defiance of *Menehune* law, King Hootano ordered her thrown from the cliffs."

Jack could imagine Scarface doing the honors.

He shook off the thought. "What does Hootano have to say about all this?"

"He does not know I am talking to you. That is why I brought you here when my people are in their dwellings, sleeping. It is Hootano's belief you all must die. The council of elders agrees. But there is a chance I can change their minds. I must take that chance."

The group exchanged worried glances.

Jack wasn't sure he was ready to gamble on Matapolu's persuasiveness. He believed Robert would agree. If they were going to make a break for it, this might be the time.

He checked out the guards posted on each side of the entrance into the chamber. As he started to turn away, he paused, and looked again. Both *Menehune* spearmen stood facing the tunnel leading in, not the room.

Odd.

But then he realized it made sense. They were lookouts for prying eyes as much as guards to prevent escape.

Matapolu had placed a lot of trust in Jack and the others.

"I sympathize with what you're saying." He swallowed hard to maintain his composure. It was all he could do to not lash out at the high chief's belief they should be killed. "Unfortunately you're right. People will come here—partly because of what we found, partly because two men have died. And in our world questions must be answered when that happens. You must also know they will come for Lisa—and for us if we do not return."

"But she is a murderer. *Menehune* law dictates she must die."

"We're not about to let you execute her no matter what she's done," Robert spoke up. "We have laws just as you do, laws you don't understand and had no say in, but they are the laws that govern us all—even you. Lisa will have to stand trial in our court system. Not here inside this mountain."

"Your laws!" Matapolu spat. "What good are laws when they do not apply equally to everyone?"

"And your laws do?" Robert scoffed. "You just told us your high chief wants us put to death, and for no reason other than our being here. Tell me, where's the equality in that?"

"This is no time to get into an argument," Jack said before Matapolu could answer. "Before we got sidetracked, you asked for our help. What is it you think we can do?"

Matapolu straightened with resolve. "*God's Stone* told me of your coming. You will take us away from here and deliver us to a place where we can live out our last days in harmony with nature, the way life is supposed to be lived."

"And if we agree to—"

Matapolu raised a hand, palm out, cutting Jack off. "You must. But first *I* must make Hootano and the elders, understand."

"And when will that be?"

"Tonight." He looked toward the opening in the ceiling. "When the moon goddess *Hina* rises, you will all stand in judgment before the council. But I must warn you. If I fail, I cannot do anything to stop them from carrying out their decision."

"Which means death for us?"

"Sadly, yes."

Jack had to admire Matapolu for his spunk, and his honesty.

Still…

He shot Robert a sideways glance and got an affirmative nod back.

"Then I must warn you," Jack said. "We will not sit back and let that happen. Not without a fight."

"Then let's pray I can make the council understand." There was a definite edge to Matapolu's voice. "For all our sakes."

"Stop it!" Sienna spat. "Stop it! Stop it! Stop it!"

They all looked at her.

"I can't believe what I'm hearing," she continued. There was no mistaking her outrage. "This talk of fighting and killing—it's utterly ridiculous. I've heard you speak of the wisdom you've gained from *God's Stone*. Where is the wisdom in killing us, or anyone?"

"To execute those who have committed murder is not the same as what you are saying," Matapolu reasoned. "The *Menehune* do not believe in killing for the sake of killing."

"If that is true, who have we murdered?" Sienna's expression hardened. "Who did Mele murder?"

"That's right," Regan said. "Whom did any of us murder?"

Matapolu looked steadily at both women for a long moment and said, "Hootano declared that if you are allowed to leave here, other *Tall One's* will come to destroy us, which is the same as murder."

"No one will come here to destroy you," Sienna promised. "I'll guarantee that."

"Can you honestly deny there are those who will seek to exploit us?"

Sienna did not answer for a long moment. Finally she said, "Unfortunately, I cannot. But I will use my considerable influence to try and make sure that does not happen."

"I believe you would try. Even so, you must understand how we feel."

"Trust that I do. And know this. The fact that you have lived here relatively unaffected by the modern world for so long is amazing in itself. Not to mention that your very existence is an enigma." She focused on Matapolu's blue eyes. "I can't begin to describe what being here among you means to a paleoanthropologist like me. I have devoted my entire life to learning and understanding the origins and evolution of man—all mankind. There are so many questions to answer, so much to be learned from you."

"It is too bad time is short," Matapolu acknowledged

"Two days," Jack pointed out. "That's all we have—two more days. Then we need to be on that beach ready to rendezvous with Kimo aboard *Pono*. Which reminds me," he looked directly at Matapolu, "we'll need our satellite phone back."

"While you're at it," Robert added, "see that the rest of our food and equipment are returned to us as well."

"Since we're making demands," Regan said. "How about a real toilet and a warm shower? I'm sorry to say that metal pot you keep in the cell for sanitation is not going to cut it. "

Sienna and Kazuko nodded in quick agreement.

"Returning your packs and the other items you brought with you will not be easy," Matapolu said. "First we must meet with King Hootano and the Elders. The other, I can provide now. But we will have to return to the passage where my people sleep. And when we do, we must not wake them. It is important no one sees me take you where we are going."

"I'm more than ready for that bathroom run," Sienna said. "But I'm also anxious to talk more. Will that be possible?"

"After you have bathed, your questions will be answered."

CHAPTER 43

Lisa found her footing and scrambled around the stone bench to put it between her and Topena. "I want to live, but know this. I'm not marrying your king or any of you disgusting animals."

"You should not have spoken so quickly. You forget, my blood runs hot."

"So, what?" she scoffed. "Now you kill me?"

"Do not be in a hurry to die."

She caught a look from him she recognized, but couldn't believe. "You can go fuck yourself, Scarface!"

"Wrong, it is you who will pleasure me and my men."

Lisa stood up straight, recoiling from the threat. But there was nowhere she could go. The *Menehune* spearmen quickly closed in around her. These were not the industrious, fun-loving *Menehune* talked about in Hawaiian folklore.

But then, she wasn't the beautiful, helpless little woman she appeared to be.

She had never had a problem dealing with men, not even the ones who thought they could force themselves on her. If she could handle a full-grown man, she could handle one half that size.

"Don't even try it!"

"You talk as though you can stop me and my men from doing whatever we want with you."

Lisa hissed and sprang like a rabid wildcat, claws and fangs bared.

Topena dodged, but not fast enough.

She was on him in an instant, digging her nails into his face. Blood oozed from parallel scratches on his cheeks.

He stumbled into the guard behind him, lost his footing, and grabbed hold of her right wrist, pulling her on top of him as he fell to the floor.

She lashed out at his good eye with the nails on her left hand, missed, and raked his cheek a second time. More blood trickled down his face.

Before she could recover enough to strike again, the strong hands of the five *Menehune* spearmen pulled her off of Topena.

The short cave dwellers were stronger than she had given them credit for, and she found herself pinned spread-eagle to the cold stone floor. She had expected them to kill her with their spears. But that wasn't going to happen. Not yet. And she couldn't stop them.

Unless…

She tried to pull free, couldn't. "Let me live and I'll do what you asked me to do."

Topena regained his feet, stepped between her legs, and peered down at her with contempt in his one good eye. He brushed a trickle of blood from his cheek with the back of his hand. "It is too late for that."

She looked at him with her big brown doe eyes and smiled. "I wasn't referring to marrying your king. I can do things to you that will bring you pleasure you've only dreamed about. Your men, too."

"You'll do that anyway." He withdrew a knife from the scabbard strapped to his waist.

Her eyes widened. "No—!"

Her scream was muffled by a calloused hand pressed hard over her mouth. She watched in terror as Topena stooped down and cut away her clothing. She was sure he intended to slice her with his knife.

Surely, he would make her bleed as she had him.

But that didn't happen.

Topena stood, returned his knife to the scabbard, and waved away the hand clamped over her mouth. "What I didn't tell you is, that night when I lost my eye," he pointed to the scar on his face, "I was caught pleasuring the daughter of *The Tall One* who cut me."

This couldn't be happening. She squeezed her eyes shut at the humiliation of being stripped naked, and moved her head from side to side, not wanting to look at him—at any of them.

But it did no good. Even with her eyes clinched tight she could see Topena and the other vile creatures staring at her with their lips pulled back in a smirk of animal lust.

She opened her eyes and peered down at her bare breasts in disbelief. Her smooth, creamy skin stood out pale in the torch light.

When she got the nerve to look at Topena, she noticed—from the protrusion beneath his loincloth—he was aroused by the sight of her naked body.

Or was it the violence?

The thought of Topena and the other nasty little cave dwellers grunting and groaning on top of her made her want to throw up.

But then why didn't it sicken her to screw that fat, sweaty, pig-of-a-man in New York who paid her a thousand dollars?

Surely that should have been just as revolting.

And what about poisoning that man who thought he could force his twisted sexual appetite on her just because he paid off her on-line gambling debt? Not to mention killing her brother and that poor, dumb cave-jockey Michael Tomkin.

She'd had her moments of lust and violence.

But they were all of her choosing.

She had never felt as dirty or violated as she did pinned there, naked to the cold stone floor with six disgusting cave-dwelling animals about to take their turns with her.

She had to believe she would still get her chance to escape.

Screaming—she was sure—would not get her a thing except another strong hand clamped over her mouth. And to make them force themselves on her would most likely get her hurt. She couldn't chance that. She'd need her strength.

There was only one answer.

She swallowed her revulsion and said, "Wouldn't it be better if your friends let go of my arms and legs so that I can pleasure you the way I promised?"

"Remember, my blood runs hot." Topena smiled sadistically. "I like it when I force myself on a woman."

"You're not really going to do this?"

Topena's answer was a nod at his men and a tightening of their grip on her wrists and ankles.

She began to think Topena had set up this whole marry-the-king proposition knowing—or at least hoping—she would refuse, giving him an excuse to carry out his perverted pleasures.

You wretched animal!

And then again, maybe in the deepest recesses of her own, cold black heart she had hoped he would pull something like this so that it would make it easier for her to kill him when the time came.

That time would come. She'd make sure of it.

Closing her eyes, she plunged into the depths of humiliation and disgust.

She'd live through even this.

With her eyes squeezed tight, she concentrated on one thought.

Revenge.

CHAPTER 44

Jack stood his ground. He had a question to ask Matapolu before they followed him to the showers. There was still a matter of trust.

Matapolu peered up at Jack. "You wish to ask me something?"

"You told us your high chief and the Elders want us dead. And you told us you brought us here while everyone settled into their dwellings to sleep so that no one would know you were talking to us."

Matapolu pointed a finger at the sacred moldavite crystal. "And to show you *God's Stone.*"

"Right." Jack continued, "If your people are not to be trusted," he jabbed a thumb at the archway, "then what about your friends over there? They know what you're up to. And let's not forget about the guards keeping an eye on Lisa. They saw you remove us from our cell. I don't want to end up with a spear in my back."

"Etu and Otu are brothers. They believe as I do. The men guarding the woman, they do not. But they will not leave their post."

"You're sure of that?"

"They will stay where they are until relieved."

"Come on, Jack." Robert gripped his friend's shoulder. "Let's give the guy a chance."

Jack wasn't all that comfortable with the scheme. He shrugged.

Matapolu started toward the door. "Let us not waste time my

friends."

Jack and Robert followed Matapolu and the women joined them. One guard pulled a torch from the niche in the wall next to him and took the lead. Matapolu whispered to him while they walked. The other guard grabbed a torch and took a position at the rear.

The lead torch bearer set a steady pace. Jack was glad to be moving fast, and held his breath when they passed in front of the burial chambers. He couldn't imagine having to walk past that odor every day.

Then again, maybe only the bones of their dead rested there and it was Tumra's body he smelled.

A crescendo of snoring greeted them as they stepped around the corner and into the main passageway, where the dwellings had been chiseled into its rock walls. The feeble flames, from a half-dozen burning *kukui* nut lamps spaced along the floor, danced lazily in the gentle cave breeze.

A touch of guilt tugged at him while he crept along the tunnel.

Thieves in the night.

He wondered if the others felt the same way. He glimpsed over his shoulder at Robert. His friend waved him forward, clearly anxious to get to where they were going.

But where was that?

He frowned with concern when the torchbearer at the head of their procession stopped next to a doorway of one of the dwellings and pulled back the cloth flap.

Surely they didn't intend…!

He slowed and watched.

The moment the flap was pulled back, Matapolu took the torch from the torchbearer's hand and stepped inside. The guard continued to hold the flap open. It was clear to Jack they were supposed to follow Matapolu inside.

He started forward, then froze.

He cocked an ear. Voices.

When Robert edged past, Jack raised a hand to stop him. He

pointed to his ear.

Robert cocked his own ear, and after a few seconds, shook his head from side to side.

Odd...

Jack would have sworn he heard *Menehune* talking and grunting. It sounded as if the noise came from the passageway leading to the council chamber. He wondered if the high chief and his elder advisors were holding their own clandestine meeting.

He listened more intently. Nothing.

Perhaps he had been mistaken. Just his overcautious imagination playing games with him. He shrugged and ducked through the doorway behind Matapolu.

The moment he stepped inside, Jack was surprised to see this was not a dwelling like the others. He stood in a short tunnel as tall as the passageway on the other side of the door flap and—judging from the glow of Matapolu's torch at the other end—perhaps twenty feet long. There was no mistaking the constant hiss of cascading water somewhere beyond.

A waterfall.

Matapolu stood at the opening to a larger cavern behind him. He vigorously waved Jack forward.

Jack peered over his shoulder and saw Robert step inside the entryway. Realizing the rest of his team stood exposed in the passageway outside, he hurried through the tunnel, hunched over like a West Virginia coal miner, and caught up with Matapolu in the cavern.

His eyes wide open and staring, he straightened in amazement.

Forty feet in front of him, water poured from a split in the rock face. It fell ten feet into a crystal clear pool that flooded over a raised lip of rock on the far side and spilled into a seemingly bottomless fissure. Crystals protruded from the rock face around the waterfall. They ranged from perhaps an inch wide and a couple of inches long to several inches wide and almost a foot long in whites, yellows, and greens. The sediment in the bottom of the pool sparkled with color—thousands of tiny crystals washed loose over a million years of erosion.

He'd never heard of crystals of such magnificence being found in Hawaii. And yet, there they were, right in front of him. Tumra Baruti should've been there to see it all—and Michael Tomkin.

A renewed anger swept over Jack when he thought about Lisa and the dead men.

Damn her murderous hide!

He forced his mind back on track, and again marveled at the natural wonder in front of him. Truly amazing. And perhaps even more incredible was how the *Menehune* had discovered this miracle of nature.

Had they entered this magical cavern through some other passageway and dug the tunnel afterwards? Or had they blindly tunneled the twenty feet and stumbled onto it by accident? And if not by accident, how did they know the cavern was there?

What he saw next amazed him even more.

Matapolu smothered his torch in a stone bowl filled with sand. But the room did not fall into an inky blackness. Instead the cavern lit up as though the rock itself glowed.

Jack rubbed his hand on the wall next to him and examined his palm. It glowed with a cold blue light.

He heard Robert behind him and turned.

Robert scanned the stone chamber, the look on his face reflecting his astonishment. "What the—!"

Jack held out his palm. "Bioluminescent bacteria, that's my guess. I suspect it's similar to the phenomenon we witnessed in the grotto."

Robert ran the tip of his index finger across Jack's palm and examined the goo collected under his nail. "This stuff grows here?"

"'Forms' might be a better word." He nodded toward Matapolu. "We'll have to ask our guide."

They waited while Kazuko, Sienna, and Regan filed into the cavern. And grinned at each other when the women's eyes widened and their mouths fell open in unmistakable amazement at the sight before them.

"Go ahead and blink. You're not seeing things," Jack said to the women and stepped over to Matapolu.

He'd noticed a finely crafted, wooden table sitting next to the pool, and now spent a few seconds poring over the items on it. Stacked on one end was a pile of neatly folded towels, in an assortment of colors and weaves. Next to the towels sat several uniquely shaped glass bottles, similar but pleasantly different from bottles he was familiar with.

Handmade.

But by whom?

"I suppose you're going to tell us this is your shower?" he said. But he already knew the answer.

Matapolu waved a hand in the direction of the waterfall. "This is where we bathe."

"All of you, in this one pool?" Sienna asked.

"We bathe together, if that is what you ask?"

"This is quite magnificent." Regan began to dance. "But right now I need to know where the bathroom is. That waterfall is making me have to go in the worst way."

"The bathroom—as you call it—is through there." Matapolu pointed to an opening in the cavern wall, near where the water from the pool spilled into the fissure.

"You don't have to tell me again." Kazuko followed Regan, who hurried toward the natural restroom.

"I'm with you girls!" Sienna rushed to catch up.

"Guess you'd better point us to the men's room," Jack said.

Matapolu pointed at the departing women. "I will wait for you here."

Jack raised his brow at Robert.

Robert shrugged. "Perhaps we should wait until the women come out?"

"I'm sure they'd appreciate it." Jack nodded at the pool of water. "We could do some fishing if we had a pole."

"I doubt there's fish. Not any worth catching, anyway."

"Right now, nothing would surprise me."

"No shit." Robert nodded at their cave dweller friend. "There's certainly a lot more to these people than meets the eye."

"Seems kind of a shame, doesn't it?"

Robert looked confused. "How's that?"

"Two worlds," Jack said with conviction. "Theirs, ours. Their world is dying simply because they're different. We should have been able to learn from each other."

"We are, now." Robert slapped Jack on the back. "And my guess is that in a few minutes we're going to learn a lot more."

CHAPTER 45

Sienna, Regan, and Kazuko splashed, whispered, and giggled to each other across the pool from Jack and Robert, their bare backs turned to the two men. Jack scrubbed himself in the cool water and tried not to look at the women, but found it almost impossible.

"Listen to them carrying on over there," he said as he scrubbed the hair on his chest with the *Menehune* version of homemade soap. "Who'd believe they're top scientists in their field?"

"Let 'em play" Robert said. He blasted Jack with a splash of water and climbed out.

Jack quickly rinsed and followed.

Naked and dripping, they both snatched a towel from the table and dried themselves.

Jack noticed the large embossed *S* on his towel.

Sheraton Inn.

At least he knew they hadn't made the towels. He held it up for Matapolu to see. "Picked them up on holiday, did you?"

Matapolu's expression remained stoic. "At night when we enter your world we often find things we can use. But we always leave something behind: a piece of fruit, a coconut, a pretty shell, a shiny stone—something of value in exchange."

"These bottles—" Robert lifted one of them from the table "—did you find them, too?"

"They were made by our craftsmen. So were the gold plates your food was served on. *God's Stone* told us how."

Glass…? Gold…?

The wheels in Jack's mind began to turn. The *Menehune* were skilled at chiseling away solid rock to make their subterranean home, he saw evidence of that everywhere. But to do that, they needed iron tools. Stone tools would not have been enough. The problem was, iron didn't exist in the Hawaiian Islands until it was introduced by the Europeans, a little over two hundred years ago.

He had to ask.

"You talk of making glass and forging gold plates. These passages and rooms you live in are not all natural lava formations. Your people needed iron tools to chip away the rock. Can you explain where the iron came from? There was no iron here until the Europeans brought it. That goes for gold, too."

"The first iron tools came to the islands with my ancestors, when they settled here. Later, metal was smelted from small deposits of iron ore discovered in our tunnels. And, of course, there was the iron you spoke of. But our furnaces sit cold and unused now that our numbers are few."

So the industrious *Menehune* had discovered at least some iron ore deposits. "And the gold?"

"Deep inside the mountain there is a great cavern where sea water flows in through a narrow passage. We do not know why, but there is much gold found in the sand at the bottom of that grotto."

"Seawater," Robert suggested. "Several years ago a microbiologist discovered that many microorganisms derive their energy from breathing in dissolved toxic metals—like uranium and cadmium—and converting them to solids. They use metals to sustain life as we do oxygen. Lab experiments showed that iron-reducing microbes placed in a gold solution, similar to that found in seawater, rapidly converted the dissolved gold to solid gold. Massive numbers of those same iron reducing microbes—or ones like them—must occur naturally in that grotto."

"It is written," Matapolu continued, "in the engravings you've seen, that our skill with metal was passed to the tall, yellow-haired ones with horns on their heads."

Jack furrowed his brow. This was the second time Matapolu had mentioned the tall, yellow-haired people with horns on their heads. They had to be the Celts. He'd also talked about the three interlocking circles—showed them where they had been carved into *Menehune* history—the three layered nature of the human soul: the earth, sea, and sky.

Now he wished he'd given more credence to his mythology class in college.

He frowned thoughtfully.

The Celts, he remembered, believed three was a sacred number. Triadic phraseology was common in Celtic mythology. The Celts even had their own version of the three interlocking circles he'd seen carved in the ceiling of Matapolu's chambers: the triskel, three interlocking spirals.

He wondered why he hadn't made the connection till now.

The Moldau Valley of Czechoslovakia, tall yellow-haired people with horns on their heads, the three interlocking circles, Matapolu's own blue eyes.

The connection was too close to be ignored.

Celts.

He put his mind to work, dredging up his knowledge of ancient history. The Celts were renowned for their metal technology. It's believed they pioneered the Bronze Age. But if his memory served him correctly, no one could say for certain who came up with the idea of mixing ten percent tin with ninety percent copper to forge a metal twice as strong as any prior to that time.

Was it possible the *Menehune*—or whatever name the little people called themselves in that area of the world—had discovered copper and ultimately ushered in the Bronze Age? And what about the Iron Age? The Celts had been credited with both.

"If that's the case," Jack made no attempt to hide his skepticism, "why didn't your ancestors pass their knowledge of metallurgy on to the people they encountered on their migration here?"

Matapolu stiffened. "They saw both good and evil in possessing metal. Man could hunt more successfully, but could also kill his own kind with greater efficiency. My ancestors could not undo what they had done, but they weren't going to hasten the inevitable. Not unless man learned to live by the word from *God's Stone*. But as you know, it was already too late. And even those men who said they believed, murdered each other in his name."

"We all know that story," Robert said dismissively. He returned the glass bottle to the table top. "I don't suppose you'd be willing to show us where you make this stuff?"

"We will wait for the women. Then I will show you those things you wish to see."

* * * *

Jack and Robert stood with their backs to Sienna, Regan and Kazuko while they toweled off and slipped on their clothes.

"You ladies dressed, yet?" Jack managed to keep his eyes facing forward. "Matapolu is ready to continue the tour."

Sienna gave him a peck on the ear from behind and whispered, "You can look now."

Jack turned and flashed a grin full of teeth. "I'll show you mine if you show me yours."

She punched him playfully on the shoulder, but hard enough to make him flinch. "I saw it. Tempting." She winked. And irresistible for some women, I'm sure."

"If I'd known you were looking," he said. "I'd have warmed up first."

"From what I saw, that wasn't necessary." She smiled. "You know what they call those green crystals over there by the waterfall?"

"I'm sure I don't."

"Tears of Pele." She winked. "But don't feel bad, Kazuko told me."

"You like screwing with me, don't you?"

She reached out her open hand toward Matapolu and held it

there, palm up, in an unmistakable invitation to walk that direction. "Shall we?"

"I suppose we should." Jack knew at that moment they would always be good friends.

Matapolu raised his hand over his head and focused the group's attention on him. "Six hundred years ago," he began, with a distinct hollowness in his voice, "when prejudice and exploitation by *The Tall Ones* drove my ancestors into an existence inside this mountain, they made it law that *The Tall Ones* would not be allowed to lay eyes on the world we created for ourselves. Since the last village of *Tall Ones* left this valley, my people have done much to make sure our existence here remained secret.

"And though your people tell stories about the *Menehune* and even see one of us on occasion, no *Tall One* has ventured into this mountain and returned to their world. Punishment has been swift and exact. To even consider letting you leave this place is taboo. For me, that could mean death. But as you know, I feel I do not have a choice. We as a people are dead anyway. It is only a matter of time."

Jack couldn't help feeling sorry for the *Menehune*. He was glad Matapolu had saved him, but if their law dictated outsiders must die, it would have been so much easier to let him fall, and leave his friends trapped where they were.

Why hadn't he?

"You spoke of swift and exact punishment," he said. "Yet you saved my friends and me."

"As I explained," Matapolu quickly replied, "*God's Stone* told me of your coming. You are the one who will take us away from here."

"But you don't have to leave your home," Sienna spoke up. "Can't you see that? Times change. We have laws that will protect you."

"Yes, times do change. But sadly, many *Tall Ones* do not. You said it yourself. You cannot guarantee we will be able to live here as we always have."

Jack listened to the two of them. They'd had this conversation before. Sienna had made her point. Matapolu too. He saw no reason to bandy words.

"When the authorities learn about my colleagues' deaths," Jack said, "and there's no way to keep that from happening, they will come here to investigate. And when they've gone, everyone looking to scam a dollar will flock to these caverns like locusts."

"And the laws she spoke of?"

"There are laws to protect you, yes." Jack shook his head. "But I'm not going to feed you a line of crap. It won't be enough. So let's get this done. We only have a few hours before we face your high chief. Then your job will be to make him and the others of your kind understand. And understand they must. Or things are going to turn ugly, really fast."

Matapolu opened his mouth as if he were going to say something. Jack held his hand up, palm out, to quiet the *kahuna*.

"I said things would turn ugly," he continued. "We don't want to go there, so let's say your chief and elders will understand. When they do, we will need to move forward with immediate preparations to leave this place. I'll remind you again, we only have two days. And you, my blue-eyed friend, must keep in mind that the other members of your clan may not want to leave their home."

"It saddens me to think that may be so," Matapolu said. "But yes, I understand some of my people might wish to remain here."

"And you're okay with that?"

"No I'm not. None of my people should stay behind. But if that is what they choose, I must think of the good for the many, not the few."

Jack nodded. "We'll just hope it doesn't come to that."

CHAPTER 46

Jack still had a few hundred questions he wanted to ask. He rubbed the tip of his index finger along the surface of a rock and held it up for Matapolu to see. "I'm sure the others are as curious about this stuff as I am. What do you call it?"

"I do not know what the word is in your language." Matapolu visibly brightened. "We call it *atuapohatu*. It was here when we found this chamber. There are other places in the mountain where it forms, but only where water pours from the rock."

"How'd you even know this cavern was here?" Kazuko asked.

Sienna and Regan glanced at her, then at Matapolu. They nodded in obvious agreement.

Jack had thought the same thing and also looked at Matapolu.

"The Elder, *Iteloa*, he is gifted in the knowledge of the forked stick."

A divining rod, Jack concluded. "And the glowing bacteria we saw in the water, in the grotto we camped in? Can you explain that?"

"Explain, no. I can only tell you that I make it happen when it is needed."

"You make it happen?" Robert spoke up. "What do you mean? That's not something you just make happen."

Jack eyed Robert. He'd been about to say those exact words.

Matapolu straightened. "Among the Chosen Ones, there are

those who possess special abilities—powers far beyond those of the others. I am the last of my people blessed with that gift. I cannot explain how it works. Only that I close my eyes and concentrate on the vision of what I want to happen. When I open my eyes, it is so."

"You're talking magic," Jack shot back before Robert could.

"Magic is sorcery. The power I speak of is much more than simple wizardry to bring about an illusion. It's the true power of mind over matter. Power passed to me through *God's Stone*."

"I suppose you're responsible for the bizarre fog I saw on the ocean the night I rescued Lisa?" Saying her name pained him and he quickly forced her from his thoughts. "The ocean was glowing that night as well."

"There are nights—when the tide is low—that me and my people go to the beach to collect the treasures left on shore by the retreating tide. That night was one of them. I made the ocean light up so that we could work. We did not expect to see a boat there. I willed the fog to form so that *The Tall Ones* onboard would not see us."

Sorcery? Divine power? Jack struggled with what he was being told. "You just closed your eyes and willed it?"

Matapolu nodded. "That is correct."

"If there is something else you want to show us," Robert interjected skeptically, "perhaps this is a good time to move on. I'm afraid I'm with Jack on this. It's all a little hard for me to accept."

That brought nods of agreement from the women.

"It is understandable." Matapolu started walking toward where the cavern continued past to the left of the waterfall. "If you will follow me, perhaps you will open your minds to what I am sharing with you."

Matapolu led them deeper into the cavern, beyond where the water poured from the fissure in the rock face. Bioluminescence continued to light their way. The crash of the waterfall was still loud behind them when they came to an area that served as a kitchen.

"This is where we prepare our meals," Matapolu said, bringing the group to a stop. "Though not as many as were once cooked here."

Jack could smell the lingering aroma of the meat they had eaten earlier. His stomach growled.

Damn it smells good!

He swallowed to quiet his stomach and stared, marveling at the *Menehune* ingenuity. In front of him sat a long, wide wooden table, about two feet high, lined with highly polished koawood bowls. These were stacked with fruit, coconut, taro, and vegetables he didn't recognize. Stone ovens with heavy metal doors had been chiseled into the rock and vented through a hole in the ceiling. A double row of shelves, like cupboards without doors, had also been chiseled into the wall.

He cautiously stepped forward for a closer look. Robert and the others joined him. The shelves were stacked with pots, pans, utensils an assortment of dishware and jars of what he figured were spices. And in the center of the room, sat a circular fire pit large enough to roast two full-grown pigs. Beyond that was a second table that was equal in size to the one directly before him, and more wooden bowls of fruits and vegetables.

"Check this out!" Robert called out from the opposite side of the cavern.

Jack walked over. He'd had already spied the sink Robert was pointing to. It was a six-foot-long trough, a foot deep and—like the ovens and shelves—chiseled from the solid stone wall. The elongated basin sat beneath arcs of water, pouring from holes in the rock which held back the underground stream.

When he got closer, he noticed the *Menehune's* ingenuity did not stop there. Water spilled from the sink through a notch in the lip and splashed into a duct cut into the basalt below. From there, the water flowed into the depths of the cavern to serve—he was sure—yet another purpose.

All the conveniences of a kitchen designed to satisfy the cooking needs of a village of several hundred.

He thought about that. From the way Matapolu talked, and what he'd seen so far, he figured the clan was small, maybe two or three dozen.

Were there more than that?

If so, he'd have seen them.

Looking at the size of their kitchen, he couldn't help but wonder how many people Matapolu expected him to deliver to the promise land.

That's how Matapolu saw it, wasn't it? A sort of *Menehune* pilgrimage from bondage.

"Excuse me," he said, getting the cave dweller's attention. "Just how many of you live here? My boat's not *that* big."

Matapolu stood silent for a long moment, and Jack wondered what the *kahuna* was thinking. Was he searching his memory for the answer, or was it something else: sadness caused by the question?

"There were nearly two hundred *Menehune* when my ancestors sought refuge in these caves," he finally said. "Twenty-seven of us are left."

Jack did not see a need to probe the subject further. There would be room for them all. He nodded in understanding. "Why don't you show us what else you've done here?"

Matapolu brushed away a tear that welled in his eye when he spoke of the dwindling number of *Menehune*, and waved the group forward.

Fifty feet in, the cavern narrowed slightly. Jack observed the walls closing in on them. They were entering the farthest reaches of this magnificent chamber and all its wonders. He couldn't help imagining the other marvels of *Menehune* ingenuity awaiting them there.

Carved into the wall on his left was an archway—not unlike the others he'd seen. The opening was large enough to drive a Cadillac through, and the interior of the room on the other side was only dimly lit by the bioluminescence from the chamber they were in. No bioluminescent bacteria grew there. But enough light found its way inside to allow him a glimpse of something that caught his attention.

Was this what Matapolu brought them there to see?

"What's in here?" Jack stepped to the opening without waiting for Matapolu to answer him. He stopped at the archway and peered inside for a closer look. Robert, Kazuko, Sienna, and Regan crowded close behind him, drawn there by a hint of excitement in his voice.

"What's up, buddy?" Robert craned his neck for a peek inside. "You see something in there you like?"

"That's one way of putting it." Jack stared into the room in front of him.

Robert planted a hand against the wall and leaned inside. "Shit, there're racks full of stuff in there."

Matapolu joined Jack and Robert. "*Halehoiteite*—the room of treasures. This is where we keep the many things we find."

"Find, or steal?" Jack knew the legend.

Seeing Matapolu's downcast expression, Jack realized at once he'd hurt his feelings.

Even if it were their custom to leave a piece of fruit, shell, or a stone in exchange for something they wanted, a trade done without the other person's knowledge was the same as stealing, regardless of the *Menehune* point of view.

But he wanted to help them, not condemn them.

Besides, it was quite evident the *Menehune* placed their own unique value on material possessions. To them a piece of fruit, a pretty shell, or a uniquely colored stone was every bit as valuable as a piece of gold. To them the trade was fair.

"I'm sorry," Jack said before the cave dweller could respond. "I shouldn't have said that."

"For saying what you think? Even if I do not agree, you should be able to speak what is on your mind."

Free speech. Interesting. Ancient Hawaiian monarchy law came to mind. Death to those who opposed the king. "Are the *Menehune* allowed to speak their minds to your chief?"

"Hootano listens, but his word is final."

"Even if he's wrong?" Jack probed.

"Hootano is very wise."

"I certainly hope so." Jack decided not to press the issue. "You mind if we go in? I for one, would like to take a look at a few of the things you've collected."

"You must remember," Matapolu cautioned, "we do not place the same importance on possessions that you do."

"You might find we are not all that different."

Matapolu stood silent for a long moment. "Perhaps not."

"If you two are done playing," Robert interjected, "the rest of us would like to have a look at what's in there. Remember, time's running out."

"You are right," Matapolu said. "We have wasted too much of it, already. There is a lot to see."

CHAPTER 47

Matapolu left the two brothers posted at the entrance and led the group inside. The chamber opened into a cavernous space that faded to darkness far beyond the glow of the bioluminescence. He couldn't begin to guess the room's size. Long wooden racks with shelves mounted three high lined the floor, giving the room the appearance of an immense warehouse. Everything imaginable, it seemed, had been piled on the racks.

Jack homed in on the large flag that had first drawn his attention to the room: it bore a red, stylized rising sun on a background of white silk. He pulled the Japanese flag down from where it hung from the shelf in front of him. Then he noticed the other items.

"Check this out." Jack handed Robert the flag.

Robert held it up in front of him. "Looks old. The sub?"

Jack lifted what he recognized as a Japanese WWII dagger, from the shelf and eyeballed its carved ivory handle. It must be from early in the war, before the handles were made of wood. "That's my guess."

Robert gazed at the dagger in Jack's hand. "Wonder how it got here?"

Jack let the question hang and concentrated on a folded piece of leather with papers showing along the right edge. It was the size of a pocket book.

A wallet perhaps, or diary?

He handed Robert the dagger and picked up the bound papers. He folded back the leather cover and it cracked at the fold. Brittle, old. There was no doubt in his mind about that.

He carefully leafed through the paperwork: folded yellowed sheets with faded inked lines of kanji symbols—clearly Japanese. Sandwiched in the middle was a black and white photograph of a young Japanese woman standing on a beach. Then more yellowed papers. Another black and white photograph: a Japanese sailor—an officer, judging from the uniform—standing next to a submarine. A stash of Japanese money.

Curious, he leafed through the cash—a half dozen brightly colored bills. Who knows what it would be worth today, if anything? It didn't matter. He wasn't keeping it.

Robert's question still hung in the air. "I think at least the captain from *I-16* made it ashore," he answered, showing Robert the photograph of the Japanese officer standing next to a mini-sub.

"Out of the frying pan and into the fire."

"Maybe, literally."

"I don't think the *Menehune* burn people at the stake."

"Or roast them on a spit?"

Robert returned the dagger to the shelf. "Doubtful."

"That makes me feel better," Jack said. He held onto the wallet. "They probably just bash your skull in with a club. That's how the ancient Hawaiian's did it."

"The *Menehune* are Hawaiians, the only true Hawaiians. Think about it. They were here first."

"Right." Jack hadn't forgotten about the death sentence hanging over their heads. How could he? "Maybe they're the ones who came up with the idea of crushing skulls with clubs."

"Hearing Matapolu talk, it doesn't sound like they're inherently barbaric."

"Just cautious."

"For good reason, I'd say."

"And I agree. Still…" Jack let the subject drop.

He held the photo and wallet up in front of him for Matapolu to see. Surely he'd remember taking the items from the sub's captain. "I suppose the Japanese officer you took this from was dead when you found him?"

Matapolu narrowed an eye at Jack, insulted by the accusation. "We found him lying on the beach. The sea killed him."

Robert gave Jack's shoulder a squeeze that said 'time to move on.' "Let's see what other treasures they have here."

"Good idea." Jack worked the wallet into his back pocket, careful to not let Matapolu see him do it. The wallet and its contents rightfully belonged to the captain's family. With luck he'd see it returned to them.

Robert raised a brow. "Interesting."

Jack noticed Robert's look and knew his friend was not happy with what he'd just seen. An explanation was in order. "The man's family should have it."

Robert nodded. "Let's see what the women are up to."

Jack had momentarily forgotten about them. Sienna, Regan, and Kazuko were quietly studying the items stacked on the shelves a few feet away. "Good idea."

Matapolu carried a fiery torch, lighting the way for Jack and his haggard group of adventurers while they explored the rows of wooden racks. Even trying not to linger, they moved slowly, methodically.

Jack tried to keep a mental inventory, but quickly gave up. It was impossible for him to comprehend the totality of it. He was sure the others were having the same problem.

So much stuff.

"Heh, Jack!" Robert held up a flashlight. "Look familiar?"

"The one I couldn't find?"

Robert chuckled. "Looks like it."

Jack scanned the items stacked on each side of him. The massed collection of artifacts appeared to be a timeline of *Menehune* existence there. Six hundred years, Jack recalled Matapolu saying. That's how long they had lived in these caves.

Sienna held up a wooden club studded with sharks' teeth and

beamed at the group. "There's not a museum anywhere in the world that wouldn't salivate over the artifacts stored here."

Feathered cloaks, sharks' teeth daggers and clubs, boars' tusks and shell necklaces, piles of kappa cloth, wooden idols with shell eyes had all been stashed there. Bone fish hooks of various sizes and shapes, netting made of twisted plant fiber, even an eight-foot long dugout canoe, complete with outrigger. Jack blew out a breath. Every Hawaiian antiquity imaginable.

"No doubt they would," he agreed. He couldn't help thinking the world *should* be allowed to see the priceless treasures amassed there.

He soon found himself immersed in another era of Hawaiian history. Rusted harpoons, coils of rope, an array of long bladed knives, intricately carved ivory. Tarnished silver flatware: knives, forks, spoons. Cups, saucers, plates—all fine china according to Kazuko. Jewelry: diamond wedding rings, necklaces, bracelets, watches, and pair after pair of eyeglasses. Sets upon sets of keys, too many to count. The keys seemed to possess a special fascination for the *Menehune.* Side mirrors from cars. License plates, new and old. An anchor, heavily rusted and maybe a hundred years old from the look of it. More netting, modern in comparison to that made of plant fiber.

When he came to a stack of books, he lifted one from the pile and opened it: *The Life and Strange Surprising Adventures of Robinson Crusoe* by Daniel Defoe, publication date: April 25, 1719. A first edition, priceless. There seemed to be no limit to the treasures the *Menehune* had acquired.

It was hard for Jack to return the book to the stack.

He was about to suggest they move on, when he spied a hoard of coins. He stepped closer, drawn by the glimmer of gold. They were heaped in neat little stacks about twenty high, like golden poker chips on a blackjack table. There were maybe a couple of hundred coins in all and many more in what looked like silver and copper. Piles of paper money, mostly US from what he could see. The *Menehune* had been busy little bankers.

Thieves in the night.

He shot a glance at Robert. He and the women were perusing the shelves ten feet away, working their way toward him. They'd be captivated by the sight of the money the way he was. And all those gold coins would light up their eyes, just as surely as he was standing there.

Gold did that to people.

He picked up a gold piece and eyed it in the torch light—American, twenty dollars, a Double Eagle. The coin's edges were sharp showing little wear, the engraving crisp. The date, 1859, triggered a mental picture of what Hawaii was like back then. Perhaps the coin had been brought to the islands by missionaries, a sea captain—possibly a whaler, or a rich American in search of cheap land?

"You might want to take a look at this," he called to the group.

Matapolu stood watching him. "Money means a lot to you?"

Jack flipped the coin and caught it. "In our world, money's very important. For me, it pays for what I do."

"And what is it you do?"

"I'm trying to save man from himself." Jack's eyes narrowed as he thought of the atrocities he'd seen. "We're killing the oceans."

His comment brought an affirming nod from Matapolu. "Then the coins should be yours."

"This one, for luck," Jack said and slid the Double Eagle into his pants pocket. They'd need all the luck they could get to pull off the exodus Matapolu had in mind.

"Just what is it we should see?" Robert asked Jack from a couple of steps away. Kazuko, Sienna, and Regan were right behind him.

"It seems the *Menehune* are quite the bankers." Jack plucked another gold coin from the shelf and held it up for Robert and the others to see. It was a Double Eagle just like the one he'd stuffed into his front pocket for luck.

Robert took the coin, examined both sides, and examined the shelves around him. "A thousand years' worth of everything imaginable," he nodded at the coin pinched between his fingers, "even a stack of Double Eagles. Hell, I bet if we look hard enough, we'll find Amelia Earhart's missing plane stashed in here someplace."

"Six hundred years, actually," Jack corrected. "If you believe Matapolu. But you could be right about finding that plane."

Robert passed the coin to Kazuko. "Six hundred years or a thousand, that's a long time to be collecting stuff. It'll be a shame to have to leave all this behind when we go."

Kazuko chuckled. "And I thought our garage was bad."

Robert smiled. "They could certainly have one hell-of-a yard sale."

"Well, I for one," Sienna added with resolve, "am going to come back here and spend a year or two cataloging every item on these shelves. This place is a veritable treasure-trove of artifacts."

Jack pulled a car's rearview mirror form the shelf across from him and held it up for her to see. "What do you think, early American Ford or Chevy?"

Sienna slapped him playfully on the arm. "Be serious."

Jack noticed Matapolu watching them. He realized they'd been carrying on oblivious to their blue-eyed friend. Everything in the room belonged to the *Menehune*—or did now, anyway.

"We're forgetting that all these things belong to our host here," he said, the laughter gone from his voice. He took the Double Eagle from Kazuko's hand and returned the coin to the stack.

"That was rude of us," Regan quickly volunteered. "It's just, well, we got excited seeing your collection."

"I understand," Matapolu reassured her.

"Ahem." Jack cleared his throat. "Perhaps this would be a good time to move on."

"It would be advisable." Matapolu edged past them in the direction of the doorway. "My people will be waking soon. We must not be found here."

CHAPTER 48

A rasp of rock in the tunnel stopped Jack and Matapolu in their tracks outside the treasure room. Jack shot his hand up to alert the rest of his group.

They froze.

Jack narrowed his eyes at Matapolu and they nodded in understanding. Someone was in the passageway ahead of them.

Matapolu crept forward, and Jack motioned the others to the wall, their only hiding place. He quietly flattened himself against the rock next to Robert and waited. Nobody spoke.

Jack listened hard for the slightest telltale sound.

Nothing!

He let himself breathe. Probably one of the *Menehune* milling about the kitchen, looking for a snack.

That's what he hoped, anyway.

From where he stood wedged against the rock, he could not see Matapolu or what was going on. If someone had been walking there, they had stopped or left the area.

He could only pray he and his friends hadn't been seen.

The sudden appearance of Etu and Otu at Jack's side caused him to jerk back in surprise, practically cracking his head on the rock. The brothers had crept up so silently he hadn't known they were there.

He felt like strangling them both.

When he saw them walk a few feet past him and stop, spears pointed in the direction of the threat in front of them and ready to defend the group, he changed his mind.

He wished he could see what was happening.

Matapolu appeared several tense seconds later. He paused and whispered to Etu and Otu a moment. Jack saw him motion the brothers ahead. They hurried off without any more talk.

What the—!

Jack met Matapolu half way. Robert and the others crowded behind him. He knew they wanted to ask the question he was dying to ask. But still no one spoke. Like him they waited for Matapolu to explain.

"One of the guards came for a banana," he said. "He is gone now."

A raid on the refrigerator. Jack smiled inwardly. He'd guessed it. But had they been seen?

"Do you think he saw us?" he asked.

"If he had, he would have called out to the others." Matapolu scanned the group. "I'm afraid he does not like any of you."

Robert moved to Jack's side. They exchanged worried looks.

Looking at Matapolu, Robert asked, "What do we do now?"

"We are out of time," Matapolu told him. "I have sent Etu and Otu to check the way. When they return, they will take you back to your cell. You will wait there. Jack, you will come with me."

"Shouldn't I—"

Matapolu lifted a hand, stopping Jack in mid-sentence. "There is more for us to discuss. We will do it in my private quarters."

Great. Jack hoped to avoid another trip past the burial chamber.

Etu and Otu returned a minute later and whispered briefly with Matapolu. Since they did not appear overly alarmed, Jack figured the coast was clear.

"We can go now," Matapolu announced quietly.

They took no more than a couple of minutes to reach the passageway outside the *Menehune* sleeping quarters. A chorus of snoring greeted them.

Matapolu silently motioned with a sweep of his hand for Etu and Otu to lead everyone except him and Jack back to the holding cell.

Jack did not like being separated from his friends, now that they were back together. Still, he had to trust Matapolu. There were details to work out and not much time to do it.

* * * *

Lisa sat in her cell with her knees pulled tightly against her breasts. Her tattered shirt and shorts—now tied in place—barely covered her body.

The assault replayed in her mind. Even when they were violating her, she'd known she would survive. And from that hurt and humiliation, she drew strength to make it all the easier for her to hate, and to kill.

Every one of the filthy little bastards would pay for their perverted pleasures with their lives.

Not just Scarface and the five other *Menehune* spearman who had assaulted her. Everyone would get what they deserved. Especially Jack. It would be easy, now. No regrets, no second thoughts.

She had planned to keep him around for a while. He'd proved to be mildly satisfying, unlike the previous men in her life.

But then he had left her to the *Menehune*.

Screw him! He should have died when that bridge fell!

Now that she thought about it, she was not at all surprised to find out Jack was no better than the other men she'd known.

Men were all the same. A profitable and sometimes entertaining distraction to be used and tossed aside when they'd served their usefulness.

Nothing in that regard had changed.

Her stomach growled a reminder she had not eaten the food that ugly little fucker Topena had brought her. A banana for Christ's sake! There was no end to Scarface's insults.

She would not give him the pleasure.

"You can go fuck yourself, Scarface." She balled her hand and extended her middle finger at Topena, who stood looking in at her from the passageway just outside her cell.

"You think your insults bother me." He laughed. "You have not been paying attention. If you had, you'd know I do not care what you say or do. You are already dead to us."

"Wrong, asshole. I'm very much alive. And if you think I'm going to just give up and let you execute me, you better think again. You'll die before I do."

"That will not happen. It will be my spear sticking in your guts."

"Then I will take pleasure in pulling it from my body and shoving it up your ass."

"It is I who stuck it in you, remember?"

She hadn't forgotten. Fueled by humiliation, her anger raged into an explosion of fury. "And for that, you will die." She worked up a wad of saliva and spit it in his face.

He wiped the spittle from his lips. "It seems you like to spit."

"Only when someone disgusts me."

"Too bad for you." He reached for the cell door.

CHAPTER 49

Jack stood a moment longer to watch his friends being led quietly back to the holding cell. Then he hurried to catch up with Matapolu, who was already walking off in the opposite direction, confident that Jack would follow.

Jack hated having to walk past the burial chamber. The place gave him the creeps.

But it couldn't be avoided.

Once they were inside Matapolu's quarters, Jack filled his lungs with the untainted air to rid himself of the stench of death.

Several deep breaths later, he said, "I've meant to ask you, those chambers back there in the tunnel, that's where you lay your dead to rest?"

Matapolu nodded. "Only their bones. We bury the bodies of our dead in the earth outside the mountain. When the flesh has rotted away, we lay the bones to rest in those chambers you spoke of."

"That smell?" Jack huffed a breath out through his nose and shook his head. "Surely the bones don't stink like that."

"The smell you speak of is from the body of your friend."

Jack nodded inwardly. He'd figured as much. Now that his suspicions had been confirmed, he wondered why they hadn't just dumped poor Tumra into a bottomless crevasse somewhere.

"I'm curious," he said, "why'd you bring Tumra's body here?"

"Because," Matapolu looked directly at Jack, "you'll want to take him with you when we leave this place."

Jack stared unseeingly at the *kahuna*. With longing he pictured the fresh air and wide open spaces of the world outside the confines of the mountain. And he'd only been there three days.

Matapolu casually slid a wooden chair up next to a palm mat on the floor next to the far wall. Then he stepped inside his sleeping chamber, returning a few seconds later carrying a cup of juice. He handed Jack the cup and took a seat on the chair.

"Please, join me." He motioned his hand toward the palm mat.

Jack lowered himself to the mat and sat cross-legged with his back against the stone wall.

Taking a sip of the juice, he noticed a tang that led him to believe it was fermented. Given the choice, he preferred a couple of ounces of Don Julio tequila on ice.

He set the cup aside. "I guess we should get down to business. I take it you have a plan?"

* * * *

Jack didn't know how long he and Matapolu talked, thirty minutes, an hour. It seemed nothing more needed to be said.

He felt his body giving way to exhaustion. It was all he could do to hold his eyes open. A long tough few days, or perhaps the drink was stronger than he'd thought.

He let his eyelids close.

Just for a second. So tired.

The quiet of the subterranean chamber was replaced by the rush of water and the smell of salt air. The ground under him pitched and tossed.

Not ground, the deck of a boat.

He sat cross-legged, listening to the water splash against the wooden hulls of the massive double-hulled canoe. Wind filled a single sail overhead. Matapolu stood on the prow of the boat, holding their glowing *God's Stone* in front of him as though the stone itself were guiding the way.

Behind him and around him, the voices of a hundred people, men and women. An ark. But he could only see Matapolu.

The more he watched the man holding the stone, the more he realized it was not Matapolu. They looked alike but different, too. An ancient ancestor, younger, the *kahuna* who carried their sacred stone to the islands.

He tried to rise up and couldn't. It was as if he were paralyzed. But he wasn't. He could move his fingers and wiggle his toes. He just couldn't stand or move from the spot where he sat.

Then he was looking down at the double-hulled canoe from the sky and watching it grow smaller, as he was swept high into the clouds.

A familiar voice spoke his name. Matapolu called from far away, guiding, drawing him toward the *kahuna.*

Now he stood on the edge of a vast, sparsely vegetated and lava studded plain, a tropical island, the big island of Hawaii. Only the island didn't look exactly the way he remembered it.

Smoke billowed from a mountain top far in the distance. A wild land. Rugged. Virgin.

In front of him, a *Menehune* woman crouched in the tall grass with an infant clutched in her arms. The woman's bare breasts sagged, heavy with milk. She seemed oblivious to his presence, her eyes fixed on the warriors stalking her. The woman was hiding from *The Tall Ones*.

He began to understand what was going on. He was dreaming. He wasn't really there, he couldn't be. But it scared him to have no control over what was happening to him.

It's a dream, a vision, he reassured himself.

Still, the scene was so real. He could feel the warmth of the sun, hear the child fussing.

So small.

There had to be something he could do to protect the young *Menehune* mother and her tiny baby. But like before, he couldn't move, couldn't call out.

He didn't want to watch, but his eyes wouldn't close.

Helpless.

His heart beat faster. His body tensed.

"No!" His scream echoed inside his head and was lost in the depths of his mind.

The image faded to white. A cloud again, he floated on a cloud. Matapolu's voice drew him away, saving him from having to watch the savagery unfold. It *was* a vision. And Matapolu was controlling it.

How? Why?

He was being allowed to experience the vision for a reason. Not to hurt, but to teach. So he would know and understand.

There was no reason to fight it.

Starting with his toes and working his way up, he concentrated on letting his body relax, allowing himself to sink deeper into the trance, drifting, floating into the abyss of nothingness.

"There you go." Matapolu in control again, speaking from just beyond Jack's vision.

The mist surrounding Jack disappeared and the scene before him intensified in clarity, becoming the Waimea Valley, the way Robert and he had seen it from the air that day. Then the grotto, the caves, the carvings, three interlocking circles chiseled into rock.

He moved along the empty passageways and the stench of death grew more potent.

A deep sadness gripped his chest like an iron claw tearing at his flesh. All around him skeletons—rows of tiny skeletons—stared at him from niches in the walls. Their empty eye sockets locked on him in a silent cry for help.

Bones were all that remained of the *Menehune* to mark their existence in this subterranean world.

And then Jack floated in a cloud again. This time he wasn't alone.

"Katie?" He called to her, not understanding why she was part of the vision.

She gently pressed the tips of her fingers to his lips and straddled him.

Why her? How did Matapolu know about Katie?

Now he was inside her, moving rhythmically with her hips.

His eyes widened. Not Katie. She was the *Menehune* woman who'd brought them food.

Jack opened his mouth to protest, reached to push her away.

Too late.

"It's okay, Jack." Matapolu spoke to him from a distant place. Still in control.

The woman slid off his lap. She smiled, but didn't speak.

Embarrassed, he wanted to cover himself. It wasn't necessary. He was fully clothed, now, and drifting away.

The cloud swallowed him up once again. And almost as soon as it did, he was walking, no, being led.

Where?

He concentrated, forcing back the mist, resisting.

"Jack! Jack ol' buddy, wake up!"

A familiar voice, not Matapolu's. Robert. He became vaguely aware of his friend shaking him.

Robert's face slowly materialized.

"Wha—what?" Jack groaned.

Sienna leaned into view. "We were beginning to think you wouldn't wake up."

Regan and Kazuko joined her.

Jack looked around, searching for the *Menehune* woman. He was no longer on the palm mat in Matapolu's chamber. He was back in the holding cell. He jerked his head in the direction of the barred entrance. Matapolu stood looking at him from the passageway on the other side. It had seemed so real.

He sighed in relief.

"Feel better?" Robert helped Jack sit up. "You stumbled in here half asleep and crashed the moment you sat down."

Still unsure if what he had seen and heard was real, Jack tried his legs and arms, rose to his knees and sat on his heels. He could move. This was not part of the vision.

His friends stared at him. He saw the concerned looks on their faces. After a moment he said, "I'm not sure how I feel."

"No matter. You're awake, now."

Etu opened the door and stepped back, joining Otu, who stood chin raised, and chest out next to Matapolu.

"It's time," Robert said. "Matapolu's here to take us to the council chamber."

Jack smoothed his hair back with his fingers. "Then we need to be ready for whatever happens."

CHAPTER 50

They followed Matapolu through the passageway.

Jack hadn't been able to shake the uneasy feeling left by the vision. He didn't even remember walking back to the holding cell. That bothered him as much as the vivid clarity of the scenes he'd experienced in his journey through time and space.

The emptiness in his loins suggested it had been more than a vision.

He still wasn't sure he would tell Robert about it. Better yet, he wanted to put the whole experience behind him.

And to be out of there.

The more time he spent inside the tunnels, the more the rock walls closed in on him, making it hard to breathe. And what about Regan? She had to feel the weight of the entire mountain pressing in on her.

Right now he wanted nothing more than to be on his boat in the open ocean.

Soon, he promised himself.

A few meters ahead of them, torches lit up the arched entrance to the council chamber. The room on the other side was lit.

Time to get down to business.

Matapolu remained confident he could persuade Hootano to go along with the plan, or so he'd told them. Perhaps he could, perhaps not.

Jack hoped for the best. But whatever it took, he and the rest of his friends were not spending another night underground

The muscles in Jack's arms, shoulders and neck tensed as he and the others were led into the chamber. He saw Hootano and the elders sitting at the head of the room. Their flinty expressions did not give him much hope.

Had they already met and made up their minds?

He shot a nervous glance at Robert and caught an understanding nod back. He did not like the looks of the situation, either.

Doing his best to believe in Matapolu's confidence, Jack led his friends to the stone bench in the center of the room. Matapolu had told them to kneel and bow before the king.

They did.

A stamp of the high chief's staff brought them to their feet.

What now?

Jack watched and waited, prepared. He wasn't overly concerned about Etu and Otu and did not see them as the problem. Scarface was the *Menehune* he worried about. Him and his five friends wielding their spears.

Scarface stood a few feet to their right, a deadly barrier between them and the exit. For a moment they locked stares. The instant their eyes met, he saw the fire of hatred flair in the ugly man's one good eye. One of them would be dead before the night was over.

But what about the other five spearmen?

If it came down to a fight, Robert and he would have to face them all. He noticed only two of Scarface's five sidekicks standing with him, spears in hand.

Lisa?

The other three must be guarding her. And why wasn't she in the room? Part of the deal was that she be released with them to stand trial in a real court of law. She should be here.

Matapolu pointed to the bench and said, "*Taiamu*."

Back to speaking *Menehune*. Matapolu had told them that would happen. No problem with Kazuko there to interpret, but they didn't need her to translate that they'd been told to sit. They each took a seat on the bench. Jack sat on the end closest to Scarface. Robert sat next to him. They were ready if it came down to a fight.

A few seconds later, the three missing *Menehune* guards paraded Lisa into the council chamber at spear point.

Jack noticed her tattered clothing. He knew what it meant. The thought turned his stomach. She had murdered Michael and should answer for killing him, but she didn't deserve to be raped.

He nudged Robert in the ribs with his elbow and nodded in her direction. He didn't need to say anything.

Robert leaned close and whispered, "When we were escorted back to our cell, I saw that scar-faced guard over there reaching for the door to her cell. When he saw me, he jerked his hand back and hurried the hell out of there. I guess he'd already done his dirty work."

"The one who cut me," Jack muttered.

"Cyclops did that to you?" Robert's expression hardened. "I knew there was a reason I didn't like him."

Jack narrowed his eyes at Scarface. "The nasty little fucker deserves to have his balls whacked and handed to him on a platter."

"Perhaps we can arrange for him to be left behind."

"Sharks need to eat, too."

They watched the three *Menehune* guards force Lisa onto her knees a few feet in front of Hootano. Jack struggled to keep his anger in check, but came off his seat when Scarface grabbed a fistful of her matted brown hair and made her bow to his king.

Robert's strong hand pulled his friend back down. "Not yet."

Jack glared at Scarface who smiled back at him. "The fucker."

Robert tightened his grip on Jack's arm.

"*Lima toto*," Scarface announced to Hootano. "*Mate!*"

"He called her a murderer," Kazuko translated. "And demanded death for Lisa."

Jack hadn't expected Scarface to serve as prosecutor.

He shot a questioning glance at Matapolu, but Matapolu was already stepping forward. Kazuko translated his words as he spoke.

"She is a murderer, yes. And by our law she should die. But to execute her would only bring more *Tall Ones* here to destroy us."

"She must die," Scarface demanded. "It is the law, our law!"

A murmur of voices and nods of agreement arose among the *Menehune* onlookers seated in back.

"I have said that is true," Matapolu's voice quieted the crowd. "The law was created to protect us from *The Tall Ones* who threatened our existence. But even with our laws we have continued to perish. *God's Stone* has shown me the way to preserve our future."

"Death to all of *The Tall Ones*," Scarface chanted. "It is the only way to protect the few of us who are left. *The Tall Ones'* arrival on these islands, and their unwillingness to allow us to live as equals alongside them, drove our ancestors into these caves to live as outcasts. He pointed his spear at Jack. "They must die, as so many of us have."

Hootano and his council of elders exchanged nods of agreement.

Matapolu took a nervous step forward, as the mood in the room turned against him. "Again, I must agree with Topena. Too many of us have died because of *The Tall Ones*. And more of us will die because these people came here. They are responsible. I will not deny that."

Kazuko's hand shot to her mouth, but only after she'd finished translating his words.

Jack couldn't believe what he was hearing. Kazuko had to be wrong. Her shocked expression told him there was no mistake.

Matapolu had betrayed them.

Jack scowled at Matapolu, who tried to continue speaking. An outburst from Scarface cut the *kahuna* off.

"Death!" Topena yelled. He raised his spear over his head and shook it in a sign of triumph. "Even the keeper of the all-knowing *God's Stone* agrees."

In spite of what he heard, Jack couldn't and wouldn't allow himself to believe Matapolu had turned against them. Clearly, their blue-eyed friend had more to say. He needed to be allowed to talk.

But that was not going to happen.

Jack stood up and took a step forward. "Listen to me, Hootano. I know you understand what I'm saying." He looked at the *Menehune* clan. "You all do."

The room erupted in an outburst of angry shouts from the spectators. Jack cast a worried look at Scarface and his buddies before refocusing on the high chief.

Hootano rose to his feet and strode toward them, cracking the bottom of his staff on the rock with each step. "Silence," he demanded, outraged by Jack's boldness.

The high-chief's use of English startled Jack.

Hootano stopped a foot from Lisa, who was on her feet now, and pointed his staff at Jack. "*Mate!*"

Lisa was on Hootano before the guards could stop her.

Jack stood there, stunned. He hadn't expected her to make a grab for the enraged high chief. And neither had the chief or the *Menehune* guards watching over him.

With the fluidity of a carefully choreographed attack, she jerked Hootano's knife from the scabbard slung from his waist, wrapped her free arm around his neck, forced his head back, and lifted him onto his tiptoes with the sharp point pressed to the side of his throat.

CHAPTER 51

Lisa maintained her death-grip on Hootano, the knife blade held tight against his leathery skin. A drop of blood pooled around the sharp point and trickled down his neck.

She realized the desperation of her act.

For a moment, she surveyed the chamber. She'd wanted to be closer to the exit when she made a run for it. Now she needed to rethink her plan.

The unexpected appearance of Hootano next to her had been too good an opportunity to pass up. And even though she wasn't sure where to go from here, she knew she couldn't stick around a second longer.

She scanned the intense faces and eyes glaring at her. Thanks to that scar-faced Topena, she, too, knew the *Menehune* spoke English.

"Stay back and I'll let him live," she ordered.

Topena leveled his spear at Lisa. His five co-conspirators fanned out around her and held their positions, ready.

Etu and Otu stepped in front of the archway and aimed their spears.

Matapolu was shocked speechless.

"Lisa, no!" Jack took a half step toward her. Robert followed.

Topena spun on them and jabbed his spear.

Sienna, Kazuko, and Regan all screamed.

The sharp metal point sliced the air.

Jack jumped back, just in time to avoid being stabbed in the gut.

Topena whirled around and again faced Lisa.

"Back off!" Lisa worked the tip of the knife in a little deeper and took a step toward the archway. "I swear I'll kill him!"

More blood oozed from around the blade.

Hootano winced at the pain, and the spearman moved back a step.

Matapolu recovered. "You can leave here unharmed, but spare Hootano's life."

"That's all I ask." She continued to step towards the archway, dragging Hootano with her.

Matapolu waved Etu and Otu out of the way.

Topena narrowed his one good eye and inched forward.

Hootano's eyes bulged. "*A oe!*"

Topena did not appear to be concerned about his king's life. He moved even closer.

Lisa tightened her grip on Hootano. "I said I'd kill him and I will. You know I'll do it. Now back the fuck away!"

Matapolu reached out with his hand as if to pull Topena back. "Let her go, Topena. She doesn't matter now."

Topena slapped Matapolu's hand away, re-gripped his spear, and took another step.

The five spearmen behind her closed in.

She felt the circle around her tighten. Topena was determined to kill her no matter what. Even at the expense of their high chief's life.

There's got to be a way...

Frantic, she swept the room with her eyes.

There!

She spotted the carved disk on the wall by the archway. Perhaps...? But she still had to get to it.

Lisa spun on her heels, taking Hootano with her. "Back off!" she yelled at the guards behind her.

The plan worked better than she had hoped. The sudden appearance of their high chief, with a knife to his neck, was enough to move the spearmen back several steps. They did not share Topena's hot-headedness.

For the moment, the pathway out of the room was clear. But she doubted she had more than a second or two to make it to the disk. Topena wouldn't allow her more than that before he shoved that spear into her stomach.

She reached the disc in three long steps.

Out of the corner of her eye, she saw Topena close in on her.

Another second was all she had.

She pushed on the disk and it slid back with a grating sound of rock on rock. The mountain around her began to rumble.

At the same time, she shoved Hootano at Topena.

His scarred face showed the same narrow-eyed determination it had the moment before and he extended his spear in front of him.

"No!" Jack and Matapolu yelled in unison from across the room. But it was already too late.

Topena's spear pierced Hootano's body at mid chest and exited through his back. The high chief collapsed against Topena, stopping the scarred cave dweller in his tracks.

Lisa had not paused to watch. She stepped in the direction of the archway just as a huge boulder fell from the ceiling of the passageway on the other side, blocking her exit.

Her eyes widened in horror. She was trapped.

Unless…

She turned. The chamber crumbled around her.

* * * *

Jack jumped backwards when a falling rock smashed onto the stone floor, inches from his right foot.

The ground under him rumbled and shook.

Small rocks and gravel, that had been raining down around them, vibrated on the smooth cobble stone floor.

They couldn't stay inside the chamber.

He scanned the room.

Ten feet away, Topena pulled his bloodied spear from Hootano's limp body and turned his angry face toward Jack.

They glowered at each other, and Jack saw that same fiery hatred he'd seen every time he stared into the scarred cave dweller's coal black eye.

The time had come for one of them to die by the other's hand.

More slabs of stone broke loose from the ceiling and crashed to the floor in chunks.

Scarface sidestepped one of the falling rocks, crouched, and charged Jack.

Etu yelled in anger at Topena from across the cavern and threw his spear. It ricocheted off the floor, bounced off the far wall, and rattled to a stop a couple of feet from Jack.

Jack grabbed the spear and turned it on Scarface.

He lunged forward.

Their shafts met with a *thwack* of wood against wood.

Jack dodged to avoid Topena's sharp point and felt his own spear tip pierce soft flesh.

Scarface's spear rattled to the floor.

Jack let go of his and stepped back.

The embittered cave dweller gripped the shaft protruding from his stomach. Bright red blood flowed between his fingers and dripped from his hands.

Shock paled his face.

A deeper rumbling echoed through the chamber.

Time to go!

Jack looked around for his friends, and saw Lisa on her hands and knees near the archway. She'd fallen and her big doe eyes were staring helplessly at him.

The floor under his feet quaked.

His peered briefly at the stone tiles, then back at her. She was on her feet again and staggering toward him, alone. Everyone else had scrambled from that side of the chamber.

"Jack, we gotta go!" Robert yelled, from a few feet away.

Jack saw his friend—hand outstretched—motion for him to

move. They were getting out of there.

Before he could take a step toward Robert, Jack felt the strata beneath them quake again, only this time more violently. The floor between him and Lisa fractured and fell away into a deep crevasse.

He wobbled and flailed his arms at his sides to keep his balance.

It wasn't just a rock slide this time. The *Menehune* booby-trap had triggered an earthquake.

He peered across the chasm at Lisa on the other side.

Still on her feet, she jumped.

Unable to make himself turn away, he watched her crash against his side of the crevasse.

Her fingertips gripped the lip of rock in front of him.

"Jack!" Someone shouted his name from behind.

It was Robert again.

Jack stared at Lisa's hands a fraction of a second longer.

She would not be able to pull herself up. He knew. He'd been there. And she'd been content to let him die.

Not this time.

She was a murderer. He wasn't going to let himself be pulled in by a pretty face.

He turned to join his friends, but stopped.

Sonofabitch!

No matter what Lisa had done, he couldn't leave her hanging there.

Dropping onto his stomach next to the precipice, he reached for her hand closest to him.

She peered up through the rocks and gravel falling around them. A freaky calmness swept over her.

Jack picked up on it.

Strange.

And even more strange, she hadn't yelled for help. She knew he'd come for her.

"There's a toehold just above your left foot!" he hollered. "Get your boot on it and push up. I'll pull you out of there."

The waffled soles of her hiking boots clawed at the wall of

crumbling rock. Her toe found the crevice.

"There," he said. "Now push up."

"Not quite." She jammed the toe of her left boot into the crack.

"I can't hold…" He strained to lift her.

The crevice crumbled under her weight.

He managed to hold on, his jaw clinched under the effort.

Again, she dug the toe of her left boot into the crevice.

His grip on her hand slipped.

She pushed up and this time the stone beneath her foot held. The fingers of her right hand closed around a protruding rock next to Jack's foot.

In the instant he felt her weight slacken, he adjusted his grip.

Gotcha!

He held her solidly by the wrist. She could almost climb out on her own now. Another inch, maybe two, was all it would take.

"Just a little higher," she said.

He struggled onto his knees and flattened the palm of his free hand against the floor, then straightened his arm and lifted.

At the same time, he felt her pull hard against the effort.

His eyes widened. Was she trying to drag him into the crevasse?

"No!" he yelled.

She looked up at him and her full lips spread into a broad smile as she increased the strain on his arm. "It's too bad," she said. "We could have shared all this."

"Lisa, don't!"

"You're such a fool." She heaved backward, lips pulled tightly against her teeth under the strain.

He felt himself going over the edge, but somehow managed to hold his ground.

Something. There has to be something…!

He worked his right leg under him for leverage and support and braced himself. She wanted him dead—he knew that—but he remained determined not to release his hold on her wrist.

Sweat dripped in beads from his brow and forearms.

She had her right foot planted firmly atop a protruding rock now, her left wedged in the crevice. She could climb out on her own.

Still, she pulled.

His mind whirled from the insanity of her actions.

He knew he should let go and end the madness, but for some reason, couldn't. Even knowing what she was.

A second passed, and another.

Her hand slipped into his, then her fingertips.

He fought to maintain his grip. No good.

She felt him loose his hold on her, because she wrenched her hand free of his grasp and made a desperate grab for the rock lip.

Missed.

Jack reached for her hand.

Too late.

She cartwheeled backwards into the pit, and he fell solidly onto his butt.

Stunned, he watched her disappear into the blackness below.

"Jack, we've got to get out of here!" Robert grabbed him by the shirt and tugged.

Jack glanced up at his friend, and then peered into the pit.

"You can't help her." Again, Robert tugged on Jack's shirt. More rocks rained down. "The room's coming apart. We gotta go. Now!"

Kazuko rushed to Robert's side, followed by Sienna and Regan. All three women screamed Jack's name, pleading.

Kazuko yelled for him to move his ass.

She knew the magic words.

The ground under their feet shook in a constant rumble now. The wall by the archway fractured into a web of cracks.

More rock collapsed into the chamber.

Jack sucked in a breath. They had to get out of there.

And fast!

But where could they go?

Jack spied several *Menehune* as they scrambled through the opening he'd seen King Hootano and the elders enter the room through, that first day. They knew something he didn't.

Or did they?

Screams from the injured and fleeing filled the chamber.

Matapolu?

He spotted him a few feet away. The *kahuna*—his expression betraying bewilderment—stood gripping the fragment of *God's Stone* on the chain draped around his neck.

Jack couldn't believe the cave dweller was just standing there, stunned by the carnage. The world he had so desperately wanted to save was collapsing around him in a jumble of rock.

He reached Matapolu in a single stride and grabbed him by the arm. He squeezed to get the *kahuna's* attention and pointed. "Where does that opening lead?"

Matapolu appeared to awaken from a horrible dream that refused to surrender its hold on him. He looked with glazed eyes first at the opening, then at Jack.

"Where?" Jack yelled. Time was up.

Matapolu swallowed. "The chamber where Hootano and the elders meet. And—"

Jack squeezed harder. "And what?"

All at once, Matapolu's eyes cleared. He focused them on the opening. "A passageway out of the mountain."

CHAPTER 52

Matapolu ran to the opening, yelling and waving for the rest of his people to get out of the council chamber. Jack followed at a trot. Robert was close behind him, with Kazuko in tow. Sienna and Regan were right on their heels.

With his long legs, Jack could have easily passed the *kahuna*. But there was no way he or any of his group would leave their blue-eyed friend behind, or even one of the remaining *Menehune* scrambling toward the exit.

Matapolu skidded to a stop at the entrance to the antechamber and waited for his people to scurry inside.

Jack took a step back and let the members of his group go ahead of him. He would be the last one out.

The floor under his feet vibrated, drawing his attention to the stone tiles. When he looked up, he noticed a jagged crack appear above the opening. The archway wouldn't hold long. The whole place was collapsing on them.

It was definitely going to be close.

Shards of rock and gravel rained down.

Jack ducked, out of reflex, and covered his head with his arms and hands.

A woman screamed.

Regan?

He whipped his head to the side and saw her cradling her left arm tight against her body, as blood oozed from a gash on her forearm. A melon-sized, jagged rock lay at her feet.

Sienna examined Regan's arm. Kazuko, too.

"It's broken," Sienna said, looking at Jack.

Jack tore off his shirt. "Tie a sling with this."

Finally the last of Matapolu's people scrambled from the crumbling chamber.

"Go!" Jack shouted to the women.

Robert pushed Kazuko through the opening before she could object. Regan—with Sienna's help—went through next.

"Show them the way," Jack yelled. He planted the palm of his hand against Matapolu's back and shoved him through directly behind the three women.

Robert shot a look at Jack that said: *You're next.*

"No time for heroics," Jack said with a slap on his friend's back. "I'm right behind you."

"You'd better be." Robert ducked through.

Jack pulled a flaming torch from a notch in the wall next to his head and followed.

Once through, he paused to scan the room. It was coming apart, too.

He choked on a cloud of dust that billowed in from the chamber behind him. Others coughed and hacked on the haze of dirt already hanging in the air.

More dust spilled from above.

More hacking erupted among the *Menehune*.

Jack wiped his eyes with his fingertips and continued to scan the ruins. Five feet away, a gray-haired *Menehune* woman lay crushed and bleeding under a slab of rock. Several more little people milled around, with blood streaming from cuts on their heads and arms.

Only a few lucky ones remained unhurt.

Then Jack spied the *Menehune* woman who'd joined with him in his dream. One of the lucky ones, she stood against the far wall, looking straight at him as if she had been waiting for him to appear.

His concentration faltered. The vision had seemed so real.

It just wasn't possible.

Regaining his composure, he wondered why she was just standing there.

Again, he glanced around the room.

And the others, why wasn't everyone on their way out of the mountain? The whole place was about to cave in.

He heard a shout from the far end of the chamber. "Jack, hurry!"

It was Robert.

Jack sprinted across the floor. And even before he reached his friend, he could see the problem. Robert, Matapolu, and several *Menehune* men struggled to push aside a large stone disc blocking the passageway.

Their doorway out.

Jack handed his flaming torch to Sienna and added his muscle.

The stone refused to move.

Behind him, the archway they had just passed through collapsed.

There was only one way out, now. And it was blocked.

He adjusted his leverage—getting lower on the stone—adding his muscled legs and broad shoulder to the effort, and shoved.

The stone moved, but only a couple of inches.

Staying with the effort, he heaved.

The muscles in his back bulged.

With a sound of rock grinding on rock, the gigantic stone rolled aside.

Kazuko jammed a shard of rock into the track to block the stone from rolling back into place. Sienna and Regan huddled close, arms reaching in an attempt to help.

Robert and the *Menehune* men collapsed against the stone and sucked in a deep breath.

"Get the hell out of here!" Jack yelled to the three women.

Kazuko shot a glance at the *Menehune* behind her and said, "What about—"

"Go!" Jack hollered, cutting her off.

The women hurried into the passageway and Sienna passed

him the torch on her way out.

Robert rushed in behind them, then stopped and waved Jack through.

"Go," Jack told him. "I'll catch up."

The remaining *Menehune* rushed past Jack and spilled into the passageway, taking Robert with them.

Jack looked to make sure everyone had got out. Matapolu remained, and the woman in the vision. He'd planned to be the last one to leave. Evidently, Matapolu had the same idea.

But why had the woman stayed?

No time to worry about that.

Behind them the walls fractured and caved in, and the ceiling was collapsing in great huge slabs of basalt.

"Run!" he shouted.

All three of them took off down the passageway.

Jack hurdled a jagged outcropping of basalt jutting up from the floor of the tunnel, stumbled when he landed, regained his footing, and kept going.

A hundred feet in, Robert, Kazuko, Sienna and Regan stood looking in the direction of the collapsing chamber. Jack saw them and realized they were waiting for him. Not a good idea.

"Move it!" he yelled when he was still fifty feet away.

Robert and the three women were preparing to go when he reached them. Together, they followed the string of fleeing *Menehune*.

Without slowing down, Jack quickly glanced around. The walls here were not hand-hewn smooth like the passageways and sleeping chambers of the *Menehune's* subterranean village. They were virgin basalt with toothed, uneven outcroppings. No stone tiles paved the path they followed. This was a natural lava tube that showed little use compared to the tunnels he'd walked along.

The rumbling quieted.

They were going to make it out of the mountain alive.

Suddenly, a third hard jolt rocked the ground under their feet.

The group staggered, but managed to keep their footing.

Everyone sprinted hard now. The fleeing *Menehune* were no more than a hundred feet ahead, with Matapolu running hard at the rear.

Jack's group narrowed the gap.

Behind them came deep groans and the sound of grinding rock, followed by a hiss that sounded as if someone had turned on a fire hydrant.

Jack recognized the sound.

Not good.

He glanced over his shoulder and saw water spray from a fissure in the wall. He remembered the waterfall. The aquifer had erupted.

Robert must have heard it too, because Jack saw his friend twist his body and peer back at him.

"Don't stop. Run!" Jack jabbed a thumb at the new threat.

A deafening *crrrack* sounded above the hiss. The fissure opened up, and with a loud *whoosh*, released a deluge of water.

Jack did not need to look back to know a wall of water was rushing toward them. He just sprinted.

Ahead of him, Robert yelled to the women. "Hurry!"

His urging wasn't necessary.

All three of them barreled down the passageway with Regan in the rear, hugging her arm suspended in the sling.

They rounded a corner in a tight group and Jack saw the *Menehune* racing across a wooden bridge which spanned a crevasse fifty feet away.

Shit!

Ankle deep water circled his feet.

His mind spinning with possibilities, Jack splashed toward the crevasse, his eyes locked on the wooden structure spanning the gap.

Another bridge.

CHAPTER 53

Water raced up Jack's leg and swirled away as he waited for the women to cross to the other side. He knew what too much weight could do to the bridge. He wasn't going to chance it.

Unless...

The torrent washed over the edge, threatening to take Jack with it.

Kazuko hollered back at Robert to follow.

Robert shot a questioning look at Jack.

Jack knew his friend felt like he was running out on him. He wasn't.

"Right behind you," Jack said with a look of reassurance.

Robert nodded and took off across the narrow span, with water flooding onto the boards behind him.

Five long strides—Jack counted them in his mind as he watched his friend hurry across.

The wood creaked under Robert's weight.

Shit!

Jack swallowed hard to get rid of the lump in his throat and stepped onto the planking.

The bridge broke when he still had ten feet to go.

He felt it slip from under his feet.

Air and a dark rock wall appeared in front of him.

But he'd anticipated the bridge coming apart and jumped. With the style and determination of a practiced broad-jumper, he continued to peddle his legs as if he were running through air.

His right foot landed hard on solid rock six inches from the edge and his left foot smacked down directly next to it.

But his shoulders were too far back for his momentum to carry him forward. The yawning pit seemed not to want to let him go.

All three women screamed.

He barely heard them. Resisting the urge to peer over his shoulder into the crevasse, he cartwheeled his arms to keep from falling backwards. The flame from the torch in his hand made a circle of fire in the dimly lit chamber.

He felt himself going over the edge.

Fuck!

He felt a strong hand grab hold of his belt and haul him onto solid ground away from certain death.

"Careful," Robert said. "Those aren't wings you're flapping."

Jack gripped his friend's forearm, sucked in a breath, and blew it out. "No shit."

The torch in his hand sputtered a reminder that he had somehow kept hold of it. He collapsed onto his butt and stared back at the newly created waterfall.

Matapolu stepped over and rested his hand on Jack's shoulder. "Come, my friend. It is not far now."

The other *Menehune* crowded in closely, the woman from his vision out front. Etu and Otu stood on each side and slightly behind her. The torch Etu held lit up their faces.

Jack pulled himself together and groaned to his feet. The *Menehune* refugees had stopped, he guessed, to wait for them to cross the bridge. It turned out they had watched him make his leap of faith. Without a doubt, a real show.

He'd had enough of crossing bridges.

He raised his torch high to extend the light past the expectant faces and into the passageway ahead.

In all the chaos and panic of running for their lives through the maze of this underground world, Jack had no idea whereabouts they were inside the mountain, or where the tunnel ahead of them led. He had to trust that his cave dweller friend knew the way out.

"After you." He waved Blue Eyes forward.

Matapolu nodded. The gathering of *Menehune* parted for their *kahuna* as he stepped to the front of the troop.

They walked the tunnel as a single group now, choosing their steps carefully. There hadn't been any more tremors, but Jack knew they weren't out of danger. Not yet. Rock had been cracked and shaken loose. More of the ceiling could come down on them at any minute and they needed to get out of the mountain. Only then would they be safe.

The seconds ground by. Two minutes had passed, at least.

A rock clattered to the stone floor behind them, another to the side of them. Jack jerked his head in the direction of each one when it fell.

Geez!

Matapolu had said it wasn't far. He strained to see into the tunnel ahead. There was only darkness.

"What do you think?" Robert asked over Jack's shoulder.

"I think I'm ready to get out of this place. That's what I think."

"This reminds me of a joke I once heard. Remind me to tell it to you when we get out of here."

"Right," he scoffed. "Once we're outside."

The next minute passed quickly. Maybe it had been Robert's mention of a joke. It didn't matter. Jack was just glad to put another hundred feet behind him.

They had to be getting close.

Then he saw it. On the fringes of his torch light, a huge stone disc, like the one in the ante-chamber, blocked the passageway ahead.

His spirits had risen at the prospect of finally getting out of there, then slumped at the thought of the trouble they'd had rolling the first one aside.

But they'd managed. They would manage here, too.

Jack passed his torch to Sienna and he and Robert hurried forward to muscle the barrier aside. All the barrel-chested *Menehune* men put their backs into it as well. They heaved.

Stone ground against stone and the massive disc rolled away to reveal an opening barely big enough for them to duck through. And on the other side, total darkness.

Jack blew out the breath he'd been holding.

Damn! Another tunnel!

He couldn't believe it.

He took the torch from Sienna and stepped through. Robert followed. While the others filed through and gathered around, Jack held his light high to study the passageway. There was something familiar about it.

He'd walked there before.

Matapolu appeared at his side. "You know where you are, now?"

"Looks familiar."

Matapolu pointed. "The entrance to our village is right down there."

Of course, they'd gone full circle.

He nodded in that direction and added, "That means the end of the tunnel is right down there, too."

"The way out," Matapolu reassured him.

Jack furrowed his brow. "I know it's night time. But shouldn't we see *some* light, from the moon or even the stars?"

Matapolu shook his head. "There is one more stone disk to move. We keep it closed when we sleep."

Another stone door to move. He remembered the opening, it was at least ten feet high. The stone disc would be gigantic—at least twice the size of the ones they'd already moved.

He took a deep breath and walked toward the exit.

Fortunately, the passageway here had not collapsed. Only a few slabs of rock had fallen on the path. They easily stepped around them. And when they arrived at the exit, Jack peered up at the twelve-foot in diameter stone door standing between them and the night air: twenty tons of solid rock, at least.

He wondered how the *Menehune* moved such a massive chunk of rock—how *they* would move it.

He put his legs and shoulder into it and pushed. The stone disc didn't budge even a fraction of an inch.

They were screwed.

He looked at Matapolu. "We'll never move this."

Matapolu knelt down and removed a wooden wedge.

He held it up for Jack to see. "Try it now."

Jack tensed the muscles in his arms and legs, leaned into the edge, and heaved with all his might. It didn't move.

He straightened, confused.

"Not that way." Matapolu corrected. The *kahuna* calmly placed the palm of his hand flat against the gigantic stone disc and pushed. The door moved easily. Only instead of rolling aside, it pivoted on an axis top and bottom. The fresh night air from outside rushed in to greet them.

Robert chuckled. "A regular Hercules, Jack, that's what you are."

Jack frowned at Robert. "Right!" In the next instant, he peered down at Matapolu. "I don't understand."

"The door has been carefully balanced," he explained. "When *The Tall Ones*—your people—venture here it is important that the door can be closed easily, and only by one of my people."

"But what about the other big-ass stones we moved? It took three men and a mule to roll them aside."

Matapolu cocked his head.

Jack realized the cave dweller—with all his wisdom—did not understand the euphemism. He clarified, "It took all of us men pushing as hard as we could to roll them out of the way."

Matapolu nodded. "Those stones were not made to move so easily."

No shit.

Jack couldn't believe the crafty cave dweller. Matapolu had stood there and let him make a fool of himself even though this was definitely not the time to be playing games with each other. He sure hadn't expected that from the *kahuna*.

Mischievous little buggers.

Jack wanted to laugh, but resisted. So the stories *were* true. He didn't press it. "Let's get out of here."

CHAPTER 54

Jack stumbled to a stop under a canopy of *ohia* trees at the base of the mountain and huddled there with the remainder of his scientific group and the two-dozen surviving *Menehune*. He could go no further. And from their haggard looks, the others couldn't, either.

But they had made it out alive.

Maintaining his grip on the torch with his right hand, he rested his left hand on his knee and closed his eyes. He could have collapsed right there. When he opened them a full ten-count later, he noticed that Sienna, Regan, and Kazuko had closed their eyes, too, as had several *Menehune*. Robert stood next to him.

Jack straightened, and for a few somber seconds they all stared back at the large black hole that marked the entrance into the subterranean world that had been home to the cave dwellers for six hundred years. No one spoke.

From outside, Jack couldn't see any sign of the massive cave-in. It was as if nothing had happened.

A slight tremor on the Richter scale, maybe. Nothing for the scientific community to be alarmed about, he was sure.

But for the *Menehune*, the quake had been cataclysmic.

The full moon peeked at them through openings in the leaves. Its cool blue light drew Jack's gaze upward where he searched out the night sky, taking in the vastness of its beauty. Out here they wouldn't need the torches for light, but they'd be glad to have the fire to ward off the chill of late night.

For the first time in days he felt he could breathe, really take a breath. And for a minute he did just that, filling his lungs to capacity and letting the air seep out, then doing it again, and again. Never had fresh air tasted or smelled so good.

"What ya think?" Robert clapped Jack on the shoulder.

Jack took in another cherished breath and let it out with a smile. "I think I'm going to enjoy sleeping under the stars tonight."

"You took a lot of chances in there, making sure everyone else got out all right."

Jack was still shaking inside. And in all likelihood, he would for a long time. He was sure everyone's nerves felt like his. But he'd done what he had to do. If need be, he'd do it again in a heartbeat.

He shrugged. "In the tunnel, after the bridge collapsed—when you saved my ass—you mentioned something about a joke. I could use a good laugh."

Robert beamed. It might not be all that funny, but it sure fit. Clearing his throat first, he said:

Fred and his dog were walking along a road. The man was enjoying the scenery, when it suddenly occurred to him he was dead.

He remembered dying, and that the dog walking beside him had been dead for years.

He wondered where the road was leading them.

After a while, they came to a high, white stone wall along one side of the road. It looked like fine marble.

At the top of a long hill, the wall was broken by a tall arch that glowed in the sunlight. As you might guess, Fred was quite curious.

He hurried up the road. And when he was standing before the arch, he saw a magnificent gate in the arch that looked like mother-of-pearl, and the street that led to the gate looked like pure gold.

He and the dog walked toward the gate, and as he got closer, he saw a man at a desk to one side. When he was close enough, he called out, "Excuse me, where are we?"

"This is Heaven, sir," the man answered.

"Wow! Would you happen to have some water?" Fred asked.

"Of course, sir. Come right in, and I'll have some ice water brought right up." The man gestured, and the gate began to open.

"Can my friend," Fred pointed at his dog, "come in, too?"

"I'm sorry, sir, but we don't accept pets."

Fred thought about that a moment then continued along the way he had been going with his dog.

After another long walk, and at the top of another long hill, Fred came to a dirt road leading through a farm gate that looked as if it had never been closed. There was no fence.

As he approached the gate, he saw a man inside, leaning against a tree and reading a book. "Excuse me!" he called to the man. "Do you have any water?"

"Yeah, sure, there's a pump over there, come on in."

"How about my friend here?" Fred pointed to his dog.

"There should be a bowl by the pump."

They went through the gate, and sure enough, there was an old-fashioned hand pump with a bowl beside it.

Fred filled the water bowl and took a long drink himself, then he gave some to the dog.

When they were full, he and the dog walked back to the man standing by the tree. "What do you call this place?" Fred asked.

"This is Heaven," the man answered.

"Well, that's confusing," Fred told him. "The man down the road said that was Heaven."

"Oh, you mean the place with the gold street and pearly gates? Nope. That's hell."

"Doesn't it make you mad when they use your name like that?"

"No, we're just happy that they screen out the folks who would leave their best friends behind."

Jack didn't have to think about this one. He would have died before he left his friends behind. And Robert knew it.

He smiled. "We should get some rest."

"And the climb out of here?"

"First light. Don't know how you feel about stumbling around out there in the dark, but I'm not about to make the four thousand foot climb over this mountain by torchlight if I don't have to."

"What we need is my satellite phone, to give Kimo a heads-up."

Jack laughed. "You can go back inside and get it if you want. I'll wait here."

"Nah, we can get by without it."

"Have you seen our blue-eyed friend?"

"Matapolu?" Robert glanced around. "Saw him talking to Etu and Otu a minute ago. Don't know where he is now."

"How are the women doing?"

"Kazuko's sitting with Regan. Sienna wandered off over there." He pointed his chin over Jack's shoulder.

Jack stiffened and peered into the plants and trees behind him. "We need to stay together. Did she say where she was going?"

"She's a big girl. Maybe she's looking for the ladies' room."

Jack relaxed a bit. He had to stop worrying about everyone else. They were safe. "They did good, ya know?"

"Did good?" Robert chuckled. "You and your English. And to answer your question, yeah, I know."

Jack smiled, but his heart wasn't in it. Not everyone had come out of the mountain alive.

"I still can't believe what happened to Michael and Tumra," he said. "Makes me feel like shit to think I was in a way responsible for their deaths."

"Tumra's death was an accident. Lisa murdered Michael. You can't blame yourself for something you had no control over."

"I invited Lisa along, remember. They're both dead because of her."

"You didn't know she was a killer. None of us did."

"Maybe, maybe not."

"She's dead, Jack."

And buried, Jack finished silently. He filled his lungs with the night air and exhaled with a loud sigh. "So tell me, regrets? Besides people dying, I mean."

"Now that we are out of there and safe," he shook his head from side to side, "not a one."

Jack arched a brow. "Not even one?"

"Well, maybe one," Robert admitted. "It would have been nice if each of us could have walked out of there with a pocket full of those gold coins."

Jack remembered. He dug into his pocket. "At least I have the Double Eagle Matapolu let me keep for luck."

Robert nodded. "Probably what saved us."

"Interesting. I—"

"I believe you wanted these," Matapolu interrupted.

Jack and Robert turned to look. They looked at each other, confused.

"Our packs," Robert said, before Jack could get the words out.

"Don't tell me you went back in and got them?" Jack added.

Matapolu motioned for Etu and Otu to hand them over. "I was not convinced Hootano would agree to my plan, so before the council meeting—while you were asleep in the cell with your friends—I instructed Etu and Otu to conceal your packs out here where you could get to them."

Jack didn't know what to think. Matapolu had told them he could convince Hootano to go along with the plan. Now he was saying he'd had his doubts.

Crafty devil.

He narrowed his eyes and pointed his index finger at the *kahuna*. And with just the hint of a smile said, "You led us to believe your high chief would go along with the plan so we wouldn't try to escape, didn't you?"

Matapolu shrugged.

"And you weren't going to betray us?"

Matapolu winked a blue eye at Jack and handed him his watch. "You'll want this."

His Seiko. Jack took the watch, glanced at the second hand to see if it was running, but didn't pay attention to the time. He was past caring, at least for now. He slipped it on.

"*Hoa pili*," he said, remembering what Kazuko had taught him, and reached out.

They clasped hands.

"Friend," Matapolu repeated in English.

"Cleaver," Robert said. He recognized his pack and took it from Etu's hand. He reached inside and dug out his satellite phone.

He switched it on. "We're in business."

Jack put his mind back on what needed to be done and rummaged through his pack. "Looks like everything's here." He held up a couple of power bars and a plastic bottle of water. "Including dinner and cocktails."

Together, they sifted through the six other packs. Jack felt a sad hollowness, knowing to whom three of the packs had belonged.

"More water and power bars here," he said, forcing aside his feelings for his dead teammates.

Robert removed a bottle and a handful of paper-wrapped bars from a pack and held them up. "Here, too. And you can use this."

He tossed Jack a spare T-shirt.

Now that his adrenaline rush had worn off, the cool night air was seeping into Jack's bones. He shivered.

Jack slipped on the T-shirt. "Jimmy Buffet, thanks."

The chill gone from his body, he gathered all the water bottles and handed all but three of them to Matapolu, Etu, and Otu. "Pass these among your people. I'm sure they need a drink as much as we do." He kept one for himself and passed two to Robert. "Make sure Regan gets a full one. I'll share this with Sienna."

Jack found her standing in a small clearing in the trees and strolled over to her, with her pack and the bottle of water in his hand. She held her gaze upward.

"Nice isn't it?" she said without taking her eyes off the sky.

"Nothing like a full moon and a carpet of stars."

She lowered her eyes long enough to flash him a wry smile.

"Being alive, Jack."

His expression sobered. "I've been trying not to think about how close we came to dying."

"What happened, anyway?"

"The cave-in that killed Tumra—the one that separated us—Lisa triggered it accidentally when she pressed on a stone disc next to the tunnel. Later, at the *Menehune* village, I noticed several more discs just like it, always by the entrance to a chamber. I figured our industrious cave-dwelling friends had rigged the passageways with booby traps to protect their existence there. Lisa must have figured it out, too."

"Let's not forget the one I saw."

"The one that gave me my sore nose," Jack joked.

The corners of her lips arced upward then the smile disappeared. "But that cave-in at the council chamber backfired. A couple of *Menehune* died. In fact, it was lucky any of us came out of that alive."

"I don't think the place was supposed to collapse like that. The mountain is honeycombed with lava tubes. There must have been one they didn't know about, directly under the floor of the council chamber. When Lisa set off the initial cave-in, the falling rocks must have triggered secondary cave-ins that caused the floor to collapse and the ceiling to fall in."

"So what story do we tell the authorities?"

"We'll come up with something we all agree on."

"Lisa was a murderer," Sienna said matter-of-factly. "Do we tell them that?"

"She died in a cave-in, so did Tumra. Michael could have, too. It'll go much more smoothly if we don't complicate things with a homicide investigation."

"And the *Menehune*? You promised Matapolu."

"I'm coming back for them."

"Your destination?"

Jack eyed her a moment. "I thought I'd keep that a secret."

It was her turn to stare into his eyes. After a second or two she asked, "Have you told the others you're coming back?"

"I'm sure Robert already knows I am, Kazuko too. And if my guess about Regan is correct, she's aware of it as well."

Once again, Sienna peered into the heavens. "A lover's moon, Jack. I never dreamed anything could look so beautiful."

He took in the sight, imagining what it would feel like to hold her tight in his arms. He wished circumstances were different.

"Remember," he said. "You promised to keep me on the top of the list."

She arched a brow at him. "What list is that?"

He grinned. "The list of men you'll call if you decide to switch sides."

She leaned in and kissed him on the cheek.

He touched his fingertips to the stubble where she'd kissed him and returned his gaze skyward. "It's good to be alive."

EPILOGUE

For the second time, Jack pointed *Pono's* twin bows into a heavy mist hugging the water. Ahead of him an unearthly glow lit up the darkness. This time he wasn't cruising into the phenomenon out of curiosity for the unknown. The plan he and Matapolu had hatched was for him to return at midnight on the first night of the new moon.

Two weeks…

He thought about Robert sitting at home sulking because he hadn't been invited along on the return trip.

"After all we've been through together, it just isn't fair," he protested.

"You whine like a mule," Jack told him. "Besides, someone has to take care of Rebel."

"You're making excuses," Robert insisted. "She can come along."

The conversation ended with a firm shake of Jack's head. "Not on this trip, my friend."

Rebel plopped her belly onto the floor, ears spread flat on the tile like wings, content to remain behind. She had adjusted well to life at the Fosters' home—Robert spoiled the flop-eared hound rotten.

Kazuko, Sienna, and Regan were also content to be left out of this trip. They were anxious to get back into their normal routines. Kazuko said she had a ton of work waiting for her at the University of Hawaii. Sienna and Regan looked forward to getting home and letting Regan's arm heal. After a stop at the hospital in Lihue on Kauai they had grabbed the first available flight to Vancouver. At last report, Regan's broken arm was on the mend, with Sienna's incessant fussing driving her crazy.

The days had flown by, yet it seemed like forever since his ragtag scientific expedition had walked onto the beach to rendezvous with Kimo, who'd stood just above the tide line with a Zodiac ready to ferry them aboard *Pono*.

And Rebel had been there with Kimo, the hound's ears flapping in the wind when she raced across the soft sand to meet them.

Perhaps he should have brought the dog along, even if it would have made Robert mad.

God, it is good to be alive!

And now he looked forward to seeing his blue-eyed cave-dweller friend and the rest of his clan. Though he wasn't sure how he'd feel looking into the eyes of the *Menehune* woman. The vision he had in Matapolu's chamber continued to haunt him in a recurring dream.

When the time was right, he'd ask Matapolu for the truth.

The mist closed in around him, and he throttled back to dead slow. He kept his eyes on the depth finder and the compass.

It wouldn't be long, now.

His thoughts wandered over events yet to come. The National Underwater Marine Agency's state-of-the-art salvage ship *Deep Blue* would arrive in ten days to take charge of the recovery of *I-16*.

Thanks to the documents in the wallet and the story Matapolu told him, there was no question the captain had survived long enough to get out of the mini-sub before it went down. The fate of the second crewmember, however, remained a mystery. Perhaps he had chosen to stay aboard. The sealed hatch suggested he had gone down with the sub when it sank.

No one knew.

And there was the question of what had caused the mini-sub to sink. Had *I-16's* batteries simply run out of power, leaving the boat adrift in a hostile sea? Had the captain and his lone crewmember scuttled it when they could go no further? Had the U-boat been damaged, and ultimately sunk by depth charge or artillery fire from American war ships?

The answers to these questions and more lay with the sub.

And then the truth may never be known.

The job rested in the capable hands of the NUMA crew.

The mist thinned. Now he could hear waves breaking and see the white ribbon of sand in front of him.

For the next few anxious seconds, he kept a wary eye on the depth finder as the bottom rose under him. He dropped anchor in twenty feet of water, just outside the line of surf. He'd bring the *Menehune* aboard in the fourteen foot Zodiac tethered to *Pono's* stern.

Robert deserved to be there to help. It hurt to leave him out of this final leg of the journey. But it was better that way.

Jack sucked in a deep breath and blew it out. He alone would bear the responsibility of keeping the location of the last surviving *Menehune* a secret.

Not even his best friend would know.

That would drive Robert crazy. And perhaps that was the only good part about leaving him behind. They'd have plenty to argue about during the years to come.

Ten minutes later, Jack ran the bow of the Zodiac onto the wet sand of the beach and stepped ashore. Matapolu stood a few feet above the tide-line, waiting for him.

"It's good to see you my friend!" Jack called out.

Matapolu raised his hand in greeting. "Good to see you!"

Jack noticed the *kahuna* cradling the *God's Stone* in the crook of his left arm. He'd obviously ventured back into the mountain. In a tight group behind him, stood the last of the *Menehune*.

Jack's stomach tightened. The woman from his vision stood at the front of the clan.

Jack tried not to stare at her, but couldn't look away. She had a glow about her that he could see, even in the dim bioluminescent light.

Or were his eyes playing tricks on him? An unconscious desire on his part to see something not there.

Part of him hoped that was the case. And part of him believed what his subconscious told him.

It had been real.

Matapolu stepped forward and smiled. "You kept your promise."

Jack offered his hand. "Did you think I wouldn't come?"

Matapolu took Jack's hand in his and shook it. "When so many *Tall Ones* have violated your trust, it is hard to remain confident."

Jack nodded in understanding. "Trust in this, my blue-eyed friend: nothing would have prevented me from keeping my promise to you."

"I believe that." Matapolu turned and waved Etu and Otu over.

Jack watched them lug a wooden chest the size of an old steamer trunk toward him. The lid was tied in place with a stout rope. He could tell the chest was heavy by the way they carried it.

"Is that your luggage?" He nodded at Etu and Otu as they approached.

Matapolu shook his head. "That is for you. Perhaps you can undo some of the harm man has done to the oceans."

Jack couldn't believe it, but he had an idea what was inside. What else could it be? He'd open it later and find out.

"I assure you I'll do my best." He unclasped the wristband on his SEIKO and handed the dive watch to Matapolu. "And this is for you, my friend." He meant what he said. He'd continue to work hard to reverse the damage done to the world's oceans, even if he were wrong about the contents of the chest.

"I know you will." Matapolu held the watch up in front of him. "You are a true friend. Now I think we should go. The mist will disappear soon."

Jack stared pensively out to sea. The fog hugging the water had begun to lift. This was the last time it would be seen shrouding the Napali Coast. "Fog's already dissipating. Grab your stuff and we'll get under way."

A second thought made him pause. He gripped the *kahuna's* arm to keep him from walking away and nodded to indicate the woman standing in front of the other *Menehune*. "Before we go, tell me the woman's name."

Matapolu smiled. "Manaolana."

* * * *

Jack sipped a Corona on the lanai at Robert's house. He'd been back four days and still he hadn't opened the chest, or even told Robert about it. When the time felt right, he'd do both.

He watched his friend peel the label from his bottle.

Shit!

He sighed and set his beer aside. The time was right, anything to bring a smile to Robert's lips.

Jack slid his chair back and stood up. "You going to wipe that sour look off your face or wear it until the cows come home?"

"I might."

"Which one?"

"Depends on you."

"Well then, cheer up and give me a hand."

Robert shot him a quizzical look. "Doing what?"

"There's something we need to check out."

"Like what?"

Jack didn't like it when Robert got into one of his moods. "Just get up and help me."

Robert sighed and heaved himself out of his chair. "Whatever."

Fifteen minutes later, they set the heavy chest on the lanai and squatted in front of it.

"You say you haven't looked in here?" Robert questioned.

"Waited to do it with you."

"And you thought that would make up for leaving me behind?"

"You're reading too much into it. I merely thought opening this chest was something we should do together."

"And you're still not going to tell me where you took Matapolu and his people?"

Jack huffed. "Just untie the damned rope and let's see what's inside."

Adding her own curiosity to the unveiling, Rebel trotted up, nuzzled the rope, and settled back on her haunches.

Jack gave her a quick scratch behind the ears, and together they watched Robert work the knot loose.

"*Pono*," Robert said. "The name you gave your boat. Making things right, that seems to be your destiny in life."

"Still mad," Jack asked as the rope fell away.

"What do you think?'

Jack grinned at his good friend and slowly lifted the lid.

His breath caught in his throat.

So much…!

It was all there: the gold coins and the cash, gold ingots weighing maybe two pounds each, perhaps a dozen of them: the first edition printing of *Robinson Crusoe*, the jewelry, necklaces, bracelets, rings. He felt bad for the people who'd lost them.

His next thought was that he should return the money and jewels, but to whom? Many of the rightful owners were long dead. As for the ones still alive, how would they ever be located? And for the *Menehune*, money was only a curiosity to them—something pretty to look at.

Looking in at the contents of the chest, Jack could see Matapolu had put a lot of thought into what went in it. He'd paid attention.

Jack could tell because Matapolu had included the sharks' tooth war club Sienna found fascinating—he'd see that she got that. The *kahuna* had even gone so far as to include the rearview mirror they'd joked about.

Everything.

"The money, the gold, the jewelry," Robert said. "I don't understand."

Jack lifted the Japanese dagger from where it lay on the folded flag and slid the blade out of the sheath. "Matapolu wants me to save the world's oceans with it."

Robert removed one of the Double Eagles and eyed the coin in the sunlight. “There’s a lot of money here, but I don’t think it’s enough to do that.”

Jack shoved the dagger home. “Perhaps not, but there might be enough to make a difference.”

THE END

ABOUT THE AUTHOR

William Nikkel is the author of four *Jack Ferrell* novels and a steampunk, zombie western featuring his latest hero Max Traver. A former homicide detective and S.W.A.T. team member for the Kern County Sheriff's Department in Bakersfield, California, William is an amateur scuba enthusiast, gold prospector, and artist who can be found just about anywhere. He and his wife Karen divide their time between California and Maui, Hawaii.

www.ingramcontent.com/pod-product-compliance
Lightning Source LLC
Chambersburg PA
CBHW051231260626
47162CB00002B/369
* 9 7 8 0 6 1 5 9 8 8 1 6 0 *